A TRIAL OF SORCERERS

ELISE KOVA

Silver Wing Press

A Trial of Sorcerers

ELISE KOVA

Published by Silver Wing Press
Copyright © 2021 by Elise Kova

Cover Artwork by Marie Magny
Developmental Editing by Rebecca Faith Editorial
Line Editing and Proofreading by Melissa Frain

ISBN (paperback): 978-1-949694-19-2
ISBN (hardcover): 978-1-949694-31-4
eISBN: 978-1-949694-30-7

ALSO BY ELISE KOVA

A Trial of Sorcerers

A Trial of Sorcerers

A Hunt of Shadows

(More to Come)

Also set in the Air Awakens Universe

AIR AWAKENS SERIES

Air Awakens

Fire Falling

Earth's End

Water's Wrath

Crystal Crowned

GOLDEN GUARD TRILOGY

The Crown's Dog

The Prince's Rogue

The Farmer's War

VORTEX CHRONICLES

Vortex Visions

Chosen Champion

Failed Future

Sovereign Sacrifice

Crystal Caged

Married to Magic

A Deal with the Elf King

Married to Magic #2

(More to Come)

Loom Saga

The Alchemists of Loom

The Dragons of Nova

The Rebels of Gold

See all books and learn more at:

http://www.EliseKova.com

for the Tower Guard

TABLE OF CONTENTS

T HE WALLS COULD talk, and they had secrets.

    …where…going…

    I don't…

  …keep this just between us…

Eira ignored the mutterings, keeping her head down and her nose in her book. The words were nothing more than magically trapped whispers of people who weren't there—people who might not have been there for hours or even decades. They were her companions and her torturers. Eira fought to suppress and ignore the voices because when she'd tried to talk about them, no one believed her.

No one else could hear them.

She ascended the main walkway of the Tower of Sorcerers, a sloping path that wound like a corkscrew between lecture halls and libraries in the center and apprentice dormitory rooms on the outside. People brushed past her, quiet in contrast to the cacophony that threatened to deafen her if she let her magic run awry and unchecked.

Instead, Eira tried to fill her mind with the words of the book she was reading. They painted pictures of a land far away—the Crescent Continent, Meru. A land filled with magic vastly different than hers, and peoples that seemed as if they were straight out of a folktale. It was easy for her to place herself beyond her body, imagining standing on those distant shores, until a voice said—

  …kill our sovereign…

She stopped in her tracks. Two apprentices emerged from a storeroom, whispering amongst themselves. The man wore Tower robes like her—no collar, loose sleeves to the elbows, hem falling at the small of his back. The woman's robes had capped sleeves and a high collar. A Waterrunner and Firebearer, Adam and Noelle, also known as the Tower's "power couple"—and the last people Eira ever wanted to see.

"What're you staring at, freak?" Adam, the Waterrunner, said.

"I'm sorry, what?" Eira asked calmly, slipping her book into her satchel so they couldn't turn her reading about Meru— her passion—into more ammunition to be used against her.

"Is she deaf now? Wasn't she the one who 'heard voices' all the time?" Adam scoffed and looked to Noelle, who gave a snicker and tucked a length of dark tresses behind her ear.

"Perhaps she was talking to her imaginary friends and couldn't hear us?" Noelle suggested.

"That it?" Adam took a step closer to Eira.

Eira looked at him from toe to head. She stared at the tip of his hooked nose to avoid his dark brown eyes. Just like Alyss had told her to do so she wouldn't be intimidated. "I thought I heard one of you say something about the emperor."

He laughed, a grating and terrible sound. A laugh Eira knew well…a laugh he reserved for *at her*. "Do I look like someone who would talk politics?"

"No." Eira shook her head. "I suppose not. You'd have to have half a brain to have an opinion on politics." She tore her eyes away and started back up the tower.

Adam grabbed her elbow, snarling, "What did you say?"

"Let me go," Eira said quietly. Her magic swelled at the offending contact; if he held on to her much longer he'd be swept away by it, as helpless as a child in a rip current.

"You think you can just insult me and walk away?"

"Come on, Adam." Noelle grabbed the arm not holding Eira in place.

"It's not insulting you if it's true," Eira said softly.

"Say that again!" Tides of magic rolled off of him, uncontrolled, unstoppable. Eira felt like the moon, spinning around him with her words. Pulling him from one direction to the next was all too easy. Making him feel whatever she wanted him to feel—

Stop.

Eira closed her eyes and sighed softly, trying to ward off the dark depths she was sinking into. It was a place she could never risk going. "I'm sorry. Now let me go, Adam, please."

"I'm not—"

"She's not worth it." Noelle regarded Eira warily from the corner of her eye. "You know what she did three years ago."

Because of you. I didn't mean to. If you hadn't... The words still bubbled up in her, as horrible and dark as the memory of that day. But Eira was eighteen now. She no longer had to say everything that crossed her mind.

Silence was often the best path forward in a noisy world. Stasis and quiet and *numb*.

"What's going on here?" a familiar voice interjected. All three of them turned to face the speaker. Adam's hand quickly fell from Eira's elbow.

"Nothing, Marcus."

"It better be," Marcus said with a note of warning. "Come, Eira, we don't want to keep the Minister of Sorcery waiting." Marcus breezed past her and up the Tower. Eira followed dutifully behind.

"Run along, coward," Noelle hissed, just loud enough that Eira could be sure it wasn't a magical whisper from the wall, or door, or floor.

Eira paused, glancing over her shoulder and meeting Noelle's black eyes.

"Isn't it nice to have Mister Perfect for a brother, who always comes to your defense? Wonder what would've happened to you if you didn't have him to keep you in check and your uncle as the minister. The senate would have eaten you alive." She sneered, her pretty face twisting into something that more resembled the ugliness in her soul.

Eira simply stared. She kept her mind vacant—as though she were sinking deeper and deeper into the bitter cold of the ocean that rolled within her. Underneath the water, everything was muted, distant, and dull. Voices couldn't carry. No one could reach her.

"Eira?" Marcus called.

Snapping back to reality, Eira followed swiftly behind, leaving Noelle and Adam standing in the walkway. "I don't need your help."

"I didn't do anything." Her brother rolled his eyes.

"Yes, you did."

"Well, what do you expect?" He sighed. "I'm not going to just stand by and watch them harass you."

Because you're afraid of what will happen if they push me too far, Eira added mentally. "If you keep standing up for me, they'll never stop."

"That something Alyss told you?" He arched a dark blond eyebrow at her, knowing he had her pegged. Marcus had hair more like their parents—a honey gold, darkened with bronze. Whereas Eira's hair was a platinum shade, so bright it looked nearly stark white in sunlight.

"Maybe." Eira twisted the strap of her bag. "But she's not wrong."

He sighed. "Eira, I told Mom and Dad I would protect and look after you. I promised Uncle Fritz and Uncle Grahm, too."

"I just turned eighteen. I don't think it's really *necessary* to protect me anymore."

"Yet I always will." His large palm landed heavily on the top of her head and Marcus shook it back and forth.

"You're going to mess up my hair." She swatted his hand away.

"How will anyone tell the difference?"

Eira scowled at him, which only made him laugh.

"Don't give me that look. Come on, Eira, smile. It's been so long since I've seen you smile."

"Let's just get our assignments for the day." Eira crossed to the second-to-last door in the Tower of Sorcerers, nearly at the very top—the office of the Minister of Sorcery. She knocked quickly.

"Come in."

Within was a room as familiar to her as her home back in Oparium. A large desk was situated in the center, facing the door. Two chairs were positioned on one side, set up for conversations. Expansive windows provided breathtaking views of the jagged peaks that topped the mountains surrounding the capital of the Solaris Empire. All manner of worktables and storage were crammed around the windows. Something was always bubbling softly on their surfaces.

Behind the desk was a man with rich blue eyes and hair that matched Marcus's. He was as much a fixture of this room in Eira's mind as the beakers or cauldrons.

"Ah, hello, you two!" Fritz, the Minister of Sorcery, stood.

"Minister," Eira said with a polite nod.

"Always so formal." Fritz rounded the desk with a shake of his head. He scooped up Marcus in a bear hug, even though Marcus was head and shoulders taller. "It's good to see you both."

"Good to see you, too, Uncle," Marcus said.

"You saw us two days ago." Yet Eira relented to her eager uncle, giving him a gentle squeeze as he crushed her so hard her back popped.

"Oh, there you go, I heard that." Fritz chuckled. "Feel better?"

"Yes, actually." Eira stretched, forward and back.

"And just because I saw you two days ago doesn't mean I don't miss you. It feels like just yesterday you two arrived at the Tower, hand in hand, playing in my office—"

"Yes, we know, Uncle." Eira gave him a smile and a pat on the shoulder. "Now, may we have our assignments?"

"Are you running off to meet Alyss?"

"If our assignments happen to coincide again," Eira admitted.

"*Happen to*," Marcus repeated with a snort and a chuckle.

"Here you go." Fritz handed her a slip of paper and then one to Marcus…twice as long. "Now, off with you; it's getting late already and there's work to be done."

"Thanks, Uncle." Marcus gave a playful salute with his paper before heading out the door. Leaving Eira in his dust, yet again.

"What is it?" Fritz asked thoughtfully.

Eira looked down at her list. Five names were penned underneath the words, *West Clinic*. Her brother had at least ten—no, fifteen.

"He has a longer list than me again," she murmured.

"I want to give you time to spend with Alyss." The words sounded sincere. So why did they feel like a lie?

"I want to do more."

"In time." He said the two words she hated the most.

"When will it be my time?" Eira asked softly. "I want to—"

He didn't give her an opportunity to finish. "Don't rush. You're young. There's plenty of time to come into your own. It's best to take things slowly, given how *unique* your magic is." Eira pressed her lips into a hard line. When she didn't say anything, he pressed, "All right?"

"All right," she echoed, resigned, and slipped away before the conversation could continue. Instead of fighting, she pulled out her book once more, reading over pages she'd read so many times she could recite the words from memory.

Words of places Eira knew she'd never get the chance to go because she'd be stuck here her entire life, chaperoned and shepherded.

She wound once more down the tower, the whispers filling her ears. As a girl, she hadn't understood the voices; she'd thought they were imaginary friends. Her parents had thought the same.

Then, her magic had begun to manifest in different ways and it became apparent that she was a sorcerer, like her brother and uncle. Eira knew from that day she was destined for the Tower of Sorcerers in Solarin, capital of the Empire. It was the place all sorcerers in the Empire were sent. She'd hoped that she'd find a solution, or even an explanation for the voices in the Tower. But she'd yet to have any leads. All she could show for her efforts was learning how to silence the voices—if she focused.

She'd arrived six years ago, young for an initiate, but not unheard of. Exceptions could also be made for the niece of the Minister of Sorcery…a fact her peers rarely let her forget.

At the base of the Tower of Sorcerers was the main entry— the only entrance non-sorcerers knew of and could access. There was a waiting area, tables and chairs, and sofas, usually vacant. No one came to visit sorcerers. Emperor Aldrik Solaris and Empress Vhalla Solaris had done a lot to push sorcerers toward being accepted in common society. But hatred and prejudice were self-feeding vines, constantly digging two new tendrils into the hearts of man for every one that was ripped out.

"I was just about to leave without you," Alyss grumped as she jumped up from the seat she'd been occupying. She sent the clay she'd been magically sculpting back into the pouch on her hip with a thought.

"Sorry."

"I saw your brother come by, so I knew you wouldn't be far behind."

Marcus's shadow. That was all she ever was. Even Alyss, her best and truest friend, knew it.

"I just got delayed with Uncle. What were you making?" Eira quickly changed the topic.

"Nothing, just messing around." Alyss grinned. Her fingertips were always stained by clay, or stone dust, from whatever project she was "messing around" with. "What you really should ask me is what I'm reading."

"You find a new book?"

"Yes, and it's a truly scandalous story." Alyss spoke low and fast. "I found it in the back corner of the used bookstore on Flare Avenue. It has things you wouldn't believe someone penned…much less committed to print!"

"You're too smart to be filling your head with such things."
Eira rolled her eyes.

"And you're too fun at heart to be so prudish and off-putting
all the time." Alyss braced her hands on her hips. Dozens of
small, long, dark braids Eira had helped weave into her hair a
week ago slipped over her shoulder. Beads Alyss's mother had
sent from the North clanked softly at the ends with every turn
of her head.

For Eira, a trip home was a hard day's travel. For Alyss, it
was a week to the northernmost region of the Solaris Empire.

"You know nothing about me." Eira mirrored her friend's
motion, putting her hands on her hips.

"Wh-me? Me? *I* know nothing about *you*?" Alyss scoffed
loudly, her voice echoing around the iron chandelier overhead.
"I am the only one in this whole Tower who knows you."

Eira hummed but said nothing. A grin threatened to split
her lips. Alyss dug her elbow into Eira's side and freed the
expression with a laugh.

"Now, we're going to the West Clinic today, right?"

"Looks like."

Together, they set off into the brisk spring dawn.

Ice still clustered around gutters and hung from awnings,
sparkling like magic given form in the early morning light.
Alyss's breath plumed before her like a chimney in the cold.
But Eira's was invisible.

Eira closed her eyes, imagining for just a second that
she was the spirit of winter itself. She was the crisp air. She
lived in the snow banks. Her heart was buried deep, deep in
the icy blue of the frost-covered peaks of the mountains that
surrounded her.

"Spring can't come fast enough," Alyss muttered from
under her scarf.

"Winter can't hold on long enough." Eira sighed
contentedly, stretching her arms high overhead.

"You're crazy."

"So they tell me."

"Lucky for you, I like crazy." Alyss hooked her elbow with Eira's. "Now, you didn't tell me." She held out the book. "Hear anything?"

"It's not something I can command..." *Smother at best.* "You know that."

"That's because you don't *try* and command it. You just suppress and sink into your 'ocean.'"

"Because I'd rather *not* hear the whispers." And there was no sound in the bubble of water Eira imagined herself within.

Alyss sighed dramatically. "You have a gift and you do nothing with it. So it falls on me to encourage you. Just hold the book and see if you can make it talk?" Alyss pressed the book into Eira's hands. "Anything?"

Eira turned it over and flipped through the pages. Despite Alyss's enthusiasm, she kept her magic bundled away. "No, it's quiet."

"Damn." Alyss took the book back and shoved it into her bag, fitting it amongst the salves and potions that she was carrying to the clinic. "One day I'll find something truly special for you to listen to."

"I hope not."

"You have a *gift*," she repeated. As if Eira would suddenly agree on the one millionth time.

"I have a *curse*."

"Stop being so down." Alyss jostled her lightly. "It's positively frigid out here. I know you can't scowl when it's this bloody cold."

Eira cracked a smile. Then, it fell. "There *was* something, earlier..."

"What?"

...kill the sovereign... That was what the voice had said. A voice as cold as winter's midnight. Eira shook her head.

"Nothing."

"I know when it's something, now tell me."

"I ran into Noelle and Adam by the Waterrunner's

storeroom." It was at least partially the truth.

"Oh, Mother above, no doubt mashing faces." Alyss scowled, and proceeded to rant on something Adam had done during one of her history classes the entire walk to the clinic.

The West Clinic was a three-story structure located on what Eira considered to be the center level of Solarin. There were two others in the city, but this was the largest and always the busiest by default. It was where new clerics were trained in the arts of potions and salves, and Groundbreakers assisted them. It was also where Waterrunners, like her, studied how to use their magic to help the dying transition into the next world.

For every five non-magical people flooding in and out of the clinic—Commons, as they were called in the Tower—Eira saw one sorcerer.

Sorcerers were easy to spot for two reasons. The first being that most, like Eira and Alyss, wore black robes of varying styles depending on their rank and type of elemental affinity. The second being that Commons would take wide steps to avoid being in a sorcerer's path.

Eira and Alyss entered through the main lobby, but stopped off in a side room, where they prepared for the day. They both tied masks over their faces and covered their hands with thick gloves before bidding each other goodbye. However, before Eira left, she couldn't help but notice even Alyss had more people on her list than she did.

Sighing, Eira tucked her hair behind her ears and forced herself to focus. She may be the runt, the outcast, the weird one…but these people still needed what comforts she could bring. She looked at the first name on the list, cross-checked it against a cleric's ledger, and then proceeded to a room in the far back wing where all activity was hushed by the presence of death itself.

Eira drifted from room to room, her magic at service to the people of the Solaris Empire. It had been the idea of the empress, they said, to make sorcerers at the behest of the people. To make use of magic beyond times of war and bring it into the sun from the shadowed corners and back alleys sorcerers had been repressed into for as long as time was counted in the Empire.

The tools of her trade were simple—a bowl and some wooden tokens. Eira would fill the bowl with water and then place the token at its center. Using her magic, she could record the words of the sick into the token and turn it into a vessel for his or her family to listen to later, just in case the worst befell them.

When Eira was finished, she returned to the Tower alone. Alyss would take at least double the amount of time. As a Groundbreaker, she was actually trying to heal the people. She could do that much. All Eira functioned as was an assistant to a friend she knew well—death.

Eira wandered the empty halls. Classes were in session and the sorcerers who weren't attending were out in the city. People were tired of being cooped up, and they were eager for spring.

… I can't believe… I'll get him back…

… Prince Baldair is dead…

Eira paused at the familiar voice. The Tower Library was unassuming in the afternoon sunlight streaming through the back windows. It was completely silent—just her and the murmurs.

"Who are you…were you?" Eira whispered, taking a step inside. A tendril of magic reached out through the air without her permission, grasping, searching. Seeking that familiar voice that she'd heard so many times in these halls.

For the first time, Eira didn't try and stop her magic. She dared to let her power wander, as Alyss would encourage, just to see what it would find.

…All of this…end very soon… The voice whispered from somewhere across space and time.

Eira paused by the back windows, looking out over the city.

Someone had been here. Someone immensely powerful. Someone with magic strong enough to imprint their words onto the very fibers of the cushions, or the stone of the walls, without even realizing it. Unintentional vessels, such things were called, and they were regarded as being highly uncommon. Eira had tried to tell her teacher otherwise once and was reprimanded. Her theory on unintentional vessels being far more common than anyone realized—if you knew how to listen for them—was of the many things she now kept silent on.

"That reminds me..." Eira started back up the Tower, pausing at the storeroom across from the Waterrunners' workroom. Instruction echoed out through the cracked door. She used one particularly zealous order to hide the soft squeal of the storeroom's hinges as she slipped inside.

Luckily, Noelle and Adam were off elsewhere. Eira did a quick round of the dusty shelves. A single bulb of glass—a flame magically hovering within—danced with the long shadows cast by Watterunner tools.

"All right, Alyss. Fine. Let's see if you're right. If this is really a gift." Eira gathered her courage and asked the air, "Who were you trying to kill?"

...just imagine, Emperor Solaris... the icy voice from earlier whispered as if in reply.

Eira spun, heart racing. She wasn't used to the voices replying. The traces of magic were ornery things, difficult to pin down in the best of times. They spoke to her on their terms, never on hers.

Or, maybe Alyss was right. Maybe she'd never really tried.

"When?" Silence. "*When?*" Was there a plot to kill the emperor? Her heart was in her throat now. Surely no one would—

*No one knows about this place...our secret...*The voice was fainter, vanishing. Eira could almost feel the ghost of the woman with the icy tones passing through her and heading... no, that couldn't be right...heading to the back corner of the room?

Eira scattered the cobwebs and dragged her fingers through years of dust along a groove she had never noticed in the back corner. It was half-hidden by a shelf and a barrel. There, concealed by the shadow of an alcove, was a small handle. She gripped it and tugged. Then pushed.

Just when Eira was about to give up, unseen hinges groaned. She pushed harder. The door released at once, swinging open.

Eira went head-over heels and toppled into a secret chamber.

COUGHING DUST, EIRA pushed her hair from her eyes and tried to get her bearings. The storeroom door latch disengaging drew her attention to the room she'd come from. Jumping to her feet, Eira grabbed the hidden door and snapped it shut before anyone else could see her...or her discovery.

She leaned against the door, holding her breath and listening. Supplies clanked in the other room as the person rummaged around the Waterrunner supplies. Eira prayed to the Mother above that they didn't notice the door as she had— that she hadn't left behind some clue as to its existence. The rummaging stopped and Eira bit her lower lip, bracing herself to hold the door closed if the person tried to open it. There was the rumbling of the storeroom door slamming shut and then... silence.

Eira exhaled slowly and wiped the hair from her face. It fell out of the loose knot she'd tied half of it into. The wispy strands hung limply between her fingers as she tried to tame them back into place.

Speaking of out of place...where was she?

Straightening, Eira took in the room for the first time. It reminded her of a Tower apprentice's dormitory, simple and relatively unadorned. A bed, a desk, a bookshelf with some crumbling journals stacked on it. The remnants of a pennon clung to the stone wall. The majority of the fibers had long since given up and were now a heap of cotton on the floor.

"Who lived here?" Eira dared to ask—dared the room to answer.

...I will...the best they've ever known... the siren voice that had guided her in here answered.

Eira looked to the bookshelf. The voice had come from one of the books on the top shelf. Delicately, she hooked one with her index finger and pulled it down. By some miracle, it didn't crumble in her hands.

Placing it on the desk, Eira slowly opened what turned out to be a journal. There was no name on the book; whoever had been its author had taken care not to give any indication of who they were. Eira could see why within the first five pages.

"Vicious," she whispered, mostly in horror as she lingered on one particularly drawn-out instruction. But part of her, a dark, cold, and wretched place that she had chosen to ignore for the past two years, was impressed.

Laid out neatly on the page, void of judgment or emotion, was the start of what appeared to be clear instructions on how to completely freeze a person solid. Some Waterrunner had gone to great lengths, or very illegal experimentations—likely both, given the detail—to show how it could be done so that the person was frozen in stasis. They would be neither alive nor dead, completely trapped.

"Unless they're a Firebearer, of course," Eira mused, and then promptly shook her head. She shut the book and put her back to it. The deep currents within her stirred at the writings. Currents she needed to keep still.

As Eira worked to void her mind, she noticed the bookcase was slightly ajar. Pressing her face into the sliver of darkness, Eira confirmed her suspicion—fresh air and damp earth lay beyond. Eira pulled, revealing an opening. No, it was more of a crack in the wall that led into a rough-hewn passage. Eira couldn't tell how far it went from here. But judging from the icy air, it progressed deep within the mountain the city and palace were built on, around, and in.

There were many hidden passages in the palace. Eira herself knew of a good few being a part of the Tower of Sorcerers. Most of the entrances and exits to the Tower were hidden in plain sight from the Commons who worked and lived in the palace.

But this didn't look like any of the usual passages. The

walls looked like they were naturally formed. And there were no flame-bulbs illuminating their depths. As such, she could only see a short distance before the unknown was consumed by the void.

"Just who were you?" Eira asked again. But this time, silence was her only reply.

She returned to the journal, curiosity daring her to open it once more. Her mind objected. But her hand disobeyed. She flipped back open to the page on freezing people solid and began reading.

The day dragged on and the pages slowly turned a deep orange with the fading light. Eira blinked, rubbed her eyes, and looked out the window. The sun already hung low in the sky. She was so accustomed to the flame bulbs that lit the majority of the Tower, constantly lending their glow, that the darkening of this forgotten chamber was an oddity.

She muttered a curse under her breath. Time never moved faster than when she was engrossed. Pressing her ear to the door that connected this secret room with the Waterrunner storeroom, Eira listened closely. She heard muffled voices and footsteps. There was a brief thundering of what sounded like a group running by.

Running to dinner, likely. Classes for younger apprentices and those not sent out to the city for the day, like her, would be ending for the afternoon. She needed to slip out now or risk someone catching her in the workroom while she exited.

Gathering her courage, Eira said a prayer and opened the door. She squeezed around the large barrel and pulled the door shut behind her. Scanning the room, Eira looked for something else she could use to obscure the opening. Something that people wouldn't notice was out of place. Something like…a large bag of wooden tokens.

Grunting, Eira hefted the bag, placing it on the barrel. It obscured the small opening where the handle was hidden. But would it be enough? Now that Eira knew a door was there, it was all she saw. How had she never noticed it before? Surely, someone would now—

The door to the storeroom swung open. "Eira?" Marcus blinked at her. "Did you just get back, too?"

"Oh, yes," she lied to her brother. Something Eira didn't usually make a habit of because it was dangerously easy. He believed every word that came out of her mouth. "I finished earlier, of course, but I took a walk around the city." As Eira spoke, she placed her bowl and leftover tokens on the shelves.

"You do like taking walks on frosty days." He chuckled and began putting away his leftover supplies as well. Of course, he had much less than her. Eira watched him from the corner of her eye. "What is it?"

"Do you…notice anything different?" Eira dared to ask. She had to know if the door was as obvious to someone else as it was to her.

"Different?" Marcus faced her, hands on his hips. "Oh, you took your hair down. I like it."

"That's…that's right. Yes." Eira raked her fingers through her hair, making sure none of the dust or cobwebs from the room she'd spent half the day in were caked on her scalp.

"In any case, I'm headed to dinner. Want to come with?"

"I really should try and catch up with Alyss." Eira laced her fingers tightly. She had half a mind to grab some candles and hunker in the room for the rest of the night. There were at least eight more journals for her to work through. And the tunnel to explore.

"Alyss was still at the clinic when I left."

"I didn't think you were sent to the West Clinic today?"

"They called me in last minute to help with pain management during a procedure and I had time." Marcus smiled.

Pain management… That meant her brother had already been taught by someone—their uncle, likely—how to use his magic to cool flesh without damage, enough to make it numb.

"When did you learn how to do that?" Eira dared to ask, wishing her voice would cooperate and be stronger while she did it.

"Oh…" He paused. His shoulders slumped a bit and he ran

a hand through his mop of hair. *Guilty*, every movement he made screamed *guilty*. "I suppose a year ago?"

"A year ago? When you were supposed to graduate the Tower?" Apprentices usually graduated at twenty. But Marcus had turned twenty last year and was still an apprentice for some inexplicable reason.

"Yeah, around then, I think. Maybe that's why Uncle taught me. He knew I should have graduated and could've learned then."

"He taught an apprentice," Eira murmured.

"I'm sure he'll teach you soon." Marcus rested a hand on her shoulder. "Come on, bird-blue eyes, don't look so down. Give your brother a smile."

Eira forced a smile as she doubted Fritz would teach her anything.

She followed Marcus down the Tower, just behind him, in his shadow, as was her place. Marcus was the star. He was the Waterrunner who shone, the one who was always in control. He helped the young apprentices and teachers alike. He was a healthy blend of academic and practical.

And she…she was…there. Always just a step out of the spotlight.

But if she actually got into the spotlight, what would she do? She didn't know. It was a question she'd posed many a night, alone in her room, and still didn't have an answer to. Some people were made to be loved and doted on. Others weren't.

Being in the shadow might make it easier if she ever did try to slip away. Those late and lonely nights usually set her mind to wandering across the sea to the Crescent Continent. She'd fantasize about striking out and making a life for herself there. She'd wonder how easy it would be to stow away onto a trading galley. Surely a few of the sailors she'd met as a girl in Oparium were still on the seas…

"Marcus?" Eira paused at the entrance to the dining hall. In a circular, central room of the Tower, apprentices and teachers alike gathered around tables, clustered in conversation. The smell of freshly baked bread and roast hog filled the air. "Aren't we—"

"We just have a quick stop to make first."

"Where?" Her heart sank.

"We're getting Cullen from the training grounds. I promised—"

"No, I'm finding Alyss."

Marcus rushed back to her, grabbing both shoulders before she could turn away. "I promised him we would have dinner together tonight. There's something he wanted to tell me."

"Good, you two can have dinner. We will catch up some other time."

"But it's midweek. We always have dinner midweek."

"You should have thought about that before you scheduled dinner with Cullen." Eira folded her arms.

"Please, Eira. He's not that bad."

Cullen was *that* bad. And worse. Cullen was more terrible than Noelle and Adam combined. He was the "Prince of the Tower," for the Mother's sake. As far as Eira was concerned, he was the worst. He rarely spoke to anyone. And when he did, it always served to remind everyone else that they were far, far beneath him.

"Marcus—"

"*Please.*" Marcus leaned forward and met her eyes. His were a darker shade than hers, like his hair, and more of a sea blue than ice. His eyes were warm and inviting, like him. Hers were brisk, almost unnaturally bright, and off-putting… like her.

"Fine." She sighed. "Fine, fine, fine." Eira added a groan at the end for good measure. "But you owe me something good from Margery's Bakery."

"A sweet bun?"

"*Two* sweet buns, whenever I request."

"Done." Marcus clapped his hands and started down the Tower. Eira watched, debating one final time if she should follow or just escape while she could. With another groan, she caught up to her brother. A promise was a promise, especially between siblings.

They left the Tower through an unmarked door. Every apprentice had their name emblazoned on their door with a silver nameplate, lovingly made by a young Firebearer of the Tower as one of their early tasks. But the unmarked doors signified passages that connected with the palace proper.

"Marcus."

"Yes?"

"Have you ever found a Tower passage that wasn't marked?"

"What do you mean?" He glanced over his shoulder. The lone flame bulb of the long hall cast deep shadows on his face.

"A door, or passage, that wasn't obvious?"

"What're you talking about?" Marcus paused at the opposite end of the hall. It looked like a dead end, the mortared stone of the palace rounding out where an exit should be.

"I—" Eira tried to gather her slippery thoughts. "—I just thought that there's so many secret, but not secret, passages... Maybe there's one or two that are *actually* secret? Maybe there are passages that people have long forgotten about?"

Her brother chuckled. "Is this a plot from one of Alyss's novels?"

"Yes." Eira forced a laugh. "Never mind, ignore me."

And he did.

Life had taught Eira over the years that she was an easy one to ignore—to forget, even. Sometimes, she wondered if she had an illusion cast over her at all times that made her blend in with the walls around her. An illusion like the one they passed through.

Marcus went first. He submerged himself without fear into the dead end of the tunnel. It was as if fog consumed him whole. Eira went after, passing through the illusion of a stone wall and into a palace hall. The only marker of the illusion was a small symbol—two halves of a circle, broken and offset from each other. It was the old symbol of the Tower, called the Broken Moon. That symbol had persisted for more than a hundred years before the crown princess, Vi Solaris, had decreed it must be changed to the marking of four circles and triangles that was now on the back of Eira's robes. A sudden and strange demand, for sure. But Eira favored the new symbol over the old.

They walked down through the palace hallways to the training grounds. Uncle Fritz had told her that sorcerers were once an oddity on the grounds—unwelcome, as sorcerers had been in most places. It was a strange thought, because one wouldn't think it had ever been true now.

The dusty training grounds of the palace had a whole section dedicated to sorcerers. They practiced alongside the palace guard and remnants of the Solaris army. Now, the vast expanse was empty, save for six people.

Marcus paused at a rampart, staring down at the small group that trained more by torchlight than sunlight. He rested his hand on the tall stone railing, looking on with what Eira could only describe as awe. She came to a stop alongside him, watching as well.

Three children sat off to the side. They were the newest class of Tower apprentices. Eira had heard the youngest was seven. The children watched as two young men practiced their sorcery, facing off against each other. They lobbed gusts of air that dug trenches into the packed earth. They dodged with unnatural grace, bodies hovering in the air for longer than should be possible. Their feet and hands moved like the wind. Because that's what they were...Windwalkers.

Windwalkers were the rarest of all the elemental affinities of the Solaris Empire—sorcerers thought to be extinct until one emerged from the ashes of a dark history: Vhalla Yarl. The woman who was born a commoner, thought to be a Commons, and then ascended beyond her station like a bird soaring against gravity to become the empress.

The same woman who was currently instructing both young men in the sparring ring.

"Just think of it," Marcus whispered. "Learning from the empress herself."

"You learn from the Minister of Sorcery himself." Something Eira yearned for. Even though she had the same blood as Marcus, she had never received the same privileges as her brother. Fritz had never pulled her aside for time one-on-one.

"It's not the same."

"Fate would have seen you born as a Windwalker if it wanted you to learn from the empress." Eira watched the two combatants dance. She didn't know the name of the younger, but she knew the older—Cullen.

Cullen was the oldest Windwalker. The first to awaken after Empress Vhalla. He had been treated with all the care that would be given to a quail egg from the moment he'd arrived in the Tower. Nothing was too good when it came to him. He was the darling child of every instructor.

Even the city had been enamored with him when he'd arrived. Being the first Windwalker after Vhalla Yarl had created an air of mystery and allure surrounding him. He'd even been granted a place in the Solaris court just for being a Windwalker. And because his father had gained a swift senate appointment.

He was first-generation money and nobility, and he acted like it.

"If only." Marcus sighed wistfully, dropping to his elbows and leaning against the railing.

Eira couldn't stand watching her brother daydream over being in the prick's shoes. Instead of watching, she placed the small of her back on the stone, leaning on her elbows and turning her gaze to the frosty mountains beyond. Her brother, the epitome of perfection in her eyes, hoisted Cullen up on a pedestal as if he were the Mother's gift to all sorcery. As if Cullen were somehow even better than the empress.

"You have a lot, Marcus. Don't wish it away," Eira murmured.

"What was that?"

"Nothing," she said quickly.

Any further conversation was cut off.

"Marcus, is that you?" Cullen called up.

"Hello, friend!" Marcus waved furiously. "Don't let me interrupt."

"We just finished; it's all right, come down."

"Are you sure?"

A pause to no doubt check with the empress. Then, "Yes, it's fine."

Marcus wheeled to face her. "Come on."

"I don't want to go."

"*Come on*. We have a chance to meet the empress!" Marcus grabbed her hand and nearly tore Eira's arm from her socket as he tugged her down the stairs pocketed into the wall that surrounded the training grounds.

Had this been his plan all along? Eira wouldn't exactly be shocked if it had been. Her brother was good at getting what he wanted. Perhaps befriending Cullen years ago and slowly working his way closer and closer to the other man was a long game to this moment. She stared at the back of her brother's golden-bronze hair. Whatever went on in his head was a mystery to her. But if only she were half as talented… half as determined…and half as loved as he was…

The world would be hers.

They emerged out of a side door and onto the training grounds. Cullen was already making his way over to them. The empress hung back, giving instructions that couldn't be heard to the other Windwalkers.

"I'm sorry, friend. Time got away from me," Cullen apologized with a suave smile. He said the words, but he didn't look sorry in the slightest. Eira had no doubt he was used to people being at his beck and call.

Marcus finally let go of her and Eira gladly fell behind. She laced her fingers, watching as Marcus gave his friend a firm pat on the shoulder, exchanging pleasantries.

Cullen, the Prince of the Tower, as the ladies called him. He looked the part in all his fine court clothes. His hair was a deep brown, so dark that in the fading light it nearly looked black. But Eira knew from a past excursion she had been forced on that, when the sun hit it, there were strands that glowed almost as gold as her brother's hair. Cullen's eyes were a hazel sunset color—piercing, almost uncomfortably bright, like hers. Eyes that now turned to her.

"You brought your sister." Cullen's expression fell, the warmth leaving it.

"I can go," Eira said easily. "In fact—"

"In fact it's our weekly dinner tonight," Marcus interjected. "You won't mind if she eats with us, will you?"

"Not at all," Cullen said with the grace one would expect of someone who'd received finishing lessons. The smile he forced objected.

Unwanted Eira. The ice wraith of the Tower. Sorcerer colder than winter. Eira was so busy beating herself up that she nearly missed the whispers.

…you and I…

…sure it's safe…

The second voice belonged to the icy woman she'd heard earlier. The same woman who had occupied, or at least passed through, the mysterious room she'd found. The same woman who had spoken of killing the emperor. Eira turned her head, looking toward the wall where the whispers seemed to come from. She hadn't heard the voice ever before, and now the woman was haunting her.

"What is it?" Marcus asked, a worried note seeping into his tone. He whispered, "Is it the voices?"

"It's nothing," Eira said quickly. "Nothing. Sorry, I thought of something I have to do, that's all. I should—" Eira was interrupted once more, this time by the empress.

"Cullen." Empress Vhalla Solaris crossed over to them. Her brown hair had been carefully coiled and pulled into braids that framed a golden circlet around her brow. One would expect an empress to be lofty and off-putting. But Eira found her more approachable than Cullen. "Are these your friends?"

"Yes, Marcus is a very good friend." Cullen motioned to her brother. Eira took half a step back, as if she could become one with the shadow and fade away. She didn't miss that he purposefully didn't mention her.

"It's good to meet you, Marcus," the empress said kindly.

"Your Majesty." Marcus sank into a low bow. "I apologize for the interruption."

"Not an interruption at all." The empress's eyes promptly turned to Eira. "And you are?"

"Eira, Your Majesty." She kept her eyes on her toes as she pinched her dress with three fingers and curtsied. Or, at least did her best approximation of a curtsy. Marcus seemed so natural among them. He was born for this. She was...a continual liability to his aspirations. What could her brother achieve if he wasn't saddled with her?

Eira hated the question, but she hated the answer even more.

"A pleasure to meet you both," the empress said politely, and promptly turned to Cullen. "You need to be better about not telegraphing your attacks. That's how Gregor got in so many surprise hits to you today."

"Yes, Your Majesty." Cullen nodded.

Despite her scolding tone, the empress smiled with what Eira would dare say was fondness. "You remind me of myself. I had the hardest time with telegraphing, too. It's natural, after all. We want to flow with the air."

"I will do better," Cullen vowed, nonetheless.

"I know you will. Now, if you will all—"

Horns echoed over Solarin.

All of them paused, holding their breath. Horns blared for two things and two things only. The first was war. But Solaris had been in peacetime for over twenty years. The second... was for the royal family.

"Vi." Vhalla whispered the name of her eldest daughter,

completely forgetting herself. Eira watched as the empress's royal facade crumbled and a mother's adoration shone through. Vi Solaris, admiral of the Solaris armada and crown princess, had been gone now for almost two years. "Please excuse me," she said hastily and started across the training grounds, meeting guards already emerging from the castle.

Cullen placed his hands in his pockets, a thoughtful and unreadable expression on his severe features. "We should go to the Sunlit Stage; it seems the crown princess has finally returned from the brutal lands of Meru."

"**M**ERU ISN'T A brutal place." The words sprung from Eira's lips before she could think better of them.

"What?" Cullen seemed startled that she was still there. "Oh, that's right, you're the one who's obsessed with the Crescent Continent, aren't you?"

"It's called Meru," Eira murmured, reminding him even though he'd just used its proper name.

"Let's just go to the Sunlit Stage," Marcus suggested. Her big brother saving her did have its perks. Marcus knew every topic Eira wanted to avoid and *usually* used that power for good. It was only a terrible ability when he was the one pestering her about said topic. "The crown princess hasn't been home since the announcement of the engagement."

"And what an announcement that was," Cullen said with a shake of his head. "I can't believe our princess will wed one of those pointy-eared folk."

Eira remembered that night. It was the only time she and her brother had been permitted to a state function. Their uncles had brought them to a winter ball where the crown princess had announced her engagement.

"They're called elfin." She couldn't stop herself from pointing out Cullen's mistakes.

Cullen glanced over his shoulder at her. "Are you going to correct me at every turn?"

"If you keep being wrong then it's my burden to bear."

"Such tact." An unkind smile spread on his lips. "I would love to see you for a day at the royal court. It would certainly be a sight to watch."

"Keep your courts, I don't care for them."

"I suspect the feeling would be mutual."

Eira glared.

"Be nice," Marcus said with a note of combined warning and scolding to both of them. "Don't talk to or about my little sister like that."

"Apologies to you both." Cullen didn't sound sorry at all. Eira glared daggers of ice into the back of his skull, stopping just before they manifested in thin air and actually hurt the man.

She didn't *want* to hurt anyone. Even if her magic insisted otherwise... Eira couldn't deny a dark and curious corner of her wondered what it would feel like to freeze him slowly, just like the journal described. Could she hold him in a frigid stasis without killing him?

"You too." Marcus didn't exempt her.

"I'll be nice as long as he is." This was why she never had spent time with Cullen and Marcus.

She'd met Cullen years ago and didn't like him in the slightest, avoiding him like the plague. Every story she'd heard whispered about him since affirmed the decision. Cullen was a polarizing person and Eira knew she was on the right pole when Alyss had agreed with her assessment. Then, after the incident three years ago and his involvement...Eira had all the more reason to be skeptical of his intentions.

The Sunlit Stage was the royal receiving area and largest, grandest public entrance to the palace. A wide stage connected the palace with an arena below. Common folk flooded in while palace servants and staff began to fill tall risers that stretched up and away from the semi-circle like sunbeams.

Luckily, they were among the first to arrive and secured good placement on the lower risers right above the archway that the crown princess would ride in through. The younger Windwalkers packed in around them, staying close. The other palace servants gave them a good step's worth of distance, even when it became crowded. The wariness that prevailed in public consciousness around sorcerers was a stubborn weed—

nearly impossible to rip out from the roots.

Eira ignored the servants, as usual, gripped the railing before her tightly, and stared at nothing. She submerged herself deep into the ocean of her magic, down and down until everything was muffled. This was a noisy place. The people were as loud as the brick and mortar. Everyone and every*thing* wanted to speak all at once in a din that only grew in volume the moment the emperor, empress, and younger prince emerged with their royal detail and took their place at the edge of the stage.

"Imagine what it's like..." Marcus sighed wistfully. His voice brought her back. "To have people screaming your name."

"It gets old," Cullen japed.

"Oh, quiet, you." Marcus elbowed his friend.

Eira kept her eyes downcast toward the archway below them. Any moment now, there would be—

The rumble of hooves brought the crowd to a hush. With the flutter of pennons catching on torchlight, moonlight, and the last dregs of sunlight alike, a group of twenty people rode through the center roadway and into the heart of the Sunlit Stage. Eira inhaled slowly, as though she could breathe in the unbridled air of a land across the sea...a land filled with unimaginable magic and peoples beyond her current comprehension. As if the people before her radiated that very air off their velvet-clad shoulders.

Elfin. They looked almost like humans, but weren't. From their pointed ears to brightly colored eyes, they were something different. A race of people that had been unknown to the Solaris Empire for hundreds of years until Crown Princess Vi Solaris formed the Imperial Armada and sailed across the sea three mere years ago. In three years, the world changed for the Solaris Empire.

A fact Eira sometimes felt like she was the only one who understood.

"Where's Vi?" Marcus whispered at her side.

Eira tore her eyes away from the ethereal creatures that

were the elfin to take in the greater group. Sure enough, she saw the elfin's delegation in their rich fabrics and careful stitching. There were the humans from Solaris in plate armor and the bland style Eira was familiar with.

But neither the princess nor her elfin betrothed were with them. A deathly silence had fallen over the assembled crowd as the masses seemed to acknowledge her absence and its possible implication. The dark eyes of the emperor were a blank slate as he regarded the group. The warmth Eira had seen earlier in the empress had vanished into something unreadable.

"Your Majesties." A man with pitch-black hair tied back into a small ponytail at the nape of his neck spoke. Judging from the bars on the shoulders of his nautical coat, he was some high-ranking member of the armada.

"Ambassador Cordon." The emperor's voice was surprisingly frigid for a man who the stories painted as the Fire Lord. "We were expecting our daughter's return."

"I regret that I do not bring our crown princess, but I do bring good tidings on her behalf." The ambassador ascended the stairs and sank to his knee, holding out a bound scroll to the empress.

Vhalla accepted the offering, broke the seal, and read it before passing it to the emperor. Everyone waited with bated breath. Waited to see if they were about to watch a massacre for the lack of crown princess…or if there was truly good news.

"People of Solaris." The emperor stepped forward, eyes still on the scroll. "These are good tidings indeed." A smile cracked his lips. Eira recognized it as the smile of a proud father. She knew it because her own father had given the same smile to Marcus countless times. "Our crown princess has succeeded in brokering a deal—not just with the Queendom of Meru, but with the Twilight Kingdom, the Kingdom of Draconis, and the People's Republic of Qwint. They are calling it the Five Kingdoms Accords."

"Kingdoms?" Eira repeated. "Wasn't one of them a queendom?"

"And one a…republic?" Marcus looked to Cullen and then

her.

Eira shook her head. "I've never heard the term before."

"It's something like the East used to be, I think. Back before Cyven was a part of the Empire—a government run by the people." Cullen was Eastern and the son of a politician; it would figure he'd know.

"How strange that there's a larger state run that way," Marcus murmured.

"How fascinating." Cullen leaned forward, hanging on the emperor's next words. Eira didn't place him as someone who would have an interest in anything beyond his scope of influence.

"To celebrate the finalization of this deal, each sovereign state will send a delegation of their finest sorcerers to compete in the Tournament of Five Kingdoms, set to begin at the start of the year 375."

"A tournament for sorcerers?" Cullen whispered in eager excitement. He met Marcus's eyes, completely overlooking Eira.

Eira stayed focused on the emperor, ignoring the young men.

"Arrangements for the tournament are to begin promptly." The emperor rolled up the scroll. "It will be a celebration of unity and strength between our cultures. This will be an opportunity to show both the might and grace of Solaris!"

Cheers rose for victors not even yet decided. Eira wasn't sure it had settled in on the people yet that they were cheering for sorcerers.

"In the meantime, Solaris welcomes Ambassador Ferro." The emperor motioned to the elfin man currently dismounting.

He had dark green hair that looked almost black or purple under the young night sky, long and unbound. The waves of his hair didn't hide his pointed ears. A cape was situated around his shoulders, held in place by a gold chain thicker than Eira's wrists. Ferro ascended the stairs and bowed with a flourish that had Eira suppressing a gasp of delight. Every movement the elfin made was magic.

"It is our honor to be here, Your Majesty. I come on behalf of Queen Lumeria, with good tidings and gifts to lay at your feet." At a sweep of his arm, two men hoisted a chest forward, placing it at the feet of the emperor. From her vantage, Eira could see gold, spices, and the most precious item of all—books—inside.

"We welcome you humbly and gladly. Come, Ambassador, you and your party are welcome at my table tonight as we discuss further details of this tournament."

The royals and delegates alike retreated across the stage and into the palace. Eira watched until the doors closed behind the last guard. Excitement rushed through her with the force of a tidal wave.

There were elfin in the palace.

The last, and only, time Eira had seen an elfin was two years ago. Uncle Fritz and Uncle Grahm had taken her and Marcus to the ball celebrating the engagement of Vi Solaris and Taavin—the Voice of Yargen. Which, as far as Eira could find in her books, basically made him the leader of their religion.

He had certainly looked noble that night in the moonlight. Eira had been so overwhelmed by the sight of him that it had made her lightheaded. She couldn't even speak when she had been introduced to the princess and elfin in a moment she'd treasure for the rest of her life.

That was the moment when she knew she had to see Meru with her own eyes, no matter what.

"Come on, Eira." Marcus shook her. "We have to get back to the Tower!"

"What?"

"Wake up! A tournament for sorcerers." She could tell from Marcus's demeanor, he was already expecting to compete. They didn't know how the tournament would happen, or where. They didn't know the requirements of participation. Yet Marcus, and all his endless confidence, knew he would go. "Let's get to Uncle!"

They raced back to the Tower. But they weren't the only ones with the idea. A roar of noise echoed through the spiral of the Tower. They followed it down to the main entry, where every student and teacher had packed in. Eira stayed up on the walkway, looking down over the railing that sloped into the sea of people.

Cullen led the Windwalkers; Marcus went with him. The apprentices of the tower parted for him naturally in wary regard. Cullen situated himself by where Fritz stood in the center of the masses.

"Listen, listen," Fritz said, waving his hands, trying to calm the crowd.

"I've been looking for you."

Eira nearly jumped over the railing, startled. Instead she spun and grabbed both of Alyss's hands. "You heard?"

"Who didn't?"

"Listen, please," Fritz tried again.

"A Tournament of Five Kingdoms. It sounds like something out of a fantasy story." Alyss squeezed Eira's fingers. "One way or another, I'll have to see it."

"We will," Eira said without thinking. The tide of excitement was rising in her as well, washing her out into a thrilling sea of possibility.

"Silence!" A voice demanded attention, booming above all others and resonating between the chandeliers overhead. Eira and Alyss both jumped. Grahm motioned to his husband, taking a step back. Fritz might be the Minister of Sorcery, but it was his husband who really kept the Tower from falling apart.

"Yes, thank you." Fritz cleared his throat and continued louder, "I know you all have a lot of questions. That's understandable. *I* have a lot of questions. But none of those questions are going to be answered tonight."

"Is it true? Will there be sorcerers from Solaris competing with these other kingdoms?" someone shouted.

"Since the emperor said it, I assume it must be true," Fritz answered. Then added hastily, "But again, let's not get ahead of ourselves. Until we know the details of this tournament there will be no way to decide who will get to partake in it or what partaking will mean.

"For now, every apprentice is to continue their classes and duties as normal. Every instructor will do the same. I will seek a meeting with the emperor or empress as soon as possible and will reassemble the Tower with an announcement hopefully in the next week. In the meantime, please remain focused on your obligations. And I had better not hear any of you harassing or questioning anyone about this.

"Am I understood?"

Muttered agreement.

"Good. Look after each other in the meantime." What Eira really heard Fritz say was, *keep each other in line.* "For—"

"The Tower takes care of its own!" every student and teacher said in one unanimous voice.

"Now, your dinners are getting cold." Fritz shooed the room.

Talk of the tournament was the only thing on every sorcerer's lips the entire way to the dining hall. Alyss and Eira bypassed it, too full of excitement to think of food. They'd find something in the pantry later to snack on so their stomachs didn't eat themselves before morning. Instead, they ascended the curving, central path of the Tower, looking for a corner to talk in. But everyone else had the same idea. Even the library was noisy with discussion.

Ultimately, they retreated to Eira's room.

It was a cramped place, like every apprentice's dormitory chambers. But Tower apprentices didn't have to share their rooms with others, which was better than most of the servants and staff in the palace. Alyss plopped herself on Eira's bed, immediately producing a blob of clay from her pouch and beginning to magically manipulate it. Eira chose to pace instead.

"What do you think it will be?" Alyss asked as she wriggled her fingers, watching the clay writhe and dance. "A tournament, so there must be games of some kind."

"I wonder how they'll manage to have us compete against each other... The elfin's magic—Lightspinning—is so different from ours. And I don't know anything of the Twilight Kingdom or the others."

"If *you* don't know it then no one in Solaris does." Alyss laughed. "Aren't you excited to find out?"

"I could burst." Eira curled and uncurled her fingers. Every icy wall she'd built up around her emotions had thawed. Magic seeped from her pores. She was surprised she wasn't leaving wet footprints behind her with every step. "I wonder if the tournament will be here. If we'll get to see them and whatever magic they do have."

"Of course it will be. Solaris is the center of the world," Alyss proudly proclaimed.

"You don't honestly believe that propaganda."

"Even with the new maps, it's just Solaris and Meru out there."

"The world is so much larger, Alyss." Eira stopped, staring out past the leaded glass of her window. The frosty peaks of the mountains teased her with that jagged horizon line. The world was out there, calling to her. Whispering from the great unknown. "Solaris *was* the center of the world, until trade opened with Meru. That was just three years ago. Now look, there's three, *three* other kingdoms! Think of how many more there could be."

"I'd rather not." Alyss laughed. "History class is already unbearable. Think of how much worse it will be if we keep making or discovering new history."

"Either way, I just want to see their world," Eira said wistfully. "I want to see Lightspinning in person. They say it's like weaving sunlight."

"And the Crones of the Mother say it's sacrilege to compare it that way."

"The Crones of the Mother hate progress." Eira shook her head and dismissed the notion.

"You know, there's one way to ensure you see them."

"What?" Eira turned to face Alyss.

"Go to the tournament."

"Obviously." Eira rolled her eyes. "But I'm not going to be able to get there if it's on Meru. Unlike the crown princess, I don't have a whole armada to carry me back and forth."

"There's a way to get there." A bright grin crossed Alyss's cheeks, nearly from ear to ear. "Compete."

"What?" Eira whispered.

"Be a competitor."

"We don't even...we don't know how."

"You could ask your uncle. You'll likely be the first to know," Alyss said eagerly. "Think, you and I could have a leg up on all the others."

"It'll likely be the instructors, or sorcerers far better than us." Eira hated how disappointingly logical she was inclined to be.

"We can be just as good as any of the instructors and are better than half—you know it."

"*You* might be just as good."

"*We* are," Alyss said firmly. "And if you try and fight me I'll throw this clay in your face and make it stick in your hair."

"I'm sure my brot—" Eira was interrupted by a deep growl of her stomach.

"Ha! You are hungry." Alyss sent the clay back into her pouch just as it was beginning to take the shape of a bird. Eira was grateful it didn't end up on her head. "I knew it."

"I only said I wasn't because it was so crowded."

"It's likely calmer now; let's go." Alyss linked her elbow with Eira's and pulled her into the hall. "We'll go. We'll eat. And we'll plan our training," Alyss decreed.

"Training?"

Alyss tossed her braids over her shoulder dramatically. "Of course. We want to be in top shape if we're going to be competitors.

FOR A WEEK, Eira went along with Alyss's pushing to turn themselves into "top competitors." Predictably, by day seven, their morning jogs ended up being more of a stroll around the city and ending either at the bookstore or the sundries store for Alyss's crafts. Not that Eira was complaining. The more she had time to think about the possible logistics of this competition, the more she doubted she would have any chance of actually participating.

She and Alyss were sitting in one of the Tower lounges, enjoying a peaceful, quiet evening, when a young apprentice approached.

"Eira Landan?" He stayed a few steps away and kept his eyes down. Eira had learned just how quickly rumors of her could spread in the Tower.

"You know it's me. What does the minister want?" She avoided calling Fritz her uncle and drawing any more attention to the familial bond.

"He'd like a word. He sent me to tell you he'd be in his chambers."

"All right, I'll head over." Eira closed the cartography book she'd been flipping through—looking at maps of Meru's crescent-shaped coastline and the city of Risen nestled within it—and slipped it into her bag as the young man left.

Alyss caught her hand, yanking her close. "I swear to the Mother above, if you get the opportunity to sign up early for this competition and don't write my name down—"

"Alyss." Eira stopped her friend with a laugh. "This likely has nothing to do with the competition. We don't even know what 'signing up' means yet, or if we can."

"Minister Fritz said he should have word in a week. I bet

he already does," Alyss whispered excitedly, glancing around. Of course, no one was sitting remotely close to them.

"Even if he knows, I'm not going to get to sign up early. I doubt he'll tell me anything. You know Uncle doesn't actually give me that kind of favoritism. Marcus, maybe, but not me."

"He loves you both, you know." Alyss gave her hand a squeeze.

"Yeah, I know." Eira didn't like talking about her family problems with Alyss. Her friend saw her parents only two, maybe three times a year. Meanwhile Eira had her brother, her uncle, and an aunt, all in the palace. The rest of her large, extended family were all within a day or two depending on how fast she traveled. "I'll see you at breakfast."

"See you then."

Eira left her friend and headed up the Tower for the door right before the minister's office, and gave a firm knock.

"Come in!" Grahm, Fritz's husband, called from within.

"Uncles?" Eira poked her nose around the door.

"Fritznangle is getting changed out of his robes." Grahm sat in a wingback chair by the large windows opposite the door on entry. "I made milk and chocolate, if you'd like some."

"You know I won't say no." Eira went to a table where a large silver kettle was warmed by a happy little flame. She topped off a cup and brought it with her to the sofa opposite Grahm.

"How have you been, Eira?" he asked.

"I'm fine."

"Excited by the presence of elfin in the palace, I bet?"

"I haven't exactly run into any elfin." Eira's lips quirked into a smile before she took a long sip of the decadent drink. Grahm's chocolate was one of the few things that could make her feel warm down to her toes. A rare time when Eira didn't mind being hot.

"I didn't hear a denial about being excited." Grahm gave her a knowing smile.

"Well, it is a bit exciting," Eira admitted, trying not to

overplay her hand. She'd taken an extra round of the city with Alyss, passing by notable landmarks, just hoping to see the elfin out sightseeing.

"Sorry to keep you waiting." Fritz emerged from a side door in his loose leisure clothes and headed right for the kettle.

"I wasn't waiting long. What did you want to talk with me about?"

"Well…" Fritz paused, mid-pour.

"Uncle?" Eira said when the silence dragged on.

"I'm not sure how to say this."

"Your cup, Uncle."

"Oh, *oh!*" Fritz quickly mopped up the spilled chocolate. Grahm tried to hide his smile with an expression of annoyance. He failed. Fritz could light his hair on fire and it would only make Grahm love him more. Eira had always admired her uncles' relationship. "Sorry about that."

"What's all this about?" Eira watched him as he came over and sat on the sofa next to her.

Fritz gave her a light pat on the knee. "I wanted to see how you're doing is all."

"I'm fine." Eira glanced between the two of them. "If that's all—"

"That's *not* all," Grahm interjected with a pointed look at his husband. "Go on, Fritz."

"We, no, I…*I* wanted to discuss the upcoming Trial of Five Kingdoms with you."

Alyss had been right. Fritz had information. Tingling ran down Eira's arms like a brisk winter wind, chasing away the warmth and bringing alertness. "Go on."

"I'll be making an announcement tomorrow morning with sign-ups starting for those interested in being a competitor in the tournament." Fritz took a sip of his chocolate and Eira remained poised at the edge of her seat, hanging on his words. "I wanted to ask, would you be interested in signing up to be a competitor for Solaris?"

Eira glanced between her uncles. "I… It's hard to make

a decision right now, without all the information." It wasn't. Eira already knew her answer. Anything that got her closer to Meru, the elfin, and Lightspinning was something she wanted to do. "Would it be such a bad thing if I did?"

The silence was deafening. Moments like these were the rare times Eira hated the quiet she usually longed for. Fritz and Grahm exchanged a look.

"Well—"

"Fine, I won't." Eira finished the last of her cup in a large gulp. She already knew what they were going to say. She didn't want to endure hearing it. "That's settled."

"Eira, we're just looking out for your best interests," Fritz tried to placate.

"So you tell me, but…" She now hated the warm chocolate in her stomach, radiating heat and a familial love she wanted to resent in that moment. "What *are* those 'best interests'? You give me half the work of Marcus at best. I'm only ever in basic classes and workshops. I know you tell me to take my magic slow but I have been for years. I can do more."

"We know," Fritz said calmly.

"And then there's Marcus being held back." The words spilled out like chocolate from Fritz's cup. "He's still an apprentice when he should be an instructor—or gone from the Tower and out in the world working. If you're keeping him here just to keep an eye on me then graduate him and give him a proper position in the Tower. He deserves *at least* that much."

"Marcus's status as an apprentice has nothing to do with you," Grahm said.

"Really?" Eira arched her eyebrows.

"Yes, really."

She didn't believe it. Not for a moment. "Look, we all know that I wouldn't be chosen as a competitor anyway."

"Eira, that's not—you see—" Fritz fumbled for words.

"It's fine. I know I'm not up to par." Eira set her cup down slowly and with fluid grace. It didn't even clank against the saucer as she slid it onto the table. The water within her was slowly churning, hardening into ice, and grinding against her chest. It sent cold daggers prickling under her fingers and swirled in her mind like a blizzard. Cold, constant, protected. "But even if I wouldn't be chosen, I would've loved to at least try out for a spot. The Mother knows you could have found a way to eliminate me anyway."

"I thought you'd prefer I ask you not to sign up directly, rather than eliminate you behind your back."

Eira pursed her lips. That was true, she supposed. "Well, now you have. If you'll excuse me, I've had a long day in the clinic and I should go rest before classes tomorrow."

"Eira…" Fritz said in that *don't be mad* voice unique to him alone.

She halted at the sound. "Tell me one thing."

"What is it?" Grahm was the one to ask.

"Is this request because of three years ago?" Eira looked them both in the eye. "You've told me this much; if it is, I want to know."

Friz opened his mouth to speak.

Grahm cut him off. "Yes."

The incident three years ago—her inescapable burden, the crime she could never expunge.

"I thought so. Excuse me, uncles." Eira departed with a bow of her head.

It stayed bowed as she descended the Tower. Eira walked without direction, eyes on her feet, not paying attention to where they were carrying her. The light shifted as she crossed through a hallway, connecting the Tower to the palace.

…*my father*…

…*how is he*…

The whispers followed her throughout the back halls of the castle, snippets of conversations long gone. She paused, listening to a particularly chatty vase just outside the guard offices—some scandalous affair. But the voices were just whispers on the wind, gone almost as soon as she heard them.

Eira pushed down her magic, silencing them once more.

"What do you need, sorcerer?" the man stationed at the entrance to the palace guard's barracks questioned her.

"I'm here to see my aunt. Don't mind me."

He gave her a wary look, but let her pass. She'd come here enough that she was reluctantly welcome. Eira went up the main stairway and entered into a giant room. Beds were stacked in bunks, three tall. They were so close together that Eira could barely pass through without brushing her shoulder against someone's hand or foot hanging off the edges.

On the outer rim, the beds were stacked only two high, and they had curtains hung—a bit of rare privacy for the higher-ranking guards like her aunt.

The curtains were already pulled for the night on her aunt's bed. Eira knocked on the bedpost anyway. Luckily, her bunkmate wasn't present.

"Go. Away," Gwen Charem seethed from behind her bed curtains.

"You said I could always come to you no matter what the time, Auntie."

The curtains snapped back. "Is that my favorite niece?"

"Goodness, don't let Rose or Lily hear you say that." Eira sat on the edge of the bed. Rose and Lily were her younger cousins, the daughters of one of Gwen's older sisters.

"Those girls are as unbearable as their mother." Gwen pulled herself upright with a yawn. She slept in her training clothes—always ready.

"You don't mean that."

"I do and Nia knows it." Gwen grinned. "And if she doesn't, I'm confident you won't be the one to tell her. You know a thing or two about unbearable older siblings."

The Charem family tree branched out wide from underneath Eira's grandparents—Orel and Tama. The two had five children over the span of sixteen years and Gwen was the youngest, only twelve years older than Eira. Two of their daughters had married and had kids—Eira's mother, Reona, and her sister Nia. The eldest daughter, Cass, was unwed and still lived with their parents just outside of Rivend. Fritz, their only son, had yet to have any children.

"So, to what do I owe the pleasure of an evening visit? Did I get it right? Does it have something to do with Marcus?"

Eira kicked off her shoes, pulling her feet onto the bed and sitting opposite her aunt. "You've heard about the tournament, right?"

"*Everyone* has heard about the tournament." Gwen grinned. "Are you thinking of becoming a candidate? Trying to beat the trials to win a spot as competitor?"

"Trials?" Eira tilted her head.

"*Oops.*" Gwen grinned sheepishly. "I forgot announcements weren't going to be made until tomorrow morning." Her aunt winked and Eira doubted she'd forgotten at all. Gwen had always been good to her. "Well, do you want to be in the tournament?"

"I…" Eira sighed, the conversation from earlier still turning her magic frigid.

"I think you should know, the Tournament of Five Kingdoms will be held on the Crescent Continent."

"What?" Eira leaned forward, her voice dropping to an excited whisper. "The tournament will be on Meru?"

Gwen looked a little too smug and proud to have shared that morsel of information. "That's the word I've heard."

Eira chewed on her bottom lip, picking at a loose seam on the hem of her dress. The competitors would get to go to Meru. Every fantasy she'd ever had about seeing that distant land with her own eyes suddenly had the chance to come true.

"Uncle doesn't want me to compete," Eira admitted softly. "Because of three years ago." When Eira dragged her eyes upward to look at Gwen, she was met with a deep scowl.

"Your uncle needs to remember you're a woman grown and to mind his business. You paid your time marvelously. That incident is done and over."

Eira let out a soft laugh. "Yes, but—"

"Three years ago was a grave and horrible mistake. You know that, but Eira, listen, look at me." Gwen leaned forward, covering Eira's picking fingers gently with her own. "You think I've never hurt anyone by accident before?"

"Hurting someone and killing them are very different," Eira whispered. Her aunt ignored the remark.

"Listen, when I first got here, I was sparring with another student. I was just older than you were. I was sixteen and stupid and thought I was in control of not just myself but the whole damn world. Sound familiar?" Gwen tilted her head and Eira forced a nod.

She didn't have the heart to correct her aunt. She hadn't had an illusion she was in control back then. She *hadn't cared about control*. She'd wanted them to hurt, just like they had hurt her—worse. She'd wanted the whole Tower to drown, to blister with her chill, whatever it took.

"In any case, I took it too far. I challenged him to a duel of forfeit. Do you know what that is?"

Eira shook her head.

"It's a duel that only ends when someone forfeits or dies."

"Duels to the death aren't allowed in Solaris."

"It's not *technically* to the death. Though I still got a strong reprimanding for it from my superiors. Anyway, to spare you from a long and gruesome bedtime story... Things got out of hand and I nearly took off the arm of one of my fellow guards. If the swing had been slightly different, I might have cleaved him to the heart."

"I didn't know," Eira whispered.

"I'm not exactly proud of it." Gwen laughed lightly. Eira could hear a bitter note she recognized in herself. "So it's not like I went home and told it around our Yule hearth that year. But it did happen. What do you think my punishment was?"

"Obviously you weren't kicked out of the palace guard."

"No. I was disciplined with hard lessons and service. But I served that time and I even rose through the ranks of the guard. Look at me now—I'm one step from major." Gwen yawned and leaned away. With her hand free, Eira resumed picking at the hem of her dress. "Look, I don't understand all the sorcery stuff of you and my brother. But I do understand what it's like to be young, and make a mistake, and feel your life is ruined. But, if you're breathing and are willing to work hard, there are not many mistakes that you can't recover from."

Eira kept her objections to herself. Certainly, if Gwen's story was true, it was pretty serious. But the person she had hurt willingly stepped into the sparring ring. They accepted a chance of injury.

They also walked away with their life.

Three years ago, Eira had stepped into a classroom with a heart filled with naive hope. She had confessed her love—a love she'd thought was true and real—to Adam and he'd decided to make a game of it. He'd lured her in with a note of false promises. He'd given her the idea that he might actually have feelings for the awkward and gangly girl she'd been.

Noelle and the others were hidden when she'd arrived. Just as he'd gone to kiss Eira, they'd leapt from their hiding places with jeers. The jest had been on her.

Worthless…ugly…not even your mother could love you…

Eira could hear a thousand voices and she would never forget those. Ice had replaced the blood in her veins that night. Their cruelty had exposed her fragility and her power ran rampant. She'd covered half the Tower in frost, two sleeping students in the thick of it. One experienced severe frostbite and never returned to the Tower. The other was young, and had a weak constitution… She never woke up.

It was a wonder Eira hadn't been expelled. Her actions were met with severe punishment, but since she'd been young, and not in control, she was spared irons—*barely*. The senate had certainly called for a more severe punishment. After that, most of the taunting happened from the shadows, rather than outright. And Eira could never look at any of her classmates the same.

"I hope you're right," Eira said softly to placate her aunt, shaking her head and sending the dark rats of her past scattering back to their usual shadows.

"I can tell you don't believe me. But I am." Gwen was settling back down underneath the covers so Eira stood. But her aunt caught her hand. "You have to move on eventually. Throw your hat in the ring. Fight to be a competitor."

"I'll think about it."

"No one—*no one* loves the Crescent Continent—"

"Meru," Eira corrected. The land had been mostly forgotten to time. Those who did know of it referred to it as the "Crescent Continent" not knowing any better. But it had a name now; as far as Eira was concerned, people needed to start referring to it properly.

"My point exactly." Gwen smiled and pulled Eira's hand so she was leaning over her. "No one loves that place more than you. You were born to go there, to see the wide world and find your place in it, I can feel it." Gwen kissed her cheek. "So sleep well, niece of mine. When you wake up, follow your heart. I'll help smooth things over with your uncle if needed."

"Thanks, Auntie."

Eira retreated back to the Tower, the shadows of her past and the possibilities of the future trailing her every step.

The next morning, she met with Alyss as planned and they suffered through classes.

After instruction was done for the day, Eira, Alyss, and the rest of the Tower met once more for an announcement in the main atrium at the Tower's base. Every student and teacher hung on bated breath to the minister's words.

"We all know why I have summoned you, so I will not make you wait." Fritz stood on a table to address them all. "This week, I had lunch with the empress, which sparked many meetings with both the empress and emperor, as well as the head of the Guard and Minister of War on this upcoming tournament. In addition, I have met with Ambassador Ferro and his delegation, discussing the details further."

"Get to the point," Alyss hissed under her breath.

Eira *shh*'ed her. She was having a hard enough time

focusing on Fritz over the murmurs, the voices that haunted her from the walls, the remnants of Gwen's encouragement, and the frantic beating of her heart.

"It has been decided, after much discussion, that one sorcerer of each affinity will be sent from the Solaris Empire as our competitors in the Tournament of Five Kingdoms. This will mean the other four kingdoms—territories—will send four of their best sorcerers as well to compete."

Whispers of excitement scampered across the room like eager children during the autumnal celebrations at the Festival of the Sun.

"Four of us, they're sending four!" Alyss shook Eira's shoulder.

"Only one of each affinity though."

"Don't be a downer."

Fritz continued before Eira could say anything. "Any apprentice over the age of fifteen or instructor is welcome to sign up as a candidate to be considered for competitor. To make the selection of final competitors fair, there will be a series of five trials to take place over the next three months that will determine who our champions are. Trials will begin after sign-ups here in the atrium. Firebearers will be able to sign up tomorrow. Groundbreakers the day after. Waterrunners will be last. Sign-ups begin at dawn and last until sunset."

"No mention of Windwalkers," Alyss muttered. "He's not going to have to compete in these trials, is he?"

Eira knew exactly who Alyss meant when she said *he*. "Of course not; they're not going to send the empress. And Cullen is the strongest, oldest, and most skilled of the Windwalkers that have awoken. He's the only viable option." Eira grimaced. "Maybe we shouldn't sign up. If we were chosen, we'd have to compete alongside Cullen."

"It'd be worth putting up with him as a teammate for a chance to compete against the other sorcerers from other kingdoms," Alyss said with a shake of her head.

"If you have any questions, please direct them to your

instructors. Good luck, everyone. You have a chance to represent Solaris on the greatest stage ever known," Fritz finished, his voice echoing overhead with the weight of destiny.

CHAPTER · FIVE

E IRA AND ALYSS weren't the only ones curious about what
"sign-ups" meant. The next evening they hovered with other
apprentices up on the walkway where they'd listened to Fritz
the night before. All eyes were focused on the board surrounded by
a ring of fire.

"I wonder if this counts as the first trial," Alyss said.

"*Hmm?*" Eira had yet to look away from the sign-up board.

"The minister said there would be five trials to narrow
down the candidates to four final competitors. I wonder if
crossing the fire counts as the first trial."

"I don't think so. He said the trials would begin after sign-
ups."

"Oh, right. He did." Alyss glanced up from the wood she
was magically whittling away, a rain of sawdust pooling at her
feet. "*Look*, he's going to try."

A young apprentice walked forward, hesitating at the edge
of the flames. He had the capped sleeves of a Firebearer. Yet,
apprehension radiated off of him. He looked like he was barely
fifteen.

Naturally occurring fire, water, wind, and earth couldn't
hurt sorcerers within their own affinities. A Firebearer couldn't
be burned by the flame of a candle, or flames they created.
However, if the fire was created by another sorcerer, then it
became a battle of strength.

Focus overcame the young man's face. Sweat dripped
down his neck as he stared intently at the flames. They
flickered, wavering a moment. He stuck his hand forward and
pulled it back with a hiss. The fire roared, brighter than before.
The young man walked away, dejected, giving up on signing

his name.

"Not strong enough." Alyss clicked her tongue. "Interesting. I wonder who's making that fire."

"Does it matter?" Eira asked, watching the next young woman approach.

She was a little older, and far more confident. She raised her hand and the flames parted, shrinking to a dull smolder around the board at their center. The apprentice passed over them, unharmed, and wrote her name on the list. From where Eira was standing, she counted about ten Firebearers' names.

"Of course it does." Alyss frowned. "Because it means they already have front-runners for competitors."

"How do you figure?"

"Think about it. Someone is making that flame that they're using as a benchmark for power. Who? Likely the person that they think would be strong enough to represent the Tower."

"So that's it then. We have no shot." Eira wanted to feel relieved. But the fantasy of being a competitor and going to Meru clung to her with determination.

The young woman left the circle of flames to a small round of applause. She bowed with a flourish and then stepped aside for the next person to try.

"Of course that's not it." Alyss glared at her. "We're going to be competitors, you and I. You have two days to practice for whatever they're going to throw at you. I only have one."

"Right..." Eira murmured. But her mind was already on what would block her sign-up board in two days. No... her mind was on *who* was behind it. Was it Fritz? That was the likely choice. But Eira had a nagging feeling deep in her gut that she knew who would be making the barricade for the Waterrunners. She pushed away from the wall.

"Where are you going?" Alyss called up after her.

"To see my brother."

Marcus was with Cullen in the library. They sat facing each other, each on a different sofa, huddled around the fireplace on the right-hand side of the room. Eira could see them well before they would see her. Perhaps because of the bookshelves. Most likely because she was an unwanted person and they were too engrossed in each other's conversation to notice her.

"...I'm just not sure if my parents will really let me go," Marcus said quietly.

"Of course they will," Cullen whispered back. "Look, you said you wanted to make a name for your family, right? This is the chance of a lifetime, and a supreme honor. You'll be representing all of Solaris. This is what you've been waiting for."

"But my sister... I told my family I would—"

"Your sister can look after herself."

Eira never thought she'd find herself agreeing with Cullen. But it turned out impossible things were happening left and right.

He continued, "You can't keep letting her hold you back."

"She's not."

"She is. That's why you're still here, isn't it?"

Eira crouched down, creeping the long way around and stopping behind a bookcase. From this vantage she could peer over the tops of the books to spy on the small sitting area. She barely breathed so she didn't make a sound.

"I'm here because I want to be."

"And you 'want to be' because you feel like you have to look after her because she's not *all there* and you're worried that if you're not looking after her then she'll do something that hurts her or others...again."

"It's not just that—"

"Look, it's admirable." Cullen continued to prevent her brother from getting another word in. "You really care for her. You love your sister. That's a wonderful thing and I'm not trying to discourage you from doing so. But you can't let her keep you from looking after yourself and doing what's best for Marcus."

Marcus was silent for a terrible amount of time. Eira wished she could see his face, but she didn't dare move. Finally, he said, "I know."

Her brother grabbed his head with both hands, ruffling his hair with his fingers. A searing needle inserted itself into her gut at his tortured motion. He was hurting. Not that she didn't see it—hadn't seen it. But he'd never let her even try to make it better. He'd always seen her as a pitiable thing, too helpless to even share some of his burdens.

"It'll be you, me, and Noelle. We already know who over half the team is based on who Minister Fritz asked to create the barriers."

Well, now Eira had the question she'd come to ask answered.

"We don't know that."

"Oh, he asked you and Noelle specifically just because he thought you both had free time on your hands?" Cullen rolled his eyes and leaned back in his chair. He propped one knee on the other, spreading out and dominating the space. Cullen could fill a room with his presence alone. "Be serious about this. We have an incredible opportunity and we would make a stellar team no matter who the Groundbreaker is. I will be the leader and you will be my second; we'll run the show. Think of the glory."

Cullen's hazel eyes glowed almost orange in the firelight— almost like a Firebearer peering into the future. They were alight with ambition and a pride that was almost frightening. Eira didn't entirely disagree with what he was saying. She wanted the best for her brother and certainly didn't want to be the cause of him holding back.

But she didn't fully believe Cullen was acting in Marcus's best interests either. The only person Eira could be certain Cullen stood for was himself.

"I already told Uncle I'd sign up. We'll see if I get past the five trials." Marcus shrugged.

"We know you will. No Waterrunner is better than you in this Tower, not even Fritz himself."

"Don't insult my uncle." Marcus stood with a stretch and

a yawn.

"I'm stating facts, not making insults."

"You're just buttering me up because you want to make sure I go to Meru with you."

"Can you blame me?" Cullen paused and there was a brief moment of vulnerability that Marcus seemed to miss as he turned. But Eira saw it. She saw his tired eyes and the brief slump of his shoulders. She saw something underneath the "Prince of the Tower" that he projected to everyone. "I need this, Marcus. It's victory or nothing for me."

"I know." Marcus wrapped his arm around Cullen's shoulder. "You'll triumph. You always have; so no matter what, I'm sure of that much."

As the two men started out of the library, Eira retreated into the shadows on all fours. She pressed herself against the back wall and felt her magic condense in the air around her. Invisible water droplets—present everywhere—grew fat with her power. They shimmered, changing the way the dim light was refracted, bending it to Eira's will.

An illusion surrounded her. If either young man were to look her way, they would only see wall and shadow. Neither did. They were too engrossed in continuing their discussion.

Eira dropped her magical shield and sat in the darkness. Whispers drifted around her from the books and shelves. Some spoke of love, some of sorrow, most of nothing important at all. Ever since she'd stopped trying to completely shut out the voices, they'd grown more articulate.

She blamed Alyss. The Tower was becoming so noisy she could hardly hear herself think.

There was one place that was quieter than the rest. And, shortly, Eira found herself in the Waterrunner storeroom, pushing on the hidden door and slipping into a forgotten Tower room. She hadn't visited the mysterious place in days, but it was exactly as she left it. The journal she'd been reading was out on the table, moonlight striking it in a thin line. A candle she'd lifted from the servants' storerooms in the palace was set out alongside it, half-burned.

"What would you do?" Eira whispered to the journal.

Silence was her only reply.

She knew the answer though. Whoever had written these journals and occupied this room had been someone bold and powerful. Someone who didn't care about what the world said they should or shouldn't do. Someone who, at some point, had said the words, *Kill our sovereign.*

They'd obviously failed. Emperor Aldrik was still alive and well. And his father had died at the hands of the Mad King Victor. So whomever this woman had been, she hadn't murdered any emperors.

Unless... Eira shook her head. The thought was too impossible to entertain. There was a woman made of pure evil and wrath who had been in the Tower of Sorcerers many, many years ago. At least, so the rumors claimed.

But she was more lore than fact. A ghost whose name was bad luck to even *think.*

Eira sat on the edge of the bed. It creaked underneath her, but held her weight. She lay back and stared at the ceiling, trying to envision herself as this woman. As someone bold enough, crazy enough, to say the words...

"Kill the emperor," Eira whispered aloud, trying it on. The words were uncomfortable, sending tingles up her arms. But there was bravery in them. They were dangerous and wild. They weren't something people who acted appropriately said or even thought.

She shook her head, casting them aside. Eira wasn't winning any awards for patriotism. But she also didn't wish the emperor dead.

Still, the boldness those three words flushed her with remained.

Eira turned her head, coughing as a plume of dust escaped the pillow. Her eyes watered and the desk came back into focus. She had two choices. One was to continue lying there, doing nothing. The other was to get up and defy all odds. To reach and try for something that the world didn't think she should have.

She knew what her uncle and brother thought she should do. Her parents were likely on their side. Alyss and Gwen were on the opposite side.

But what did *she* want?

Taking a deep breath, Eira sat up and crossed to the desk with a step. She opened her tinderbox, lighting the candle on the desk. There was enough wax to get her through the night; tomorrow she could look into procuring a flame bulb for the room. Or at least a better stock of candles.

Eira flipped open the journal and began reading. Alyss was right. If she wanted to make herself a contender for the tournament then she should start practicing now.

THE NEXT DAY, Eira watched as Alyss waited her turn in line. The sign-up board was completely encased in a thick, granite cube. The walls were unnaturally smooth—which indicated they had been made by magic, and not human hands.

One by one, Groundbreakers approached. They would plant their feet and shove their palms into the granite. Most of them did nothing at all. The rock was unforgiving. For some, it cracked under their hands. Or it wobbled, as though the rock had turned into gelatin, but the stone ultimately didn't yield.

But a rare few approached the stone and parted it like a curtain, then slipped inside to write their name before reemerging. Alyss was one of those few.

"I told you," Alyss said proudly as she sauntered up to where Eira was waiting, "it would be no problem."

"You were nervous at breakfast this morning," Eira pointed out with a grin. "But congratulations. I never doubted you."

"Tomorrow is your turn." Alyss started up the Tower, Eira following silently. Alyss glanced at her from the corner of her eye. "Don't tell me you're going to back out."

"I'm not," Eira said with more confidence than she felt.

Two factions had been warring in her since the night prior. One said to follow the path people were laying out for her—to not let her family down and to step away from the trials. She'd already seen what happened when she tried to make waves. She wasn't designed for the greatness that Cullen, or the mysterious Waterrunner who had found a secret Tower room to make their own, or anyone like them, so clearly sought.

But the other side of her spoke with Gwen's voice. *You were made for this.* The trials were hers for the taking. No one was better suited to go to Meru—no one would want it more than her.

That night, she returned to the hidden room when everyone else in the Tower was asleep. Eira practiced her magic into the small hours of the morning and crashed on the bed, not even bothering to go back to her room. She was jolted awake a short time later by the sound of someone rummaging through the storeroom.

Eira held her breath, fully expecting whoever it was to finally see the hidden door. But they didn't. The sounds stopped and the rumble of the storeroom door closing resonated through the castle stone to her.

She raked her fingers through her hair on the way to breakfast and tried to beat the dust out of her clothes.

The dining hall for the Tower was in the center. Apprentices took turns cooking, so the food was always different…and of varying quality. This morning was cuisine from the western portion of the Empire—a tomato-based stew with an egg poached in it, served with two points of toast.

"You weren't in your room this morning," Alyss observed, situating herself across from Eira at a long table. No one else dared to sit near them. "And you look a mess. Did you sleep in your clothes?"

"I did."

"Why?"

"I was practicing all night."

Alyss's face lit up. "I knew you had it in you." She leaned forward, her braids slipping over her shoulders. "I don't see your brother this morning. I think you were right. He is the one making the barrier today."

"Have you gone and seen it yet?"

Alyss shook her head. "I'll go when you sign up. Want to do it on the way to the clinic?"

"I'll do it after the clinic."

"Sign-ups are only until sundown," Alyss needlessly reminded her. "Be sure you're not out too late."

"I should say that to you. You're the busy one who always holds us up."

Alyss stuck out her tongue and made a face.

It turned out that Eira's jest had been wrong. Alyss only had a few patients to help the clerics with. Meanwhile, Eira's list had tripled.

Fritz handed over the list as though it were nothing. There was no mention of her brother from either of them, but Eira knew. She had this list because he wasn't going out today. He couldn't go attend the clinics if he was making the barrier. And if she was kept busy until sundown as a result, likely all the better as far as her uncle was concerned.

"There's one more thing," Fritz said before she left his office.

"If I'm going to get through all of these I'd better start now." Eira waved her list through the air.

"In a rush?" His words held an accusatory tone.

"Just want to make sure that I don't besmirch the Tower by being late or not getting to see everyone." Eira pressed her lips into a thin smile.

"Well, here. You can read this on the way." Fritz passed her a folded letter, sealed with a familiar glob of wax. "It arrived this morning."

"Thank you," she murmured and excused herself. Eira flipped over the letter. Her name was written in her father's handwriting on the front with the words "Apprentice of the Tower" scribbled beneath it. She slipped her finger under the seal, but instantly thought better of it. This wasn't something she wanted to read in the middle of the Tower's main hall.

Retreating to the Waterrunner storeroom, Eira gathered the things she'd need for the clinic, her bag three times as heavy as normal. Taking a breath and hoping everyone was already focused on their classes or the barrier, she opened the letter.

It read:

Eira,

Word of the trials has reached us and we couldn't be more excited! This seems like an incredible opportunity, one that shouldn't be missed.

She smiled, but the expression slipped from her face as she read on.

As you know, your brother has dutifully looked after you for years. He's supported your time in the Tower from a very young age. Now, we would like to ask you to support him.
These trials will mean a lot for him.

"Mean a lot for *him...*" she read out loud, seeing if the words felt any better when heard. They didn't. They felt as bad as they were to read.

Please make sure you give Marcus space to shine. Your uncle tells us that you're eager to prove yourself. But now isn't your time. Support your brother as dutifully as he's supported you.
We're planning on making the journey to Solarin to see him compete in the second trial. We can't wait to cheer his success alongside you. Listen to your uncles and focus on your studies.
We love you,

Mother & Father

She read the note twice, willing the words to change. *Support Marcus. Step aside. Wait your turn.*

"When will it be my turn?" Eira whispered, her voice thin with a pain she couldn't quite describe. Eira shook her head and shoved the note in the bag. The words were becoming blurry, and if she looked at it any longer the letter would tear her up into smaller pieces than she could hope to put back together.

Trying to put it from her mind, Eira started back down the Tower. But the trials lived on the tongues of every excited apprentice. And the barrier she saw on her way out was yet another weighty reminder.

The Groundbreaker's cube had been smooth and polished. Her brother had gone for a more…organic approach. Spears of ice wove together into a wicked-looking cage. It radiated plumes of frost. The whole lobby was frigid with its presence.

She had to admit, she was impressed. It looked formidable. And it seemed to be effective at keeping most of the Waterrunners out. Two attempted as Eira wound down the walkway and out of the Tower. Neither could make a single blade of ice budge.

The day dragged on, and on. Yet, somehow, it was over all too soon.

The sun hung low as Eira made her way back to the Tower. She was breathless by the time she arrived, winded by a light jog, determined to beat the sun. As Eira entered the Tower she saw Alyss seated in the back corner, waiting. Fritz had taken up a position by the cage of ice.

Eira froze. She hadn't accounted for an audience. Alyss, maybe. But not the twenty others who milled about. And certainly not her uncle.

Fritz didn't notice her. He was focused on his timepiece— no doubt counting down the minutes until the barrier fell and he could collect the board and be done with the sign-ups.

Alyss rose to her feet, summoning Eira's attention. *Do it*, she mouthed. Eira swallowed hard. *Do it*, Alyss insisted silently.

Her parents' request was still at the forefront of her thoughts. It had been there all day, worming away at her resolve.

With a slow shake of her head, Eira tucked her chin and started up the pathway. *It's better this way*, she tried to tell herself. She'd been wrong; Gwen had been wrong. She wasn't meant for this, Marcus was. He was the shining star of the family—the one who would no doubt follow in their uncle's shoes. Competing in the Tournament of Five Kingdoms was a good start toward Minister of Sorcery for the Empire, maybe even a lordship like Cullen.

If he did this, he wouldn't be held back by her anymore.

Eira's footsteps slowed. She looked over her shoulder, down at the cage of ice. Fritz caught her eye and smiled, giving a small wave.

A surge of wild, and likely misguided, bravery overtook her. No. There was another way to show them all Marcus didn't need to hold himself back because of her. She could *prove* she could stand on her own. Swallowing down her nerves and allowing the courage to rise, Eira stalked back down and crossed to the cage of ice.

"Eira? Might I help you with something?" Fritz blinked at her.

"Please excuse me, Minister." Eira gave a bow of her head and stepped around him.

"Eira—"

Before she could second-guess herself again, Eira held up her hand. The cold sank into her fingers, familiar and welcome. She allowed the tethers of magic to wrap around her forearm. Eira took a step forward and her hand met the bitter ice. She fused to it, magic and flesh.

There was no doubt; this was her brother's magic. Eira had spent all of her life looking up to him, wanting to be like him. She knew his power better than anyone. She took a breath, and closed her hand into a fist.

The deep-blue ice crunched under her fingers like it was nothing more than frost. The whole barrier fractured with a crack that echoed through the Tower. The ice fell to the floor as water.

Eira lifted her skirts and stepped over the puddle. It rippled and writhed against her magic, trying to reform. Spears of water rose from the ground, frost cracking through them before they fell back down under their own weight. Her brother must be tired from holding the barrier up all day. Because he couldn't put up much of a fight, wherever he was.

Eira lifted the pen and inked her name, last on the list. Fritz's gaze bored holes into her skull, but Eira ignored him as she returned the pen and retreated up the Tower, heart racing in her ears.

"T HAT. WAS. BRILLIANT." Alyss grabbed both of Eira's hands and spun Eira around her room. "The way you didn't just move the barrier but shattered the whole thing! I didn't know if you had it in you to even sign up. But, wow, what a statement. You just walked in there and *pow*—" Alyss thrust out a hand, punching the air. "Barrier gone. Look out, other Waterrunners. Eira is here to stay!"

Eira laughed nervously. "I don't think my uncle was as amused as you are." Her parents wouldn't be either.

"He didn't stop you."

"He *couldn't* stop me, not really." Eira paced back and forth between Alyss and the window. "At the end of the day, he can't show me favoritism, or the opposite. I have to be the same as any other apprentice." And if that were true, why was Eira so nervous? Likely because she had just, very publicly, disobeyed the request of her entire family.

In the three years since the incident, Eira had worked to honor every expectation set out for her. But Gwen was right. Wasn't she? Eventually Eira had to stand on her own. She had to break away from her family's desires of her and show them who she really was without being tethered to Marcus.

"I'm sure it'll be fine."

"I—" Eira didn't get to finish. Fate decided to explain for her instead.

A flurry of four knocks on the door, a pause, and then two slow knocks interrupted her. Before she could tell her brother to come in, he entered. Marcus's eyes glossed over Alyss and landed on her.

"Uncle wants you."

"I bet he does," Eira mumbled.

"Don't let her be in trouble." Alyss wedged herself between Eira and Marcus. "She's allowed to compete in the trials if she wants to."

"Go back to your room, Alyss," Marcus said in his no-nonsense tone. "Convincing her to sign up was no doubt your *brilliant* idea."

"I *am* brilliant, thank you for noticing." Alyss completely ignored the sarcasm that hung on the word "brilliant" when Marcus said it. She squeezed past Marcus and called back from the hall, "Good job, Eira. Can't wait to be your teammate for the Tournament of Five Kingdoms!"

Eira didn't say anything; she was too focused on guarding herself against the daggers that Marcus was glaring into her.

"Let's go." Marcus put his back to her and started up the Tower.

Eira scampered behind him. "Marcus—"

"Save it, Eira."

"Marcus, I know you're angry with me."

"You have no idea what I feel." Marcus's voice pitched upward and then took an immediate dive. He rounded on her. "There's no way you could because *I* have no idea what I feel."

"I know you didn't want me to compete." Eira stared her brother in the eyes. After her growth spurts the past two years, she was nearly his height.

"Of course I didn't. I don't want you to do anything that could put you at risk. I *can't* let you do anything risky. That is one thing that's been made very clear to me by Mom and Dad and everyone else, so I thought it was to you, too." Marcus continued upward again.

"Life is full of risks," Eira hissed, dropping her voice as they passed by other sorcerers. "You can't protect me from all of them."

"Don't tell me what I can't do," he grumbled.

"Yeah, it's not fun, is it? Someone telling you what you can and can't do."

"Eira—"

"Maybe you'll get it now." She glared at him. "I am my own person. I don't just jump when asked and I won't neatly exist only where and how you or anyone else wants me to."

"You don't think I know that? That *we* know that?" Marcus shook his head. Disappointment radiated off of him with more strength than his magic earlier. "But you also have to trust us when we're looking out for your best interests."

"What about *your* best interests?" Eira hated that she was echoing Cullen. "When will you stop worrying about me and start focusing on you?"

"When I can trust that you won't accidentally kill people!" he snapped, and then instantly backed away.

"I didn't mean to, you know I didn't." Eira wrapped her arms around herself, as if she could ward off the waves of guilt that crashed down on her with every reminder of that day. "It wasn't—"

"I know. I'm sorry, I shouldn't have brought it up." Marcus shook his head. "But…there is that incident. And the 'voices' you hear all around."

"I really do hear voices. You know I do," she whispered, breathless. One remark after the next was a gut punch, hitting harder than he likely intended and leaving her windless. Out of everyone, he was the one who said he believed her. She needed someone in her family to believe her, and if not Marcus, then who? "I've told you, the voices come from unintentional vessels made by people's magic without them realizing… That's why the Tower is nosier than anywhere else."

"Eira." He sighed and slowed to a stop. They were nearing Uncle's office. Marcus's hands clasped over her shoulders and he looked her in the eye. "I know you believe that, but no one else has ever heard voices like that. Not one Waterrunner. And unintentional vessels are very difficult to make."

"Maybe not as difficult as people think. Maybe someone else heard the voices and they were too afraid of being treated like this to say anything."

Pain flashed across his expression, chased by guilt. Still, Marcus didn't relent. "Which do you think is more reasonable? You have some kind of ability that no one else has ever had? Or that you're hearing things that…"

"That aren't real?" she finished, as frigid as the tides within her.

"That you want to hear," he said firmly. "I know things haven't been easy for you. It's natural to want friends. Or to want to feel special."

"I'm not making this up. And I don't have imaginary friends." Eira pulled away from him. Pain seared up her chest, infiltrating the numbing barriers she tried to submerge herself within. "You really don't believe me, do you?"

"I believe you believe what you're saying. Eira, wait—"

She wrenched open the door to the office of the minister, done with this conversation.

Fritz sat behind his desk, head in his hands. Grahm leaned against the edge of the desk, arms crossed. Whatever conversation they had been having came to an abrupt end as well.

"Let's get this over with." Eira sat in one of the two chairs opposite Fritz, bracing herself to be chastised further.

"Close the door, please, Marcus," Fritz said wearily. Marcus obliged and Fritz turned to her. "You said you wouldn't sign up."

"I changed my mind."

"We asked you specifically not to. Your *parents* asked you specifically not to," Grahm said. Frustration made his voice harder than his arm made of ice. He'd lost the arm in the war against the Mad King Victor and now used his magic as a prosthetic.

"It's fine," Fritz said with a sigh.

"It is?" Eira asked cautiously.

"Yes. The first trial is meant to cut the field in half. You'll be in the half that's cut."

"Are you saying you'll really cut me regardless of how I

perform?" She couldn't believe what she was hearing.

"No, unfortunately the trials are going to be made public at every stage. So I can't interfere behind the scenes without raising questions. I'm saying you will throw it."

"Why don't you want me to do this?" Eira pushed herself off the seat with a slap. "Why don't any of you want me to do this?"

"We told you why," Grahm said without looking at her.

"Because of three years ago? It was a mistake—an error. I'm not the girl I was then. I'm a woman now. I'm stronger and I have more control."

"Do you?"

"Of course I do!"

"Do you?" Grahm gave a nod to the chair.

Eira followed his gaze back to it. The entire chair was soaking wet, dripping on the floor. She glanced at her hands, at the water there already condensing into ice.

"Yes," Eira insisted, letting go of her power and frustration with one exhale. The water evaporated. "And maybe this is the only way to prove it to all of you. It's clear to me now, if I don't do this, you are all going to continue treating me like a child to be handed off and managed for the rest of my life. Even if I'm not chosen as a final competitor, I'll show you all that I can handle myself."

"Stop being unreasonable." Grahm rolled his eyes.

"Wanting some control of my life is the least unreasonable thing I could ask for." Eira started for the door.

"Don't be selfish, Eira," her brother murmured.

Eira pinned him with her stare. "Don't you see? This is as much for me as it is for you and your freedom, too."

"Please sit down. We're not finished," Fritz said.

"I am." Eira slammed the door behind her.

She stormed down the Tower, working to keep the dark currents whorling in her under control. Her ocean was churning with ice, grinding into bitter stillness. Ice. Ice all the way down. Ice from the top of her head to her toes. She'd freeze the entire tumultuous ocean in her.

"Well, aren't you the ice queen tonight?" Cullen's voice was like a lightning strike, arcing through every corner of her.

Eira stopped dead in her tracks. Cullen was right down the hall from her. Hair perfectly coiffed up and off to the side. Hands in pockets and wearing that lazy, arrogant smile of his.

"What?"

"You'd better calm down or you're going to freeze the whole Tower...*again*."

When she scowled, he pointed to her feet. Sure enough, ice was spreading from where she stood. Cursing under her breath, Eira pressed her eyes closed and exhaled deeply. When she opened her eyes, the frost was gone.

"There."

"What has you so worked up?" Cullen asked before she could leave him behind. "No, wait, let me guess, you're coming back from talking with Marcus and you've realized that you embarrassed him in front of the whole Tower with your little show today."

"What I talk about with my brother isn't your business, Cullen." Eira turned, glaring up at him. The light of the flame bulbs cast almost sinister shadows on the hard lines of his jaw and nose. His brown hair was outlined in orange. His eyes were a warm amber color, as threatening as they were beautiful.

"Let me give you a bit of advice." He took a step toward her. Eira didn't back away.

"Let me tell you I don't want your advice." She gathered her height. But he was farther up on the slope of the Tower's main walkway. And he was just slightly taller to begin with.

"Your brother is going to be a competitor, with me. Some people are just born for this." He gave a small shrug and his eyes dragged down her body, head to toe. "Nothing to be bothered by or ashamed of when you don't measure up. But I will have the team *I* choose for this competition. You're not going to get very far challenging that."

"The final team is chosen based on merit."

"The trials are a formality."

"You arrogant man," Eira seethed. Cullen had been born with his powerful magic, his perfect hair, his up-and-coming family, and his handsome face. He'd been handed everything without ever having to work for it. He had been the first Windwalker after Vhalla's ascension to power. He had been hand-trained by the empress herself. He was risen to lordship; his father had become a senator, welcomed with open arms into the Solaris Court—no wonder he thought the world revolved around him.

"It would be more correct to say, 'You arrogant *lord.*'"

"Now you're going to start flaunting your title?" She narrowed her eyes at him. Cullen historically hadn't demanded the use of his title in the Tower. He was modest, or claimed to be. Of course, the humility had also been an act.

"I'm just correcting you. As long as you get things wrong, it'll fall to me to do it." He threw the words from their last interaction back in her face.

Eira scowled and didn't take the bait. "You have no control over this. The trials will be public."

Cullen seemed genuinely surprised at that information. But the expression quickly vanished on an unseen breeze. "All the more reason for you to back out when you can. No reason to make your humiliation a public affair."

"I'm going to compete and I'm going to win," she vowed as much to herself as to him.

His face twisted with disgust. "Think of your brother."

"I think I'm the only one in this Tower who is. Good night, Cullen. If you need me, you can find me at the first trial." Eira stepped away, heading in the opposite direction as him. He continued upward, no doubt to go to Marcus's room and tell him of Eira's lack of control and her sour demeanor.

Think of Marcus.

How dare they. The statement was a betrayal on two fronts. The first was a betrayal to Marcus, as if the world was content to let him be her keeper. If Eira never stepped out of his shadow then he would forever be saddled with responsibility for her. The second was a betrayal to her. None of them believed she had a shot. They didn't even have the decency to pretend they did.

For a second night, Eira didn't go to her bedroom. Instead, she went to the mysterious room behind the secret door. She read into the late hours and, for the first time, dared to attempt some of the stranger, magical instructions in the long-forgotten journals.

"What's wrong?" Alyss said the moment she sat next to Eira at one of the long tables in the lecture hall.

"I didn't sleep well," Eira murmured, flipping through the blank pages of her notebook and envisioning the pages of the journal she'd been reading an hour ago.

"This is more than that." Alyss grabbed her hand. "You're staring at blank pages; you look a mess; *and* you weren't at breakfast. It's skillet cake day. There is nothing you love more than when they stop serving us that gruel and make us hot, buttery skillet cakes."

"The explanation of how wonderful the skillet cakes were was really not necessary."

"Tell me what's going on and you'll get one."

"What?" Eira straightened.

"I sneaked one out of the mess hall—now tell me what's going on."

"Cake first."

"No, *you* first."

Eira groaned. "Fine. You know my uncle called me last night to meet with me…" Eira recounted the events with Marcus, her uncle, and even Cullen in the hall after. When she finished, Alyss blankly passed her a grease-stained parcel. Eira put her bag in her lap and rested the skillet cake on top—the last thing she wanted was butter stains on her dress.

"What absolute dolts," Alyss said, finally. "The whole lot of them are idiots."

"Easy on the insulting, they're still my family. Except for Cullen…have at him," Eira said between bites.

"We're going to show them, you and I." Alyss nudged her with her shoulder. "I'm proud of you for not backing down."

Eira licked her fingers and said, "There's something else I need to tell you about." She'd been debating when was the right time to tell her friend of the secret room. But since it seemed like it was going to be more than a passing fascination, now was as good a time as any.

"What?"

"Well, showing you would be easier…"

"Now you have me on pins, what is it?"

They were interrupted by a shrill laugh. Noelle entered the lecture hall with Adam and their usual posse. They never seemed to go anywhere without their admirers and accomplices. Eira brought her eyes back to her notebook, wiping her mouth with her fingers.

"They all signed up, too," Alyss said softly.

"Good," Eira whispered back. "I'll really enjoy crushing Adam in the trials." Even if Eira wasn't chosen as a competitor…showing her family she could look after herself *and* putting Adam in his place would be a good consolation prize.

"All right, everyone," their instructor, Mister Levit, said as he walked in. "We have a lot to cover today, and so you're not all distracted during class, I will address what is no doubt the most pressing thought on your minds—the trials."

Murmurs were exchanged by just about everyone in the lecture hall. Most eyes went to Noelle and Adam's group. But a few wary glances were cast Eira's way.

"The first trial will be held over the next week. As you all know, there will be one sorcerer of each affinity sent to the tournament. So every participant is really competing only against the others who share their affinity. Thus, each affinity will be tested on a different day."

As he spoke, Mister Levit wrote in chalk on the board. In four days, the first trial would begin with the Firebearers, then Groundbreakers, and then Waterrunners on the final day.

"Now, I know the candidates among us are all burning to know the details of their first trial. And I know that even the non-candidates of the Tower are already invested." He wiggled his fingers in the air, sparks of fire dancing between them on the word "burning." "I will tell you everything I know and we'll leave it at that. Since the Tournament of Five Kingdoms is meant to celebrate a joining of cultures and mutual respect, there will be many events and opportunities for cultures to mingle. Naturally, we want to send the best among us, who are not only skilled with magic but who also will display tact and grace in navigating the cultures of Meru.

"Thus, the first trial is indeed…a test. A written examination that will assess the competitors' knowledge of Meru, its cultures, and customs."

"*HA!*" Alyss blurted.

"What?" Noelle nearly shrieked at the same time.

"Ladies, please." Mister Levit sighed.

A written test…on Meru. The blank expression Eira had trained on her face in the presence of Adam and Noelle cracked into a smile. This first trial was *hers*. No one in the Tower was more fascinated with Meru. No one else had read, for years, every limited scrap of information there was.

No wonder her uncle had tried to convince her to throw it. There would be no way she'd be culled, otherwise.

"Mister Levit, this simply isn't fair," Noelle said. "We are to be measured on our skills as sorcerers, aren't we?"

"The details of the tournament have yet to be decided," he reminded them. "As I was saying, the best thing Solaris can do is send well-rounded competitors who have exceptional skill, grace, knowledge, courage, determination, and, of course, people who won't put their feet in their mouths the moment they arrive on Meru."

"I told you," Alyss whispered and slapped Eira's leg. "You were made for this." Eira gave her friend a small grin. "And now you're going to have to help me study. I only have five days to get all of what's in your head, in mine."

Eira held back a snort of laughter.

"If you're worried about your scores, Noelle, might I recommend you pay closer attention in today's lecture. We will be discussing the end of the War of the Crystal Caverns, which will lead us nicely into a discussion on the opening of Meru…"

Eira listened attentively to Mister Levit. But it was all information she already knew. The Crystal Caverns fell with the end of the short reign of the Mad King Victor, and the location where the Caverns once stood became one of the first sites dignitaries from Meru had demanded to visit.

The Crystal Caverns had been a place of mysterious and powerful magic. Magic that, in Eira's opinion, the world seemed better off without. Based on the stories, exposure to the crystals turned men into monsters and unlocked other impossible, evil magics. After the Mad King Victor had been defeated, the crystals of the caverns were said to have turned dark and collapsed into a fine black dust—like ash. It was a page in history well before her time, and one that read more like Imperial propaganda for how great the emperor and empress were in bringing about the fall of the Mad King Victor and the Crystal Caverns.

When the lecture was finished, two whole hours later, the majority of the room departed in a swarm that trailed after Noelle's poor attitude like flies on scat. Eira and Alyss packed up slowly, giving ample time for everyone else to depart. They didn't have to discuss why—the last thing either of them wanted was to run into Noelle and Adam in the hall when they were already in a poor mood.

"Eira," Mister Levit called as she was just finishing putting her journals away. "A word?"

"Yes, sir?" Eira walked down the short stairs to where he

was.

"Privately, if you please, Alyss."

"Sure thing." Alyss squeezed her shoulder lightly. "I'll wait outside for you."

Eira nodded, and her friend left. "Yes?"

"I have something for you." Mister Levit held onto his worn leather satchel with both hands. He was a young man, Eira suspected a mere ten years older than her. His dark hair had yet to be peppered with salt, and his deep brown skin showed no signs of wrinkling. "Though, now I feel I shouldn't give it to you."

"What is it?" Eira asked, trying to keep any emotion from her voice. She was curious, but she wasn't going to pry.

He sighed, clearly making up his mind, and shoved a hand into his bag. Mister Levit held out a leather-bound book to her. It had a symbol emblazoned in gold on the front—shining circles, interconnecting with woven lines in a pattern that was magical simply to look at.

Eira let out a gasp, taking the tome reverently with both hands.

"This is not favoritism," he insisted, though Eira wasn't sure if it was to her or himself, "as I have been sharing my collection with you for years now." Every time Mister Levit got his hands on a book from Meru, he lent it to her. After he was finished with it, of course.

"Are you sure? You just got this one, didn't you?"

He nodded. "Two weeks ago, when the ambassador returned. They brought back a small chest of books again. There's more, but they're still circulating between the Tower, Imperial Library, and imperial family. This is the only one I've managed to get my hands on so far."

"Are you really sure?" she repeated, clutching the book to her chest. "I don't want to prevent you from getting other books by holding onto this one."

He shook his head, wearing a warm smile. "Give it back to me when you're done and you won't."

"Thank you, thank you!" Eira could hug him. She didn't. But she could.

"Of course." He chuckled and slung his bag over his shoulder. "If there's any new information in there, there won't be time for it to appear on the test. And any old information, you likely already know. But...I'd still recommend you keep it private. Otherwise it may complicate things during the trials with claims of unfair advantages."

"Yes, right, I will." Eira peeled the book off her chest and put it in her bag. She peeked, twice, on her way to the door, as if it might somehow disappear.

"One last thing." He paused right before the door. "Good luck, Eira. I'll be cheering for you. No one deserves this more than you do." Mister Levit clapped her once on the shoulder and left before Eira could say anything else.

CHAPTER
EIGHT

IVE DAYS LATER, Eira sat in the risers that overlooked the Sunlit
Stage alongside other Tower apprentices, instructors, palace
staff, and Commons that she presumed came from the city
to watch. Today, the stage truly looked its name. Every banister,
column, seat, and slab of marble was polished between each day of
testing, and they glistened in the morning light.

Below, where the masses usually gathered, tables had been
set up. Tower apprentices sat several paces apart as three sheets
of parchment were placed in front of each. Eira and Alyss had
come to watch the trial take place yesterday, she knew what to
expect, but seeing Alyss's below set her nerves ablaze.

She'll be all right, Eira tried to reassure herself. Alyss
hadn't taken to the study of Meru and its history like Eira had.
But she'd certainly been forced to listen to Eira's enthusiasm
over the years. Surely something—or several somethings—
had sunk in. Plus, they had done nothing but cram for the past
five days in preparation for the test.

Mister Levit stood in front of a table up on the actual stage.
A large board was behind him, two Groundbreaker instructors
on either side. Mister Levit waited to speak until the assistants
finished passing out the examinations.

"You will have one hour to complete the exam. If you finish
early, you may bring up your finished papers to me. Once you
stand from your seat, you may not sit again. Any cheating or
other foul play will be punished by both the Tower and the
palace guard. You will be scored on what you complete within
the hour. Those in the top fifty percent of scores will proceed
on to the next trial. Are there any questions?"

No one spoke.

"I ask those in the audience to please remain silent as anything you say, even encouragement for a candidate, could result in their disqualification. If there is nothing further, Groundbreakers, you may begin." Mister Levit flipped a large hourglass and went to sit behind the table. Just once, she could've sworn his eyes darted her way.

Eira grabbed the bench beneath her and tapped her feet, already restless. From her vantage, she couldn't see a word of the actual examination, so she was left to guessing what had Alyss shaking her head and pausing. But, more often, Alyss's quill moved quickly across the page.

About fifteen minutes in, a small group emerged from the back of the stage. Eira recognized the ambassador for Solaris, Cordon, and the pointy-eared ambassador for Meru, Ferro. They each had a guard in tow. Gwen stood near Cordon, a hand lazily resting on the pommel of her sword. And an elfin woman with black hair and dark skin was a step behind Ferro.

They walked to the edge of the stage, observing the competitors. Some paused their work, gaping up at the elfin. But most, including Alyss, remained steadfast, focused on the exam. Eira wondered if the presence of elfin wasn't some part of the test—to see who could remain focused when presented with a distraction. After a brief, whispered discussion, the group crossed to Mister Levit to continue their conversation.

The first apprentice finished five minutes later, almost halfway through the examination time. She was young and Eira could tell by the way her shoulders slumped that she knew she was going to be cut. Eira admired her for deciding to try at all.

The girl walked up and handed her exam to Mister Levit. He scored it with both ambassadors and their guards looking over his shoulders. It had been the same the day before with the Firebearers—no doubt an attempt to curb any claims of favoritism from the proctor.

Mister Levit went to the Groundbreakers back by the blank stone tablet. They nodded at him, and then turned to the tablet. With a quick hand motion, a name magically appeared etched at the top with a score alongside it.

One by one, others finished and rose for their judgment. Mister Levit scored them silently, and their names were embossed in stone by the Groundbreakers for all to see. About forty minutes in and they had passed the halfway mark of total scores. At this time, a line appeared—the apprentices who made the cut were above. Those who didn't were below.

The names continued to shuffle as the sand in the hourglass trickled down. Eira bit her lip, watching Alyss. Her friend had gone through her answers several times over. Finally satisfied, Alyss stood and approached the stage.

Eira held her breath for what felt like forever as Mister Levit went through Alyss's scores. Yet, all too soon, it was over. Alyss's name was shuffled on the board.

Top twenty percent.

Eira pressed both hands over her mouth to stop herself from shouting in excitement. There were only a handful of students left. Even if all of them did better than Alyss, she would make the cut.

She didn't wait to see the final examinations be turned in. Eira jumped up from the bench and raced down through the palace wall, coming to a stop at the barricade erected by the palace guard.

"That concludes today's examination. Congratulations to the competitors who are moving to the next round," Mister Levit was saying as apprentices began to make their triumphant or disappointed path back to the Tower.

"You did it!" Eira hissed with excitement as she yanked Alyss her way. "You did it!"

"With your help!" Alyss wrapped her arms tightly around Eira and they jumped up and down together. "*We* did it."

"You would've passed without me."

"Maybe. But I certainly wouldn't have scored so high. It would have been a nail-biter." Alyss finally released her from the bone-crushing grip. "Now, you're next."

"We'll see." Her parents' letter was still in her mind,

stewing with the conversation she'd had with Marcus and her uncles.

"No false modesty. We both know you're going to ace whatever is put in front of you with flying colors."

Eira stretched out on her bed, flipping through the pages of the book Mister Levit had given her. It was a book on the strange magic of Meru—Lightspinning, they called it. Unlike the affinities of the Solaris Empire, which functioned on instinct and intention, Lightspinning was governed by a series of words. It was a logical, elegant system that Eira was constantly in awe of.

"Duro... Durroe." She tried out the magic words like a new dress. They were awkward and didn't fit quite right across her tongue. Moreover, they did nothing for her own magic. But she practiced them anyway. Saying them felt good, like some part of her could belong on that distant land.

A knock on her door stopped her—four fast knocks, a pause, and then two slow.

She scowled and closed the book, sliding it under her bed and replacing it with one of her other notebooks. "Come in, Marcus."

Her brother slipped inside, closed the door behind him, and leaned against it. He ran a hand through his golden hair uncertainly, as if questioning why he came. Eira was about to do the same.

"What do you want?" She flipped a page of her notebook nonchalantly.

"I wanted to talk, one-on-one."

"All right, we're talking." She could see him frown from the corners of her eyes.

"Grahm, Fritz, Mom and Dad, we're all just trying to protect you. We don't mean to upset you."

"I can protect myself."

"Eira." He sighed. "I know you can…but these trials—the tournament—is more than surviving the day to day of the Tower. It's more than helping people at the clinic or conducting research with Mister Levit. If you try to be a competitor *everyone* will be watching you."

"So?"

"I thought you didn't like attention drawn to you?"

"It's not my favorite," she admitted, then flicked her eyes to his. "But Meru *is* my favorite."

"We don't even know if the actual Tournament of Five Kingdoms will take place on Meru."

"Aunt Gwen told me it would be." Eira glanced at him. Marcus cursed softly and shook his head. The dark waters in her churned violently at the sight. "You knew, too."

"Uncle asked me not to say so that—"

"So that I wouldn't be more motivated to compete?" Eira arched her eyebrows.

"So that people wouldn't accuse him of favoritism and giving me special information."

It sounded like a lie, but Eira looked back at her journal and pretended to ignore it. *Move aside for Marcus; let Marcus have a chance.* The words were in her depths, rising to the surface as ugly, primordial beasts.

"Listen, Eira… I know what you care about most is going to Meru." Marcus pushed away from the door to stand at her bedside. "If I'm selected as a competitor, I'll bring you along."

"You can do that?" She searched his expression for another lie.

"I'm sure there will be assistants to the competitors in some fashion. Between me, Uncle, Auntie, and their connections, we'll find a way to get you there."

"And all I have to do is step aside and let you win?"

Marcus glanced at her notebook, flipped it closed, and slid it away from her so he could sit on the edge of the bed. Eira pushed herself upright as well.

"Think about it. You don't *really* care about competition. You want to learn more about Meru. Right?"

"You're a fool," she whispered with a shake of her head.

"I'm doing this for you, too." Eira grabbed his hand, pleading, "Uncle, Mom, and Dad, they're all going to expect you to keep looking after me. You're never going to feel free to go off and live your own life. Even if I'm not chosen as the final Waterrunner, getting far in the trials will show them that I can stand on my own without you."

Marcus clasped his hand tightly with hers. "That's it, then? That's what you want?" He chuckled and shook his head. "Fine, take the test and pass the first trial with flying colors as we all know you will. You can always throw in the towel later, after you've proved your point."

"I..." Was that all she wanted? If Marcus could bring her with him, then wouldn't it be easier to allow him to be the final Waterrunner? She'd have more time to focus on experiencing, studying, and learning if she wasn't a competitor in the Tournament.

But if she didn't compete...she had no guarantees she would go to Meru. He *thought* he could get her there. But that might mean very little.

"Love you, sister." Marcus leaned forward and planted a kiss on her forehead. He stood and left before she could say anything else.

Eira was restless that night.

She tossed and turned in bed, dreams haunted by beaches on faraway lands churned up by frigid gray seas. She woke, sweat-slicked and in a panic, more than once. The Tower was noisy tonight. Her usually silent room was filled with whispers that she forced away.

Come morning, she was ready to face the test if for no other reason than to have something to focus her mind on. Eira could be her own worst enemy when left alone.

She was the first to arrive, nearly an hour early. Mister Levit was already there and he permitted her to have the seat of her choice. Eira picked one off to the side and toward the back. She wanted to see everyone else who came in.

Other Waterrunners slowly filled the tables. There appeared to be thirty of them in total that signed up—the largest contingent compared to Groundbreakers and Firebearers. Fifteen would be cut today. Eira could pin about five or six who had no chance, just based off her brief interactions with them in classes.

Marcus entered, sun shining off his hair in a way that made it look almost as light as hers. The way he strode in with purpose, shoulders back and chin high...he walked like a prince. He'd no doubt been studying Cullen. Eira could almost hear the whispers and swooning of ladies in the stands, and she fought rolling her eyes.

His gaze swept to hers and Marcus gave her a small nod, one Eira returned. To him, it was likely a gesture of a plan they both knew. For Eira, it said, *Let the games begin.*

"You will have one hour to complete the exam. If you finish early, you may bring your exam up to me. Once you stand from your seat, you may not sit again. Any cheating or..." Mister Levit began to go through his explanation as the assistants passed out the written portions. He changed the examination each day with the help of the Master of Tome from the library. That way it was impossible for anyone to relay answers.

Eira ran her nail along the corner of the page, heart racing.

"If there is nothing further, Waterrunners, you may begin." Mister Levit flipped a large hourglass and Eira flipped her pages.

There were seventy-five questions in total. Each question had a blank for the answer; some were just a word, some demanded a few sentences. Eira skimmed them, turning the pages over.

That's it? She blinked. She'd been expecting more. She'd been hoping for an actual challenge.

Eira dove in.

Capital of Meru? Risen. Primary religious organization?

Faithful of Yargen. Other kingdoms once a part of Meru? The Twilight Kingdom and Kingdom of the Draconi. Average lifespan of the elfin? About 175 years. Magic? Oh, they didn't give her nearly enough space to write about Lightspinning.

Her quill flew across the page, nearly scratching holes with her ferocity. Before Eira knew it, she'd answered every question. Nearly breathless from the cocktail of nerves and excitement, she looked up, expecting the time to be expired and most others to have turned in their papers.

Only about ten minutes had passed.

Eira looked back down at her work and inhaled deeply. She should check her answers. But Eira had a strict policy when it came to her studies—never second-guess herself. Whenever she doubted her gut, it usually resulted in her changing from the correct answers. The first choice was usually the right one.

Setting down her quill, Eira stood and gathered her examination.

She could feel the eyes of her fellow apprentices and those assembled. Marcus was right—she hated the feeling. The papers crumpled slightly in her fingers as her grip tightened under the weight of her nerves.

Eira was nearly at the stage when the ambassadors and their guards emerged from the palace doors. She faltered, staring at them. They were early today. They usually didn't come until about halfway through.

Mister Levit held out his hand expectantly. It prompted Eira to gather every last scrap of her courage and ascend to the top of the stage. She handed the papers to her teacher.

"You're sure?" he whispered, hardly moving his lips. Eira gave a small nod and he picked up his quill, scoring it right before her.

The elfin approaching were a welcome distraction. Today they were fitted with clothes that matched the tailored styles of the Solaris Empire instead of the swooping necks and dropped sleeves of Meru. Ambassador Ferro had lightly teased his dark green hair back, placing his ears even more on display.

Between the clothes and hair—or perhaps just up close—he looked younger than Eira expected. He looked even younger than Mister Levit. Only a few years older than her, if she had to guess.

But he was elfin, a people graced with unnatural youthfulness. He could be fifty for all Eira knew. The weight of a second set of eyes drew her attention to Ferro's right. The same guard he'd had yesterday was there, peering a hole into Eira. She quickly brought her eyes back to Mister Levit.

"Someone's already finished?" Cordon appraised as he drew near. "Didn't the examination only begin ten minutes ago?"

"It did. But Eira is one of my best students," Mister Levit said proudly. He was on the last page. Eira had completely missed how the first two pages scored.

Ambassador Ferro stepped to the side, folding his arms behind his back and looking over Mister Levit's shoulder. His face was passive and betrayed no emotion. His violet eyes flicked up to her.

"Eira, was it?" he asked with the smooth accent of Meru.

She nearly melted in place. "Y-yes?"

He just nodded, mostly to himself, and strode off to the far side of the stage to look out over the apprentices still testing. His guard followed and the two engaged in a whispered conversation.

"All right, then." Mister Levit stood, papers in hand. He showed them to Cordon, who let out a low whistle and then gave her an assessing look.

Eira folded her arms before her, afflicted with a sudden wave of discomfort.

Mister Levit handed the paper to the Groundbreakers by the board. They exchanged a few words. She held her breath as her name magically appeared, embossed in stone, at the top of the board.

Eira Landan - 75

A perfect score. She'd passed the first trial.

NINE

"**W**ELL DONE," MISTER Levit whispered as he sat.

Eira turned, descending to the back wall underneath the risers that circled the Sunlit Stage. She tried to ignore the glares her fellow apprentices were shooting her. If looks could kill, she'd be skewered several times over.

Out of the sunlight, Eira could breathe a little easier. The shade was a familiar place for her to be in. Relative darkness was a cool and welcoming embrace. Eira tucked her hair behind her ears several times and waited, watching, as the rest of them finished.

One by one, other apprentices went up. They turned in their papers and Eira watched their names shuffle on the board like cards. But one name didn't move—hers.

Her fellow Waterrunners formed packs along the back walls. They murmured with hushed breaths, glancing her way. But none of them crossed the gap to her. Eira thought of globe-trinkets she'd seen at the Festival of the Sun last year, filled with water and fake snow. She had an invisible sphere like that around her always. A barrier that kept others away…even Marcus.

When he finished, he went to a group of friends, met with pats on the shoulder and praise. He ended up ranking fourth, all told. The closest person to Eira scored sixty-four out of seventy-five correct.

"That concludes today's examination," Mister Levit announced when the last name appeared on the board. "Congratulations to the competitors who are moving on. There will be a special dinner held in the Tower tonight just for you all, where you'll learn about the details of the second trial."

The clapping of those assembled, cheers and reassurances, faded away. Eira's eyes had drifted to the stage, where Ambassador Ferro still stood, leaning against a column, arms crossed. His gaze was locked on hers and, for a breath, the world stopped.

It was as though she could almost feel him in the back of her mind searching for something she didn't know if she wanted to give, whispering quietly for entry. The icy barriers that were just under her skin thickened, pushing away the sensation. His mouth quirked into a smirk. Eira gave a tip of her head and he returned the motion.

Ferro pushed away from the column, his guard's eyes flicking back to Eira twice as they left.

"Mother above, woman, a *perfect score!*" Alyss nearly tackled Eira to the ground with her embrace. Eira was so focused on Ferro that she hadn't even noticed they'd begun to clear the Sunlit Stage. "I knew there was no chance you wouldn't pass but this proves you're someone to watch out for."

"They're doing more than watching me." The glares had yet to stop.

"Ignore them, they're just jealous." Alyss linked her arm with Eira's and began leading them back toward the Tower. "Now, you mentioned wanting to show me something the other day?"

"Oh, right."

"Since we have the rest of the day free, why not now?"

They went back to the Tower. Eira tried to set a slower pace than Alyss's excitement wanted. As they returned, apprentices were settling in for their afternoon sessions—lessons and practicals. The library was full as they passed, as was the Waterrunners' workroom.

Eira brought a finger to her lips as they approached the archway that was open to the workroom. An instructor's voice echoed down the hall to them. Glancing around, Eira lifted a hand. She felt the moisture in the air shift at her beckoning. The light wavered ahead of them and a thin, watery line appeared between the opening to the workroom and storeroom.

Any apprentices in the workroom who had a view of the storeroom would continue to see the door shut tight and an empty hall. An illusion obscured the truth. Eira and Alyss slipped behind her magic facade, opening the door wide enough to sneak in. She shut it softly behind them and relaxed her powers.

"All right, the sneaking has my attention," Alyss whispered.

"As will this." Eira went to the back corner. She was getting familiar with where the lever was, and the door had been opened and closed so many times that the hinges were silent now.

"What in the Mother's name?" Alyss stared at the secret room.

"Come on, before anyone checks the storeroom." Eira had already squeezed around the barrel and into the room, holding out her hand for Alyss. When her friend was in, Eira shut the door behind them.

"How did you? Why? *What?*"

"I found it by accident. I don't know why this room is here, or what it was used for." Eira attempted to answer her friend's questions in order. "Well, sort of don't know what it was used for. I know another Waterrunner was here, at least based on these journals." Eira took one of the journals off the shelf.

"This…Eira, this is dangerous magic." Alyss flipped the pages. She paused on one. "Can Waterrunners do this?"

"I'm not sure, I haven't tried."

"Nor should you. It'll just spell trouble if you fill your head with wicked ways to use magic." Alyss closed the journal and put it back on the shelf. "I don't know who was here but they—" She stopped, distracted by the opening in the back of the bookcase. "What's back there?"

"I don't know."

"You haven't explored it?" Alyss gasped.

"It looks like a natural passage so I was worried about getting stuck. I didn't dare proceed without my favorite Groundbreaker."

"Well, all right then, let's go." Alyss grabbed the candle on the desk and lit it.

"And here I thought the room was off-putting to you."

"It's a bit creepy, only because of those journals of magic that borders on torture." She pointed to the bookshelf. "But flattery is going to get you everywhere, Eira. Trust your favorite Groundbreaker and we'll explore."

Eira laughed and squeezed into the passage behind her. The uneven floor was damp and slick. The rocks shifted under Alyss's feet, always giving her sure footing. Eira followed suit, using her magic to allow an icy chill to radiate off her shoes. She left behind frozen footprints as arcs of ice covered her boots and melded with the floor.

The silence was heavy in the tunnel, almost eerie. Eira wasn't sure why, but she had the distinct sense that they were the first souls to traverse this path in many years. The candle Alyss held only gave them a small aura of light to see by, so the void they marched into set her thoughts racing with a mixture of fear and excitement of what would finally emerge from the darkness.

They came to a fork in the tunnel.

"Which way?"

"Let's go down."

"Farther into the depths? Crazy woman." Alyss shook her head but carried on downward. Thick algae covered slick, rough-cut steps that opened up to a large underground spring. Alyss's breath collected as white in the air. She spoke with chattering lips. "We must be in the heart of the mountain now."

"Maybe. Come on, let's go back. There's no way forward here." At least not for Alyss.

As the light retreated, Eira stayed focused on the perfectly clear, icy waters. Deep beneath the glassy surface was an underwater tunnel. Where did it lead? And did a Waterrunner dare to explore those dark depths?

They backtracked, heading up the other fork in the road. The passage came to an abrupt opening in a dust-covered hall. A statue was slid to the side of the opening, thanks to a hidden mechanism on the floor.

"Where are we?" Alyss whispered as she set down the candle on one of the wide windowsills by the opening.

"Somewhere long forgotten," Eira murmured. There were no signs of anyone having existed here for years. Yet they still spoke with hushed tones. As if by being too loud they'd scare the ghosts.

"This looks like the former emperor." Alyss stopped by a faded and cracking portrait. Oil had flaked off to the floor like dying flower petals.

"Earlier." Eira pointed to an inscription. "That's the last of the Solaris kings."

...I don't see any mark of Adela though... The whisper came from the painting. Eira inhaled sharply.

"What is it?" Alyss asked.

"Nothing, just, distracted." Eira shook her head.

"Voices?"

"Yes." Eira didn't dare say what she'd heard. To say the name of the pirate queen aloud was to bring misfortune and ill luck on you and everything dear to you. That was the lore the sailors had drilled into her down by the docks and beaches of Oparium.

Alyss seemed to pick up the need for a shift in topic. "Do you think these used to be the royal apartments?"

"Perhaps." Eira shrugged. The palace of Solaris had been built into the mountain, and then built on again. There were certain to be many forgotten places and passages over the years.

"I wonder how long they've been abandoned."

"It may be in a book somewhere on the history of the palace...the date the current imperial quarters and their ostentatious gate were finished."

"Careful," Alyss playfully scolded. "It's rude to insult the royals and their tacky obsession with gold."

Eira laughed softly. But too quickly, the silence and oppressive atmosphere swallowed the sound.

They walked among forgotten specters, past bedrooms and parlors. The only occupants had been rats and spiders for decades. Still, it was a capsule of history. A more accurate representation of the end of the Solaris Kingdom and early Empire than any book or painting could ever portray.

The voices of the people who had once lived here filled her ears. Her jaw was set against the sounds of every painting, curtain, and decrepit piece of furniture trying to say something all at once.

...Father, do you have time now?...

...come to me...you are able, my love...

...show me, Solaris... The icy voice. She'd been here, whoever *she* was. Eira paused, looking around a small parlor and waiting to see if the disembodied speaker had anything else to say.

"What is it?" Alyss asked.

"Another voice. It's nothing." The icy woman was gone once more. But others filled in the silence as she walked. Alyss cast more than one worried stare.

...Don't play games!...

...there wouldn't be adornments in an escape passage...

Eira rounded the corner of the hall and froze, Alyss bumping into her.

"What the—" Alyss stopped mid-sentence.

A pair of bright blue eyes turned to them. The woman was standing at one of the doorways, still as a tomb. She had dark hair, pulled into a high bun, and a severe, unforgettable expression. Eira had met these eyes merely an hour or two ago.

"Eira Landan and another Tower apprentice," Ambassador Ferro's guard said softly. "I thought the rats were a little too noisy today."

"We're sorry! We'll be going now!" Alyss grabbed Eira's

arm.

"What're you doing here?" Eira dared to ask.

A smirk cut the guard's lips. "I should ask you the same. This is a forgotten place of fate, not meant for people like you."

"That's why we're leaving now. So sorry. Let's go, Eira." Alyss tugged and Eira felt the earth tremble under her friend's determined steps. They dashed back to the long hall they'd entered from.

Alyss's hasty footsteps didn't stop until they were all the way back in Eira's room in the Tower. For once, Eira was sitting and Alyss was pacing, looking over her shoulder every now and then. She twirled a piece of wood in her fingers, too anxious to carve it.

"I don't like it. Nope. I don't like any of it." Alyss shook her head several times.

"What was all that about?" Eira finally demanded.

"Something we don't want to know."

"What?"

"Eira, think, and don't let your fascination with Meru cloud your judgment here." Alyss rubbed her temples. "There's a secret room with really, really shady magic outlined in journals that were probably locked away for good reason. This secret room has a secret, *secret* passage connecting to what looked like old royal apartments? Either way, it's all been long forgotten, and hidden, likely *for a reason*. And then there's one of the two elfin in all of the Empire who just happens to be wandering those abandoned halls because *who knows why*."

"Perhaps she was exploring the palace and got lost?"

"Did she look like someone who was lost?" Alyss threw her hands in the air. "She was up to something."

"Alyss, stop. She's here as part of the delegation from Meru. They're friends of Solaris. She's not a danger to anyone."

"I asked you not to let your Meru obsession cloud your judgment." Alyss pointed the wood at her.

"I'm not. I'm just sure there's a perfectly reasonable explanation." Eira shrugged.

Alyss tugged at her braids in frustration. "How did you even find that place to begin with?"

"I...heard a voice," Eira admitted.

"What did it say?" Alyss had never doubted the voices Eira heard, or her theory on why she could hear them. Eira pursed her lips. "Eira, what did it say?"

"Kill the emperor."

"Oh, great. This is... Wow, Eira. You." Alyss was at a rare loss for words. "You followed a voice talking about killing the emperor to find a room with deadly magic, connected to a passage—"

"Yes, I know how it looks now," Eira cut her off. "Curiosity got the better of me." She vowed to never bring up the mention of Adela in the ancient halls. It'd just be another log on Alyss's fiery hatred of that place.

"What else is new?" Alyss sighed and crossed over to the bed, shoved the wood back in her bag, and sat heavily at Eira's side. "I want you to promise me you won't go back there."

"What?"

"There's nothing good there, Eira. I can feel it. That's a place better forgotten by time."

"You're just on edge—"

"Promise me." Alyss grabbed both her cheeks, forcing Eira to meet her eyes. "Don't go back there."

"I'm not going to lie to you, Alyss."

Her friend heaved a mighty groan and flopped back. "You are hopeless."

"I think it's part of my charm."

Alyss playfully dug her fist into Eira's side. "Promise me you won't go back there *alone*, then?"

"Fine, deal." Eira relented. "But that just means you have to go back so I can."

"Hopefully we'll be too busy with the trials for that to ever happen. Which, speaking of...we should get ready for dinner."

The candidates' dinner was held in the usual mess hall following the regular dinner hour. Eira and Alyss were some of the first to arrive and Eira didn't miss a few of the envious looks non-competitors cast their way. A rift was already forming between the apprentices who were candidates to be competitors and those who weren't.

A rift that would no doubt grow worse thanks to the pins instructors were handing out. They stood on either side of the mess hall entry, giving a single pin to every current candidate, and instructed that it was to be worn on their right breast underneath their collarbone.

The pin bore the symbol of the Tower—four circles interlocking in a diamond shape. There was a triangle in each that corresponded with the elemental affinity from each of the four different regions of the Solaris Empire. In the center of the circles there was a fifth circle that was usually solid and unadorned. But on this pin it had the number 5 embossed into what would've been a blank space. No doubt to represent the Tournament of Five Kingdoms.

Eira inspected the shiny gold pin throughout dinner. Its glint caught her eye multiple times and Eira touched it more than once.

"It's not going anywhere," Alyss teased.

Eira knew it wasn't, but she still couldn't believe it was there to begin with. Even if nothing else worked out for her, she'd made it this far. That counted for something, didn't it?

Dinner was not made by other apprentices, but catered by palace staff. As such, the quality was leagues better than any of them were accustomed to. Every plate was cleaned, even Eira's, despite her having a second helping of the largest hunk of cake she'd ever seen.

"You seriously have a gift for packing sweets away. It's unnatural," Alyss said, glancing up from the book she was reading. There were two things Alyss was rarely without—some kind of over-the-top romance novel and some kind of clay or wood to mold. It was normal for them to fall into easy silences over meals as Eira got lost in her head, or a book of her own, and Alyss tinkered away making something.

"Maybe one of these days it'll stick to my hips and make me look more like a woman, rather than a pre-pubescent boy." Eira scraped icing off her plate.

Alyss snorted. "You're beautiful."

"As are you."

Another snort and a turn of her head. Alyss gazed over to a group of people clustered about. It was obvious that the favorites for the tournament were beginning to coalesce. Marcus and Cullen sat together. Noelle and Adam were at their table, along with a few others that Eira recognized but had never spoken to.

"I can't believe he's not sitting with you," Alyss murmured.

"It's fine."

"He's your brother. He should be celebrating your accomplishments."

"It's complicated." Eira recalled her uncles' expressions and the uncomfortable conversation with Marcus in her room. She hadn't told Alyss yet about the letter from her parents, either.

"Is it? It seems pretty simple to me. You're both great. You're both talented. Let the best man or woman win. Support each other along the way." Alyss brought her gaze back to Eira, thankfully before anyone in the group noticed her staring. "You're happy for him, right?"

"Yeah, I am," Eira said softly. She was well and truly happy for her brother. "If he's the one to beat me in the end, I'm okay with that. I just want the chance to put up a fight. To show them what I can do."

"Well you certainly did that today." Alyss snickered.

Eira couldn't fight and win against the grin that spread across her cheeks.

"Congratulations, all," Fritz said as he walked in. The echo of his voice in the rafters mingled with his applause. "Well done to each of you. You've made it through the first trial." He went to the front of the mess hall, where the buffet had just been cleared away. "I know you all have questions about what's next. So let's get right to business, that way you all can get to bed.

"Foremost, the pins you were given are to be worn henceforth. Every candidate for competitor has been given one. Part of being a competitor will be to represent Solaris and that means you will always have eyes on you. Your actions will be judged around the clock."

Eira grimaced at the notion.

"Consider these pins the beginning of that. Any conduct unbecoming for a representative of Solaris will get back to me and you will have your pin *and* candidacy revoked."

"We can get eliminated when we're not in a trial?" Noelle asked.

"Indeed." Fritz continued, "Now, speaking of trials, your next one will take place in three weeks, as we will need ample time to set up and prepare. To assist you in these trials, your classes, workshops, and other Tower responsibilities are not mandatory for pin holders.

"For the next trial we will be testing your magic in an obstacle course. The field will be cut by a third after this trial. Those who complete the course with times in the upper two-thirds of the pack will proceed on."

"Minister—"

Fritz held up a hand, stopping the interruption from a Firebearer. "I know what you're about to ask. There are fifteen Waterrunners and six Groundbreakers still in competition. These numbers are easy to reduce by a third. But what happens to the Firebearers, who have eleven candidates? We will be rounding down in such instances. So three Firebearers will be eliminated by next week's course."

Eira leaned toward Alyss and whispered, "There will be

only four Groundbreakers after next week. You'll have a good shot!"

Alyss *shh*'ed her. There was a nervous smile on her face. As if she couldn't believe either how close she already was to being selected as a competitor.

Eira did a quick scan of the room, seeing if she recognized the other five Groundbreakers still in the trials. She knew their faces, but nothing about their abilities. Was one of them the one Fritz had chosen to make the barrier? If so, that was the person Alyss needed to watch. Then again, it was also possible that person didn't make it past the first trial. They could have been strong, but knew nothing about Meru.

"Minister, are there still to be five trials in total?" Cullen's deep voice was auditory velvet. He didn't need to speak loudly to command a room to a hush.

"Yes. The first three trials are decided on by the Tower and Imperial family," Fritz continued. "The final two will be decided by the elfin ambassador from Meru."

Murmurs at this. Eira's heart raced. Even Alyss shot her a knowing grin. If the elfin determined the last two, then she had to have a leg up, right? No one knew more about Meru than her, as was shown by her score today. She *must* have an advantage on whatever the elfin came up with.

Alyss wasn't the only one looking her way. Other candidates were casting glances over their shoulders. Eira was forced to wonder if the reason her family had pushed so hard for her not to compete was because they knew it was the only way she wouldn't be chosen.

"More information will follow in the days and weeks to come. For now, enjoy your celebration and rest well on your laurels."

The room cleared out shortly after. Apprentices parted ways. Marcus and Cullen headed toward the library. Alyss declared she wanted to focus on "finishing her cat because she actually liked this one"—the one she had started sculpting over dinner—and departed.

Eira returned to her room alone, pin still glistening on her breast. She was so distracted with it that she didn't notice the sealed envelope on her bed until she was reaching for the book on Lightspinning still tucked underneath her bed frame. She glanced around the room, as if the person who sent the note could be hiding somewhere in a dormitory that was three steps wide.

The wax seal was a deep purple. The symbol was simple—three circles, stacked vertically, with a line drawn through them. It was the symbol of Yargen, and of Meru.

Eira slid her finger under and opened the letter. It was one line long:

Meet me at the Sunlit Stage.

THE SUNLIT STAGE at night was beautiful in an unnerving way. The moon turned the marble and alabaster into bone and the gilding silvery. Long shadows clung to the seats where people should be sitting—where they'd watched her test hours ago.

Eira moved silently through the empty hallways and stairwells, emerging onto the lower arena space. She stepped timidly into the moonlight. The letter was clutched in her hand as she spun, searching for a sign of its sender.

"You came."

Eira nearly jumped out of her skin at the man's voice. She turned. Even though she'd only seen him four times, Eira knew Ambassador Ferro by accent alone, no pointed ears necessary.

"This was from you?" she asked softly. Yet her words echoed across the empty stage.

"It was."

"How did you get in the Tower?" Eira doubted an elfin ambassador would be able to sneak in without being noticed. Then again, if he'd used Lightspinning… Or perhaps his guard had been the one to deliver it, through the secret passage Eira knew about, and that was why she'd been there in the first place?

"I have my ways." He smirked, as if reading her mind. "Let's sojourn to somewhere more comfortable so you and I might have a word." Ferro turned, walking under the shadow of the colonnade of the back half of the stage. He didn't once look back at her.

Eira worried her bottom lip between her teeth. Should she go with him? She could already hear Alyss saying no. Even if the elfin were friends of Solaris and he was clearly a nobleman, she should definitely *not* sneak off into the night following a stranger.

So, of course, Eira did.

She raced through the moonlight and into the shadow as Ferro opened one of the large doors on the back of the stage. He disappeared inside, leaving her sprinting to keep up with him. He was already several paces down a long palace hall as she closed the door behind her.

Eira had never been in this section of the palace before— she didn't even know if she was *allowed* to be—but she kept up anyway. She followed him deeper into the palace, up a flight of stairs, down a sculpture gallery, and through a gaming parlor. Eventually, they came to a sitting room where a fire crackled warmly in the hearth, fighting against the night's chill.

"You're bolder than you look," Ferro said softly as he closed the doors to the parlor behind her. "I didn't expect you to actually come all this way."

"Should I be nervous?" Eira was grateful her voice didn't quiver.

"No, I mean you no harm. Please, sit." He motioned to the chairs situated around the hearth with a smile.

Eira did as instructed. She bunched her dress in her fists and then forced herself to relax. The new room was filled with sounds she'd never heard before and she had to guard herself against. It was an easy task whenever Ferro spoke, because her focus was solely on him.

"Why did you send me this letter?" Eira asked. He held out his hand and she passed the letter to him. Ferro cast it in the fire. Eira barely resisted the urge to snuff the fire instantly with her magic. "I'd been meaning to save it as a keepsake."

"Were you?" He chuckled. The sound made her toes curl. "Why is that?"

"Because..." She hated every way the truth could be phrased. She'd wanted to keep it because he—an elfin—had written it. So, instead, she lied. "Because I'm trying to save everything I can to commemorate the trials."

"Is that the reason? Or is it because someone from Meru gave you that letter?" Ferro sat back in his chair. She pursed her lips and that only made him laugh. "Your curiosity about my homeland is no secret. If you'd intended for it to be, you would've intentionally thrown at least one question during your examination today."

Eira sighed and admitted, "I am fascinated with Meru, yes."

"I'm flattered."

"What?" She met his amethyst eyes.

"So many of Solaris take a stance of begrudging acceptance toward what you once called the Crescent Continent. To know that there are those who wish to learn about us with a genuine interest warms my heart."

"I see."

"Where does your fascination come from?"

Eira shifted uncomfortably in her seat. She didn't want to keep lying to the man. But she also hated feeling bare and exposed. Her curiosity surrounding Meru hadn't earned her a good deal of favor from her peers. At best, it'd earned her teasing.

"I think I've always thought it was fascinating. I grew up in Oparium—it's the closest port to Solarin in a valley to the east."

He nodded. "I'm familiar with it."

"I grew up seeing the ocean and all its vastness every day. It seemed to beckon to me. I wondered what was out there. Then, when I was twelve, I learned the crown princess was speaking with the Crescent Continent—as I knew it then. In the years that followed, there was an explosion of information in Solarin about a wide world we never even knew we were a part of. Who wouldn't be excited?" Ferro smiled a little at this and Eira returned the expression. "And then…"

"Then?" he encouraged.

"Then, when I was fifteen, I was privileged to attend the ball where our princess announced her betrothal to the Voice of Yargen." Her voice dropped to a whisper. "I saw him."

Ferro chuckled. "Taavin has made quite the impact on our world, as has your princess. It's fitting they have ended up together."

"That's what I say! But you're right. Most people in Solaris don't seem to grasp how perfect they are for each other." The engagement had been met by resistance, to say the least. Which had prompted their marriage to be postponed longer than normal by royal standards.

"So, a young girl's fascination, fueled further by a romantic whim on meeting a handsome elfin—"

"I said nothing about romantic," Eira interjected, a flush rising up her neck.

Ferro ignored her. "—turned you into one of the leading experts in Solarin on the subject of Meru…if your instructor Mister Levit is to be believed, and as your test scores support."

Eira wondered what Mister Levit had said. Perhaps the kind man had been the one to help arrange this meeting for her. She didn't dare let herself think that Ferro had been interested in her of his own accord. "I just try and learn what I can."

"How would you like to learn more?"

"Are you offering?" There was no way she could say no.

"I admit, I am just as much fascinated by you as you are by me." Ferro's eyes roved across her. Eira fought a shiver. No one had ever stared at her so intently, with so much focus and fascination, void of any judgment or harshness. It was a little uncomfortable, but not entirely in a bad way. "I worked hard to ascend to the rank of ambassador as quickly as possible so that I might come and explore this previously closed-off land I now know as Solaris."

"It never occurred to me that Meru might be as fascinated by us as we are by them."

"Your island—no, continent, you call it, correct?" Eira nodded and he continued, "Your continent has a storied history in both our records and lore."

"It does?"

"Indeed. A fascinating place where the legends say the gods and their champions once walked." He chuckled and Eira followed suit. "Of course, such a thing is ludicrous. But I imagine the stories were grounded in some truth surrounding the now-gone Crystal Caverns."

"Perhaps." They had been a mysterious place of even more mysterious powers.

"In any case, I think that we could help each other." Ferro's smile was dazzling. "If you are open to it, I would love to have these little chats with you as we're able. You can tell me of your life here, and I'll share with you my life on Meru."

"That sounds wonderful." Eira didn't see any reason to refuse. There was no harm in merely talking. Was there? "If you don't mind, I'd love to hear more about these legends—"

"One more thing," Ferro interjected. "Before we get to that, I'd like to make sure that you and I are aligned. I have no intention of telling anyone else of our discussions. While nothing untoward is occurring, I wouldn't want to give the look of impropriety or favoritism, since I will be designing your final two trials."

"Oh, that's right." Eira tucked her hair behind her ears, thinking a moment. "Well, as you said, we know we're doing nothing wrong. I don't see why our meeting needs to be public knowledge." The only person Eira might tell would be Alyss. And Eira knew that Alyss would keep it secret, and not judge her too harshly...hopefully.

"Good!" Ferro clapped his hands together. "Now, I want to know more about your magic, and then I will tell you a legend."

"Mine?"

"The elemental affinities fascinate me. I've been told that sorcerers of a particular affinity cannot be harmed—at least not lethally—by elements of their affinity."

"That's true."

"So, I wonder, can a Waterrunner drown?"

"Yes, though not easily." Eira's mind wandered to the

underground spring she'd seen earlier, deep in the depths of the palace. She imagined a Waterrunner, far bolder than her and with a voice like ice, diving into those equally cold waters, never to emerge again. "It's not *easy* to drown a Waterrunner, as our innate sorcery will spring to action, preventing water from harming us. Our magic forms a bubble around us, underneath the surface. But, that very act, however instinctive it is, saps our power." Eira pursed her lips. "It's difficult to explain. But, if kept under long enough, we would run out of magic and strength. When that happens, yes, we would drown."

"And the air in that bubble?" he asked.

"I suppose it could run out..." Eira had never really considered it. "It'd depend on how prepared the Waterruner was before going under, I think."

"Ah, I see." He laughed, though Eira wasn't amused by the conversation in the slightest. "I have witnessed your crown princess walk through fire and come out unscathed. So I thought that all Solaris sorcerers were impervious to their elements."

"Completely impervious, no. But thankfully, as I said, it's not easy for us to be harmed by the same element as our affinities."

"Indeed." Ferro smiled. "Now, I promised you a legend about your continent. Let's start with how Meru and Solaris were once one."

Eira settled back in her chair as Ferro told her a story of a long-ago time when Meru, Solaris, and the Shattered Isles between them were one unified continent. He told her of a great godly war between the ultimate good—Yargen—and ultimate evil—Raspian. In that battle, the continent was torn asunder.

It was more fiction than fact. But in his rich tones, the words came to life. They painted pictures before her eyes like no one ever had before. Ferro was a skilled orator and Eira listened to him speak long into the night. She eagerly answered his every question about her magic just in exchange for his voice.

By the time they stood, the fire had died to smoldering embers that cast them in red outlines.

"I believe that is our signal." Was that lamentation Eira heard in his tone?

She stood from her chair at the same time as him. "I enjoyed tonight." She was surprised by how much she meant the statement. Her voice was hoarse. Eira wasn't accustomed to speaking with anyone so much. By now, she and Alyss would've long fallen into a comfortable silence as they focused on a book and a wad of clay or bit of wood, respectively.

"As did I, more than I expected." Ferro hovered and Eira followed his lead. "Thank you for telling me so much about your magic, and the Tower."

"Of course. I look forward to our next exchange."

"As do I." Ferro's attention dropped. Before Eira could figure out what gained his focus, he swept her hand up in his. In a fluid motion, the ambassador brought her knuckles to his lips.

Eira was grateful for the warm glow of the room, because the flush on her cheeks was worse than if she spent an hour in the sun.

"Until next time, sweet Eira." Ferro left her standing in the growing darkness, trying to collect her breath and find her knees.

Over the next week, the whole encounter felt like it had been a dream.

It couldn't have been real. A clandestine meeting in the middle of the night with Ambassador Ferro? Things like that didn't happen to Eira.

Then again, perhaps they did. In the past month she had discovered a secret room and passage. She had defied her family and become a candidate for competitor in the Tournament of Five Kingdoms. Why couldn't she also secretly meet with a dignitary from Meru? She was becoming someone new, perhaps someone she'd always been meant to be.

Every night, Eira returned to her room, waiting for another letter. But none came. She wished she could've kept the first letter he'd sent and vowed to keep the next. It would be the only proof she had that she really hadn't dreamed the whole encounter.

"All right, what do you know?" Alyss looked up from the clay that was coating her fingers. Her bowl of porridge was pushed off to the side, mostly empty.

Eira made a low humming noise, bringing her attention back to the real world.

"You've spent the better part of breakfast daydreaming while staring out the windows. Spill it."

"I'm thinking of the next trial."

Alyss snorted. "I don't believe that for a second."

"Well, it's true." Just not the whole truth.

Alyss leaned forward, her voice dropped to a whisper. "You haven't been going back to that place, have you?"

"No, I promised you I wouldn't."

"Good." Satisfied, Alyss settled back with the clear intent of returning to her sculpting—a fox, today. But her eyes didn't make it. Instead, they looked over Eira's shoulder, narrowing slightly. "Well, if it isn't the Prince of the Tower, gracing us with his lordly presence."

"Good morning, ladies." Cullen gave a nod. His hair was free and tousled today, falling into his eyes. "Eira, I was hoping to have a word with you."

"Why?" Eira didn't bother hiding a grimace. Alyss snickered.

"Because I would like one."

"And I would like a boat to Meru. Get me that and I'll think about giving you a word."

"May we speak, *please*?" Cullen ground out the word. He clearly wasn't accustomed to people not jumping at the opportunity to bask in his glory. "I'm here on your brother's behalf."

That brought her attention back to him in an instant. "Is everything all right with Marcus?"

"Yes, please, just a word before I meet with the empress." Cullen, per usual, never missed a chance to mention he got to train with the empress. Or dine with the empress. Or just get to bask in the empress's glory because he was *so* special.

Eira rolled her eyes. "Fine."

She followed Cullen out of the mess hall and up the Tower. They wound around, past the library and Waterrunners' workshop, eventually entering a door not far from her brother's room—between the workshop and the minister's office. It was a strange little room, indeed. As if the space couldn't make up its mind on what it wanted to be.

A small wood-burning stove had two chairs positioned next to it. Eira could see the smoke it piped through the wall streaming by the stained glass window. Two bookshelves were crammed full, a desk wedged between them. The right half of the room was dominated by a large table and stools with cramped curio cabinets behind them, almost like a miniature version of the Waterrunners' workroom.

"What is this place?"

"We call it the Windwalkers' study." Cullen motioned to the chairs by the stove. "Make yourself comfortable."

"I think I'll stand," Eira decided when he leaned against the table rather than sitting.

"If it pleases you."

"Where is my brother?"

"Already out for the day. I think he was sent to the East Clinic, if you're curious."

Even though competitors weren't supposed to have duties, Marcus apparently still did. Eira didn't envy the work. But she did envy the idea of being so important that people didn't want to even afford her a day off. "I thought you said—"

"He asked me to speak to you." Cullen gave her a hard stare. He oozed discomfort from every pore as he gripped the edge of the table, clearly debating what he was going to say next. Eira allowed him to stew in his agony. She was used to awkward situations; she'd been the herald of awkward for years, so the circumstances weren't having the same effect on her. "I am going to invite you to court tomorrow. I mean, I *am* inviting you to court tomorrow."

Eira blinked several times, shook her head, and tucked her hair behind her ears. "I'm sorry, I don't think I heard—"

"Tomorrow, I would like you to be my guest at court," he rephrased. The eloquence Cullen could usually muster had returned the third try.

"Why?"

"It's not because I want to be around you."

"Obviously." Eira rolled her eyes. "Given my shock, I thought you'd realize I know that."

Cullen's lips curled into a thin smirk. There was a mischievous glint to his hazel eyes that Eira wasn't used to and didn't know how to read. "Your brother asked me to do it."

"Still unclear as to the why."

"Rumor is, the obstacle course for our next trial is being set up in the training grounds. They've been closed off for the entire week, so it seems likely. The training grounds aren't far from court and there is a back entrance to them where, sometimes, the nobles will go to observe the guards running drills."

"Why would they want to do that?" she blurted.

"The things boredom can drive wealthy people to do would shock you." Cullen shrugged. The way he said it made it clear that he didn't count himself among those "wealthy people," which struck Eira as odd, given his status. "In any case, if I slipped out of court to go take a look, it would be noticed. But if I brought you…well, you're pretty good at being overlooked."

"Thanks," she said dryly.

"I meant no offense, just a fact."

"Well, the fact is offensive."

"Mother above, you are abrasive." He put his hand over his face and sighed.

"Only to people who are abrasive to me."

"I have been nothing but kind to you."

Eira snorted at his remark.

"Oh? How have I been unkind?"

Eira folded her arms over her chest and turned to the windows. She hated the memories the mere question dredged up. "You know how."

"Eira." His tone softened some. His eyes searched her and she felt vulnerable under his gaze. "I had no idea what Adam's letter said. I didn't know what he was planning to do to you. Don't shoot the messenger."

"Stop."

"I didn't support them."

"Lies."

"Don't call me a liar," Cullen snapped.

"Then don't lie to my face! You and Adam were inseparable. You still are. There's no way you didn't know."

"I seriously had no idea!" He pushed away from the table and advanced on her.

"*Lies*," she repeated. Eira jutted out her chin as he crossed the threshold of her personal space. Her heart raced. Cullen opened his mouth to speak but she cut him off. "Even if you didn't know, you let it happen. You were—and still are—complicit to him torturing me. You stood by him after, and everyone in the Tower looks up to you, so you told *everyone* with your actions that what Adam did was all right."

Her words seemed to shake him, but only for a moment. "Just let it go. Everything will be better for you if you do." He almost sounded sincere. Compassionate? The notion soured her stomach further.

"I will not. Not until justice has been properly served."

"Justice?" He scoffed. "Says the woman who killed someone and still walks free."

Eira took a step back like he'd struck her.

Cullen looked away guiltily. "I shouldn't have said that. I'm sorry."

"What do you care?" Eira grabbed her elbows, holding herself.

"Eira, I—" He faltered. His hand hovered in the air, as if he'd been about to reach for her. Eira looked between it and his face and Cullen dropped the offending appendage. "I can understand."

"Oh, you can? The perfect Prince of the Tower."

"I can more than you know."

"Just stop." Anxiety was welling up in her at the memory of the incident. She hadn't meant to, but she had killed someone. It would always make her feel cold, clammy, off-balance. It should. That was her punishment.

Her usual mental barriers were weakened and the voices began to slip through.

...I don't think I can master this technique. It's hopeless...

...You like her! Gregor has a crush...

...I know I have no choice. I'll do whatever it takes to keep up this game. If the truth ever got out, my family would be ruined... Cullen's voice.

The last voice was his, resonating from the mantle. Who was he speaking to when he said that? How long ago had it been? What dark secret was he carrying? He could understand more than she knew? Suddenly the ascension of his family to nobility, his father's senate seat, everything was cast in a slightly more nefarious light.

The door opened and both of them turned to find the empress.

When the startled expression wore off Vhalla's face, she smiled almost a little too sweetly. "I apologize for interrupting, Cullen. If you need to reschedule our lessons today I'd be happy to do so."

"We were just wrapping up." Cullen cleared his throat and hastily stepped away. It wasn't until then that Eira realized how close they'd been. She pushed ice under her cheeks to keep them from warming and making the whole situation look worse.

"Apologies, Your Majesty." Eira curtsied as best she could.

"It's no trouble," Vhalla said warmly. She crossed the threshold and placed a heavy tome on the table. *Windwalkers of the East* was its title. "Are you certain, Cullen?"

"Yes. I was inviting Eira to court tomorrow. Since she accepted, we were just wrapping up," Cullen said smoothly.

"Oh, you will be a delight at court." Vhalla beamed. "The emperor and I hope for more and more sorcerers to be around the nobility."

He involved the empress, the bastard. There was no way Eira could back down now. "It's my honor," Eira forced herself to say. "Now, if you'll excuse me."

She had to go and use every hour to mentally prepare herself for the viper pit that was the Solaris Court.

THAT NIGHT, A courier arrived in the Tower with a box for her. Inside was an impeccably tailored gown of a deep blue velvet and sea-foam satin trim that Eira hated herself for admiring. Especially given who sent it.

She marched straight to her brother's room, box and letter in hand. The moment Marcus opened the door, Eira launched into him.

"It's one thing to sign me up to do something with Cullen, of all people. It's another for that thing to be going with him to court. But did you have to give him my *measurements*?" Eira pointed accusingly to a section of Cullen's note that smugly read:

I do hope the color pleases you. I tried to find something that matched your personality. Based on the numbers I was given, it should fit. Luckily, things only needed to be taken in since you don't have much in the way of hips or bust.

Marcus burst out into laughter.

"Marcus, this is serious!"

"Eira, it's fine. Come in and sit."

Marcus's room was identical to Eira's and every other apprentice's dormitory. She sat on the bed in a huff, the box a whisper of rustling fabric beside her.

"Listen, he's doing it as a favor to me. I knew you were free tomorrow, I'm not. Uncle has me still going to the clinic despite being a candidate. He says they need me there and that it'll help my overall prestige and appearance as a candidate. I would've gone if I could."

Eira still chose to ignore that her brother was *so important* he wasn't getting time off like the rest of them. "Why don't you go to court the next day?"

"Because the court only meets once a month, usually. We're lucky the timing works at all. We might not have had a chance to catch a glimpse of the course early otherwise."

Eira stared at her toes. That was the real reason why she'd come. "You know you're talking about cheating, don't you?"

"It's not *really* cheating." Marcus rolled his eyes.

"You're going to know elements of the course before anyone else. How is that not cheating?"

"But we won't know how they're going to make us run through those elements. And it's only partway built; they might change something. So it's not really any kind of leg up."

"If it's not a benefit to you then why am I doing this at all?" Eira stared him down. "And if it's not cheating, why am I sneaking around to do it?"

"Eira..." Marcus grabbed her shoulders. "Please? As a favor to me?"

"Why are you stooping to this level?"

He released her with a sigh. "I need to win."

"You don't need to cheat to do that." Eira stood. "Marcus, you're the best Waterrunner I know. You're even better than Fritz," Eira echoed Cullen's words. Maybe if enough people told her brother, he'd believe them. "I'm sure that's part of why he's allowed you to stay in the Tower as an apprentice. You can learn more without all the limitations of an instructor on your time." At least, she hoped that was part of the reason he was still here. It couldn't *all* be because of her, could it?

"I'm not as good as you think I am." He looked at her with weary and sad eyes. Eyes Eira didn't recognize from her brother.

"Yes, you are. I've spent my whole life looking up to you. If anyone knows how great you are, it's me."

Marcus pulled her in for a tight hug, one Eira returned. "You really are the best sister a guy could ask for."

"You're an okay brother, I guess."

"Okay? You *guess*?" He pulled back in mock offense.

Eira laughed. "Fine, you're pretty great."

"I thought so." Marcus shared her laughter. "So, will you do it? Please? For me?" Eira bit her lower lip. "I also thought… it'd give you a chance to see the course, so you could see when you'd throw your run and how to make it look believable when you did."

"Throw my run?"

"So you wouldn't keep being a candidate for competitor?"

"Oh, right," Eira murmured. The levity in the room vanished and was replaced with a lead weight on her shoulders.

"Mom and Dad are coming to watch the second trial, remember? They'll be watching for you to fail like they asked."

Watching for her to fail, while he succeeded. Their letter still had yet to sit right with her. The words became harder to bear by the day.

"Yeah…right." She sighed heavily, but no amount of exhaling could relieve the pressure growing on her. It felt like two separate weights were on different halves of her body and if she kept trying to hold them steady they'd rip her in half. "Fine, I'll do it for you. But think about if you *really* want to know any information I gather. You don't need to cheat."

Eira collected the dress box and left him to think about what she'd said.

She paced the hallway Cullen had instructed her to wait in, her ankles getting tangled in the tailored skirt of the gown. Her usual hems were looser-fitting pieces that actually gave her room to move. This clung to her frame, giving her shapes that Eira hadn't realized were there.

Ah, the illusions that could be wrought with good tailoring.

The door on the Tower side of the hall opened, finally,

and Cullen strode through in all his court finery. He came to a sudden stop, as if walking into an invisible wall, and just stared. Eira's feet halted as she did the same.

Cullen was dressed in deep purple trousers that clung to legs far more muscular than she expected. The hours he spent on the training grounds with the empress clearly weren't for show. His long, gray coat had a sheen to it that looked almost like liquid metal. Two lines of buttons trailed down the front, ending just above the hem at his mid-thigh.

"I...hello."

"Hello, Cullen." Eira wasn't accustomed to being more eloquent than him. He must be more nervous about what they were going to do than she was. "I did as you instructed." She smoothed her hands over her skirts.

"I see that, and you—you look..." He trailed off, staring once more. Cullen shook his head. "You look perfectly acceptable for court."

"Ah, I'm so glad I look 'acceptable' for the Prince of the Tower." She could've sworn she caught the ghost of a grimace at the mention of his moniker this time. "Shall we get this over with?"

"Let's." He breezed past her. The entire walk to the court, Cullen kept his eyes forward. Not once did he glance her way.

The hall for the Solaris Court was a stately building set between the training grounds and water gardens that stretched out from the grand Mirror Ballroom. The lavish gardens leading up to it were a menagerie of topiaries trained into winged and hoofed beasts in cages of heavy flora. Eira had seen the hall from a distance before, but she'd never had a reason to explore closer—this was a place for the Lords and Ladies of Solaris. Common folk like her weren't made for this hallowed ground.

Yet, as she crossed the marble threshold, no one rushed over to *shoo* her away. Eira let out a soft chuckle under her breath. She was surprised Cullen heard.

"What is it?"

"Nothing." Maybe something of her uncle's lordship had

brushed off on her. Maybe she could navigate these waters.

"You have an almost worrisome smile."

"I am not worrisome." Eira shot him a glare, surprised to find a lazy grin hanging on Cullen's cheeks. "*Fine.* I begrudgingly admit that I am grateful Marcus shared with you my measurements. It felt like a betrayal of trust yesterday. But now I feel like I blend in as well as the statues or drapes." Eira kept her voice to a hushed whisper.

"You do," he said softly. "As long as you can refrain from opening your mouth and exposing just how unpolished you are." Eira jabbed her elbow into his side, a little harder than even she intended. He grunted and hissed, "What was that for?"

"Sorry for my *unpolished* movements. Clumsy me," Eira said sweetly.

"You are seriously—" Cullen began to growl. But he was cut off by a singsong voice belonging to a woman dressed in a red ensemble finished with actual western rubies.

"Lord Cullen, it's so good to see you." The woman gave a bow of her head. "I see you've brought a guest with you today. How peculiar."

"Lady Allora, this is Eira. She's a fellow apprentice in the Tower of Sorcerers."

"A delight to meet you, Eira."

"And you as well, Lady Allora." Eira tilted her head as she'd seen Allora do, hoping she didn't break any etiquette. For all she made jabs at Cullen's finishing lessons and the airs he put on, Eira suddenly could appreciate their necessity if he had to survive in this world. Every movement here was under scrutiny. Eira had never felt so many sideways glances cast her way, and she was one of the most unwelcome people in the Tower of Sorcerers.

"I see you're a candidate as well." Allora's eyes dropped to her pin. "You don't intend to try and beat our Cullen, do you?"

If I wanted to, I could, Eira barely resisted saying. She said instead, "I am a Waterrunner. We're not in competition."

"How good for you." She turned her attention back to Cullen. "It's not common for you to bring a lady with you. What should we think of this development?" Allora adjusted the furs around her shoulders with a serpentine grin. Eira noticed a few other conversations slowing around them so people could listen in.

"Think what you will. Far be it from me to deny you any delight you may glean from rumors to pass the hours of your day." Cullen's response had the tone of a rapier being drawn from a sheathe. Strong, deadly, and elegant. "Eira, if it pleases you, I would love to share with you my favorite pieces of art here in the hall."

"I'd be delighted," Eira said, hoping she read the situation correctly and he was looking for an out.

"Take care, Lady Allora." Cullen bowed his head and escorted Eira away. Her hand had yet to leave the crook of his elbow since entering, and what had originally been a reluctant touch now felt like a lifeline.

"It's not a problem that you brought me, is it?" Eira went to glance over her shoulder.

"Don't look back," Cullen hissed under his breath. She snapped her head forward once more. "You'll give her the satisfaction of knowing she put you off guard."

"The rumors are true, this place really is a viper pit," Eira murmured. Cullen ignored the remark.

The hall was split into three stretches. The main stretch, which aligned with the grand entry, had a soaring, vaulted ceiling supported by square columns. On the outside of the columns were two other stretches, lined by windows and art. Men and women drifted throughout with nothing better to do with their time than be beautiful, stare at pretty things, and spread gossip.

"The door I mentioned in my instructions is ahead." Cullen gave a nod toward a small side door, tucked in the corner. "Do you have any questions about the plan?"

"No." Eira shook her head. He'd been fastidious with his

instructions on how the day would play out.

"Good. In the meantime, there is something I think you'll enjoy."

He guided her over to a small painting of a city divided by a river. Hills of shimmering gold sloped behind it, soaking in sunshine. On either side of the river were two rises. One rise supported a grand castle, the other a temple.

Eira let out a soft gasp, stepping closer to the piece. It was as if someone had cracked her skull and the yolk of her dreams had oozed across the canvas in all its splendor. She knew this place, knew it as well as Solarin or Oparium, even though she had only ever visited it in her daydreams.

"This is…"

"It's Risen"—*the capital of Meru*—"or so I'm told. Ambassador Ferro brought this as an offering for the Imperial collection."

"Why is no one else looking at it?" Eira glanced around. The painting was framed by velvet curtains. Two flame bulbs on either side gave off perfect viewing light. It was treated respectfully. Yet…no one seemed interested in the treasure that was among them.

"It's been hanging since Ambassador Ferro arrived. There was a special soiree to unveil it, even."

"But…it's magnificent."

"Anything gets old the longer you look at it."

"I would never grow tired of seeing this," Eira insisted. "I could stare at it every night before I slumbered and still be eager to wake up and have it be the first thing I see."

Cullen took a step toward her. In her trance, she hadn't realized she'd stepped away from him to admire the painting more closely. He stopped at her side. But rather than being fixated on the painting, Cullen focused on *her*.

"What?" Eira straightened away. Her nose had been nearly touching the oil and canvas.

"You really love it, don't you?"

"It? Meru?" Eira tucked her hair behind her ears. She

wasn't accustomed to being anyone's sole attention, not in a good way. First Ferro, now…whatever this expression was from Cullen. Perhaps something about her *had* changed these past few weeks since she'd dared to enter the trials. "I love it more than anything, save for my family."

"I…" Cullen trailed off, finally looking to the artwork. His expression wasn't delight as she would've expected.

"You what?" Eira touched his elbow lightly—the only part on his body she felt permitted to come in contact with.

"It's admirable," he said, finally. Eira noticed he didn't immediately withdraw or flinch from her touch. "To be so passionate about something. To not care what anyone else thinks of that passion."

Eira laughed softly. "It's not that I don't care what they think. It's that I *can't* care. It hurts too much when I do. It's easier to encase myself in—"

"Walls. So they never see the real you. If they don't really know you, then they can't really hurt you."

She had been going to say ice, but… "Yes." The echo of his voice in the Windwalkers' study pulsed through her. "You know about that, don't you?" Eira whispered. "Having to keep people away at all costs just to survive?"

A look of shock, tinged with panic, raced across his face. It was an emotion so raw and real that all the finishing classes in the world couldn't keep it hidden. Eira stared up at the man, as if she could see him—part of him—for the first time. She'd thought she hated him…but what did she really know about him?

Cullen had his secrets.

"What do you know?" he breathed.

"I don't know—"

Their conversation ended abruptly as a set of golden doors, emblazoned with the sun of the Empire, opened. They were opposite the main entry and were gilded not just with gold, but with the invisible and palpable aura of *royal*. From the shadows behind the doors, Prince Romulin emerged with Ferro. The prince made a formal introduction of the ambassador to the court at large. Eira was transfixed by the elfin, as though he had finally emerged from her dreams. Seeing him in the cool light of day after their last meeting was unexpectedly jarring.

"Eira, it's time," Cullen whispered to her, underneath Prince Romulin's introductions.

Right. She gave Cullen a nod and stepped off to the side, moving behind the people who were just as transfixed by Ferro's presence as she had been.

With a wave of her hand, Eira summoned a wall of illusion in the back corner—a mere step behind the oblivious courtiers. Much like how she had sneaked Alyss into the Waterrunners' storeroom, Eira stepped behind her illusion. Anyone who took their eyes off Ferro would see an empty corner and a shut door as Eira slipped into a back hall.

The first set of doors led to a place for the lords and ladies to relieve themselves. Farther down, the hall was chained off. Eira ducked underneath the harmless barrier, continuing to a T intersection at the end.

As Cullen instructed, she headed right. Two doors down, Eira entered into a narrow passage that connected with a stair. He'd said that nobles used these chambers to observe people training on the grounds, but Eira couldn't imagine the ladies and their expensive skirts pressing through these dark halls that wove between palace walls.

Finally, the hall spit her out into a musty room. A skinny window extended like a horizon, splitting a line in the wall opposite her. Her feet came to a stop right before the window; Eira stared at the blinding line of sunlight.

She could turn around. She had no interest in cheating. Eira worried her lower lip between her teeth. But if she did leave…she'd let Marcus down. She'd promised him.

Her thoughts wandered back to her conversation with Cullen. She wanted this more than anyone else in the Tower. She wanted it not for glory or prestige. She wanted it for knowledge…because something far across the sea tugged on her heart more powerfully than the pull of the tides.

Eira left her doubts behind her, and looked out the window.

The training grounds had been completely transformed. Deep ditches had been dug into the packed earth, creating small lakes and valleys. There were wooden and stone structures— some looked like they had been built by craftsmen. But most had the "too-perfect" appearance only magic yielded.

She swept her eyes across the field several times, committing as much as she could to memory. In the back of her mind, there was the phantom ticking of a clock—incessantly reminding her that she had to hurry. Cullen had made it clear that him bringing a lady to court would be noted, thus her absence would be eventually noted as well.

Eira turned away from the window and fumbled back into the passage, nearly blind until her eyes adjusted. The tailoring of her skirts would only permit her to move agonizingly slowly down the stairs. Eira cursed with every step. She'd just closed the door to the passage when Cullen's voice echoed down the hall.

"Ah, yes, I'm just waiting for my guest," he said.

"We didn't see her powdering her nose," an unfamiliar woman's voice replied.

"Perhaps she left you, Lord Cullen." That was Allora. "It was too kind of you to bring her, but you should join us instead."

"Waterrunners can craft illusions, ladies. Perhaps she merely did not want to answer any of your prying questions and hid."

Was that a huff she heard in reply? A door closing echoed back to her. Eira began moving again and nearly tumbled face-first into Cullen as he rounded the corner.

"What took you so long?" he hissed.

"You didn't tell me how far it was." She glared at the tone he took.

"Come on, we have to—"

Just as Cullen was about to wheel her around the corner there was the sound of doors opening and closing again. His face crumpled into panic and Cullen spun, yanking her back into the shadows. Eira opened her mouth and Cullen pressed his finger over her lips.

She was mildly tempted to nip at it in offense. At least until she heard the voices of those he'd caught a glimpse of.

"Here are the washrooms, Ambassador," Prince Romulin said.

"Ah, my apologies, I was actually intending to retire to my chambers." Ferro was with him.

"Did someone in the court commit an offense, sir?"

"Not at all." Ferro chuckled. It sounded fake to Eira. "It's only that I have planning to do for the fourth and fifth trials. I want to make sure I've designed them just right."

"You are very diligent in your work."

Footsteps neared. Panic was on Cullen's face as he pulled them a step farther from the intersection of the hallways. He leaned forward. Eira stepped away but her back hit the wall.

"That is the passage to the royal wing," he whispered against her ear. Eira shivered at the feeling of his lips moving against her skin. Cullen was oblivious and pointed down the third, unexplored hall. "If they catch us here it's going to arouse suspicion that we can't have."

"I can illusion us."

"That assumes they won't walk through the illusion and bump into us. They might head this way to inspect the progress of the trial."

Eira bit her lip. "We can just—"

"They might take our pins for this," he interrupted sternly.

I'll do whatever it takes. If it ever got out, my family would be ruined. His words echoed in her mind. Was the mysterious "it" what had Cullen so panicked at the idea of being caught out of place? What risks did he keep hidden behind his walls? Or did they have more reasons to be afraid that Eira didn't yet understand?

Her heart beat so hard against her ribs, she was shocked that Ferro couldn't hear it with his long ears.

"I want to make sure everything goes smoothly," Ferro said over the clanking of the chain that barred entry being hung against the wall.

Cullen cursed under his breath. He looked to her, wide-eyed. Eira stared up and mouthed the words, *What do we do?* If they tried to flee down the hallway, they would be seen. There was no way they'd make it to the nearest door before Ferro and Romulin rounded that corner. And even if they did make it to the door, they would no doubt hear the door closing and investigate.

"Kiss me," Cullen breathed.

"What?" The word was a soft gasp.

He put his arms around her waist, pulling her to him. The feeling of his palms sliding smoothly over the silk of her dress melted every wall of ice she'd ever erected. The tides of her magic were raging. They were going to boil her alive.

"Kiss me and we'll both make it out of this unscathed."

She had two seconds to debate. Two seconds to decide. There was movement in the corner of her eye as a booted foot crossed into the intersection of the halls.

Eira wrapped her arms around Cullen's shoulders and brought her lips to his.

CHAPTER

TWELVE

THE MOMENT HER lips touched his, all caution was thrown to the wind. Her back was flush against the wall as Cullen pressed forward, claiming her mouth with all the bold tenacity of a lover. Eira's eyes opened in shock and then she forced them shut once more. Her fingers dug into his shoulders, surprised to find sturdy muscle underneath all the lux fabrics he wore as armor to guard against the lessers of the world.

Lessers like you, a nasty voice in the back of her mind whispered.

His hand was in her hair. Eira didn't know when it had moved from her waist, but his nails were now against her scalp, threatening to draw out a sound that Eira—under no circumstances—had ever intended to make. Especially not with Cullen.

Prince Romulin cleared his throat with a soft, "*Ahem.*"

Cullen pulled away abruptly, panic in his eyes. The panic she believed to be real. They weren't out of the woods yet. The faint flush to his cheeks was certainly an act. However, her own flush, that was very, very real.

"I, uh…Mother above," Cullen groaned with embarrassment. "Forgive us, Your Highness." He bowed low.

"These things happen." The prince wore a grin as if he could relate all too well to sneaking off into dark hallways. "But this area is technically off limits."

"I know…I, we…"

"I won't report you to the guard for trespassing into the royal wing. Take your time, collect yourselves, and head back to court. Though I recommend you find a different dark corner for any future urges that can't be ignored."

As the two men spoke, Eira's attention was on Ferro. His violet eyes shone brightly, as if amused, but his brow was furrowed. The elfin's face was in conflict, as if it couldn't make up his mind on what reaction he wanted to have toward this discovery.

Eira bit her lip to keep herself from saying something to Ferro and ruining Cullen's effort. She could still taste Cullen's mouth on hers and, for some reason, it only made her want to assure Ferro more that things weren't as they seemed.

"You are too generous, Your Highness." Cullen bowed again.

Eira mumbled apologies and curtsied. When she raised her eyes, she only caught one more glimpse of Ferro before he disappeared through a door.

Cullen heaved a sigh of relief. "That was close."

"Would he really have reported us to the guard?"

"Technically, he could've. Or he could've investigated further and figured out what we were really doing and revoked our pins. Or, just revoked them because trespassing is unbecoming of competitors." Cullen pressed a finger into the pin over her chest. "And I doubted you wanted to risk that."

"No."

"Still, I apologize for the kiss." Cullen took a long step away and started back toward the court.

Eira raked her fingers through her hair, making sure it was in place. The motion brought back the memory of his nails on her scalp. She shivered and barely resisted telling him not to apologize. It had been a long time since she was kissed...and she'd never been kissed like that.

"It's all right. I understand."

As he was putting the chain back in place, he paused. "That wasn't your first kiss, was it?"

Eira rolled her eyes. "Of course it wasn't."

"Oh, thank the Mother, I would've felt awful. I knew you were inexperienced but—"

"How did you 'know I was inexperienced?'" Eira grabbed

his elbow, stopping him.

"Well, given how you were all over Adam…and he said…" His eyes were shifty, looking anywhere but her.

Eira gave him a jerk, summoning his full attention to her. "Listen, here's the thing that I don't even think Adam grasped—he was the first man I *loved*." The words were like glass, every last one. They tore up her throat and made it hard to keep speaking. But something about airing her truth felt good. Felt long overdue. Perhaps she could only say these words because they had crossed a line that put Cullen closer than anyone had come to her in a long time, even if that line had been crossed by acting and nothing more. "I didn't desire him in a carnal way. If I merely wanted satisfaction of that nature I'd find it elsewhere or give it to myself."

Cullen stared at her in what Eira could only describe as morbid fascination.

"I'm not fragile. I'm not ignorant to the ways of the world. I was hurt that day; not because I didn't get a man, or because he cared for someone else—I was hurt because he made a mockery of me and my feelings. Feelings I had cherished. He dared to make me never want to feel again," Eira finished.

Cullen stared at her. She waited in silence for his judgment for an agonizing minute. When it was clear he had nothing more to say, Eira left him and the court gladly behind.

She'd been prepared for her brother to say something about how things had ended with Cullen. But he never did. Not when she told him everything she'd seen about the course. And not in the days that followed.

Either Cullen had told Marcus and sworn him to secrecy, or Cullen had kept their encounter, and all she'd said, solely between them. Eira didn't know which she liked least. The idea Marcus would take Cullen's side over hers and keep his secrets over checking if she was okay. Or the idea that Cullen may have the ability to respect her—that he may be a better man than she'd given him credit for. And if that was the case, that opened the possibility that she'd been wrong about him in other ways.

Those thoughts about Cullen being decent were born from the lingering haze of the kiss, surely. It had been a *good* kiss. The best she'd had. Eira's more sensual experiences had been limited to a few summers of explorations with one of the handsome young sailors who were in and out of port. Nothing serious…but a few good nights in the bunch that were worth thinking about from time to time.

So Eira strove to put the whole day from her mind. She focused on her work and studies. She spent time with Alyss, sharing space quietly in their own corners. And all too fast, it was the night before the second trial and a letter was waiting on her pillow after dinner.

It had arrived as mysteriously as the last. No sign of its sender. Just like before, it was unsigned, but the seal told her as much who it was from as the elegant script within that read,

Meet me in our lounge.

Our lounge. For some reason her eyes kept snagging on those words as Eira waited for the right time to sneak out of the Tower and through the palace. It wasn't really "theirs." It was a random lounge that Ferro had found, or been given for his time in the palace.

But she had to admit that after their first night there it had become a special place in her mind. It had seemed more magical than the Tower then…and now, as Eira stood in the doorway, staring at the back of Ferro's head.

"Come in," he said in that smooth accent of his.

"How did you know it was me?" Eira asked and closed the door behind her.

"Your heartbeat." Ferro looked up from the book he was reading as she rounded the chairs.

"My...heartbeat?"

"Yes, it has a flutter unique to you. I think I'd notice it anywhere." He motioned to the seat she'd assumed last time. Eira sat once more.

"If you could hear it from across the room, then—"

"I noticed when you sneaked out of the court...and I heard you before Prince Romulin and I reached the end of the hall." Ferro didn't mince words. It was what she'd expect of a dignitary. But that didn't stop Eira from cringing inwardly. She quickly vowed to tackle the situation head on.

"About that..."

"I wouldn't judge someone for a kiss in the shadows." Ferro chuckled. His eyes shone intently in the firelight, accented by the orange like a purple sunset right before nightfall. "However, all week I've been mulling it over. I can't seem to escape the image."

"Why?" Eira's throat felt tight. He'd been thinking about her all week—more specifically, her kissing Cullen. What did that mean?

"Because you do not strike me as the sort of woman who scampers into the shadows to steal kisses."

"What kind of woman do I strike you as?" she dared to ask.

"A woman of purpose and goals. A woman who wouldn't be afraid to kiss whomever she chose in the open." Ferro rested the book on the table between them and settled back in his chair. Eira noted the title of the manuscript—*History of the Crystal Caverns*. Ferro continued before she could make note of his topic choice. "Which led me to investigate, and I think I found the answer to my question of why Eira scampered off the moment court was distracted by my arrival."

"Which is?"

"You were looking for a leg up on the next trial." Ferro's mouth curled into a grin as Eira felt panic crash down on her. "And I think you found your advantage in an old court viewing room that overlooks the training grounds."

Her stomach churned around the dinner she'd eaten,

turning it into bile that threatened to escape. She'd known cheating had been a terrible idea and she'd done it anyway. But he didn't have to know that she'd already told Marcus of her findings. She could take the fall and Marcus would still have the edge he wanted. He'd take her as some kind of page or assistant to Meru. She could salvage the situation.

Eira stood, pulling the pin from her breast. She held it out to Ferro. He dragged his eyes from the offering to her face.

"What do you expect me to do with this?" He arched his eyebrows.

"You're right," Eira admitted. "I went and saw the course. I know some of what's waiting for me tomorrow and because of that I have an unfair advantage. I acted—"

"As I would expect a candidate to act," Ferro interrupted firmly. A mischievous glint had spread from his grin to his eyes. "Put your pin back on. I'm not going to disqualify you."

"But—"

"Let me assure you, I haven't told anyone else of this discovery." He chuckled as Eira returned the pin to her breast and sat. Ferro leaned in his chair, resting his elbow on the armrest, chin on his knuckles. "You amuse me, dear Eira."

Dear Eira. The words swirled around her. She wanted to duck her head under and spend forever in the currents of this feeling. A game of pretend was beginning—Eira knew it was. She would pretend that Ferro had a genuine interest in her. She would bask in this fantasy as long as he would let her, knowingly or otherwise. Doing so wouldn't hurt anyone, so why not?

"I suppose I could say the feeling is mutual," she said. "I would expect anyone else to revoke my pin."

"It is part of my role here to make sure the Trial of Five Kingdoms is an impressive display of power, and is entertaining to watch for the gathered masses. To that end, I do not want to see competitors be chosen who are unwilling to fight. I want competitors who are resourceful, cunning, and *hungry*. Competitors who want victory or nothing and will do anything to get it."

Eira turned the words over in her head. Would she hunt victory at all costs? She supposed she already had her answer. She'd made that choice at court.

"To that end, I want to help you." Ferro ran the tips of his long fingers across his lips in thought. Eira was fixated on the unintentionally sensual motion. "How about we make another exchange tonight? What do you know of the forests and mountains around Solarin?"

"A good deal. My grandparents live in the woods on the outskirts of Rivend."

"Rivend isn't far from where the Crystal Caverns once were, by my recollection."

"They're not." Eira glanced to the fire, distracted by a memory she hadn't thought of in some time.

"What is it?" Ferro, of course, caught the motion. She wondered if his pointed ears could hear her thoughts almost as well as her heartbeat.

"A family story… The mention of the Crystal Caverns made me recall something my mother told me once. After the rise of the Mad King and the sacking of Solarin, Empress Vhalla—though she was still a commoner, then—and Emperor Aldrik actually took shelter in my grandparents' home."

"An impressive page to have in the tome of your family's history."

"I thought so when I first heard it. But it seems normal now."

Ferro chuckled. "It's funny how quickly things can become normal. I have already grown accustomed to the mountain chill and Solaris cuisine."

Eira nodded. "In any case… Yes, I know about the rebuilding. My grandparents are still in that home. One of my aunts is in Rivend. And I grew up in Oparium, which is to the—"

"Southwest," he finished. "You mentioned last time that you hail from Oparium." Eira couldn't recall if she had or hadn't. But she must've. How else would he have known? "I took the liberty of reading up on Solarin's port and that's what prompted my fascination of the time following the downfall of the Crystal Caverns and the rebuilding. So, if you tell me what you know through your experiences and family's stories, I will impart some additional knowledge that will assist you tomorrow."

"You'll help me cheat?" Even though they were the only ones in the large room, Eira's voice dropped to a whisper. Every shadow felt like it was listening.

"I am technically an organizer. I don't think it can be counted as cheating if I give information to whomever I deem fit."

Eira mulled this over. Perhaps he was right? Ferro had no reason to show her favoritism. Marcus had his own advantages from Fritz already. Really, she was just leveling the playing field as her brother was her only real threat. Eira's logical contortion stretched far to justify her actions.

"But," Ferro continued, "I do want to stress again that no one can know of these meetings."

"I doubt anyone would think you'll help me cheat."

"I don't want anyone to think poorly of you at all," he said smoothly. "If anything, I'd like to protect you."

"Protect me?" she repeated, heart fluttering.

"Yes." Ferro shifted in his seat, glancing away from her as conflict took over his features. "You know how a young woman meeting a man in the dead of night might look."

Did she ever. That was exactly what was becoming the foundation of some of her new fantasies. Her imagination went wild when his violet eyes returned to her and Ferro gave her an almost longing look through his lashes.

"I want to see that your honor as a competitor and a woman is preserved."

"Thank you," she somehow managed to say. Her throat was gummy.

"So we will continue keeping these meetings secret? No

matter what's said?"

"Of course," Eira said quickly, perhaps *too* quickly. "You have a deal, Ambassador. I don't want these meetings to stop."

"Good. I knew you wouldn't let me down. Just like I know you won't let me down tomorrow in your run." He eased back in his seat, relief taking over his face. Pride swelled in her. "One last thing."

"Yes?"

"Call me Ferro. Ambassador seems too stiff to be used between friends."

"Are we friends?" Her heart might not be able to handle the answer.

"I would like to be, if that's all right by you?"

"More than." Eira couldn't stop a smile and it only grew larger as Ferro returned it.

"Now, about this obstacle course. There are a few tricky segments you'll want to think about how you'll tackle before going out there…"

Eira tried to commit his every word to memory. She repeated several of the key elements back to him to make sure she understood. The entire time Ferro was patient, allowing her to phrase things several ways and question the more particular parts of the course. Especially the parts that seemed…shockingly dangerous.

But this competition was a friendly display to celebrate unity. Eira trusted that they wouldn't allow anything too dangerous to transpire.

After, she answered his questions about the aftermath of the Mad King Victor and what happened to the Crystal Caverns. Solarin had been in a rough state, as was most of the southern tip of the Empire. Oparium had remained fairly insulated, which helped get the capital back on its feet faster, since Oparium could support sea trade with Norin—the old capital of the West.

On Eira's second yawn of the night, Ferro stood and said, "I should allow you to turn in. It won't do if you're too exhausted to perform tomorrow."

Eira stood and stretched. "I wish we could talk all night." She sighed wistfully and, as Ferro's expression shifted into something thoughtful, her words registered. "I…I didn't mean… What I meant to say was—"

"I feel the same," Ferro said softly. The words had a tender ache that hollowed out something in her gut. Something she desperately needed filled. "It is lonely here. You're one of the few who will speak with me. And, among those who will share a word with me, none do so candidly as you."

"I apologize for how Solaris is treating you."

He shook his head. "It's understandable. I am still seen as the strange outsider." Ferro forced a smile. She knew it was forced, because she had practiced such smiles in the mirror many times. "It will get better. Hopefully, the tournament will help ease tensions between our nations. I shudder to think of what might happen if Meru and Solaris had picked up swords rather than the pen."

"As do I." Eira crossed, starting for the door, but she stalled. Ferro slowed to meet her pace. "Your guard…you and she could—"

"Deneya?" Ferro let out a deep laugh. "Deneya is not someone with whom I make conversation. She's much too cold for that."

Eira chuckled softly. "Usually I'm the cold one."

Ferro hummed and reached for her hand. Eira didn't stop him as his fingers closed around hers. Once more, he brought her knuckles to his lips, holding them there for several long seconds more than normal. Then, he shook his head.

"Warm, just like last time. I could never think of you as cold." He certainly made her feel hot all over.

"How do you think of me?" Her voice was a whisper.

"As my light in this dark land of Solaris."

Eira swallowed, her throat tight. "I hope—" she cleared her throat "—I hope that you will be able to return home soon, so it's not so lonely for you. Good night, Ferro." She forced herself to move, walking through the door, head down. Playing pretend was fine as long as she guarded her heart and didn't get in too deep.

"I hope when I go home, you will come with me."

The words brought her to a halt. Eira turned, looking back for one last glimpse of his stunning eyes. But Ferro had already slipped between the shadows.

Yet, the thought of him lingered with her all the way back to the Tower like the remnants of a delicious dream.

Eira was too awake to even think about going to sleep. His words were in her head, emboldening her. She was a competitor and she had people in high places looking out for her—just like Marcus and Cullen. They might have the empress and Minister of Sorcery. But she had the ambassador from Meru, Instructor Levit, and a series of notebooks that might help her survive the next day.

She didn't quite recall leaving her bed, but she must've. Because Eira now stood at the entrance to the secret room and debated with herself. She had promised Alyss she wouldn't "go back alone." Alyss had just meant the tunnels, right? Certainly not the room. She had been here enough times that it was markedly safe. Yet something about standing there felt like she was breaking a promise and making a new secret.

Alyss didn't know about the day at court, either. Well, she knew Eira had gone with Cullen. But Eira had dodged all the follow-up questions this past week until Alyss grew bored of the topic.

She was already keeping secrets from her friend, what was one more? She'd already crossed more lines than she could count. Eira pushed ahead.

In the dim room, Eira scavenged the bookshelf, skimming the journals. There were techniques in here that might help her with the trial—now that she knew what she was looking for. Eira spent the rest of the night reading, pulling herself from the text only at the last moment.

By the time Eira emerged, she had to rush through bathing

and dressing for the day. Instead of wearing her hair loose, as usual, she plaited it down her back and then coiled the braid into a disk on the back of her head. She wouldn't have it catching or snagging on any part of the course. She'd just finished when Marcus knocked on her door—four fast knocks, pause, two slow knocks.

"You ready?" Marcus asked, hovering in the hall.

"I think so." Eira stood, adjusting her apprentice jacket over a sleeveless shirt underneath. She wore leggings today and her sturdy boots. "What?" she asked, catching Marcus tilting his head this way and that.

"You look like you could actually be a real competitor."

"Of course I do." Eira breezed past him. "Let's get Alyss."

"Good call. It'll be more realistic for you to look like you're making an effort before you throw your attempt."

Eira just hummed, ignoring the remainder of his nervous chatter.

They went with the rest of the candidates to a holding room not far from the training grounds. There, all thirty-two Waterrunners, Groundbreakers, and Firebearers spent the day sequestered so they couldn't watch each other's runs before completing their own. The atmosphere was thick and charged, like before a summer's lightning storm. Eira perched herself in one of the seats by the windows with Alyss and they passed the hours reading two books they discovered forgotten on a bookcase in the study.

Around lunchtime, they were brought food. But the majority of the candidates just picked at the spread. No one's stomach was up for eating.

It was around two when the first Groundbreaker was taken away. Gwen arrived in her formal palace guard armor, called a name, and then escorted the individual without a word. The room became quieter after that. In part, because the trial had become real. But also because their numbers quickly dwindled.

Eira bid Alyss farewell with a fierce hug and a whisper of vague advice. She was the fifth Groundbreaker to leave out of six. After, the eleven Firebearers were escorted away one by one. Soon, there were only the fifteen Waterrunners. By then, Marcus had made his way over to her.

"Are you nervous?" Eira dared to make small talk.

"A little." He chuckled. "But I'm reminding myself that I just have to be better than five people. Four, really, since you don't count." Eira looked out the window, avoiding his quickly probing stare. "You are throwing it, right?"

She said nothing.

"Eira, tell me you're going to throw your run," he demanded.

She pressed her lips into a line. She should just tell him. He would accept it, surely? Eira brought her eyes back to him just as the door opened once more.

"Marcus Landan." Their aunt's voice cut through the tension.

"Good luck." She grabbed for and squeezed both his hands. "I know you'll do great."

Marcus gave her a wary look and pulled his fingers from hers. "I look forward to seeing how your run goes. Mom and Dad will be watching, too."

She stewed on his words as the rest of the Waterrunners were escorted away. Eira was the last one called. She was waiting when Gwen opened the door.

"Are you ready?" Gwen asked.

Eira nodded. "How did Marcus do?"

"He's in third place. He'll be progressing," Gwen said with a smile that quickly fell. "But he didn't seem too pleased…"

He was worried about what she would do. Eira nibbled on her lower lip.

Gwen slipped her hand into Eira's, giving it a tight squeeze. "Don't worry about him."

"But—"

"This is *your* run, your chance. Don't throw it away. Do it for yourself and no one else. Whatever it is you're called to do."

Eira gave a small nod and Gwen released her. There wasn't time for any more words of assurance as they emerged from the long, dark hallway and Eira stepped into the blinding sunlight that illuminated her next trial.

CHAPTER

⊕HIRTEEN

THE TRAINING GROUNDS were even more transformed than she'd last seen them. The obstacle course ran the length in four columns, three switchbacks between them. She stood on a raised platform at the starting point.

Opposite her, on an even higher platform, sat the Imperial family plus the Ministers of Tome and Sorcery, the head of the palace guard, and Ferro. Underneath their balcony was a stone tablet, much like they'd used for the first trial. On it were fourteen names with a line drawn above the lower third—the cut-off line. Four names at the bottom had dashes instead of times. Four people hadn't even finished. Eira swallowed and gathered her courage. All she had to do was be better than the one person beneath the cut-off line with a time and she'd make the cut.

Eira skimmed the crowd made up of her peers from the Tower, courtiers, and strangers alike. Men and women were packed into the ramparts that surrounded the training ground. But, even among the masses, fate played a cruel trick on her.

Somehow, out of everyone, she found her parents.

The sun picked up the honeyed tones of her mother's hair, cut short around her ears. Her father had a closely cropped beard, a darker shade that was almost brown—the only indication of what his hair color had once been, as he kept his head completely shaved. Her mother gave an eager wave and her father clapped his hands.

For a moment, Eira pretended they were here to cheer her on. They were here supporting her. They weren't here as overseers to make sure she threw her run at their request. The thought was like a blow to her stomach, stealing the wind from her; Eira brought her eyes back to Fritz as he began to speak.

"Eira Landan," Fritz projected over the field. "Today you will partake in your next trial as a candidate for competitor in the Tournament of Five Kingdoms. Your goal is to cross the course in the fastest time possible. To progress, you must do so while always stepping on, grabbing, or using elements of the course that are marked in white."

Underneath her feet, a thick, chalky paint had been slathered over the platform. That paint topped various pillars, grips, and walkways.

"Should you, at any point, no longer be in contact with the white parts of the course, you will be disqualified."

Her heart sank. She'd been planning on crossing the moat near the end with ice. Eira glanced toward the sixth obstacle out of seven and then quickly brought her eyes to Fritz. She'd worry about that when she had to. There were five obstacles she had to tackle first.

"You may use any magic you want, so long as you observe the aforementioned rules and wear your pin the entire time. If, at any point, you wish to stop, you may do so either by stepping off the course or by removing your pin. At that time, your run will be considered forfeit. Do you have any questions?"

Eira shook her head and then, realizing he may not be able to see her clearly from the distance, shouted, "I do not."

"Do you still wish to partake in this trial as a candidate?"

Her eyes darted to her parents. Her mother slowly shook her head. Her father stared on with a severe expression. Even Fritz, from what Eira could tell at her distance, seemed to be holding his breath.

They all wanted her to say no. They wanted her to back down like a coward—to do whatever they told her without question. She couldn't back down now... If she did, she'd accomplish nothing. They'd see her as retreating at the last second and as incapable of standing up to them. She'd go on being someone to manage and oversee.

"I do!" Eira shouted, her voice echoing in the vacuum of

the hush that the eager spectators had created.

"Then, on the emperor's mark." Fritz frowned but stepped to the side as the emperor stepped forward.

Aldrik cradled something in his hand connected by a chain to his coat—a pocket watch, likely. She sank into her legs, staring down the obstacles before her. Eira knew she wasn't the strongest, or the fastest. She had never spent copious time on the training grounds, like other apprentices would. A few days of jogging with Alyss when the trials were announced wasn't going to make up for years of books over push-ups.

But she was light on her feet. She was clever. And she'd prepared for this in a way no one else had. A way that was far more valuable than running laps around the palace. She'd had Ferro. Plus, she only had to beat one person's time. There was no way she was going to lose. Eira repeated these things over and over, convincing herself of them. She'd show them all here and now just what she was capable of.

"Begin!" the emperor boomed. Eira launched forward and the crowd erupted with cheers. Were they cheering *for* her? Or against her? Eira couldn't tell and she allowed her racing heart to drown them out.

The first obstacle was a wall that was just slightly taller than her. White was painted up the side and over the top. A simple test of strength. She could imagine her brother getting a running start and vaulting over the wall with ease. But the benefit of being last was knowing that four people hadn't even finished the course. She just had to beat that one person, and their time was abysmal. She could move slowly and deliberately.

Eira placed her foot on the smooth paint of the wall. Ice grew underneath the toe of her shoe, extending back to her heel, and creating a ledge for her to support herself on. She shifted her weight and brought her other foot higher. The entire time, she kept her grip on the top of the wall.

At all times she had to keep her hands or feet on the white.

After three steps, she was high enough to double over the wall and hoist herself over. Eira fell hard on the other side and stood with a groan. Immediately as she found her feet, a burst of flame had her pressing her back against the wall.

Before her was the deep ditch she'd seen during her day at court. Columns of rock rose up from the deep crevice; their tops were white, making stepping stones across. However today the moat was not empty. Curling flames swirled around the columns like an angry tide. A river of fire separated her and the first switchback; the only way across was jumping between the columns.

Eira pushed off the wall, creeping toward the edge of the platform she was on. Sure enough, the moment she neared the first gap, a column of fire shot upward. Eira jumped back, watching and waiting.

"Go. Go!" the masses watching her chanted. She wasn't making for good entertainment taking her time. Eira didn't care.

She watched every geyser of fire erupt, counting the time between each of them. Sure enough, there was a pattern. Eira took a deep breath, holding it until the flames rose right before her.

She ran.

As Eira leapt, she twisted her wrist. Steam surrounded her, smothering her as ice met fire. Eira wavered, dizzy. She'd gone from a brisk spring day to a sauna. She had to cool herself or she'd faint.

More ice.

More steam.

Eira pushed her power down the column she was now on—as much as it took to completely snuff the flames. She could feel the Firebearer manipulating the bursts of fire fighting against her. Eira closed her eyes and continued pushing against that raging power. Firebearers always teetered at the edge of control. She'd slip her magic underneath their tethers, severing the source of their flames. If it were possible, she would've cut off their magic.

There wasn't one, but three Firebearers. *Fine, no matter,*

one, three, ten, it didn't make a difference. Her ice crackled against the flames, finally gaining traction. She pushed until the entire moat was filled with a shimmering blue and a blast of cold hit her face.

She stood, head spinning. Eira wasn't sure if it was because of using so much power, or because of the deafening roars that erupted from the crowd. The way they carried on, one would think that no other Waterrunner had tried to extinguish the flames.

Wrap your magic around your fingers, one of the journals in that secret room had read. *Hold it in place with an unrelenting grip*. Eira did as instructed, as she'd been practicing for weeks. The ice stayed in place as she jumped to the second column, and then to the third. By the time she was at the fourth, her hold on the ice was beginning to weaken. The Firebearers hadn't relented their assault. The edges of the frost were steaming.

But Eira made it across to the next platform that served as the switchback. She released the magic and the ice evaporated as she scanned the crowd. Her father looked down on her with shadowed eyes. She couldn't bear the sight of her mother, hands clutched with worry.

The better she did, the unhappier they looked. Eira focused back on the course rather than spending too much time distracting herself with them.

She now stood at another ledge. A giant gap separated her and the next platform. There was nothing between the two, just a sheer drop. They hadn't even hung a safety net.

Ferro had told her during their discussions that safety precautions were taken behind the scenes. The illusion of danger was part of the test. They were challenging the candidates' bravery and steel will—not trying to kill them.

This obstacle was the embodiment of that. There was white on her platform, and on the steep incline she was expected to land on and then scramble over. She couldn't use any magic between the two as that would put her in contact with something other than the white paint. Somehow, free fall didn't break those rules.

Eira backed up as far as she could. The shadow of the balcony where the royals sat was overhead—where Ferro was. *He's watching*, Eira reminded herself. Her parents sapped her will. But Ferro restored it, giving her the courage she needed.

Before she could think better, before she could hesitate, Eira sprinted forward. She charged to the ledge and put all the power she could into her long legs as she leapt. For a moment, her heart stopped, her stomach sucked into her ribcage on her inhale of terror. She was weightless, vulnerable. It was terrifying.

It was thrilling.

Time crashed around her, pulling her down with gravity. Eira kicked her legs, as if she could move the air like a Windwalker. As though she could place herself closer to the distant platform. She tipped forward, stretching out her arms.

She fell *hard*. Her chin snapped against the wood of the incline and her teeth sang. A woman—her mother, likely—let out a yelp. The taste of blood exploded in her mouth and Eira ran her tongue along the backs of her teeth to make sure she hadn't bitten it clean off.

But gravity wasn't done with her. She was sliding down the incline. Eira scrambled, digging her nails into the wood at the top of the triangle-shaped platform. Panic had her scratching, splinters embedding into her skin.

She couldn't find purchase. She was going to slide off into the jagged rocks below. Eira scrambled, her arms screaming with agony as she struggled to use them to support herself.

Stop panicking and think! A lone voice shouted from the back of her mind—her better sense. *Use your magic!*

Eira gave one final, mighty hoist and brought up a foot. She slammed her toe onto the wood, gaining as much grip as possible. Ice exploded under it. Eira shifted her weight, quickly doing the same with her other foot. Repeating the process from the first obstacle, she tipped over the third and rolled down the other side of the triangle ramp.

An arrow whizzed past her face.

Eira jumped back on instinct. The arrow bounced harmlessly off one of the rocks between the rows of obstacles. It had a blunted tip, coated in a harmless, tacky substance.

The illusion of danger, that's all it is, she reminded herself. This was the one obstacle that Ferro had warned her of specifically last night. Beams alternated on the path ahead with low walls. She would have to vault over the walls and duck under the beams. All the while, archers would pelt her with arrows, trying to knock her off course, or strike off her pin. And she knew they had the best marksmen in Solaris hiding up in the roosts.

Eira had scoured the journals in the hidden room for something that could help her get past this obstacle. She'd encountered a way to cover her body in ice—a skin-like armor. But she couldn't perfect it enough in one night to move nimbly. One wrong step or tumble and she'd be over the sides and out of bounds.

Covering the pin on her chest with a hand, Eira coated it in a layer of ice. She felt her magic seeping through the fabric and into her skin. She imagined its roots wrapping around her heart. She couldn't cover her whole body, but she could do that much.

"Should have done that from the start," Eira muttered, shifting her weight on the incline. As soon as she began running they would shoot. At least this way, they wouldn't be able to knock off her pin.

Blunted arrows would still hurt. They may just be the illusion of danger but—*wait, an illusion.* They couldn't hit her if they couldn't see her.

Eira held out one palm parallel with the ground, pushed the other flat against it, and slid her hands apart slowly. A fine mist spread out from her feet as her fingertips parted. The water vapor in the air condensed to her will, the light shifting in it to create whatever illusion she wanted. Her ice evaporating earlier gave her a lot of moisture to work with.

Raising her hands, Eira pushed up the moisture, watching the sunlight shift within it. As she held out her palms like an offering, a map unfurled over the entire arena. Eira's brow furrowed with focus as she made sure every nook and cranny of Solaris and Meru was detailed on it. The map condensed, leaving her in a twilight haze underneath.

Judging from the shouts and cries of the crowd, her plan worked: no one could see her. An arrow whizzed harmlessly through her illusion. The mist curled around it, creating a momentary shaft of sunlight.

Eira pushed forward. More arrows punctured her veil as she leapt and ducked. One lucky shot found its mark on her thigh and a cry of pain escaped her. Her leg stung, pain searing all the way up her spine and reminding her that her teeth still ached and her hands were bloody from the leap of faith.

Over and under. Over and under. She wasn't going to let pain stop her. She was more than halfway through.

Emerging up onto the second switchback, Eira released the illusion with a wave. The crowd cheered as they saw her on the other side. Arrows whizzed harmlessly.

"Eira," Fritz boomed over the noise, "with our view obstructed it is impossible to know if you stepped out of bounds." He was trying to get her disqualified.

"You have my word, I didn't!" she shouted back.

The crowd began to jeer and chant for her to continue.

The empress stepped forward with an approving smile. A smile Eira wished she could've seen in her own mother. "Given the nature of that obstacle, we'll assume you didn't step out of bounds. Continue, Eira, but don't use an illusion like that again."

Fritz stayed at the edge of the balcony, watching her with wary eyes. Eira tore her attention from him. Whatever he thought of her attempt, let him think it. No matter what happened, they'd never think she was helpless and desperate for her brother's protection after today.

The next two obstacles were tied together by water. The sixth obstacle was a moat cradled at the top of a miniature mountain. To get to it, she had to climb up the fifth obstacle—a waterfall—using only the marked handholds.

Really, number five was a break.

Her muscles were exhausted and reminded her of the fact with her every push and pull upward. But the water curved around her hands. It washed over her and Eira relished in its force. She turned her face to the sky and imagined the roaring currents peeling away her skin to reveal something harder, stronger. To reveal someone she'd never been given the opportunity to discover before now.

When Eira cleared the top of the waterfall, she was breathless. But she felt the best she had since starting the trial. She nearly felt reborn, emerging soaked and panting.

White ropes were suspended over the moat. It was clear that they intended her to grasp the first and then swing across. But her arms were too tired. The chances she'd slip off and fall into the water were too great.

Eira took the first rope in her left hand and backed up so it became taut. The crowd cheered her on, expecting her to run and swing to the next. Instead, with a flash of magic, Eira summoned a wicked sharp dagger in her right palm and she pushed it through the rope with one motion, severing a piece.

The crowd hushed.

"Eira, if you wish to forfeit, you must remove your pin," her uncle was too eager to say.

She ignored him, stepping to the edge of the water. Ice spread out from her feet, forming a bridge as Eira walked. The crowd exploded with chaos.

"Can she do that?"

"Is that allowed?"

"But the rules…"

They volleyed questions to the balcony of royals that Eira was approaching once more as she neared the third and final switchback. Eira stepped back onto the white mark of the platform and released the rope. She looked up to the balcony, waiting.

The emperor and empress watched her, both now wearing

the hint of a smile that Eira would dare risk saying looked... delighted? Romulin looked as though he was holding in laughter. Fritz gave her a smoldering glare that would've been more befitting of a Firebearer.

Ferro grinned openly. The roguish quirk of his mouth had her heart racing once more. It would give her the strength to continue. He was in her corner, even if no one else was.

None of them said anything, and Eira took their silence to mean permission. She'd followed their rules. They'd intended her to grip the white ropes to get across. They'd never specified the ropes couldn't be cut. And she'd had a handhold on the white markings the entire time.

Eira faced down the final obstacle—several slacklines suspended across another void. They crossed over and under each other, making no one clear path available. She paced back and forth at the edge, carefully selecting her route. Before setting out, Eira crouched down, unlacing her boots.

"What's she doing now?" someone above her asked.

Eira couldn't hear the answer. She wondered if someone responded with, *getting better balance.* She wanted full movement of her feet on the lines.

One foot after the next, Eira shuffled along the thin line she'd selected, keeping it in the arches of her feet. She carefully placed her foot and then shifted her weight. Her progress was agonizingly slow. But she could use two other lines for balance until about halfway.

A gust of wind burst out of nowhere and Eira let out a startled cry as she doubled over the line she'd been using for support. Her balance tipped and she spun.

The crowd cheered as another gust of wind tried to rip her from the lines. Of course it wasn't going to be as easy as walking across some rope. The Windwalkers loved playing on their slacklines. This was their doing.

No, this was one man's doing. She'd bet anything Cullen was behind this. Somehow, his magic buffeting against her felt familiar already. She'd only been forced to watch her brother admire him for years. It made sense she could pick him out of a crowd. Moreover, the empress certainly wasn't behind this magic and no other Windwalker was strong enough to make these gusts. No one else would toy with her like this.

Eira cursed Cullen under her breath as she struggled to find her grip. She swung like a tunic on the drying line. Pumping her feet, Eira struggled to get them back on the first line. No matter how hard she strained, she couldn't find any stability.

Her arms were going to give out soon. Sweat dripped off her face. The white lines were stained red from her bloodied hands.

He was going to blast her again. Eira made herself look as vulnerable as possible—she had one last, crazy attempt. The moment he acted, she used Cullen's winds against him. Expending a monumental amount of her nearly depleted energy, Eira used the wind to help her hoist her feet up. She locked her heels over the line, hanging upside-down.

Hand over hand, she dragged herself along the line. Blood rushed to her head, roaring in her ears as loudly as the wind. But Eira just focused on the platform that grew closer and closer.

She was almost there. One more—

A burst of wind, stronger than all the others, tore her hand from the line. It was as though he'd targeted just her grip. Eira let out a cry. Her legs weren't strong enough. She was going to fall.

Pressing her feet against each other, line between them, Eira made a clumsy lunge for the platform. A gust pushed her sideways. Her shoulder smacked the wood. Eira grabbed for something—anything. But there was nothing.

With a cry of determination, she raised her fist in the air, as if cursing every last person who had ever told her no, who had ever dared to hold her back, and slammed it toward the platform. Ice spread up from her hand and down in a three-pointed spear. It sank into the wood with a satisfying thud. Grabbing the spear—no, it was a *trident*—with both hands, Eira pulled herself onto the final platform.

She rolled onto her back with a groan that was drowned out by the jubilant cries of the crowd.

TWO HANDS HOISTED her up. Eira blinked, the shadowed face cut against the sunlight coming into focus.

"Auntie?" Eira croaked. Why was her voice so tired? Had she been screaming more than she thought? The sudden image of herself shouting and screaming through the course mortified her.

"You were *astounding*!" Gwen praised as she slipped Eira's arm over her shoulders. If her aunt had been a sorcerer, Eira had always envisioned she would be a Groundbreaker. She was sturdy, stubborn, and secure. Everything Eira needed right now. "Come on, let's get you to the recovery room."

"I want nothing more," Eira mumbled, shuffling off the platform and back into the palace. It wasn't until the sunlight left her shoulders that she tried to look back and see what expression Ferro wore. But by then, it was too late. All Eira could catch a glimpse of was her name on the board—she'd passed.

Gwen helped her along the short walk to a stately office that had been repurposed for clerics tending to candidates. A sheet was laid out on a leather sofa where Eira was placed. A kind and sage-looking old man inspected her injuries, expressing relief that they weren't too severe. He tried to make small talk about how he'd seen her working in the West Clinic and was impressed that she was such a fierce candidate while he mixed her a potion and spread salve over her hands, but Eira wasn't up for talking.

Her mind was reeling. She'd done it. It had taken every ounce of strength from a well she didn't even know she could tap into. And she'd been the very last name above the line. But her name was above the line; she'd made it through.

A muffled argument on the other side of the door brought Eira back to the present. She blinked, several times, the room coming back into focus. At some point the cleric must have stepped out. She thought she vaguely remembered him mumbling something about drinking her draught and then resting. A warm mug of fortifying broth was cradled in her hands and Eira took a long sip, leeching the strength from it.

"...no circumstances can she know." *That's Father,* Eira realized.

"You are being ridiculous." Gwen's whisper was, as usual, not very quiet. Eira could hear every word through the door. But her father's soft reply had Eira standing and padding softly over to the room's entrance, pressing her ear against the wood to hear better.

"This is not your decision," her mother said.

"Leave it be, Gwen." Fritz was there, too.

"You're being stupid." Gwen grumbled something nasty sounding. "You have a big head for such a snail-sized brain."

Her mother sighed. "I see you never outgrew your childish taunts."

"Stop fighting, you two," Fritz scolded, reverting to the big brother. "No matter what you think of Reona's decision, it's hers to make."

"She's going to find out," Gwen insisted.

Find out what? Eira wondered and pressed even closer to the door.

"She will not," her father said sternly. "Especially once we put all this to an end. You saw her today."

"You three can't be serious." Eira heard stomping she presumed to be Gwen. "You're going to try and disqualify her after the fact? You're going to punish her because of something she has no control over?"

"You saw what happened!" Her mother's voice cracked with sudden volume. Eira jumped. Her heart was beating harder than it ever had in the trial. But she couldn't step away.

A terrible curiosity was holding her to the door. When her mother spoke again, her voice wavered. "Her…her magic. She made the trident."

"Fritz filled in the gaps between the prongs with ice before anyone could notice," Gwen countered.

"*We think no one noticed*," her father hissed.

"And I won't always be there." Fritz sighed.

"What will happen if someone saw?" her mother whispered.

"It isn't a crime for a Waterrunner to make a trident," Gwen said.

"You and I both know the implications run deeper than that. Where she comes from…there's her hair and eyes, too. Her power. You saw it today. People will be watching her, and if she continues on this path someone will discover the truth." What was her mother talking about? The way she spoke made Eira sound like some stranger.

"Which is why you should tell her so she'll be ready," Gwen insisted again.

Eira couldn't bear listening in any longer. She yanked open the door. "Tell me what?"

Her family stood in the hall, looking like small children caught filching warm cookies from the cooling rack. Fritz took a step back. Gwen folded her arms over her chest and glared at her siblings. Her parents exchanged a glance.

"Well?" Gwen motioned between her parents and Eira.

"Whatever it is, I want to know." Eira took another sip from her mug, hoping the broth would give her strength and courage in equal measure. Unfortunately, there was no courage potion. All she had was slightly chicken-flavored hot water that smoothed over the aches in her muscles.

"We were debating who would tell you to drop out of the competition." Her father's words were a glancing blow. Why would he lie to her?

"That wasn't what you were discussing, and I know it." Eira's nails dug lightly into her mug. "I know it wasn't because you've all had no problem telling me to drop out already. Save for Gwen." Her aunt gave her a weak smile. "Now, what were you talking about?"

"It's not something you need to worry about," her father said.

"Tell me!"

"If none of you will do it then I will." Gwen turned to face her. She opened her mouth and took a breath.

"Stop, Gwen," her mother snapped with a voice usually reserved for when Eira broke something. "You and Fritz leave. We'll handle it from here."

"But—"

"This is our family's business." Her mother cut Gwen's protest with a glare.

Gwen just rolled her eyes and crossed over to Eira, wrapped her arms around her shoulders, and gripped her tightly. "Eira, we love you very much."

"And we always will." Fritz's expression crumpled.

"I...I never questioned that." Eira stared down at her mug as her aunt released her.

"Good." Gwen and Fritz started down the hall, Gwen hesitating as she stood by Reona. "Tell her. She deserves to know. Don't back away from the truth."

Her mother just sighed as they retreated into the recovery room, the door closing them off from the world. Her parents exchanged a look before their attention ended up back on Eira. There was a strange and inexplicable sorrow filling them.

"Just, tell me," Eira demanded again, softer this time. "Whatever it is, I can take it."

"You don't know what you're asking," her mother said, eyes shining.

"Stop treating me like I'm fragile! If I say I can do something then it means I can." If the trial today didn't prove that, Eira didn't know what would.

"Very well," her father said. She could tell she'd worked his last nerve. But Eira didn't feel remorseful. Whatever this secret was, it was clearly long overdue to be told. "If you think you're mature enough to handle the truth, we'll give it to you."

"Herron—"

"No, Reona, she clearly thinks she's ready." Agitation dripped from her father's words.

"Eira, we love you very much." Her mother lightly took the mug from Eira's grip. Eira didn't fight as she placed it on the nearby desk. "We always will; all we've ever wanted is the very best for you."

"I know," Eira said, weaker. The first ugly blossoms of regret were poking their heads up from the bed she'd made by pursuing this question. "I don't like some of the things you've asked of me. I don't like being coddled by you both and Marcus...and the rest of the family. I don't like secrets. But none of it ever made me doubt you loved me."

Her father stepped forward, arms folded. He was the imposing mountain Eira remembered from growing up. Someone that only Marcus ever had a chance of measuring up to.

"We are not your birth parents."

She blinked, and blinked again, as if the sudden problem with her ears could be fixed by bringing the world into better focus. "I...what?" Her voice was distant, detached, and did not sound like her own. "I don't think I..."

"Eira, listen." Her mother stroked her hair thoughtfully. "We have always seen ourselves as your parents—your *real* parents. We are your family. We love you."

Eira turned her head to stare up at the woman touching her. Her mother's—*Reona's* eyes were filled with a distant pain that threatened to spill over. Eira blinked several times, trying to see her mother as she once had. But the face at her side was suddenly strange.

She turned back to her father—to Herron. "You're lying."

"Eira—" Reona began to say.

"You're lying!" Eira pushed the woman away. She staggered backward, her body aching with every step. But this wasn't from the trial. It was from a wound that had been there her whole life and she'd never known.

"This isn't easy for us to tell you. Eira, please—" Reona began to attempt to soothe.

"You said you were ready, act like it," Herron snapped. He was always brisk when he was in pain. This was like the time they were at the beach and she'd been caught in the tide. They'd thought she'd drowned. Her father had yelled at her through his worried tears. Eira stared up at his eyes, searching for warmth and finding none. She wanted to scream at him to show some kind of feeling as she cracked and shattered before them both.

"How... If you're not... Who is?" she managed to say.

"You were left on our doorstep one winter's night," Herron answered. His matter-of-fact tone was grating her ears already. "We didn't find you until morning. You were so still we thought you had frozen to death. But your mother insisted we take you inside anyway. You warmed up and began to cry."

"I might not have given birth to you," Reona said gently. "But you are every measure my daughter as Marcus is my son."

As she listened, Eira pillaged her deepest and earliest memories for some recollection of what her parents were saying—for some proof this portrait of her beginnings was true. But she could find nothing. Her earliest memories were of playing with Marcus in winter.

Her brother.

Not my brother?

Eira gripped her head with both hands. She shook it back and forth as if she could scatter this truth like snow from her shoulders. And it *was* true. She knew it was. Some part of her must have always known, because it seemed so horribly obvious now.

Her mother had the same deep golden hair as Fritz, as Marcus, and the rest of the Charem family. Her father had a darker, ashen blond. Not platinum like Eira's was. Her mother had a dusting of freckles across her nose and cheeks, which

Marcus had also inherited faint speckles of. Eira's complexion was void of any such marks.

Stop calling them Mother and Father, a voice raked against the back of her mind. *They're not.*

But they are, her heart replied.

An argument began that would split her in two.

"Eira." Two hands landed on her shoulders. She looked up to meet Reona's eyes. "I know this is hard for you."

"Hard?" She was the punch line of a horrible joke. That was why she couldn't breathe now. Someone had hit her square in the gut. Eira wheezed hollow laughter out of trembling lips. Everyone had known. Everyone had seen it but her. The whole universe was laughing at her. They'd always been anyway, she'd just never realized the true reason why. *Not even your mother could love you*, that's what Noelle had said three years ago on the night of the incident. Even Noelle somehow knew the truth. That was why it'd hurt so much. Eira had been the oblivious one. "You have no idea what this feels like."

"We don't, but we're here to help you. We love you," she soothed.

"You don't love me!" Eira stepped away. The tides roared in her. Ice crackled cold under her numb fingertips. She would keep them from touching her again by force if she had to. She could hardly think with them looking at her. "If you—if you loved me, you would've told me. *Someone* would've told me. Why did no one tell me?"

Eira's back hit the far wall. She hadn't even realized she'd been moving. A wide gap was between her and her parents. Snow fell between them magically, creating an icy line.

"We wanted to," Reona said, pleading. Tears streamed down her cheeks. "As you grew, it became harder and harder. We—"

"Hard for you?" Eira was almost shouting. "What about for me? Did you ever think of *me*?"

"Of course we did." Herron stepped forward but didn't cross her magic line. "That was all we thought about and why we were waiting."

"Waiting for what?" What could've possibly had them keeping this secret from her?

"For you to be old enough to handle the truth and understand its importance." Herron locked eyes with her. "There's one more detail about that night you were found. You had a note tucked in your blankets. But there wasn't writing on it, just the symbol of a trident."

"What does it mean?" Eira whispered.

"You know what it means," Herron said. He had grown up in Oparium. He had been the one to tell her the old sailors' stories and make Eira swear she'd never repeat the name of the pirate queen. Her promises suddenly took on new meaning.

"No, no, that's impossible. She's a myth." Eira shook her head frantically. *No more*, she wanted to beg. She couldn't handle any more revelations.

"Adela was reported to have been seen thirty years ago in Oparium," Herron said. Just the mention of Adela's name made Eira cringe. That name alone was bad luck. She'd always hated it, but maybe was now uncovering the reason why.

"My sister, Gwen, found record of the incident at the summer palace in the guard's logs, written by Prince Baldair," Reona said sadly.

"Thirty years ago? I'm only eighteen."

"Perhaps she came back. We had to keep you secret and safe."

"Adela would've been ancient by then!" Eira shook her head. "There's no way."

"Perhaps another pirate has taken her name and continues terrorizing the seas. Perhaps she's been made immortal by hate. Or perhaps you're right," Herron admitted. "Perhaps the trident was some desperate mother's way of ensuring you would be taken in by offering a threat."

"I could've been left out in the cold just as easily," Eira realized. "Adela is bad luck... You... You both had no reason to take me in."

"But we did," Herron said firmly, wrapping an arm around his wife's shoulders.

He was right. They did. And what good had she been as a daughter? She'd created a lifetime of her parents looking over their shoulders, afraid that just maybe she was the offspring of the fabled pirate queen. A lifetime of them trying to hide her and keep her secret and safe. A lifetime of worry.

"And we love you." Reona wiped her cheeks.

"I've been nothing but a burden to you." Eira looked down at her hands. Frost coated them, snow dripping down to the floor like the icy tears that streamed down her face. She'd said she could handle this truth, but she was proving by the second she couldn't. "I have caused you worry and pain. I've held your real child back."

"Do not say that again," Herron boomed.

"You *are* our 'real child,'" Reona snapped in a no-nonsense tone. "Just as much as Marcus is."

But she wasn't. That feeling of always being in her brother's shadow. The innate urge to compete, as if to prove herself worthy of love—of a moment in the sun—like there wasn't enough affection to go around, suddenly had an explanation.

Eira continued staring at her hands. The frost now covered her arms. It was as though her magic was trying to cocoon her, numb her, protect her from this horrible truth.

"Now listen to me," Herron demanded. Eira couldn't bear to bring her eyes to his. "If there is suspicion that you are somehow related to Adela then, at best, you will be ostracized."

"I already am ostracized," Eira murmured. Another explanation for everything she'd endured. Bad luck and hate was in her blood. They didn't seem to hear.

He continued, "At worst, you will be hunted. I taught you from a young age—hatred for Adela is as deeply rooted as hatred for sorcerers that still clings to the corners of Solaris. You have to keep this secret for your own sake now. And that may mean clamping down on your magic even more so there aren't any reasons for people to grow suspicious. No more incidents like the trident today. Anything that can connect you to Adela is a liability."

Eira drew up her eyes to him. "That's why Fritz always gave Marcus more tasks in the clinics. That's why I was never selected for any special training or projects. You two told Uncle to never let me be eligible. You didn't want to risk my magic taking shape. You didn't want me to have too much power."

"I know this is hard, but think rationally," Reona pleaded with her.

Eira was beyond being rational. "That's why Marcus has been...saddled with me, managing me, like he's my keeper. And that was why you didn't want to let me compete in the trials."

"Only because we love you." Reona had the decency to at least pretend to be pained. Eira honestly didn't know what was sincere anymore. "We all do and want what's best for you."

"What's best for me is a moment alone." Her voice was steel.

"And now that you know, you must realize that the best thing for you to do is drop out of the competition, immediately," Herron said.

"Get out," Eira seethed.

"Eira—"

"Get out!" Her voice rose and her magic rushed to meet it. Wickedly sharp points of ice sprouted from her line of snow, stopping just before they punctured her parents' clothes. Eira panted.

"Let's give her some space," Reona said sadly.

"Now that you know the truth, you know what you must do." Herron looked down at her one last time before allowing his wife to lead him away. "And we expect an apology from you before we leave."

Eira didn't know if she could ever bear speaking to them again.

She wanted the echo of the door closing behind them to be the last word on the whole horrible affair. She wanted to never have to think about what they told her again. She wanted it to be a lie.

She wanted so much it ached. So much that everything in the world wouldn't be enough to fill this gaping hole of want.

Eira slid down the wall, curling into a ball. She didn't want to think about it. *Numb. Cold. Pack the ice tall and tight—so thick that you can't feel anything. If you are the daughter of the pirate queen then so be it. Be as heartless as she is.*

The tears froze on her cheeks as the permafrost that covered her arms crept up her neck. Eira clutched her knees and buried her face in her forearms. Maybe this was what she felt like the night she was abandoned—cold and empty.

A voice echoed to her from a distance. It thudded dully against her mental and physical walls. There was movement as well. Something ruffled her hair. Eira was surprised to realize that hair was still exposed. Every other part of her was coated in ice.

"…get…" the voice said faintly, "…what's…okay…"

There was a howling in her ears. Eira slowly raised her face to see a whirlwind surrounding her. It ripped curtains off their rungs and peeled off chunks of ice from her body, scattering them like snow around the room.

At the center of the storm was Cullen. He pulled at the ice coating her with red fingers. Her frigid magic nipped at his skin and he cursed under his breath every time one chunk of frost that he peeled off was replaced by another that grew.

"What're you doing?" Eira murmured.

"You're not going to be able to breathe if you keep coating yourself in ice." His hands were on her cheeks, scraping away frost until his cold-blistered fingers met skin. "You mad woman, are you trying to kill yourself?" he shouted in her face over the howling wind that battered her.

"No…the cold won't kill me." It hadn't claimed her when she was a baby, it wouldn't now. It had been a part of her for her whole life. It was the only thing she knew she could trust to be real.

"Well, stop acting like you're trying to test that theory!"

Eira sighed softly and worked to get her magic under control. The ice slowly vanished into steam. Cullen's hands fell from her face. The radius around them was a wet mess from frost and wind.

"Mother above, you really are a handful," he muttered.

"I know," she whispered.

"It's no wonder Marcus is always worrying about you."

She winced. "I know."

"You're too powerful for your own good."

"I know."

Cullen's hands returned to her face. He grabbed both of her cheeks and brought her face toward his with force.

"*What?*" Eira snapped.

"Just making sure it really is you. Because, more than any of those things, the Eira I've known is stubborn, determined, and not afraid to talk back or put someone in their place. You're little more than a wet rag right now."

"Leave me be." She glanced aside. His breath was too warm on her cheeks. He was running the risk of making her feel again. And if she could feel, the tears would start once more. The whole cycle would rack her body anew.

"No. Marcus told me to check on you so I am. You took the run hard and he's worried. I'm not going back empty-handed."

"Where is he?" Eira dared to ask.

"With Fritz, I presume. He was coming to see you himself, but the minister intercepted us on our way."

Eira laughed softly. If he was with Fritz, then Reona and Herron would soon follow. Marcus would find out the truth of their relationship, no doubt much to his relief. Her mission to make sure he felt like he never had to take care of her again because of her performance in the trials had succeeded spectacularly. Just not in the way she expected.

All because of a stupid trident she hadn't even intended to make. It was those journals' fault. A shudder ripped through her.

Who wrote those journals?

"You can go. He won't care soon," Eira murmured.

"What?"

"Marcus won't care what happens to me soon."

"Stop," Cullen said firmly, bringing her attention back to him with a gentle tug of his hands. They were still on her face. Why was he still holding onto her? Didn't he realize he was holding bad luck incarnate? "I'm not letting you speak ill of yourself or Marcus. He loves you more than anything. And you, you're…" Cullen trailed off, his loss for words more telling than anything that might have followed.

"You're jealous," she whispered. Cullen's eyes widened. "Do you love my brother?"

"No," he snarled. "I'm jealous that you two have each other. That you have family who look out for one another rather than just seeing the branches of the family tree as potential kindling for the fires of ambition." He released her in disgust and stood.

"They don't really love me," she whispered when his back was to her. Cullen spun, but Eira spoke before she could. "My family is a lie. They can't really love me because I'm not one of them; I've never been." Eira shook her head slowly, the tears falling in earnest. "My parents…they're not the same as Marcus's parents. They've never been. And they kept it from me."

"What are you saying?" he whispered.

"I was abandoned. Left to die. And Marcus's parents took me in because they were afraid of who my mother might be." Eira buried her face in her hands and curled into a ball once more.

But before the ice could consume her, Cullen's arms were around her, and suddenly her frozen world was filled with his agonizing warmth.

"I—"

"*Shh,*" he whispered in her ear. Cullen pressed her face into his shoulder, as if shielding her from everything that might seek to harm her. "Just cry."

"But—"

"Stop. Let it out."

That was all the permission she needed. Eira pressed her face into his shoulder and sobbed. Cullen's velvet-covered muscle muffled her cries. When she tried to pull away, he yanked her close once more, and the crying continued.

Eira had never shed so many tears in her life. It was as though she was trying to drown the world in her agony. She didn't even know a person could cry so much. Perhaps it was just her magic manifesting her pain in a new way. If it couldn't be ice, then it would be a never-ending river of tears.

After what could've been minutes or hours, Eira straightened. This time, Cullen didn't pull her back. Somehow, he'd sensed she'd reached her limit.

Eira rubbed her face, sniffling. Cullen stood and crossed the room silently. He was no doubt ashamed for comforting someone like her. He was putting as much distance between her and him as possible. He would leave.

She concocted a number of terrible, self-deprecating fantasies as Cullen rummaged through the desk, not caring for whose it may be. He returned with a small kerchief and knelt once more before her, presenting his humble offering.

"Thank you," Eira murmured, blowing her nose.

"Of course." The way he said those words, he seemed to know she meant more than just the kerchief. "I'm…sorry." Eira let out a bitter laugh. A noise that elicited a look of confusion from him.

"The Prince of the Tower, always so self-assured. I've never seen you look so…"

"Hopeless?" He ran a hand through his hair. "If you ever got to know me, you'd find out I can be incredibly hopeless." Cullen sat and pulled his own knees to his chest, loosely situating them in his elbows. When he spoke, he didn't look at her. "And that nickname, can you not call me that?"

"Prince of the Tower?"

"Yes. I hate it."

"Why?"

Cullen turned to her with weary eyes. It was as though she was finally seeing through that perfect image he always exuded to something *real*. There was raw hurt and fierce determination smoldering within him. His clothing was disheveled. He was finally imperfect, messy, and everything that Eira knew her peers in the Tower would find unbecoming because they ruined the illusion of their perfect lord that had been lifted from the squalor they all lived in.

Yet, it was the first time she'd felt anything genuine toward him. In his world-weariness, he'd never looked more tragically beautiful.

"I honestly have no interest in being a prince, or a lord, or any other titles that came with my powers awakening and my father's ambition." This was the same Cullen Eira had heard the echo of in the Windwalkers' study. "You're not the only one with a messed-up family that has secrets stacked up to your hip, Eira. But at least yours loves you."

"I'm sure yours—"

"Don't presume anything about my family." He stopped her on the spot. "You have no idea what happens behind closed doors."

"I guess I don't." Eira had learned well today that it was impossible to really have a clear picture of a family, even your own.

Cullen patted her knee with a heavy hand. "You're allowed to feel all this. Don't try not to. Clearly that wasn't working out well." He motioned around at the disheveled room. "But don't let those feelings shake the fact that they love you. It may be hard to believe now, but their love for you hasn't changed."

"I...I'll try." She didn't want to argue. She was far too tired to try. He was right, nothing had changed, not really. And, yet, everything felt irrevocably different. She needed to find a way to apologize to her parents, but she couldn't bear even the thought of looking them in the eyes.

"Good." Cullen stood.

"Where are you going?"

"I, unfortunately, have dinner with the empress to discuss the next trial."

She laughed softly. "Cullen, you're the only man alive who would make dinner with the empress sound like a chore." That earned her a small smirk and a playful glint in his eyes as they darted toward her.

"It's certainly not a chore. But, sometimes, there are other things I'd rather do that my current position doesn't allow... In any case, I'll find Alyss and send her." Cullen ran a hand down his shirt, smoothing out the wrinkles that her body had left when he'd held her.

"Cullen—" She stopped him when he was at the door.

"Yes?" He turned in a way that almost made it look like he was...eager?

"I... Thank you for staying with me. For earlier."

His face softened and the sad eyes returned. "You're welcome. Oh, and don't worry about the room. I'll put in a word with Her Majesty and smooth it all over."

Cullen left. Eira bit her lip. *Thanks* wasn't entirely what she'd wanted to say... What she'd really wanted was to ask him to stay. Because, for a moment, in his arms, there had been something stable in her world again. He'd felt warm, and safe, and everything she suddenly found herself desperate for.

When Alyss arrived, all the ice that had covered Eira and

the floor around her had completely vanished. She didn't know where she found the strength to dismiss it. But at some point she must've, because water didn't usually evaporate that quickly in the cool halls of the palace.

"Eira?" Alyss said softly, poking her nose into the room. "Are you here?"

"Over here."

"Are you all right?" Alyss stepped in. That was when Eira noticed her arm was in a sling.

"I should be asking you that." Eira pushed herself to her feet. It was easier to move when she was focusing on someone else. "What happened?"

"Oh, this?" Alyss motioned to her injury. "I fell in the trial and cracked a few things. They gave me a bone regrowth potion—honestly the potion hurt worse than anything in the trial—and they don't want me to move it for an hour or two so everything sets up right. I'm sorry I didn't see your run though."

Eira shook her head. "Don't apologize. You didn't miss anything special."

"Not true, from what I hear. Everyone is talking about how impressed they are."

"You're lying."

"Well…no… I mean, they're saying they're impressed either by the fact that you could actually hoist yourself over a wall, or how hard you fell, or—oh, this is a good one—the creative ways you used your magic!"

"I get it." Eira held up a hand. Comparative to all the other emotional revelations, people making sarcastic comments about her physical ineptitudes was fairly benign. But she didn't particularly enjoy it, either.

"They're still impressed with you though." Alyss came over and wrapped her good arm around Eira's shoulders. "Fritz also announced another special dinner tonight for the competitors. So let's get back to the Tower and get cleaned up."

"I doubt I'll go," Eira murmured, shuffling forward at Alyss's tugging.

"Why not? I can't wait to see Noelle's expressions over dinner. I bet she's sour you're still in the running. I hear Adam didn't make it."

"He didn't?" Eira gaped. She should have noticed that it was *his* name beneath the line as the sole person she was competing against, but there were a dozen other things she'd been focusing on at the start of the trial.

"I thought that would cheer you up." Alyss laughed as they emerged into the halls.

Eira gave a wary glance around her for any of her family. Just the thought of them put a rock in her stomach now. Her brain couldn't even seem to conjure the image of their faces. They had completely shifted in her mind into something she no longer recognized. Did she know them at all anymore?

Of course you do, they're still your family, part of her wanted to say. The other part of her just felt empty.

"Why the long face, anyway? Cullen, of all people, seemed worried about you. Now I can see why; you don't look like a woman who just progressed to the next trial."

"I…" As Eira stared ahead, the halls before her seemed to elongate into infinity. They were never ending—a maze she would be trapped in forever. She had to get out. She couldn't go back to the Tower. Not yet. "Can we go to Margery's?"

"The bakery?"

"Do we know of any other Margery?"

"Fair. Sure, I can go."

"Good. I have a dire need of a sweet bun."

Alyss turned them in an about-face. With every step Eira took away from the Tower she felt lighter. When they emerged into the city streets, she inhaled as deeply as possible, trying to exhale every last bit of torturous air that was trapped in her. The palace was toxic now. Every moment within would be poison.

Margery's Bakery was between the Tower entrance and

the western clinic, if one took the long way. It was a quaint shop that was only large enough for three stools inside at the countertop. Outside, the patron, Margery, set up two wooden folding tables to accommodate the occasional rush. Today, it was blessedly empty.

They made small talk with Margery while they ordered. The rosy-cheeked owner was pleasantly surprised to see candidate pins on both of their breasts. So much so that their sweet buns were on the house. The exchange made Eira realize that she hadn't been out in the month since the trials began. It also made her realize that the last time she'd even thought about the bakery was when she'd made Marcus promise her two sweet buns before the trials were even a notion.

The memory filled her with an indescribable sorrow.

"Is something wrong with it?" Alyss asked from the other side of the table. The street was quiet, and the only other noise was the faint strumming of a lute lofting out of one of the high windows of a nearby home.

"No, nothing," Eira murmured, tearing a piece of the pillowy, glazed roll and popping it in her mouth. The creamy, sweet cheese center melted on her tongue. But Eira seemed to have lost all sense of taste.

"Are you going to tell me what's up now? Because something obviously is and please don't insult me by denying it."

Eira shook her head. "Yes. Sorry. I couldn't tell you in the palace. I had to get out of there."

"I could tell."

"You know me too well." Eira gave Alyss a weak smile.

"I'm your best friend, it's my job to know you well."

"I...I found out something after the trial..." Eira proceeded to recount everything that had transpired with her parents. Herron had asked her not to tell another soul and Eira had promptly told two people. Then again, if her family really knew anything about her, they wouldn't count Alyss anyway, since it should be obvious Eira would share her deepest secrets with her best friend.

When Eira was finished, Alyss leaned back in her chair, expression blank. She proceeded to poke at her own sweet bun for several moments as she mulled it all over. Eira gave her friend space and took her own. They both finished their rolls at the same time.

"I have thoughts," Alyss declared. "But first, all this necessitates the need for another sweet bun."

After the second round of buns were secured, Eira finally asked, "So, what're your thoughts?"

"That they made a terrible error in how they handled all of this. And when I say 'they' I mean everyone in your family who knew—your parents, Fritz, Gwen, Marcus if he knew. Did he know?"

Eira shook her head. "I don't think so."

"You need to talk to him after we finish here," Alyss decreed. "You need to first apologize to your parents and then find him."

Eira groaned and sank her face into her palms. "I can't."

"You can."

"I don't want to."

"You must."

Eira busied her mouth with a hunk of roll. Chewing slowly bought her a minute or two of time. "I don't know what I'll do if he knew…"

"Stewing over it isn't going to help." Alyss sighed. "And, if he didn't know, he's as blindsided as you. I'm not saying it's the *exact same* feeling of betrayal as you. But you two might be able to help each other through this."

"Marcus is likely still sour I didn't throw the trial today."

"Forget the trials! This is your family." Alyss said those words with such conviction that, for a fleeting moment, Eira almost completely believed them. This was the reason why Cullen had known to get Alyss, and why Eira had stolen away for a moment with her friend. Only Alyss could scatter the clouds in her world so well.

"All right." Eira swallowed the last of her sweet bun with force. Just like accepting her next plan of attack, it didn't go down easy. "You're right. I'll talk to them in a day or two."

"Tonight."

"Tomorrow."

"*Tonight*," Alyss insisted.

"Fine." Eira sighed and slumped in her chair.

"We're going to go back and get changed. You're going to find your parents and then go to the dinner with your head held high, like the future competitor in the Tournament of Five Kingdoms that you are. You're going to sit and savor good food we rarely get; I don't care how full those sweet buns made you—you're going to eat. Then you'll listen to the details of the next trial with the rest of us. And *then* you're going to pull Marcus aside."

"I don't have a choice in all this, do I?"

"Nope," Alyss said cheerfully. She was an adorable dictator.

"I'm in your hands," Eira said, resigned. She was tired, emotionally spent, and weary in body and soul. The last thing she wanted to do right now was *think*. So she'd forfeit independent thought and give in to Alyss's demands.

The rest of the afternoon progressed exactly as Alyss had decreed. Despite not feeling ready in the slightest, they returned to the Tower. The entire walk up to their rooms, Eira could feel phantom eyes on her. The magic whispers were louder and harder to control.

It felt like everyone and every*thing* knew her secret.

Alyss followed Eira to her room as they collected her things, and then Eira to Alyss's. The bone regrowth had finished mending Alyss's arm and she left the sling and bandages behind. After, they went to the Tower baths. Eira scrubbed herself within an inch of her life. She scrubbed until her skin was red and splotchy—until Alyss had to command her to stop.

When she emerged from the bath and stared at herself in the mirror, slowly combing her hair, she couldn't quite place the woman she saw. The same reflection that Eira had always known stared back at her. But it no longer felt like her.

Her face, her body, they'd been stolen from her. Taken by a truth she was quickly realizing she would've preferred to live in ignorance of forever. Whose eyes stared back at her? Whom did they belong to? Were they uniquely hers? Or did they belong to a birth mother who'd abandoned Eira in the night? Did they belong to the Pirate Queen Adela?

"Ready?" Alyss asked, breaking Eira from her trance.

Eira leaned away from the mirror. "Almost."

The sensation of no longer fitting into her own skin persisted as Eira dressed. Every stitch of fabric buttoned up as it should. But none of it felt right.

She looked like herself. She moved like herself. But the image of who she was had been smeared across the canvas of her mind. The colors were blurred and distorted. She'd give anything for a distraction from the unnerving sensation of feeling like she was a thief who'd stolen her flesh.

Eira stood in the Tower hall, staring up at her uncle's office.

"Good luck." Alyss gave her a squeeze. "I'll wait in your room for you and we can go to dinner together."

"Do I have to?" Eira murmured.

"Get it over with." Alyss gave her a light shove. "You'll feel better as soon as you do."

"I hate that you're always right," she muttered.

"It's my burden to bear." Alyss sauntered away, heading back for Eira's room.

Eira stewed in the silence until it became hot and intolerable. The ocean within her was boiling, getting ready to foam over. She had to keep her better sense about her. No matter what she felt, apologizing for how she had handled the news was the right course. That would at least smooth things over for a while so Eira could process everything—according to Alyss.

She gave a knock on her uncle's office door.

"Enter."

Eira stepped inside, watching her uncle's expression become pinched and tense at the mere sight of her. Eira shut the door behind her and stared at her feet. She'd mentally practiced everything she'd wanted to say, but she couldn't find the words now.

"Well?" Fritz folded his hands on his desk and sighed. His face was pinched—because of her, likely. "What is it?"

"I…" She met his cold and closed stare. "Do you know where my parents are?"

He gazed out the window, as if unable to look her in the eye. "They left."

All the waters within her stilled and Eira felt herself slipping beneath the surface into the bitter cold depths. "What?" she breathed.

"I'm sorry, Eira." Did he sound sorry? She couldn't tell. "Your father had some work to do tomorrow so they had to make haste back to Oparium."

"I thought they'd stay for at least a little…"

"Eira…" Fritz shook his head, burying his face in his hands for a moment. The disappointment that radiated off of him was like daggers. "The way they saw it…you attacked them with your magic."

"I didn't. I mean, not really." Did they say she had? Was that how they'd seen her frozen line? She had made spears of ice that jutted toward them. Was that really an attack?

"I assumed that was the case, but they would not listen to me."

"*But*…" But. That's all she could muster. A weak protest. How hard had her uncle worked to stand up for her?

"The last time your emotions got the better of you, you killed someone. And that was over a boy." Every word hurt worse than the last. It was a parade of her failings. "From what they told me, you didn't make any improvements in managing your emotions and magic. I didn't have a leg to stand on."

"I didn't freeze anyone but myself." Her defense was weak and small. "I didn't hurt them."

"I'm sure you didn't mean to."

"I *didn't*." She insisted. Full stop.

"Don't you see? You have to begin thinking about how your actions follow you. I won't always be here to spell it out. Because of your history, no one knows if you're one second away from unleashing your magic on them!" Fritz snapped, as though he'd been holding back the words for a long time.

Eira's back hit the door. She wanted to run from this uncomfortable truth.

His face immediately softened with remorse. "Eira, I'm sorry. This has been a burden on all of us."

"A burden on all of *you*?" she whispered.

"You are not the only one dealing with this. Do you know how hard it has been to have you in my care? To know and not be able to tell you? I have loved you like my own but have had no say in any of this because I've been forced to respect your parents' wishes."

"I… I need to finish getting ready for dinner," Eira lied, and escaped before he could say anything else. She didn't want his half-hearted excuses.

Her parents had left without giving her the chance to say goodbye. Fritz clearly thought she was one breath away from killing anyone who had the misfortune of being close to her. How would Marcus react when she finally spoke to him?

She'd find out soon enough.

"How'd it go?" Alyss asked as she shoved the tiny wooden sculpture of a bear she'd been working on into her bag, brushing sawdust from her lap.

"Not well."

"Oh." Her friend's expression fell. "I'm sure—"

"I don't want to talk about it," Eira said firmly.

"Then we won't." One of the many reasons Eira loved Alyss so much. She always knew when to push, and when to back away. "Let's go and enjoy dinner and not think about it all for a little bit."

"All right." Eira doubted how much of a distraction dinner could be. But a scuffle just above the entrance to the mess hall proved to be an unexpected relief from her thoughts.

"Noelle, please." Adam chased after his Firebearer lover like a puppy with his tail between his legs. "Let me explain."

"No."

"But—" Adam grabbed her arm.

"I have no reason to allow you to explain!" Noelle swung her free hand and sent sparks crackling in the air just before Adam's face. He jumped back. "Stop following me."

Alyss and Eira stopped just up the hall from them, watching the situation unfold.

"Lovers' quarrel?" Alyss murmured to Eira.

"Looks like," she whispered back.

The two had yet to notice them. They were too enraged with each other to have noticed a giant, northern noru cat charging up the hall.

"You're being unreasonable," Adam growled.

"And you're being an ass." Noelle threw back her head and

laughed, a grating and terrible sound. "You had me fooled for the longest time. But I'm so done with you and your games. Now get away from me."

"You are *my* woman." Adam stepped forward and grabbed Noelle by the shoulders. It was in this movement that Eira noticed Adam's lack of candidate pin. Alyss had mentioned it, but seeing his chest void of metal brought about an ugly sense of satisfaction. Perhaps the feeling of triumph was what ultimately emboldened her.

Noelle leaned forward and sneered in his face, "I am not *yours* or anyone else's. Now let me go or I will burn your skin to the bone."

"You wouldn't hurt me."

"Try me."

"Noelle," Eira called. Both heads snapped up to her and Alyss. "Sorry to keep you waiting!"

"What in the Mother's name are you doing?" Alyss said out of the corner of her mouth.

Eira ignored her and bounded down to Noelle, shooting Adam a glare. "Let's go to dinner?"

"You... You were on your way to meet these *freaks*?" Adam balked.

"Yes, you brute. I'm finally realizing who the quality people are in the Tower." Noelle slapped his hands away and, thankfully, Adam's arms fell limply to his sides. "Now get away from me. I'm not going to be late to the candidates' dinner on your account." Noelle carefully tucked strands of her long, black hair back into the braids they'd fallen from. When she walked down the Tower hall, she seemed to half-stride, half-float like a royal would.

Adam shot Alyss and Eira glares as they passed, catching up with Noelle.

Noelle glanced over her shoulder, prompting Eira to do the same. Adam was nowhere to be seen. Her dark eyes met Eira's. "You didn't have to do that. I had everything under control."

"See, we shouldn't have helped. She clearly doesn't want

us," Alyss said snidely.

Eira ignored her friend. "You burn him and they would've taken your pin for it," she retorted. "So you're welcome."

Noelle snorted. "*Fine.* Thank you, I suppose."

"I take it the Tower's 'power couple' of Noelle and Adam is no more?" Alyss asked.

"What gave you your first hint?" Noelle muttered.

"Did you dump him because he didn't pass the trial?" Alyss didn't miss the chance to question Noelle. "Did he vow to pass it to prove his love to you or something? Then you couldn't handle the shame?"

Eira barely resisted stopping Alyss to tell her she read too many romance novels.

"What're you talking about?" Noelle rolled her eyes. She sighed, shoulders hunching slightly—a movement Noelle quickly corrected. "I suppose I might as well tell you. He's going to start rumors, no doubt, and I should be ahead of them. No, it had nothing to do with the trials and everything to do with the fact that he is an ass. I made excuses for it long enough, but I woke up to the fact when I found out he's been dallying with some stable girl."

"Yeah, I can believe that," Eira murmured. "I could've told you he was an ass."

Noelle stopped short and Eira did as well. They locked eyes. For a brief second, Eira braced herself to have Noelle defend Adam. As she said herself, she always had.

But Noelle surprised her when she said, "I know now. And I'm sorry for not seeing it earlier—when I should have…when seeing it would've put me in a position to stop him."

Eira pursed her lips slightly. The movement prompted Noelle to continue.

"What he did to you was exceptionally cruel, and I'm sorry." Deeming the matter finished, Noelle charged ahead.

Not even your mother could love you. Those were the words Noelle had said to her three years ago on that fateful night. Words that hurt more than ever. Eira clenched her fists, but kept her magic under control.

"What're you sorry for?" Eira called on an impulse.

Noelle halted and glanced behind her. Her eyes narrowed slightly. "For what he did."

"Don't apologize for him. If you're going to apologize, apologize for your hand in it."

Noelle stood a little straighter, determined to not back down. "I'm sorry for what I said to you that night. I helped organize the whole affair. I was just as cruel as he was. And I should have apologized much sooner than now."

Eira pursed her lips. She wanted to gloat, basking in this moment of bringing Noelle to task. She wanted to yell, saying that two words—*I'm sorry*—could never be enough. Instead of doing either of those things, she just sighed.

"Fine, I forgive you."

Noelle's eyes widened a fraction in shock. She gave a small nod, and quickly disappeared around the corner into the mess hall—as if she didn't want to risk Eira revoking the forgiveness. A part of Eira was admittedly tempted to.

"You...you *forgive her?*" Alyss gaped at Eira. "No way. I don't believe it. You're trying to trick her, right? Lull her into a false sense of security and then strike her down right before the next trial to throw off her attempt?"

Eira shook her head. "I always knew Adam was the real leader of that whole night and…" She let out a sigh that she felt like she'd been holding in for years. On that exhale, all the tension that knotted her neck and shoulders about Adam and his cruelty vanished. The words they said might linger, but Eira would do everything in her power not to willingly carry them a minute longer. "It doesn't matter anymore."

"How can it not matter? What he did was— What she said was—"

"Terrible, I know. I'm not saying I forgive *him*. But maybe Noelle was manipulated then like I was?"

"Maybe she wasn't."

"If not, then she's clearly learned." Eira shrugged. "I

guess it just doesn't seem that important after today. I can't willingly carry that weight any longer." Alyss continued to stare strangely at her. Prompting Eira to ask, with a nervous laugh, "What?"

"I feel like I'm watching my little sister grow up." Alyss wiped imaginary tears from the corners of her eyes.

Eira gaped. "I'm older than you!"

"By a month!"

"Still older."

Alyss rolled her eyes. "We all know I'm the mature one."

Eira let out a small laugh.

"There, that's what I was hoping for, a laugh."

"You're impossible," Eira said softly.

"Takes impossible to know it." Alyss smiled up at her. This woman was the one thing that still seemed real in Eira's shifting world.

With Noelle, the colors of her world had been smeared yet again.

Cullen was being raw, and real, and vulnerable around her. Noelle wasn't being cruel or haughty toward her. Marcus was still an unknown. And Eira, she...she wasn't who she thought she was.

But Alyss was there, right where she always was. Eira slipped her arm around Alyss's, hooking her elbow and pulling her close. "Thank you."

"What did I do now?"

"You're dependable. You'll always be there when I expect you. And I need that right now more than anything."

"I know," Alyss said softly, squeezing her bicep and pressing her side flush against Eira's. "Nothing will ever take me from you."

"Good. I'll kill anything that tries," Eira said as they started into the mess hall. Alyss laughed. But Eira had never meant anything more.

Dinner was catered by the chefs from the palace again. They had clearly been working on the food for the entire day.

A whole hog roast was presented on a buffet for them; buttered rice, spring vegetables, and dishes of steamed pudding prepared alongside it.

Eira arrived before Marcus—a fact she was grateful for. She was focused on her food, head down, when she saw him finally arrive with Cullen from the corner of her eye. She couldn't bring herself to look at him outright, but she stole glances when he was focused elsewhere.

His shoulders were a bit hunched. His gaze seemed distant. Eira hated seeing her brother look so forlorn, but the distraught expression gave her some hope. If he was as shocked as she was, then he hadn't known. This wound could bond them. It would be a tether between them when everything else was called into question...she hoped.

Fritz entered the mess hall, and following closely behind were the emperor and empress themselves. The entire room jumped to their feet—all twenty-two remaining candidates plus Cullen—and bowed their heads in respect.

"Please, sit, everyone. You've had a long enough day as it is," Vhalla said graciously.

The apprentices all lifted their heads, glancing around. No one seemed to want to be the first to sit. They were trapped between what they viewed as expected decorum toward the royals, and a direct command that ran course opposite to that decorum.

Unsurprisingly, Cullen was the first to take his seat. If anyone knew the correct protocol when it came to dealing with royals, it was him. He was followed by Marcus and Noelle, then the rest of them. As they settled back onto the benches, Fritz, Aldrik, and Vhalla assumed position at the front of the room.

"The emperor and I wanted to come and congratulate you ourselves," Vhalla continued. "Each of you had an impressive run through the course today. We know many of you took hard falls, but you endured and pressed on. You have all earned your pins today, every one of you. Take pride in the fact." She brought her hands together, clapping, and the room followed suit.

"As you know, one of the goals of our reign has been to oversee the better integration of sorcerers with Commons." The emperor stepped forward, hands folded behind his back. His slightly crooked nose, dark hair, and angular features made him a harsh and imposing man. Emperor Aldrik radiated a presence up close that had the room stilling and a slight terror worming its way into the back of Eira's mind. "Because of this, we are particularly invested in finding the best sorcerers to represent our Empire. People who are honorable, strong of heart and will. Sorcerers of astonishing power and skill. Sorcerers that even the Commons who are the most steadfast in their ways will cheer for."

"To that end," Vhalla continued where her husband left off. "The third trial is one of our own design. My husband and I wished to craft a trial that will allow you and your magic to shine as only you know best." She motioned to Fritz to continue.

The minister stepped forward and Eira stared over his shoulder rather than in his eyes. She didn't dare be the one who averted her eyes entirely. She wouldn't be that rude outright. But she couldn't stare at his face after their recent interaction. After it became clear that he thought she was one breath away from killing even her own parents.

"The third trial will occur in just under two weeks. We are calling it 'the creation,'" Fritz said. "You are to create something with your magic that will impress us."

"Create something?" Alyss repeated softly.

An apprentice raised their hand. Fritz nodded at the young man. He stood with a quick bow. "Sir, Your Majesties, what is it that you would like us to create?"

"That's the beauty of this trial," Vhalla said with a smile. "Your creation is entirely up to you. What form it takes, how you present it, are all your decisions."

The apprentice slowly sat down. He looked as confused as the rest of them.

"You will be given ten minutes each to present your creations," Fritz continued. "The emperor, empress, Prince Romulin, and Ambassadors Cordon and Ferro will be your judges for this trial. The trial, as the others have been, will be open to spectators. It will be conducted at the Sunlit Stage. You will have the entire lower area—where the test was conducted—to present your creation. The rules are that the creation must be entirely housed in this area; it must not be a danger to any who are gathered or damage the Sunlit Stage; and you must create, present, and destroy it in the time given."

Everyone mulled this over in silence.

"We realize this is an open-ended trial," Vhalla said in a reassuring way. "But we want to see your creativity. We want to see what you can do without restrictions or a goal in mind. Set your minds, and your magic, free—wow us."

"Any additional questions can be directed to me or your instructors. One-fourth of the remaining pool will be cut following this trial. Be sure to do your best to get a score that places you in the top three-fourths," Fritz finished.

With that, the minister, emperor, and empress left. As much as Eira wanted to sit and continue mulling over what they just said, she knew she couldn't. The time had come for her to conquer something much more immediate, and scarier, than any trial.

She stood, said a quick farewell to Alyss, and crossed to her brother before he could escape. Marcus locked eyes with her and sheer terror seemed to swallow him whole. He shrank in his seat. His eyes were wide with panic.

"I—hello, Marcus."

"Eira." He choked out her name, swallowed, and said more smoothly, "Hello."

"Can we talk?"

Marcus looked to Cullen, who was already stepping away from the table with Noelle.

"Let's give the ice siblings some space," Cullen said casually. Noelle gave her a questioning look, but stayed silent, disappearing. Eira was left to wonder if Marcus had confided in them both.

"Where do you want to talk?" Marcus stood. Though, given the way he moved, the weight that was trying to crush her all day was also bearing down on his shoulders.

"I don't know..." Eira folded and unfolded her hands. "Let's go to the rooftop."

"We haven't been there since we were kids and new to the Tower."

"Perfect time to go, then."

They accessed the rooftop by a passageway back to the palace proper and a spiral stair that let them out onto a guard's walk. Down the rampart was an old ladder, mostly rusted off and icy to the touch. When Eira gripped the first rung, a firm coating of ice covered the ladder and the bolts that connected it to the wall. Like this, it was sturdy enough for them to climb up to the flat roof of a palace spire.

Eira walked over to the far edge, inhaling the bracing chill of the night. "From here, I always thought I could see the whole world."

"It's quite the view," Marcus agreed softly. He didn't move far from the ladder, as if he were still debating a quick escape.

Eira chewed on her lower lip as she stared out at the city, glittering in challenge to the cosmos above. At the city's far edge were the switchbacks that trailed down the mountain into the dark forest below. That was the route they would take home through the mountains.

Home. The word was a dagger, slowly peeling away the armor she'd thought she had protecting her.

"I didn't bring you here to talk about the view, though," Eira said softly. "But you already know that." She glanced over her shoulder. Marcus remained silent, staring. There was an invisible wall between them. One that couldn't be seen but Eira could feel. "I don't know if I know this city anymore, or at least my place in it... I don't know if I know who you are— who we are—who *I* am."

Marcus pressed his lips into a hard line. Eira took it as an invitation to keep speaking. As if she could talk away the insurmountable wall of discomfort between them.

"I didn't know," she whispered. "I had no idea. If I'd known I would've...I would've told you."

He still did not speak.

"Say something?" she pleaded.

Silence.

"Did you know?" Eira dared to ask outright.

Marcus looked away and Eira could almost *hear* her heart shattering. He'd known. No matter what he said next, his movements told her that horrible truth.

"Not...outright. No. I...I didn't know. I was never told, is what I mean to say." Marcus frowned. But was it at himself, or at her? "Though, I think, there's a part of me that knew."

"There was a part of me that knew too," Eira said hastily, grasping for a connection with him. She couldn't be alone now, not when the rest of her family felt so far from reach. She needed him.

"I have...a memory," Marcus continued. "I never understood it. I thought I dreamed it." He laughed bitterly. "I guess that's the memory of a three-year-old, hazy and dream like."

"What was your memory?" She didn't know why she asked. She didn't want the answer.

"I remember you coming from nowhere. I remember waking up, and you were there. Mom and Dad telling me I had a sister. I remember thinking, 'I didn't ask for a sister.' But there you were in my home."

In my *home*. Eira blinked several times over as the words replayed. *His* home. *His* family. She had been an invader. She had been the one who imposed. Marcus had no doubt been thinking how good his life would've been without her ever since Fritz's revelation.

Marcus crossed his arms, swaying slightly as he shuffled his feet. Perhaps he was cold; he'd always been more susceptible to the cold than she. Or perhaps he was debating if he wanted to run off and reclaim the sister-less life he'd been born into—the life he should have had.

"I didn't mean…" Eira shook her head.

"I know you didn't mean. You didn't mean anything. You were a baby. You had no say in it all, just like me." Marcus glared at her. "But you did have a choice today in the trial."

"This is more than the trial…this is about our family," Eira said weakly, trying to summon the strength Alyss had earlier. But the words were a cheap echo of Alyss's, void of all substance.

"Exactly, *family*. And you know what family doesn't do, Eira? Family doesn't lie." He took a step forward. "Family doesn't challenge each other." Another step. Her eyes were burning again. She desperately wanted to give in to the icy wind prickling her skin—allow it to coat her once more. "Family doesn't attack each other."

"I never attacked our parents," she whispered.

He didn't hear, or didn't care. Marcus continued relentlessly on. "Family helps each other succeed rather than trying to tear each other down."

"I just wanted—"

"You were selfish," he snapped. Marcus loomed over her. "You didn't think about me, or what I wanted. You didn't think how important these trials may be to *me*."

"And what about me?" Eira's voice rose. "What about what I want? You don't even care about Meru, or traveling, or the wide world. Maybe it's *you* who should have stepped aside. You'd be rid of me at the very least. You'd all be rid of me, and think of how much happier that'd make everyone." Maybe she should go and never come back.

"I've sacrificed so much to look after you!" he shouted, ignoring her self-deprecating remarks.

"I never asked you to!" she shouted right back. "You did that of your own volition."

"Because I *thought* you were my sister!"

Thought.

You.

Were.

My.

Sister.

...*Thought.*

The words struck her down. They stole any strength she might have had. Eira backed away. Her ribs had been cracked open and her heart was exposed. She would bleed out before him.

"Go away, Marcus," she whispered, clutching her chest. If she didn't feel her heart beating, she would've suspected it had stopped entirely then and there.

His expression softened. "Eira, I didn't mean... Look, I—"

"Go away!" she yelled with all her might. Eira didn't care who heard. She didn't care if threatening everyone's precious front-runner cost her pin.

"You're being unreasonable."

"Stop." Eira shook her head, straightening. The world was spinning. She felt like she was in a tide of black ink, spinning around a drain. But if she was going down, she would do it with her head held high. "Just...leave."

"Maybe I should, before you attack me too," Marcus grumbled and stomped down the ladder. Eira watched him go from the rooftop. When he stopped, a flutter of hope took over her that he might already try to mend this. But hope was fleeting, because then he said, "If you ever cared about me, you'll drop out. If you want to prove you love me, and Mom, Dad, and the rest of our family, don't compete in the next trial."

With that, he left her alone.

Eira shrank, crouching into a ball and clutching her knees. *He didn't mean it. Not really. He's hurting, too. He's being stupid.* She tried to reassure herself over and over and over again. But the words were hollow and they wouldn't stick.

The crackle of ice diverted her attention. It was coating her once more.

Quickly shaking the frost from her shoulders, Eira descended and took the long way back to the Tower. She went first to her room, but stopped, staring at the nameplate that read:

EIRA LANDAN

"Well, that's not really me, is it?" she murmured and wandered away.

Eira felt like a ghost—an unwanted creature, void of substance. There was no place for her here. Was there?

Her thoughts drifted like she did, as dark as the rooms she passed. The Tower was silent this late, save for a few apprentices hunched over textbooks in the library. Eira avoided them at all costs. If she was seen, then she was real. If she was real, then she could feel.

She didn't want to exist.

So she went to a place that wasn't supposed to exist.

Eira pushed open the secret door in the Waterrunner storeroom. She sidestepped around the barrel into the dark room and closed the door behind her. Breathing a sigh of relief—as if she had truly somehow escaped all the problems that hunted her—Eira lay out on the bed and closed her eyes.

Maybe she would fade away here. She wouldn't worry about trying to sort through these messy feelings. And...the world would be fine without her...wouldn't it? They'd be happier without her. It'd be simpler for them...

Something cold, and sharp, pressed into her neck right underneath her jaw. Eira's eyes shot open. Standing over her was one of two elfin in all of Solaris—Ferro's guard, Deneya. Her dark hair was tied back into a high bun. Her eyes shone in the moonlight. And she held a dagger to Eira's throat.

"We need to have a talk, you and I," Deneya nearly purred. Eira opened her mouth but was interrupted by, "Tell me...what is your relationship with the Pirate Queen, Adela Lagmir?"

*A*DELA *LAGMIR*, THE infamous pirate queen. Eira had grown up with the lore and whispered stories of her. But she'd never heard the name more than in the past day.

Narrowing her eyes, Eira pushed her magic outward. A sheet of ice grew underneath the tip of the dagger, coating her neck and chest, pushing the blade away. Deneya stepped back nonchalantly, letting Eira swing her legs off the side of the bed and sit. Frost clouded the air off her body in waves.

"Don't look at me with murderous intent. If I wanted to kill you, you'd be dead." Deneya cast aside the dagger. However, it didn't clatter to the floor as a normal dagger would. It fell through the air, unraveling into strands of light. Yet, Eira had felt it at her throat—solid and sharp.

"Mysst."

"What?" Deneya tilted her head.

"That was mysst—Lightspinning to craft weapons and shields. Wasn't it?" Eira's attention drifted from the spot where the dagger had disappeared back to the woman who had been holding it.

Deneya tilted her head to the other side, as if Eira was a complicated book to be read. When she finished her assessment, she put her hands on her hips and let out a low humming noise.

"You're not one of hers, then, are you?"

"Do you mean Adela Lagmir's?" The name was strange to say aloud. Her whole life, Eira had seen people shunned for saying the name. To do so was to bring about bad luck, they said. But perhaps it was the name of her birth mother. Or the name of her birth mother's employer. "I honestly don't know if I am or not." Eira sighed and tried to relax the ice coating her body. She couldn't let it get out of hand again. The thought evoked memories of Cullen's arms around her and the frost retreated.

"What does that mean?"

"Nothing," Eira muttered.

"How do you know of this place?" Deneya motioned around her.

"I found it by accident. How did you find those forgotten halls of Solaris?" Eira turned the question back on the woman.

Deneya smirked. "I found them, by accident."

"You're lying."

The elfin laughed outright, a hearty and fearless sound. "You are a fun one, aren't you? Not even the slightest amount of fear toward me and my magic despite being from Solaris. You remind me of a good friend of mine." Deneya started for the passage behind the bookcase. "You're right. I'm lying. But you don't seem to be. Which makes you none of my concern. Enjoy lying in Adela's bed, Eira."

Deneya slipped back into the rough-hewn passage. Eira was on her feet in an instant, following closely behind. She heard the echo of whispered words as Deneya summoned a glowing orb over her shoulders, casting a pale light on the hallway.

"It was Adela's then? That room?"

"It was." Deneya kept walking.

"How do you know?"

"I know a lot more about Solaris history than you do." Deneya didn't even turn to speak to her, or slow down. Eira had to use magic to root her feet in ice just to keep up, otherwise she'd slip at the woman's pace.

"It seems everyone knows a lot more about my history than I do," Eira said with a bitter note.

That earned an inquisitive glance, but Deneya didn't remark. Instead, she asked, "Why are you following me, apprentice?"

Eira didn't entirely know herself. Something about this

whole interaction—the whole day—was like a dream. And in a dream, didn't people go wandering secret passages with pointy-eared sorceresses?

"Why did you ask me about Adela?"

"It's best not to worry about it." Deneya emerged into the forgotten hallway that the passage connected to. Eira was close behind her. "Nothing good will come of anything involving Adela. The superstitions do have that right."

"Is…is Adela *real*?" Eira dared to ask.

"What kind of a question is that?" Deneya stopped in a square of moonlight streaming through the cracked glass of the windows at their right. "Of course she's real. You were in her room, weren't you?"

"Right. But is she still someone to worry about?" Eira rephrased her question.

Deneya's lips twitched into a frown for only a second. "Very much so."

"But the stories of her… They're from a long time ago. They mention her stealing the royal treasure of the last Solaris king, right before his death, and fleeing to Oparium." *And she likely used the passage to escape,* Eira realized, glancing behind her.

"Yes, and?"

"That would've been almost seventy years ago." Eira took a step forward, stepping into her own beam of moonlight. "Is a seventy-year-old woman really out terrorizing the seas?"

Deneya slowly raised a single finger. "One—do not presume what can and cannot be done because of age. Even for humans, like you, your mind limits you well before your body or skill does." She raised a second finger. "Two—I can assure you that Adela is alive and terrorizing. She hasn't come around these parts for a while. Thank your princess admiral for that."

"Where is she?" Eira asked as Deneya went to leave.

"Last I heard, off the west, southwest coast of Meru, causing trouble for the Empire of Carasovia." The woman quirked an eyebrow. "Why are you so interested?"

"I…" Eira bit her lip, chewing on it and her words. "Why did you ask if I was associated with Adela?" She braced herself for the answer because she already knew what it would be.

"Your performance at the trial today. You moved like her. Your magic looked like hers." Deneya ran her eyes over Eira from head to toe. "Yargen bless, you truly *look* like her."

"Do I?" Eira took a hasty step forward, as if she were rushing toward the truth. Her foot crossed out of the moonlight and once more into the darkness.

"I've answered enough for you. It's time for you to answer a question for me." Deneya continued her assessment of Eira. "What did you mean when you said you didn't know if you were Adela's or not?"

Eira dropped her eyes to focus on her toes. Her parents had asked her not to share her truth for her own safety. They'd been proved right, hadn't they? Deneya had held a dagger to her throat on suspicion of association with Adela. What would she do if she found out Eira might be…might be of Adela's blood?

She slowly shook her head, raising her gaze. "I don't know why I said that. It's been a long day. I'm not making any sense."

Deneya smiled slyly. "Now it's you who's lying." Eira went to counter but couldn't get a word in. "That's fine, Eira. Go and rest; let your head sort itself."

The elfin turned, folding her hands behind her back and started off into the darkness. Eira felt pulled toward her, like someone had knotted an invisible rope around her waist, tethering her to the woman. The Firebearers who were gifted future sight whispered of the red lines of fate, given to all mortals by the Mother herself. Was this what the pull of fate felt like?

Eira stepped backwards slowly. She was just about to put her back to the woman and leave her, and the thought of her, behind when Deneya's voice cut through the silence.

"However…should you sort things out and wish to speak

again..." Deneya glanced over her shoulder. In the moonlight the blue of her eyes took on an unnatural purple hue. "You can meet me here in two days' time."

Eira stared in a stunned silence as she watched the elfin disappear into shadows as thick as the mystery that surrounded her.

The next morning, Eira awoke in Adela's bed. She stared out the same small window that she imagined Adela did. She visualized the woman, a woman who looked very much like Eira herself, hunched over the desk Eira had been pouring over for weeks now.

The Adela of Eira's mind was cruel, cunning, equal measures wicked and...stunning. In Eira's creations, Adela was like the magic detailed in her journals. There was something forbidden, yet alluring, about her and her knowledge.

"There's no way." Eira shook her head and stared up at the ceiling. The Adela of Eira's mind couldn't be her birth mother. They couldn't share blood.

That woman was bold. She was someone to be seen and feared. Eira stared at her hands. In contrast to Adela, she was no one.

Eira spent the day in the room. She let her stomach eat itself as she scavenged the journals for something she hadn't seen before. She searched for some kind of piece of information that would slot neatly into the hole that now existed in the picture of herself.

Unfortunately, the words, *This is who you really are, Eira*, weren't written anywhere.

She emerged at dinnertime, when her stomach was growling so loudly that Eira could no longer focus. Wasting away would do her no good. There were still trials to face.

If she faced them.

Her world was tilted and uneven. No step felt certain, or fully hers. Eira was pulled in competing, oscillating directions of "all right" and "very much not."

Fortunately, Alyss was nowhere to be found in the dining hall. She didn't want to re-hash how terribly things with Marcus had gone, not even with her best friend. She just wasn't ready. Eira ate quickly, alone, and promptly left before she could run into anyone else. As she wandered back up the tower, she initially started for Adela's secret room, but quickly backtracked to her own bedroom.

There was one person she'd be open to seeing. Fortunately for her, the feeling was mutual. A small envelope was waiting on her pillow.

Eira just hoped that it wasn't leftover from the night prior.

Washed and dressed in fresh clothes, Eira made her way through the tower and palace. The warm glow of her and Ferro's study was the most inviting thing she'd seen in days. Eira was all too eager to slip inside.

"You came tonight." He sounded, dare she even think it, eager? "I was worried you didn't get my message when you didn't show up last night."

"I'm sorry." Eira sighed softly as she took her seat. "I... yesterday was..."

"It was a lot." Ferro stood from his chair and stepped around the low table between them to hover before her. Eira stared up into his bright violet eyes, swallowing hard. He knelt before her, taking both her hands in his. Ferro turned them over, looking at their fronts and backs, as if searching for remnants of her injuries. "I was worried about you," he murmured.

"Why?" she whispered.

"I invited you to come and visit with me and you didn't show. Perhaps I'm being too forward...but I feared the only thing that would keep you from me was a grave injury."

Eira's mouth quirked into a smile. Her cheeks felt warm but she did nothing to hide them. "I think that's generally a fair assumption. But no grave injuries. I'm all right." *Physically, at least.*

"Good." He didn't make any motion away from her. Eira shifted her thumb slightly, running it over the smooth curve of his knuckle. His hands were the hands of a diplomat—soft and without callus. If he noticed the movement, he didn't remark on it. Something bold made her do it again.

This time, he gently stroked the back of her hand in reply, sending shivers up her spine.

"Why did you worry about me?" she dared to ask.

"You took some brutal falls. Anyone would've been worried." He shook his head, staring off at a dark corner. "No...I was worried because I didn't want to see you hurt. Especially when I watched and did nothing to help you."

"You couldn't. If you'd intervened it would've disqualified me."

"I know, which is why I kept my magic to myself. But it..." He chuckled softly. "It physically pained me not to."

Her chest tightened. She didn't know if she could believe what she was hearing, if she should believe it. Had it been anyone else, she would allow herself to see him as...pursuing her romantically?

"I was all right." The words were thick and hard to say.

"Yes, because you're strong." He looked back at her with a tender smile.

"I don't feel very strong lately," Eira admitted, both to herself and him.

"What has made you not feel strong?"

"I shouldn't say," she whispered.

"You can tell me anything," he assured her. "Tell me and I will make it better. Anything for you."

Eira bit her lower lip. Their hands were still lightly entwined, resting on her knees. The firelight tangled in his hair, streaking it with golden strands.

She wanted to believe him with all her might.

"I...I found out that my birth parents weren't who I thought they were."

"What?" he breathed in shock.

"No matter how many times I say them, those words still don't feel real." Eira hung her head, closing her eyes. She couldn't bear the sight of him. Neither could she deny how good speaking to someone else who had no judgment, no stakes or opinions of those involved, felt. "I've had so many competing thoughts and emotions. I'm sad and angry. Yet I'm also oddly relieved? As if something I've never understood—but never realized I understood—finally makes sense."

"Do you know who your birth mother was?" he asked delicately.

"No… I was abandoned on my parents' doorstep."

"Do they have any guesses by whom?"

Eira flinched.

Ferro's fingers tightened around hers. "You don't have to say if you don't want to."

"You'll hate me if I do." Eira thought back to her conversation with Deneya. Maybe Deneya had told him of the interaction and Ferro was merely playing ignorant for her benefit. Or maybe Ferro had his own suspicions. If Deneya had pieced together the possibility from being familiar with Adela's magic then Ferro, as a delegate from Meru, surely could, too.

His hands freed themselves of hers and Eira almost grasped them back frantically. His fingertips ran along her cheeks until his palms cupped them. Slowly, Ferro turned her face upward, to face him.

"I don't think I could ever hate you," he whispered. "You are a bright spot in a dark world. When I told you that before, I meant it. I won't *allow* anything to change it."

"I was abandoned with Adela's mark pinned to my blanket."

His eyes widened, just for a second, and by only a small margin. "So your family thinks your birth mother was Adela?"

Eira nodded. "Which I know is ridiculous, because Adela hasn't been seen in decades."

"It might not be that ridiculous," he murmured. Surprisingly, she hated that he was taking her seriously. She wanted him to write it off.

"No, it is." Eira forced a laugh, trying to cut through his intense stare. "Because she would've had to have given birth to me when she was…sixty? Sixty-five? I know our minds limit us before our bodies. But that would be a fairly incredible birth."

"For a human, yes."

"For…a human?"

Ferro stood. The warmth of his hands left her face and Eira let the chill prickle her senses back to being alert as she watched him cross to the hearth. His silhouette cast a long and imposing shadow.

When he was silent for what felt like forever, Eira was drawn to her feet. She was trying to keep her question in, but it was tugging at her, pulling her upright, demanding to be asked.

"Is Adela not human?"

"No," he answered, finally. "Not entirely, at least. I don't know what her parentage is. But, from what I've heard out of the Court of Shadows in Meru, she is half human and half elfin." Ferro turned to face her, as if to watch how this revelation settled on her. Eira's face had gone numb with shock, so he knew before she did. "Which could explain why your magic is so unique and powerful."

Eira shook her head violently. "No, no. It's not possible."

"It's not, or you don't want it to be?"

She shook her head again, not knowing what she was answering. Eira balled her hands into fists, fighting against the chill sweeping through her. Her magic was out of control these days. She had to get it under control. She had to find something in those journals that would help her.

Adela's journals.

Eira moved. She was somewhere between striding and running toward the door. A blur of movement solidified into Ferro in front of her. Eira raised her hands, bracing herself to run into him. His fingers laced with hers and he held her in place.

"Eira—"

"No."

"Eira, listen…" He pulled her a step closer.

"No, I don't want to." She shook her head.

"This could explain everything for you—your fascination with Meru, your magic, how you long to be a part of a different world, because that world is *in your blood.*" He released one hand and wrapped it around the back of her neck.

Eira's eyes shot open and she allowed the world to slowly come into focus—a world that began and ended with him. "But my family…"

"They will always be your family," he said softly. "You know that, right?"

She nodded weakly. She thought she did.

Thought.

Just like Marcus had *thought*—past tense—she was his sister.

Eira shook her head. His other hand unlaced with hers and Ferro's palm was back on her cheek. Eira couldn't stop herself from leaning into it. He caressed her like she'd only allowed herself to dream of. He touched her like a lover would and it was the first thing to feel good in what seemed like forever.

"If you don't want to find out the truth, then you don't have to," he whispered softly. "But if you do… Perhaps Yargen sent me to help you do this. Perhaps this is what I see in you—I see the blood of my people and a child of Meru."

Eira met his brilliant eyes. Her eyes had been called "unnatural" and "creepy" by the school children when she was young. Her bright shade of blue, a hue so vibrant that it was more like his, like Deneya's, than anyone she'd ever met in Solaris. Perhaps that's part of what had called to and fascinated her in Taavin when she'd first laid eyes on him.

The elfin was what she had been missing and searching for all along.

"I don't know if I can search for that truth," Eira admitted.

"I know exactly how hard it is."

"You—"

"I was abandoned, too." He silenced her with the confession.

"You what?"

"I'm an orphan. I became an ambassador to try and get close to the Court of Shadows to find out who my parents were. If anyone can find out, it's them."

"Ferro, I didn't know…"

"But this isn't about me," he added hastily. "What do *you* want?" he whispered. As his breath warmed her face, Eira realized how close they were. She barely resisted wrapping her arms around his waist.

"I don't know yet," she murmured. "Beyond knowing that I don't want to stop seeing you."

"That feeling, dear one, is quite mutual."

She wanted to kiss him. *Mother above*. She wanted to kiss him. And she had kissed recently, so this was more than a lusty longing for something she hadn't experienced in some time.

She wanted to kiss him because he suddenly made sense. *They* suddenly made sense. He was the only thing that did in the world.

He'd become her light in the darkness.

"I can't talk about this any more tonight. Give me an escape, for a little while?" she begged softly.

"What sort of escape would you like?"

"Whatever you will give me."

His eyes dropped to her lips. Ferro licked his and, for a glorious breath, he seemed to lean closer. But he slowly eased away. Was there any way she'd imagined the tension between them? Had she been wrong?

Perhaps he had the sense she lacked to know this wasn't the right moment to pursue something possibly scandalous between them.

"Come. Tonight we'll talk about anything but pirate queens and families." Fingers laced with hers, Ferro led her to the chairs. This time, Eira sat next to him. "I will tell you anything you want of Meru. And, then, if you're up to it and it would be a pleasant distraction, you can tell me more about the hiking trails in the mountains with Alyss. Or anything else that pleases you."

"Thank you."

"It is my supreme pleasure." A smile spread on his handsome face. "So, what would you like to know?"

"You mentioned a Court of Shadows earlier… I've never read about such a thing."

"You likely wouldn't. It is their job to know, and to make themselves mostly unknown. The Court of Shadows is the dark hand of the Queen of Meru. They are Queen Lumera's spies and whisperers…"

Ferro lived up to his word. For the rest of the night, she thought of nothing but Risen and its ancient underground, filled with secret passages of forgotten cities that propped up modern buildings, where spymasters lurked around every corner.

"YOU ACTUALLY CAME." Deneya was waiting in the dark hall the next night, just as she said she would be. She leaned against the wall between the cracked and grimy windows, beams of moonlight framing her.

"I did." Eira folded her arms, staying right by the entrance of the passage. She wanted a quick escape if this conversation turned sour. "You sound surprised."

"I flipped a coin to guess if you would. The coin said no. Apparently my coin is a liar."

"Like me."

Deneya hummed. "Are you a *liar*? Or were you *lying*? They're different, you know."

"I suppose the latter."

"I do as well." Deneya smiled.

"Did Ferro send you to meet with me?"

"No." A look of confusion crossed her face. "Why would he?"

Eira hadn't thought that Ferro had sent Deneya. Their meeting the other night seemed to be solely of Deneya's design. There was no way Ferro would ever let someone hold a blade to her throat.

Deneya also didn't seem to know that she and Ferro were meeting—if she had, she certainly would've said something— and *that* surprised Eira. Ferro had said that he didn't tell his guard much...but Eira had assumed that she, at least, kept tabs on his whereabouts.

It made Eira appreciate her interactions with the man all the more as they now seemed twice as special. There was something to their meetings being secret that made them even more thrilling. And made the possible implications behind them set her heart to racing. Maybe he wanted to keep things private for *other reasons*? Eira didn't let herself linger on the thought for very long.

"You're his guard. I assumed that everything you do is at his order." Eira worked to sound casual.

Deneya laughed roughly. More of a bark, really, than a laugh. "No. If anyone is keeping tabs here, it's me keeping tabs on him."

"To protect him?"

"Sure, you could think of it that way."

The conversation was putting Eira slightly on edge. She was beginning to regret her decision to come. Eira couldn't shake the notion that there was some kind of game or competition being played between the two elfin. A protective edge overtook her at the thought of Deneya doing something sinister to Ferro.

"I have a question for you."

"I'm not surprised; you're full of them."

"Answer my question, and I'll answer yours—what I meant when I said I didn't know if I was Adela's or not." If Eira's suspicions were correct, Deneya might know anyway.

"All right, fine."

"Are you a member of the Court of Shadows?"

Deneya stilled. A sly smile curved across her face. She quirked one eyebrow up and tilted her head slightly as she asked, "What do *you* know about the Court of Shadows?"

"I know that it is Queen Lumeria's organization of whisperers and spies." Eira didn't dare say too much. She didn't want to betray Ferro's trust in her. Especially if he hadn't told Deneya about their meetings. "But, understandably, there's not much else on them."

"If you know that much, then you would, *understandably*, also know I certainly wouldn't tell you if I were a member of this organization."

"I think you are," Eira said boldly.

"All right. Why do you think that?" Deneya folded her hands behind her back, still wearing the amused grin.

"Because you seem to lurk in the shadows. You're quiet around groups, but have a lot to say in private. You've found these hidden passages. And...because you know about Adela." Ferro had said that it was the Court of Shadows who kept a tabs on Adela. "Were you sent here to hunt me?"

"I suspect the answer to that question lies in what you mean when you say you 'don't know' if you're one of Adela's."

"My parents suspect she was my birth mother."

"Oh?" Deneya seemed slightly eager at that. Enough that the note of unexpected delight grated on Eira. There was nothing about her circumstances that was worthy of amusement. She pushed down the sentiment, however. She needed a level head right now. "That would certainly explain some things if it were true."

"Do you think it's true?"

"Adela is as much myth as she is flesh. It's hard to say what's true when it comes to her. How old are you?"

"Eighteen."

Deneya hummed in thought. "You were born a few years after I saw her last, then."

"You...you *saw* her?"

Deneya laughed at Eira's surprise. "I rode on the *Stormfrost* itself."

"The *Stormfrost*?"

"Adela's ship. Be grateful you've never seen it. You'd know it if you did."

Eira detached herself from reality for a moment. She scoured her memories, searching for some recollection of a magical ship. She could almost imagine it...but was that ghostly imagery floating in the shroud of time real? Or just her mind trying to fabricate something that would fit into this grand unknown of the history that was a part of her?

"Are you going to kill me now?" Eira asked as she brought herself back to the present.

"Kill you? Why would I do that?" Deneya approached slowly.

"Because I might be Adela's child."

"And thank goodness that neither Solaris or Meru punishes children for the crimes of their parents if that is the case. I apologize for threatening you out the gate. It has nothing to do with your potential parentage; I merely thought you might have been one of her crew. And Adela's crew tends to be a fight first, ask questions later sort of bunch."

"I'm not."

"Yes, that's apparent. Your magic resembles hers, hence my initial suspicion; but I now believe it's because you've been reading her journals."

Relief washed over Eira, followed quickly by dread. The notion of her *not* being Adela's offspring allowed her to take a breath with a chest less tight than it had been in days. But there was a sickening sense of dread and fear that followed the relief.

If Adela wasn't her birth mother, and neither was Reona, then a whole component of her history was a dark void that suddenly wanted to swallow her whole. It also meant that her magic, every strange and wonderful aspect of it, was of unknown origin, too. And…it meant that she likely wasn't part elfin. There was no real connection between her and Meru, after all. Which meant she and Ferro didn't have some kind of fated link between them.

"You don't look happy." Deneya came to a stop before Eira, inspecting her. "Most would be pleased not to be the offspring of the Pirate Queen."

"I would be happiest to have all the pieces of who I am."

"Did you know who you were before all this?"

"I thought I did," Eira murmured. She didn't know how the conversation got to this point. She certainly hadn't expected opening up to Deneya.

Four people—excluding her family—now knew of Eira's potential parentage. Her parents' disembodied disappointment took up residence in her, scolding her for sharing it with so many so quickly. But Eira fought the notion. It was her secret to tell. At least telling it with the people she wanted, for whatever reason she wanted, gave her some control over it.

"If you knew who you were before, then you still know who you are now."

"But... This... I look in the mirror and I don't see my face anymore. I don't know whose face I see. There's this *hole* in me that I can't describe. Like a piece is missing in the picture of who I am."

Deneya sighed softly. A gentle smile crossed her lips. The woman went from warrior to sagely aunt in the span of a moment. "Listen, Eira, if there was never a hole to begin with, there's not one now. It may be hard to see that. But eventually you will. Everything you need to be your complete self is already in your possession."

"What do you know about being abandoned?"

"Most of the Court of Shadows are orphans. Most never found a loving family to raise and cherish them as you did."

Eira ignored the guilt that the remark seeded in her. Instead, saying, "Then it's true, you're part of the Court of Shadows?"

Deneya smirked. "That perked you up."

"You still haven't said yes or no."

"How about this..." Deneya made a show of thinking, but Eira suspected she was a woman who made up her mind long before she even opened her mouth. "I will tell you, if you can break my shield."

"Break your shield?"

Deneya held up her palm and uttered, "*Mysst xieh.*"

That's how those words are supposed to sound, Eira thought. They were pure elegance on Deneya's tongue. They were made for her as much as ice and water were made to be Eira's playthings.

A dot of golden light appeared in Deneya's palm that spun outward into the shape of a disk. Unlike the dagger, the glyph didn't harden into anything solid. It remained a faintly glowing light, slowly spinning through the air.

"Lightspinning," Eira whispered in awe.

"You knew these words. Now break them."

"But—"

"However you see fit. Break my shield." Deneya grinned.

Eira tentatively reached out a hand. Deneya didn't move. Her fingertips lightly brushed against the surface of the glyph. It felt smooth, almost glass-like underneath her palm. Eira's fingers splayed against the light, inches from Deneya's, against the barrier.

"Why?"

"You want to know about the Court of Shadows, don't you? Break it."

Eira pulled back her hand and balled it into a fist. A thick coating of ice covered her hand, nearly up to her elbow. She punched forward and the impact shot through her arm, condensing every joint, up into her shoulder, her neck, and straight into her teeth. Punching one of the stone walls of the palace would be softer.

She stepped back, rubbing and rotating her shoulder. "Mother above," Eira murmured. "That's…solid."

"Yes, it is." Deneya chuckled. "Now that we know punching it isn't going to work, let's try for something with a bit more…finesse, shall we?"

Eira stepped back and closed her hand around a dagger of ice that formed from her palm. She struck it across the surface in a slashing movement. The strands of light seemed to writhe around the shallow cut. But they quickly wove themselves back together.

"You can do better than that," Deneya both challenged and encouraged.

She twisted the dagger in her hand and it grew into a short sword. Eira charged again.

Attack after attack, the shield stayed in place. Eira lobbed everything she could think of at the disk—from spears of ice to jets of water. But as dawn bled across the horizon, she was still no closer to destroying it.

Deneya lowered her hands and the glyph unraveled. Cursed thing. It had been the bane of Eira's existence all evening, impervious to every attack, and then just faded away as though it had never existed at all.

"You should go back to your bed. Don't want them to find you here."

"I don't have anything to do," Eira said, breathless. "I can keep trying."

"As fun as it is to watch you attack me with all the brute force you can muster, *I* have things to do." Deneya stepped backward. "But I'll come back tonight."

"Why?" Eira called after her.

"Because you amuse me," Deneya called back. "So you're welcome to try again, Eira."

The following week was a blur of emotions.

Eira was most calm when she was with Alyss in the library in the afternoons, debating what they were going to do for their show of creativity. Alyss would obviously craft some kind of stunning, magical sculpture from a mixture of stone, clay, and wood. But Eira still couldn't decide what she wanted to do. Debating it was its own distraction, at least. She didn't have to think of anything beyond what had the greatest likelihood of impressing the judges, mainly Ferro.

And Ferro… He was a whole different set of emotions—the sort of emotions that made her blush for hours, lying in her bed, long after he'd kissed her knuckles and bid her goodnight. She met him three more times that week. Not once did he mention Deneya, so neither did Eira.

But she kept meeting with Deneya as well. The two elfin couldn't be more opposite. Ferro was as smooth as silk. Deneya was more like a dagger. She was graceful in her own way, but sharp, and at any moment could well be the last thing you saw.

Yet, for all Eira knew of the risks conceptually, she never felt at danger when it came to Deneya. Other than for a few tense seconds during their first encounter, Deneya hadn't ever given Eira the impression she had anything to fear.

Overall, Eira felt less at odds sneaking around with her elfin friends—*was "friends" the right term for them?*—than she did walking in the Tower. Much like her skin had felt those first few hours after the *revelation*, as she and Alyss had begun to term it, the Tower no longer felt like it fit. The walkways and rooms were too small. Every corner closed in on her.

When Eira wasn't meeting with Alyss, she chose to wander the city. She would often find herself walking to the clinic where she'd assisted before the trials, then to Margery's Bakery, and then often down to the city gates before finally returning to the Tower.

It was on one of these walks that she saw Marcus leaving from the clinic. Eira tried to duck behind a building. But he'd seen her. This wasn't the first time they'd crossed paths, but it was their first time outside of the Tower.

"Eira," he said.

She turned, pretending she didn't hear.

"Eira, wait!"

Eira stopped as he ran over. Every muscle in her neck was tense, pulling her shoulders up toward her ears.

"What're you doing out here?"

"Taking a walk," she answered without looking at him.

"Alyss said you go for a lot of walks these days."

"What're you talking to Alyss about?"

"You. I…I've been worried about you."

Eira glanced at him from the corners of her eyes, skeptical. "Don't you get it? You don't *have to* worry about me anymore."

"Eira, I didn't mean what I said."

She turned. Eira didn't want to hear this. She didn't want to confront it. Not when the trial was tomorrow.

He grabbed her shoulder, stopping her from leaving. "I'm

sorry. I mean that. But not...not the other stuff. Everything came out wrong. I was so confused and my emotions were a mess. That day... I..." Marcus cursed under his breath. "Look, can we just walk back to the Tower together?"

Eira gazed up at her flustered brother. Part of her wanted to twist the proverbial knife. She wanted to be ugly and throw his words back in his face. But she couldn't muster enough wretchedness to do that. She'd been craving *normal* so badly that its peaceful allure was too much to refuse.

"Fine."

They started off together. In awkward silence, at first. But it became less uncomfortable with every step. Marcus being at her side was normal, even if it usually resulted in her being in his shadow.

"I really am sorry," he said again, softer. The words had more weight this time.

"I forgive you."

"Do you?" He seemed shocked.

"I think so?" Eira shrugged up at him. "I don't..." She sighed. Deneya's words were in her mind. If she had everything before, then she wasn't missing something now. Sure, maybe some pieces had to be rearranged. But all the pieces were there. They always had been. Even if the colors on a few were too blurry to make out still. Maybe they always would be. "I want to try to forgive you. I know I can. And, most importantly, I don't want to fight with you. I never did."

"I know, I was an ass."

"Mature of you to say so."

"Mature of you to forgive me."

"You might have spoken too soon. I could just be having a good day today. Maybe I'll be angry again tomorrow and resent you for hours." Eira put her hands in the pockets of her skirts and grinned up at him. Marcus laughed.

How cute, he thought she was kidding. Still, his laughter elicited the same from her.

"I meant to apologize sooner but—"

Eira held out her hand and shook her head. "This is nice. Let's drop talk of the *revelation* for now before we ruin it, all right?"

"All right."

Another pass of awkward silence over another twenty steps. They'd just made up. Why did she still feel so uncomfortable?

The Tower looming in the distance had Eira slowing until she came to a full stop. Marcus didn't realize until he was several steps ahead, looking back at her with an inquisitive stare.

"Marcus?"

"Eira?"

"Am I still your sister, like you thought?" she asked so softly the wind nearly stole her words.

Pain flashed in his eyes. Marcus slowly marched back to her. Without a word, he wrapped his arms around her shoulders and pulled her close.

"Yes," he whispered. "I should have never said those words—never done anything to make you feel that way." Eira pressed her eyes closed and embraced her brother on the side of the street, allowing the world to go on around them. Not caring for any passersby they might inconvenience. "You will *always* be my sister. Even if you're stubborn, or annoying, or too clever for your own good, or more gifted than me with magic."

"I'm not more gifted than you with magic," Eira muttered.

"You are and you know it." He gave her a squeeze. "You're still figuring yourself and your magic out, that's all. But once you get it down…" Marcus pulled away with a whistle. "You're going to stun the world."

"The trials?" she dared to ask.

"Perhaps you'll stun the world tomorrow at the trial." He grinned. There was still pain and a bit of frustration in his eyes. But Marcus was clearly striving to put on a brave face.

"You don't want me to throw them?"

"I want you to do what you want. I guess that's something

else I need to apologize for." Marcus slung his arm around her shoulders. "Mother above, I have been a terrible brother lately, haven't I?"

"You had room for improvement." Eira grinned up at him. She realized this was the first time she was seeing her brother as less than perfect. In a way, it made her sad. "I'm glad we're okay, though."

"You and me both."

Eira didn't mention anything more on the trials as they entered back into the Tower. The truth remained that only one of them could progress to take the final spot as Waterrunner. Unless they were both knocked out. Perhaps that would be the best option?

Still, Eira couldn't bring herself to hope for it. Regardless of her prospective parentage, Meru called to her and she was going to do whatever it took to get to it.

IN THE TOWER library there was a clock hung over the mantle of the fireplace. It was a large, iron thing—an early prototype from Norin, likely over a hundred years old. The exposed gears whirred and ticked loudly, marking the agonizingly slow passage of time.

Eira paced, alone.

The Tower was silent. Everyone—instructors, apprentices, and candidates—had gone to the Sunlit Stage early this morning to watch the trial. Times were posted last night. But, like the last trial, Eira's slot was the very last of all the Waterrunners.

"You're trying to spite me, I know it," Eira muttered to the thought of her uncle. She could just see him scheduling her last in the day to try and make her nerves work against her. She wasn't going to let him win. She would keep a cool head and stay focused.

"Who is?" Cullen's voice startled her from her thoughts.

"You could've killed me from shock." Eira gripped her shirt over her heart. "What're you doing here?"

"It's the Tower... I'm allowed to be here?" He grinned, leaning against one of the bookshelves and exuding an air of arrogance like he owned the whole palace.

"That's not what I was asking and you know it."

"You're asking why I'm not with the rest of the masses at the Sunlit Stage? I had some business to attend to with my father." He motioned to his formal clothes. "I was going to change and then see who I could. Have you gone yet?"

"No...I'm the last one."

"Good, then I should see what you have decided to present."

"You seem happy about that." Eira had kept fairly tight-lipped with everyone about what her creation would be. She didn't want anyone to talk her out of it—wouldn't take much to do so.

"Should I not be?"

"I thought you wanted my brother to take the Waterrunner spot."

Cullen mulled over his next words, holding her in suspense. "I want the best Waterrunner to have the spot. I thought that was your brother."

"But you don't anymore?" Eira asked hesitantly. She was unexpectedly nervous about what the answer might be.

"I'm going to let the trials play out as they were meant to." Cullen pushed off from the bookcase and strolled over to her. His eyes turned serious, intense. "How are you, Eira?"

"I'm fine." She glanced away.

He lightly touched her exposed forearm. The contact sent shivers up her spine. For some reason, she couldn't stop herself from remembering the day at court…his fingers in her hair… his mouth on hers. The memory shifted and suddenly it was Ferro kissing her.

Eira shook her head, scattering the thoughts. She couldn't allow her focus to wane now.

"Are you?" he asked, clearly misinterpreting her expression. "Given the shock you had, it's all right if you're not."

"I am as fine as I can be."

"Ah, so not fine at all."

"Don't impose your perceptions on me," she cautioned.

"You're right. I shouldn't layer my family problems and tensions over yours." He stepped away with a grin. Cullen said the words like a joke, but there was real pain in his eyes. He hovered, halfway between the entrance to the library and her.

"Yes?" Eira finally asked.

"Speaking of my family…" he said thoughtfully. "I have a favor to ask of you."

"What is it?" Eira resisted remarking that the mighty Cullen needed *her* for something. He'd made it clear how much he disliked that sort of talk. She would respect his wishes.

"Would you come to court again with me next week?"

That was the last thing she wanted to do. Yet... "I guess I can. I suppose I owe you."

"You know what, forget it." He backtracked quickly at her hesitancy. "No one wants to go to that horrible place."

"Cullen, stop." Eira rushed over to him. When he kept moving, she grabbed his hand. Cullen turned to meet her eyes. "I'll go. It's an excuse to wear that pretty dress you gave me again, if nothing else."

"You'll need a new pretty dress. We can't let the ladies of court see you wearing the same thing twice." He chuckled softly and tucked a strand of hair behind her ear. The movement was so natural that both of them seemed to realize it happened on a delay. They stared at each other in a second of stunned silence that he had willingly touched her in an almost affectionate way.

"You don't have to get me another dress," she murmured.

"I'd like to." Cullen stepped away and Eira released him. "Besides, you're doing me the favor, remember?"

"I suppose…" It was dawning on her that he hadn't said *why* he wanted her to go to court yet. But Eira didn't have a chance to ask.

"Excellent. Good luck out there. I look forward to seeing your creation." Cullen made a hasty retreat. Almost…too hasty. Like he was *nervous?*

Eira shook her head and pushed the notion from her mind. She had to stay focused. Now, more than ever, she needed a handle on her thoughts and her emotions.

When the clock chimed fifteen minutes before her time to present, Eira finally left the Tower. She took the back passages through the palace, avoiding others as much as possible. She didn't want to see or hear anything.

She emerged out of the walls of the Sunlit Stage by one of the lower entries to the fading cheers for the person before her.

"You, there." A guard she didn't recognize rushed over. "Are you Eira Landan?"

"Yes."

"Oh, thank the Mother, we thought you'd be a no-show." The guard ushered her toward the entry.

"A no-show?" she asked.

"The minister said you might be."

"Of course he did," Eira mumbled.

"Doesn't matter, you're up."

With a small shove, Eira was thrust into the Sunlit Stage, alone, and with easily a thousand eyes watching her from the stands.

Word of the trials seemed to have spread quickly, collecting an audience from all walks of life. People of all shapes, colors, and sizes packed the stands. Eira turned, blinking, taking them all in. She didn't know if she was more relieved or hurt to not find her parents among them this time. Every pair of eyes stared down on her, judging silently.

But the real judges were the four individuals sitting behind a table on the stage portion of the Sunlit Stage. The emperor and empress sat flanked by Ferro and Cordon respectively. Ambassador Cordon was flipping through some papers, glancing at her and making a few marks. Vhalla and Aldrik both stared down at her from what felt like a mountaintop.

Ferro's eyes were familiar, but his gaze was not. He wore the expression of an ambassador—cold and cut off. Along the back of the stage were palace guards, sorcerers peppered among them—Fritz and Deneya included. They both kept a close eye on Eira as she approached the center of the arena.

Eira wrung her hands and quickly stopped the nervous motion. It was replaced by a bite of her lip. But she at least stood a little straighter.

She felt alone, laid bare, *vulnerable*. Eira took a breath and fought against the urge to surround herself in ice. That would certainly be a creation. But any Waterrunner could do something of the like.

The magic in her set Eira apart from the rest. She just had to find the courage to put it on display.

"Eira Landan," the emperor spoke, "you will have ten minutes to present a creation of your choice. It must be entirely housed within the area and cannot pose a danger to anyone gathered here or the arena itself. Do you have any questions?"

"I do not," Eira said softly. Wishing her voice boomed as the emperor's did.

"Then your time begins now." The emperor reached for an hourglass on the table and flipped it. The sand began pouring from top to bottom, no doubt carefully calibrated to ten minutes exactly.

Eira took a deep breath, held it, and closed her eyes. This was it. Time for what would likely be the dumbest choice of her life.

The muscles tightened in her ears as she strained to listen. She wanted to hear every creak of the stands above her as the excited crowd shifted. She wanted to hear Ferro's breathing. She wanted to hear as though her ears were long and pointed, not short and rounded.

No…she didn't want to hear with her ears at all. She wanted to hear with her magic.

The arena was a dry lake—her lake. It was thirsty, waiting to be filled. Eira let her power seep from her. She imagined water springing up from around her feet, quickly filling the whole place to the brim.

When Eira opened her eyes, the stage was still as dry as a bone. But she felt every corner. Her power stretched, ebbing and flowing, searching.

"What is she going to do?" someone asked loudly from above.

Someone else yawned.

More murmuring.

Cordon tilted his head, narrowing his eyes. His pen scratched loudly on his notes. The emperor and empress waited, as perfect as statues. Ferro kept his face passive.

He'd asked what she intended…but Eira hadn't told him. She'd wanted it to be a surprise. She wanted to impress him.

Eira closed her eyes again and furrowed her brow. She heard everything but nothing she was listening for. The crowd's restlessness was growing. More murmurs. Some laughter. They thought she was doing nothing when really she was trying to do something that everyone had shunned her whole life. Everyone had said it was impossible.

She was going to show them the limits of what was possible, here and now.

"Quiet," Eira murmured. They were being too noisy. So many people that the walls were silent. "Stop talking, please," she said, louder. No one seemed to hear. "Silence!" Eira shouted. Her voice felt like it echoed across the whole city.

Everyone fell into a stunned hush. And in that moment of blessed peace, Eira heard a whisper.

She opened her eyes with a start. Immediately they found the crown the empress wore. It was different from the emperor's—from what would be expected of a Solaris Empress. The Empire was gilded. Everything that glittered was truly gold under the Solaris sun.

But Vhalla's crown was silver, ornate, and adorned with western rubies.

Eira strung her magic to the crown. It was hard, from a distance. Usually, when she worked with vessels she could place them in water and directly manipulate the magic within them with her own.

She was trying to apply the same concept without actually touching the item—something she'd been doing subconsciously since birth but only began actively trying to control, rather than stint, these past few weeks. Eira imagined her magic pooling around the crown, soaking it. She was careful not to summon actual water and drench the empress.

"Five minutes have passed, candidate," Cordon said dully. "What do you intend to present?"

"The echoes of truth," Eira said. Vhalla leveled her eyes slightly with Eira's, clearly taking note of her intense stare.

The magic finally took hold. It was stable and strong. The

words were faint, but the crowd continued to wait in a hushed thrall.

She would've wanted you to have it, a soft voice said across time. Eira didn't know the time or place the moment she was tapping into had occurred in. But the connection was unwavering.

"She would've wanted you to have it," Eira echoed, praying that these words would mean something to the empress. *Fiera was not one to change who she was.* "Fiera was not one to change who she was." *Even when she married an emperor of the South, she wanted a crown of silver.* "Even when she married an emperor of the South, she wanted a crown of silver."

The empress inhaled, raising a hand to her chest, clutching over her breast. She stared at Eira in slack-jawed shock. The panel oscillated focus between Eira and their sovereign.

So, this crown truly is... Eira breathed a sigh of relief. The new voice was younger than the empress's now, but it was unmistakably Vhalla.

"So, this crown truly is..." Eira paused, her magic wavering. She'd never echoed the words she'd heard before and it took more focus than Eira expected. "You said that, in response to this woman, Your Majesty." Eira paused. "No, two women...there's another voice."

She locked eyes with the crown again, and allowed the conversation to play out as long as she could hear it.

"Our sister's, Aldrik's mother's. She was the empress this realm needed, if only she'd lived to fulfill that role," Eira said in tandem with the second voice.

Then, there was the first voice again. "But she gave us Aldrik. And hopefully he has brought us an empress who will be worthy of picking up my sister's crown."

Eira blinked. The voices were becoming fainter. She was going to lose the connection. "I will be—you said, Your Majesty."

Vhalla stood with purpose. The empress pressed both hands into the table, leaning forward. Her breath was ragged, her eyes wide and...vulnerable. Eira knew that expression because she'd worn it countless times. She just never expected to see it on her sovereign. And certainly not because of her.

"How... How did you know that?" Vhalla whispered.

"Your crown told me."

"What?" Cordon said.

The emperor leaned forward. Ferro wore a smirk, settling in his seat. His eyes shone with an approval that made Eira stand a little bit taller.

"The crown told me," Eira repeated, louder. "We change everything we touch. We mark this world with our mere existence. Especially sorcerers." She turned, addressing the crowd in the process. The emperor and empress knew this principle better than anyone, from the stories Fritz had told her as a girl. "They're called unintentional vessels—trapped bits of magic from a sorcerer in items."

"It takes a great deal of magic to create an unintentional vessel," the emperor said skeptically.

"Respectfully, Your Majesty, I have found it does not. Any bit of magic can mark an item, or a wall, or a tapestry—anything. And if there is something said while that imprint is left, then an *echo* of those words lives on."

"This ring." Cordon thrust his hand forward. On his middle finger was a large signet ring that nearly spanned both knuckles. "What do you hear from it?"

Eira glanced at the hourglass. There was only about a minute left. She shifted her focus from the crown and tried to condense her magic around the ring.

There was more murmuring from above. Whispers abounded. But Eira's senses, and magic, were now honed. She heard the voices easier than the last time.

...commissioned from the Le'Dans, a female voice said. *Wear it even when we are apart. Swear you will return.*

"It was a gift, commissioned from the Le'Dans. The woman who gave it to you told you to wear it even when you are apart and swear you will return."

"A reasonable guess," Cordon said, though panic was creeping into his voice.

Eira waited. The words continued playing across her mind. She allowed them to flow like the sands in the hourglass. It was clearly a conversation between lovers. But, given the scandalous implications...one of the lovers was already spoken for.

"Ambassador, I do not think you'll wish for me to say the rest, not here." Eira bit her lip as the conversation finished.

"I am unafraid. Surely you—"

"Who is Lucelle?" Eira asked.

It was Cordon's turn to jump from his seat. He stumbled backward, slowly shaking his head. "No," he whispered twice over. "What sorcery is this?"

"My sorcery," Eira answered as the time ran out.

The empress eased herself back into her seat. The emperor tapped on the hourglass. The whole of the Sunlit Stage continued to watch her with shock and horror.

Eira swallowed hard, trying to stand tall under the crushing weight of their judgment. No matter what happened from here—no matter how her magic was received or responded to—she finally had shown all of them that the voices she heard were real. Her theories on vessels were real.

Let someone try and deny her now. She didn't expect her uncle, of all people, to rise to the task.

Fritz stepped forward from the line of sorcerers and guards at the back of the stage. "Your Majesties, I do not know if this presentation meets the requirements you laid out."

"What?" Vhalla looked over her shoulder at the approaching Minister of Sorcery.

"The task, as you laid out, was to *create* something with magic—not *do* something." Fritz's attention drifted to Eira. Disapproval filled his eyes, tangling with what Eira believed might be resentment. She hadn't known her family could find still new and creative ways to wound her. "In the interest of fairness to the other competitors who followed the letter of the trial, I would propose a motion to disqualify Eira and remove her pin."

"You can't be serious. What she did was incredible!" Ferro's defense of her was the only thing that broke through the ringing in her ears. Sound began to slowly return to Eira and she realized the people in the stands were beginning to murmur in protest as well.

"He does have a point." Ambassador Cordon regarded her warily, as though he was looking at a completely new person. "Perhaps it would be more fair."

You just didn't like what I heard. Eira bit back the angry words.

"I am serious." Fritz doubled down. "Moreover, in the last trial she circumvented the rules with her illusion. She was already given a second chance."

"You didn't say that was against the rules before the trial began. I didn't know! I followed the rules you laid out then." Eira couldn't keep quiet and it earned her a glare from Fritz.

The emperor and empress shared a look, an unspoken conversation flowing between them in a way that only deeply bonded partners could manage. But as they debated silently, the crowd began to rally.

"You can't disqualify her!" someone shouted. "Not on a technicality!"

"Let her be scored!" *That was Alyss.* Eira looked up, searching for her friend.

"Let her compete, let her compete!" A chant was rising from the masses. They were behind her, rallying for *her*. Eira stared up in awe.

"Give her a fair chance." *Marcus.* Somehow, she found him out of the hundreds of people. She heard his voice out of the rising cheers. "She deserves to be scored like the rest of us!"

Fritz looked as though he'd been wounded. He'd no doubt heard Marcus's defense of her as well. Something in her cracked and tears threatened to ooze out. But for the first time in days, they were not tears of despair. Things weren't perfect. But Marcus was still on her side. Marcus was fighting for her to stay in the trials, even though it meant they were pitted against each other.

Nothing could've cemented her forgiveness of the way he acted during the revelation faster.

"Enough." Vhalla stood and the crowd fell to a hush. "The emperor and I have decided that Eira Landan will not be disqualified. While she did not follow the *letter* of the trial, she followed the spirit. She showed us something truly special that only her magic could do. She returned to me a memory I have not thought of in years and more than anything, for that, has my gratitude." The empress's gentle gaze landed on Eira.

"Thank you, Your Majesty," Eira forced herself to say. She didn't know how to handle random people defending her, approving of her. Having the empress also stand up for her was more than she could process.

Perhaps this was how Cullen felt all the time. Perhaps that's why he acted how he did.

The crowd erupted in cheers as Eira bowed. Their jubilance at her victory gave her the strength she needed to turn her back to her uncle and walk out of the Sunlit Stage with her head held high. Her parents, her uncle, Marcus, none of them were in control any longer.

She was the one in charge of her own destiny; and, now that she knew this feeling, Eira would never let anyone take it from her again.

CHAPTER
TWENTY

SCORES WERE POSTED later that night at the base of the tower. Once more, Groundbreakers erected a stone tablet, stamping names one by one. Once more…Eira's name was at the top.

She stared, stunned. Everyone had been giving her a wide berth. No one had even spoken to her following her display in the trial.

No one but—

"You amazing sorcerer, you!" Alyss threw her arms around Eira's neck. "You did it!"

"So did you." Eira gave Alyss a squeeze and then promptly began her retreat up the Tower. There was another dinner tonight for the candidates and she couldn't handle the stares and side-eyes of the other apprentices. Some were clearly regretting cheering for her not to be disqualified.

"I got third place."

"You're still continuing on."

"Only four Groundbreakers competed in that trial and three are moving on. I basically got last." Alyss rolled her eyes. "I should have done something more creative, like you."

"It doesn't matter. I got last in the second trial. All that matters is that we keep making it through."

"You and me, on our way to Meru!" Alyss jumped up and down, letting out a squeal.

"Don't get ahead of yourself," Eira scolded lightly with a laugh.

"We just have two more trials. I can't wait to find out what—"

"Excuse me, sorry for interrupting, Alyss." Fritz seemed to materialize out of nowhere, stopping them both. "Eira, may I speak with you a moment?"

"I..." Her uncle's face had become the face of betrayal, and it stung just to be in his presence.

"I'll leave you to it," Alyss said quickly, stepping away. Eira shot her a glare but Alyss was impervious to it. "You two should talk," Alyss insisted. It must be easy to insist such things when she got to retreat down the Tower.

Eira folded her arms. "Yes, Minister?"

"Eira, please, it's Uncle and you know it." He sighed. "Come, we have a bit of time before dinner. Let's speak in my office."

"I don't have anything to say to you."

The wounded look that crossed his face nearly set her off. How dare *he* get to look wounded after what he'd done to her?

"Please?"

"You're going to keep hounding me until I do, aren't you?"

"Yes."

"Fine, let's get this over with," she grumbled.

The march up the Tower was over all too quickly. Eira settled in the chair across from her uncle's desk, running her hands over the familiar, worn leather arms. Whatever comfort they might have once given her was gone.

Fritz sat heavily. His shoulders slumped and he folded and unfolded his hands several times.

"I owe you an apology," he said, finally.

"I think you owe me several," she snapped.

He rubbed his temples. "I'm just trying to help you. We all are."

"Stop using that excuse."

"It's not an excuse."

"You're not helping me, you're hurting me!" She gripped the arms of the chair with quivering hands. "Everyone in this whole family says they love me, but all they do is hold me back, cut me off at the knees whenever they can, and have no faith in me. You claim it's to help me...but I think you're just trying to make yourselves feel better."

"Eira." Fritz's voice raised a fraction, summoning her inner child and hushing her. "What you did today was reckless, and might endanger you for the rest of your life."

Now he believed she could hear voices. "Not everything I do endangers me."

"Think about what you just showed to the world." He slammed his palms onto his desk. "You showed that almost no secret is safe with you around. That not even secrets taken to the grave die because of these voices you hear."

Eira's back pressed into the chair as his words startled her. "I— That's not—"

"That is how every senator, every minister, every man and woman with aspirations saw your power to hear echoes." Fritz tapped his fingers into his desk with every word. "And they will either want you for their own now, or to see you eradicated, or worse."

"You're overreacting." Eira sank farther into the chair for stability.

"I'm not. None of us are. We're trying to keep you safe. You're a danger and—"

"I'm a danger?" she whispered.

"You— I didn't mean— Your magic— *In* danger—"

"I'm *a* danger." Eira repeated with a shake of her head. "You said exactly what you meant, Uncle."

"That was a slip of the tongue."

She stood. "I don't think it was."

"We're not done with this discussion." He rounded his desk as she started for the door.

"I was done with it before it began." Eira glared back at him. "Careful, Uncle, or I'll be done with you next."

Eira slammed the door as his face crumpled and started down the tower. Luckily, for her uncle's sake, he didn't follow her. With the way she felt, she'd have no problem telling him off for all the Tower to hear.

Wrenching the door to her room open, Eira saw a figure on the bed from the corner of her eye. Assuming it to be Alyss, she started right into her tirade. "I can't believe him, he really just—" Eira froze. Her eyes met Ferro's. "What're you doing here?" she whispered.

"I came to say congratulations." His words were as fluid as his movements when he stood. Eira had never been aware of how small her room was, or how close he stood. "I couldn't wait until tonight. I had to see you," he whispered breathlessly.

"What if someone sees you coming or going from my room?" she breathed. He was so agonizingly close.

"They won't. We'll be careful we're not discovered, just as we have been this whole time."

"Dinner will start soon... They'll wonder where I am."

Ferro slowly lifted his hand, fingertips trailing along her jaw to hook behind her ear. He had her in stasis with the lightest touch. The feeling of his breath, hot on her lips, had Eira's toes curling.

"I know, we don't have long. But will you come to me when I next summon you?"

"I will," she murmured, all too aware of how alone they were. What would he do if she kissed him? Would her affections be welcomed? Was his heart hammering against his chest as loudly as hers was?

"Good. I will try to make it as soon as I'm able." Ferro eased away and a low whine rose up in the back of her throat that Eira thought she strangled before he'd heard. But given the grin on his face, she was wrong. He reached into the pocket of his coat. "In the meantime, I have something for you."

Eira accepted the folded papers from his long, elegant fingers. "What is it?"

"The rough plans for the next trial."

"Am I allowed to have this?" she whispered.

"I'm the one who's planning the trial. Whomever I deem fit can see it."

Eira suspected that wasn't true. "Thank you," she said anyway.

"Thank you for your display today. It was truly a sight

to see. And for all you've done for me while I've been here.
I couldn't have designed this without you." He tapped the
papers lightly.

"It's been my pleasure."

"I assure you, the pleasure is all mine."

They stared at each other for a long moment. Her stomach
bubbled with effervescence. She felt like she wanted to say
something, or he wanted her to say something, or she *should*
say something, maybe all of them at once.

"I should—"

"I must go. But"—he caught her hand—"I cannot wait
until we are alone together again, my delicious secret."

"Neither can I," she whispered with a shiver.

Ferro brought her knuckles to his lips and slipped out of
her room, leaving her aching and wanting.

Banging on her door woke her the next morning. Between
her meetings with Deneya and Ferro at night, and her practicing
during the day, she had been burning the candle at both ends
for a week and it was finally catching up with her. She'd been
sleeping much more heavily than normal these past few days.
Blinking away the pleasant dreams she'd had following last
night's discussions with Ferro in their study, Eira got herself
upright.

"What?" she grumbled, swinging open the door.

"Really? That's how you greet someone bearing gifts?"

"It's too early, Cullen." She yawned.

"It's almost ten. It is certainly not early." He pushed himself
inside. "And if you don't start dressing now, you'll certainly
make us late for court."

Oh, that was today. Eira cursed under her breath. "Well,
get out then so I can get ready."

"Don't want me to help you with the laces?" He grinned.

"I don't want you to help me with anything involving my clothes, thank you very much. Out with you." She pushed him out the door, closing it with a smile. Since when had Cullen become someone she could laugh and joke with?

Maybe she was just in a good mood in general, these days. Anything was better than the complex and ugly feelings that the revelation had placed in her. And she clung to any distractions from thinking about her family. The dress Cullen had procured for her certainly further helped her mood.

Its long sleeves tapered to points over the backs of her hands, loops around her middle fingers holding them in place. The skirts were a bit looser this time, which afforded better movement. Though the top was more constricting and...

"Was the neckline really necessary?" Eira asked as she opened the door. With one hand she trailed her fingers down the V of the dress—just a bit more scandalous than she generally preferred.

Cullen leaned against the opposite wall in his formal clothes. He straightened at the sight of her. "It, uh—" He cleared his throat. "I'm told it's the upcoming fashion."

"I don't have the breasts to support this look." Eira adjusted the shoulders of the dress once more.

"You most certainly—" He stopped himself short. A scarlet blush streaked across his cheeks. Eira grinned. She hadn't been trying to set him up for embarrassment. But seeing Cullen squirm was too much of a delight to not enjoy. Perhaps the tension with Ferro was overflowing into a mix of more confidence and flirtatiousness than Eira had ever possessed. "You look great once more. Shall we?"

"I don't have anywhere else to be." Eira hooked her arm with his. "I'm yours for the next few hours."

He glanced at her from the corner of his eye, expression unreadable and in distinct contrast to the smile quirking his lips. "Thank you again for doing this. I couldn't go alone today."

"Why not?" Eira followed him into the same passage as

before, heading toward the main part of the palace.

"Because of who will be there."

"Who will be there?" He didn't answer and Eira stopped, holding him in place. "I'm fine to do this, Cullen. But you need to be honest with me. Is it someone I should worry about?" Because if this person made Cullen nervous then Eira certainly felt like she should be as well.

"No, no. You'll be fine. It's..." He trailed off, unable to meet her eyes when he spoke next. "My father will be there today with his wife." *With his wife—not "my mother."* "I hate it when he's there. Doubly so when she is."

"Then we'll keep you distracted." Eira squeezed his arm lightly and Cullen gave her a clearly skeptical smile.

Entering the court a second time was a role reversal of the first. Eira, even though she wasn't experienced in this world at all, was fairly calm. At least today there wouldn't be any sneaking around. And when it came to family issues, well... she was swiftly becoming an expert in those types of messes.

Cullen, however, was tense from the moment they crossed the threshold. The muscles in his jaw bulged. His eyes darted around, scanning every corner as if he were walking into a battlefield and not a fancy hall.

"He's not here yet," Cullen murmured. "Mother bless, hopefully something came up with the senate."

"Your father is a senator, right?" Eria asked. The senate always made her prickle since the incident. She could still feel their eyes on her, *judging her*, awaiting their verdict...

"Yes. Before that he served on the Eastern Council." The origins of the senate stemmed from the East—formerly Cyven. When the first Emperor Solaris took over the East, he adopted the senate. It was intended to be a bridge between the emperor and the people as well as to handle minor affairs of state with the emperor having the final say. Really, Eira just saw it as a platitude with little real power.

An opinion she usually kept to herself.

"Can we go look at the painting of Risen again?" Eira

suggested.

"I'd love to."

As they started over, they were interrupted by a familiar woman, still bedazzled with western rubies. "Lord Cullen, you brought your *friend* again today. Airra, was it?"

"Eira," she corrected. "AYE-ruh."

"Yes, of course." Lady Allora scrunched her nose slightly. Eira got the impression that she wasn't accustomed to being corrected so brazenly. Allora turned her attention back to Cullen. "Are you and *Eira* an official item?"

"Eira is a good friend, and one of the eight remaining Waterrunner candidates to be a competitor in the Tournament of Five Kingdoms," Cullen said with what Eira would dare say was a defensive note.

"I can see that." Allora took note of the pin on Eira's breast. "If you are chosen, I do hope you'll do your best to support Cullen in his glory."

"I'll do what I can." Eira smiled thinly. As if Cullen's glory was the only thing she and the other candidates were focusing on.

"Please excuse us," Cullen said stiffly, pulling Eira away. His usual grace was lacking today. No doubt due to stress.

"It'll be all right." Eira squeezed his arm lightly.

"I know; I really can't stand her sometimes," he murmured. "And I don't have the patience for it today."

Eira laughed softly.

"What?"

"You surprise me is all, Cullen. You're not the man I thought you were."

"That's mutual," he said softly. "You've surprised me countless times."

They came to a stop before the painting. Once more, the rest of the court was content to ignore the art, leaving them alone. Eira stayed focused on the canvas. But Cullen's eyes were on her. She pretended not to notice. She wasn't sure if he had intended for her to realize it or not.

Eventually, the tension became too much for her. "She likes you, you know."

"What?" Cullen seemed startled.

"Allora. She's interested in courting you."

He grimaced. "I know."

"You're not totally dense? Surprising for a man."

Cullen actually chuckled. "That's a fair assessment I suppose."

"You...don't return her affections?" Eira met his eyes.

"I thought I did once, but..."

"But?"

"She's the type of woman my father would want me to marry—that he tried to *force me* to marry." A dark shadow crossed Cullen's expression. "He claimed it'd further secure our position in society. That I have to because..."

"Because?" Eira pressed. He kept stopping himself right before saying what felt like the most important part.

"It's nothing." Cullen shook his head, retreating from the topic. Eira bit back a sigh, but didn't persist. His secrets were his own and the echo of his worried voice was still in her ears.

"Your father seems like a man who is ambitious."

"An understatement. He's—" Cullen stopped, glancing over his shoulder at a commotion.

A group of people collected by the door. A man was at their center, a spitting image of what Eira imagined Cullen would be in twenty to thirty years. His dark brown hair was salted and carefully coiffed back in a mirror of how the emperor wore his hair. Across his chest was the sash of a senator.

At his side was a woman with short, blonde hair. She wore it half pulled back, pinned with a feathered and bejeweled clip. She had the body of a dancer and the eyes of a scholar.

"He's here," Cullen finished with a grimace. "Let's keep looking at the painting."

"Shouldn't we go and say hello?" Eira asked. Cullen gave a light tug of his arm, drawing her attention forward.

"I'd rather my father come over here and meet me on my

terms."

"I'll follow your lead," Eira reassured him.

Sure enough, they only had to wait a few minutes before the senator approached. Eira was surprised to see his dark brown eyes—nothing like Cullen's bright amber. That must have been a trait he inherited from his birth mother.

"My son, it's good to see you."

"You as well, Father." Cullen gave a bow of his head. It felt as though he was greeting a stranger and not his family. He turned and greeted the woman with a stiff, "Lady Patrice."

"Hello, Cullen," Patrice said warmly. "Who is your guest today? Another candidate, I see."

"I'm Eira Landan." Eira bowed her head as Cullen had.

"Ah, Miss Landan..." Cullen's father's eyes narrowed slightly as his words trailed off. "I thought your name was familiar during the third trial."

Eira's eyes widened slightly. Her day in court following the incident three years ago was fresh in her mind, sharpening despite time. This man's face put her right back into the shoes of that girl, afraid and awaiting judgment.

"It is you, isn't it? The girl who murdered her peers."

"I... I didn't..."

"Father," Cullen said sharply. "That's not appropriate conversation for court."

"Of course not." He chuckled, but there was a sinister note to it. "You might not remember me, but I led the senate investigation on the murder of a Tower apprentice."

I didn't murder anyone, she wanted to scream. She'd killed them by accident. There was a difference. There had to be.

"Father!" Cullen's biceps tensed, drawing Eira slightly closer. "I think what my father is trying to say, is that his name is Yemir Drowel."

Yemir. Yes...she knew that name. She'd just made herself forget it. Like so much else she'd tried to wish away. Eira felt cold in the worst of ways.

"It's a good thing we didn't lock you away. After the

display of your talent, it would be a shame for the world to lose that."

"Thank you for the compliment," Eira mumbled, mostly because she felt like she had to, and immediately hated herself for expressing gratitude to a man who was making her viciously uncomfortable.

"Have you ever considered becoming an aide to a senator? I could think of a few uses for a young woman with your skills. Perhaps you could think of it as gratitude for what I did for you back then."

You tried to lock me away, Eira wanted to say. If Fritz hadn't stepped in…

"Eira is focused on the trials at present," Cullen said briskly. "She doesn't have time to become an aide to you or anyone else."

"Think about it is all I ask." Yemir shifted his focus to his son. Eira bit back a sigh of relief. "I thought you and I might take a walk about the gardens. It's been a while since we caught up, just you and I."

"I wouldn't like to leave Eira alone since she is new to court."

"I would be happy to keep her company." Patrice stepped to Eira's free side, scooping up her hand and patting the back. "I shall introduce you to my friends."

"Good, that's settled," Yemir declared. "Come along, Cullen."

Eira thought the muscles in Cullen's jaw would rupture from how tense they were. But he ultimately didn't speak any objection, leaving her behind and going off with his father. Oddly, Eira was far more worried about Cullen than she was for herself. Now that she realized who Yemir was, she didn't want to leave anyone alone with him.

"So, Eira." Patrice placed Eira's hand in her elbow, beginning to stroll. "Tell me what your intentions are with my son."

"Excuse me?"

"Cullen is a handsome young man and one of the most eligible bachelors in Solarin." She spoke with an easy smile, as though the fact was known by everyone far and wide. Eira, in fact, had not known it. But she never really had concerned herself with the power plays of nobles. That had always been more of Marcus's aspiration. "He's been hand-trained by the empress and is within her inner circle. He's a lord, the son of a senator, and is likely to be a senator—if not Head of Senate—one day. Not to mention, he is also a viable candidate for Minister of Sorcery."

"My uncle is the Minister of Sorcery," Eira said flatly.

"Oh, how charming! Well then you know how prestigious a minister position is."

"I suppose."

"You seem like a smart girl, so I'm sure you can realize that Cullen must remain focused on his future. And that extends to who he surrounds himself with, if you follow."

Cullen's mention of Allora was forefront in Eira's mind. "You're talking about who he courts, or marries."

"You're so bold. So refreshing for court." Patrice tittered as they turned the corner. "Yes, you're right, I am. So, dear, you must understand that you simply cannot get any ideas. Yemir and I have Cullen's best interests in mind, and he needs to marry of a particular station." *Which you are not*, hovered in the air, unsaid.

"Cullen is my friend," Eira said flatly. "I'm not interested in him in any other way."

"Good. We have an understanding then."

They passed the open doors to court and, from the corners of her eyes, Eira saw Cullen storming off toward the castle. She stopped. "I have to go."

"Pardon?"

"Excuse me. And, uh, it was lovely to talk with you." Eira gave a nod of her head and hiked her skirts before starting down the gravel paths of the gardens. On her way to where Cullen had run off to, she passed by Yemir. He cast her a wary glance, one Eira returned.

There would never be friendliness between them. Eira was certain of that.

A whisper in a familiar voice had her slowing to a stop. She glanced between a nearby bench and where Cullen had gone off to. She shouldn't eavesdrop, even after the fact, but...

Eira looked to the bench, reaching out with her magic. If it didn't snag on anything, she'd go. But if it did—

You're being unreasonable. Cullen's voice resonated through the tether.

The girl is a political liability at best and outright dangerous at worst. Yemir was talking about her.

She's neither of those things.

She can find out about you, us, your past.

Maybe we should stop trying to hide it?

What you suggest goes against the empress's wishes and the good of Windwalkers everywhere, Yemir snapped. *Stop this insistence otherwise and do as I say. We will find you a suitable wife and you will marry on your return as the victor of the tournament. The city will be so enraptured with you that it will be the perfect time to make your bid for the senate. Your life has a plan.*

I don't want your plan, Father.

I'm only looking out for your best interests.

What if I want to decide, just once, what my best interests are? So much pain lived in Cullen's question. Pain Eira could share keenly.

You are a child. *You can't be trusted to know what that is. Cut your ties with her and proceed as we planned—her brother will be your Waterrunner counterpart. Let me handle her. She's more of a liability than you know.*

And if I don't do as you ask? Cullen dared to ask.

Don't test me, son.

The sensation of eyes staring at her drew Eira back to the present. She looked over her shoulder, back toward the court, to see Yemir and Patrice staring her down. She knew how she must've looked, focused intently on the bench. Eira swallowed her discomfort and continued on after Cullen, her head held high—even though it felt as though they were trying to cut her down with every step.

Once inside, she didn't have to look far to find Cullen. He sat, hunched, on a bench framed by two suits of armor. He didn't even look up to confirm it was her as Eira sat next to him.

"I know," he said softly. Eira had never heard him sound so vulnerable. "I know, you will tell me to be grateful that I know who my parents are. That I didn't have them keep a profound secret from me. That what I'm enduring isn't that bad."

"I wasn't going to say anything of the like," Eira said, equally softly. "What did you tell me that day? I'm not the only one with family problems?"

He gave a raspy chuckle. "I shouldn't have dragged you into it. I fear I might have made things worse for you. My father is not a *bad* man…but he can be misguided in how he determines the path forward, especially when it comes to me."

"I can handle myself."

"So you're proving." Cullen finally looked at her. "Thank you, Eira. Having you here today…" He rested his hand on hers. His fingers curled around her palm. "I find your presence calming. As if, out of everyone, I've finally found the one person I can trust. The one person who might understand."

Eira stared at his hand holding hers. She had to fight the urge to take his fingers. "I want you to trust me," she admitted to both herself and him in that moment. "But you can't, if I'm not completely honest with you."

"What are you talking about?"

"I heard." Eira slowly dragged her eyes from his hand, up his arm, to his face. "I heard the traces of your conversation with your father." His eyes widened. "And before that I heard a whisper of you in the Windwalkers' study."

"You…you were spying on me?" he breathed.

"No, not at all!"

"Did someone put you up to it?" His grip tightened around hers, popping her knuckles. "Was it to take me down? Or my father?"

"The first time was an accident. Just now…well, I listened. But only for a little." Cullen stood, as though she'd burned him. "Cullen, please, I was worried about you was all. Given how you and your father looked…"

"What do you know?" He refused to look at her when he posed his question.

"That you have a secret. That's all. I have no idea what it is," Eira said reassuringly.

"It's only a matter of time until you do," he murmured. "My father was right." Nothing could've prepared her for how deeply those words wounded. "With that gift—that *curse* of yours, no one is safe." Cullen looked over his shoulder with a wary stare. In one expression he encompassed the voice of everyone who had teased, belittled, or hurt her over the years.

Her uncle had been right about how others would see her magic. And she hated him even more for it. She hated the whole world in that moment.

"Sometimes, I just hear things." Eira stood, stepping toward him as he walked away. "I don't mean to. Usually I try and stop it but—"

"Don't follow me." Cullen's voice was a stranger's. No, she knew it. It was the voice of the indifferent apprentice, the Prince of the Tower, lording above her once more. Distant and unreachable. "I'm done with you. Your powers…*you're* too dangerous." Cullen started down the hall.

"Cullen, wait!"

But he was too far gone. There was no way he'd turn around now, no matter how hard she willed it. Eira stared at his back, her chest knotting painfully. She wanted to tell herself that it didn't matter. That *Cullen* didn't matter. But perhaps he hadn't been alone in finding someone to trust…

Eira had never cared about Cullen before. But, somehow, now the idea of losing him—of yet another person abandoning

her—was more than she could bear.

ALYSS SAT IN the chair of the tiny desk that was wedged against the armoire in Eira's room. Her feet were propped on the desktop, crossed, as she balanced on the back two legs of her chair. It was a wonder she didn't fall over, given how transfixed she was on the latest printing of her favorite romance author. The book was perched on her knees as she furiously squished and molded clay, too distracted to make any concrete shapes.

Eira listlessly flipped through the pages of the Lightspinning book Mister Levit had given her. She'd read all the pages, multiple times, but she was now looking for a way to counter Deneya. She still had yet to break the stupid shield.

At least, that's what she told herself she was doing.

Her focus oscillated between the writing and the dark world outside. It looked like a blizzard was approaching the mountainside. But Eira's thoughts stretched beyond the horizon.

They landed first on Cullen. She'd yet to see him again since court three days ago. His eyes, however, lingered with her. They had even chased her into her dreams.

The only thing that could free her thoughts from them was Ferro. She had been seeing him almost nightly now. But he had warned her that with the trial fast approaching, he wouldn't have as much time to spend with her.

Eira felt torn between the two with emotions she'd never felt before. Both were men she shouldn't even be thinking of—shouldn't even have known. Yet fate had designed to place them both in her life at the same time.

"I can't focus on my book *or* my clay; you're being too

noisy," Alyss muttered.

"What?" Eira was jolted back to her gray Tower room. "I'm not doing anything."

"Your thoughts are loud."

"Thoughts aren't loud."

"Yours are, when someone knows you as well as I do." Alyss carefully slid her leather bookmark into her page and set the novel on the desk. She spun the chair to face Eira but her focus was now on making the blob of clay actually resemble something. "Tell me."

"Tell you what?"

"What's on your mind, since you already said you won't tell me why you summoned me until Marcus arrives."

"It's nothing," Eira murmured.

"Oh, Mother, why do you even try and lie to me?" Alyss rolled her eyes. "It's not that room, is it?"

"No, it's not." Guilt swam through Eira's tides. She hated lying to Alyss. But something about her meetings with Deneya seemed even more secret than her meetings with Ferro. "I... I have been seeing someone."

"*Obviously.*" Alyss threw her hands in the air. "I've been waiting for you to tell me the details."

"What do you mean '*obviously*'?"

"You haven't been hanging out with me as much. You're up late. You seem distracted. You have all the hallmarks of a heroine pining for her secret lover by day."

"I am not a heroine and I *do not* have a secret lover."

"Then who have you been 'seeing'?" Alyss folded her arms over her chest.

"You wouldn't believe me if I told you."

"Try me."

"Ambassador Ferro." The confession came out as a rush of air.

Alyss blinked, several times, and then a slow, eager grin crept across her cheeks. This bit of news had Alyss setting down her clay. "No," she gasped. "Tell me *everything*."

Eira did. She told Alyss of the first mysterious letter. The study that had quickly become "theirs." She told her of the burning western liquor Ferro had shared with her on their last meeting and of the comfort he'd given her following the revelation.

"You have an elfin lover." Alyss gaped with shock. Then she quickly clapped, bouncing in her chair. "You have an elfin lover!"

"Not so loud! And I do not."

"You're meeting at night. There's clandestine letters mysteriously left. He's incredibly handsome. You're obviously hopelessly smitten with him." Alyss counted on her fingers. "Own up, you have an elfin lover."

"We haven't even kissed! I think lovers would do that."

"But you have had romantic fireside chats. The kissing should come easy. Get to working on it!"

Eira groaned and face-planted into her bed. "I couldn't. I don't even know how old he is. He's elfin. He could be eighty for all I know."

"He seems young to me."

"They're a race that looks young until they're, like, a hundred. And then they only look slightly *less* young."

Alyss considered this a moment. "All right, fair. You're right. It's a lot sexier in books than when it's actually your friend being courted by an ageless creature. So figure out his age and *then* kiss him if it's not creepy."

"You're not helping!"

Eira was saved by a knock on her door. She bounced up, opening it to reveal Marcus.

"Sorry I'm late." He stepped inside. The room was cramped with three people, so Eira quickly returned to the bed. "What's with all the secrecy?"

"I have something I want to share with you both." Eira flipped to the back of her book where she'd been hiding Ferro's papers.

"Are you going to tell him?" Alyss gasped.

"Tell me what?" Marcus looked between them.

"Stop." Eira glared at her friend. "This is serious."

"I know!" Alyss looked to Marcus. "She has been seeing someone."

"Alyss!"

"Cullen told me," Marcus said, the words guarded.

Eira's blood ran cold. What had Cullen said? Was he still thinking of her like she was of him?

"Wait a minute. You didn't say anything about *Cullen*." Alyss had an expression of horror and delight. "Two? Tell me more!"

"Can we please focus?" Eira groaned. Before her brother or Alyss could say another word, Eira handed them each a sheet of paper. Their expressions quickly turned serious.

"This is…" Marcus murmured, stepping to read over Alyss's shoulder. The two compared papers and Eira handed them the third. Marcus's eyes turned up to hers. "How do you have these?"

"I can't say." Eira glanced askance. Then quickly added, "But I didn't do anything that would get me in trouble."

"Did he give them—"

"*Shhh,*" Eira made the noise with a finger against her lips and a glare at Alyss.

Alyss had the audacity to laugh.

"Who's *he*?"

"No one," Eira said quickly to Marcus, before Alyss could get a word in. "Can we focus, please? These are the notes on our next trial. They're going to blindfold us and fill our ears with cotton. We'll be taken out into the wilds surrounding Solarin and have to use our magic and wits to find our way back."

"But what are these?" Alyss pointed to various markers on the map.

"They're going to be challenges that stand in our way. Either traps laid, or actual sorcerers who will try and impede our progress."

"So with this we can prepare for the challenges." Marcus stroked his chin, exchanging pages again with Alyss.

"Somewhat… We aren't going to be allowed to take anything with us. You know how guarded they're keeping this trial. If we go in with supplies, they're going to know we had an edge."

"Then we each train in a different area of survival for the next few days."

"No, we're all going to be dropped in different spots," Eira said. "We won't go in as a group."

"The more you explain this trial, the more it seems… dangerous." Marcus frowned.

"It's only the illusion of danger, like the second trial." Eira couldn't help the defensive edge in her voice. Ferro had designed the final two trials.

"They're putting people as young as fifteen out in the wilds alone."

"If there are sorcerers out there to give us challenges along the way then I'm sure we'll be watched every step," Eira countered.

Marcus just shrugged. Alyss gave her a sly smile. Her friend had figured out why she was defensive.

"At least this way we can see the paths of least resistance back." Alyss brought a page close to her face, narrowing her eyes. "Now, if only my sense of direction wasn't so terrible."

The three of them spent the rest of the night going over the pages. They made a brief excursion to the library to get some cartography books, followed shortly after by dinner. The clocks had chimed eleven when Alyss and Marcus finally bid their goodbyes. Eira didn't allow them to take the papers, so they vowed to go over everything again the next night.

Eira was exhausted, but she pulled herself from her bed and crept up the Tower. Moving in and out of Adela's secret chambers was second nature to her now. But every time she did, she always paused by the bookshelf, staring at the journals and wondering what other secrets they held that Eira had yet to see.

It was nearly midnight by the time she arrived in the long-forgotten royal passages.

"You're late." Deneya leaned against a wall, waiting. "I was about to give up on you."

"I'm glad you didn't. I thought we might do something else tonight?"

"Getting tired of the shield?" Deneya grinned. "What do you have in mind?"

"You seem capable of making more than a shield—like the dagger, from the first night we met."

"*Mysst soto larrk.*" Deneya raised her hand and threads of light collected into a dagger in her palm.

"Teach me how to use it." Eira raised her own hand, summoning a shard of ice.

Deneya tilted her head, arching her eyebrows. "Are you asking me to teach you how to fight?"

"You know how, don't you?"

"I do." Deneya chuckled. "Why do *you* want to know, is the real question."

"Teach me something I could use to defend myself against an attacker." Ferro had given Eira the tip that their final trial might pit the candidates against each other. She didn't know the first thing about dueling.

"You're not defending anything with a stance like that." Deneya looked Eira over from head to toe. She slowly approached. "If you want to learn combat, I'll teach you. But it'll be much harder than trying to break a shield."

"I'm ready."

"Are you?" Deneya chuckled. "I doubt it."

"I have to do this."

"Why?"

"Because I must go to Meru." Eira wasn't about to let anything stop her. "There are answers for me there, I can feel it."

"A bit of advice." Deneya paused, a step away from Eira.

Up close, the woman looked ten times stronger. The moonlight outlined the muscles of her shoulders and arms. She could easily hoist much heavier weapons than the dagger. "Be careful when you go hunting for the truth. It's rarely what you expect."

"I know that better than anyone."

"So you should heed my warning better than anyone." Deneya nodded. "Now, hit me."

"What?"

"Hit me. Though I warn you it'll only be a slightly less impossible task than breaking the shield."

Eira had always known the shield was impossible. But she'd tried anyway. She'd thrown herself against it night after night and hadn't realized why Deneya had put her through the exercise until that moment.

Her magic had been honed with each attempt. Every time she'd attacked the shield, she'd summoned more strength. By day, she'd thought of new techniques. Even if Deneya was giving her an insurmountable task, Eira was striving to new heights just trying to reach it.

Determined, emboldened, Eira threw her weight behind a jab. Deneya didn't even lift her dagger to parry. She dodged backward, sidestepped, turned, and, without so much as a whisper of air, was behind Eira. The sharp blade of Deneya's weapon pressed into her throat.

"Again," Deneya whispered.

So Eira moved once more.

Everything ached. Over the past week she'd sparred against Deneya every night. Tonight had been her last showing and far from her best. Deneya had sent her back to her room early and instructed her not to return the next night.

She needed a night to heal, Deneya had said. Otherwise

she had no hope of passing the trial in two days.

Eira was forced to agree. But she hated doing so. She felt like she had years of training to make up for—years of knowledge she was lacking. She had been a diligent student, but maybe not as diligent as she'd thought. The more she learned, the more the gaps in her knowledge were becoming apparent.

She opened the door to her room and stepped inside. Eira caught movement from the corner of her eye. Perhaps it was just having come from training with Deneya. Or perhaps she really had developed new instincts. Eira acted without thought.

A dagger of ice was in her palm—icepick grip. She twisted, thrusting backward.

"*Mysst xieh.*" Light sprung from the darkness, illuminating Ferro's face.

Eira let out a gasp, trying to stop her momentum. But it was too late. Her dagger bounced off his shield harmlessly.

Thankfully, she'd never figured out how to break them.

"Do you regularly take it upon yourself to attack people?" he asked, amused.

"I… I'm so sorry," Eira said in a rush. "I didn't realize it was you, it's late and—"

"It is late," he murmured. "Where were you?"

"I was doing some reading."

Ferro released the glyph from his palm, plunging them into darkness. Eira blinked several times, trying to force her eyes to adjust. He was a shadow, outlined in silver moonlight.

"I waited for you," Ferro whispered. There was a weight to him in the night. His shape had become something instinctual—a force felt more than seen.

"How did you get here?" she whispered in reply. Her back pressed against the door. His hand landed to the side of her face as he leaned over her.

"I followed the passages you told me about."

Oh, right, she had told him about the Tower's secret passages, hadn't she? It was hard to form cohesive thoughts with him standing so close. "Why are you here?"

"I wanted to wish you luck before you set off tomorrow."

"Thank you," she said, little more than a squeak. Her heart was thundering. His lips were struck silver by the moon and she could imagine Alyss screaming, *kiss him!*, in the back of her mind.

"You're welcome." His eyes were almost luminescent in the darkness and they bore into her. "I'll be watching you. I'll be looking for *you*."

"Ferro…"

"Eira?"

"How old are you?" she blurted.

He chuckled. "I'm twenty-four."

Six years older than her. Not twenty-six. Not sixty. *Six. A perfectly "not creepy" age gap,* Eira decided. "You're so young."

"I had motivation to ascend beyond my humble beginnings as fast as I could." She remembered him mentioning he was orphaned. "We're a lot alike in that way. The Tournament of Five Kingdoms means as much to me as it does to you."

"Why?" she whispered.

It was as if she broke him from a trance. Ferro blinked several times, staring at her. The shock faded into tenderness. He cupped her cheek. "Because it brought me to you."

Ferro leaned forward and pressed his lips gently to hers. Her whole body tingled, from the top down. She shivered, shifting closer to him, wanting more. But all too soon, he pulled away, giving her nothing but a chaste peck.

"Ferro—"

"Consider that your good luck charm." He smirked lazily. "Keep us—everything about our interactions—a secret for just a bit longer and then you'll be headed to Meru with me as a competitor."

Before Eira could even think of a response, he was gone. He'd disappeared into the night faster than a pleasant dream. The only proof Eira hadn't fabricated the whole encounter was

the pent-up energy threatening to explode from her every pore and the tingling of her lips.

SEVENTEEN SORCERERS STOOD in a spot usually reserved for royalty. They lined up on the Sunlit Stage in three groups—eight Waterrunners, three Groundbreakers, and six Firebearers. The amassed crowd cheered and chanted. They waved pennons emblazoned with the symbols for water, earth, and fire. Fever for the trials had spread and was reaching its climax.

Eira stared blinking in the morning light and frantically scanning the crowd for her parents. Thankfully, they hadn't come. The other candidates smiled and waved. They made proclamations of victory to the crowd.

The emperor and empress made a series of announcements, wished them all luck, and discussed more about the tournament. Ferro stood beside them. He, too, addressed the crowd.

The people of Solaris fell to a hush as he spoke. Eira could hear their whispers and see their shifting gazes. Solaris might have grown to love the notion of the trials happening in their own lands, but the idea of sending competitors across the sea to Meru still gave them pause.

When the announcements were over, the candidates were escorted in groups of six, six, and five to wagons waiting in the center of the lower area. Each wagon had one Groundbreaker, two Firebearers, and three or two Waterrunners.

A palace guard handed out cotton, instructing them to place it in their ears. Eira was all too happy to oblige and drown out the deafening noise of the crowd. But her other candidates seemed a little skeptical about what was to come. They hadn't been afforded the same level of detail about what to expect—

an edge that would benefit her.

The next guard that came around bound strips of fabric around their heads. The cloth held the cotton in place and covered their eyes. Around and around they wound the blindfold until the world was completely dark, save for pops of light behind Eira's eyes from the pressure.

She placed her hands under her thighs to keep herself from touching the blindfold. At any time she could take it off. It wasn't tied with a knot she couldn't undo. But to remove it was to forfeit.

Right before the cart lurched forward, there was a commotion. Eira could make out hazy noise, but she couldn't tell what had transpired. Her shoulder brushed against the people next to her as the wagon jostled down the road. She didn't even know who she was rocking against. She hadn't paid attention to who was in the wagon with her. It could be Alyss and Marcus as easily as anyone else.

This trial is you against yourself; it is a test of survival, Ferro had said. *We will send you all out and you must find your way back. The fastest will progress on.*

As the cart continued to rock and rumble down the mountainside, Eira shifted her hands, folding them in her lap. She wasn't going to touch her blindfold no matter how much of a headache it gave her. Instead, she focused on Ferro and their encounter the night before. She would fight to make it back to him.

And when I return, I will be the one to kiss him, Eira vowed to herself.

The cart made its first stop. The boards creaked underfoot, sagging as one of the candidates was removed. Silence, followed by the cart jostling once more.

Eira was the fifth person let off out of six. The guard tapped her shoulders and held her hands as he helped her off the cart. He tapped her shoulder twice and she heard the faint groan of the cart through the cotton of her ears.

Two taps, count to one hundred, they'd instructed. Eira

wasn't sure how they'd know if she counted to one hundred or sixty, but she did one hundred anyway before removing her blindfold.

The world was blinding. A thick sheet of white carpeted the tundra from the mountain blizzard days ago. The wind howled down from the mountaintops that surrounded her.

Eira turned in place, trying to get her bearings. The cart tracks did a few turns on themselves around her, no doubt trying to trick her. The sun was high in the sky by now. Too high to tell with confidence which way was east or west.

Fortunately, the trees were thin here. Eira summoned a small pole of ice in the snow and she marked where its shadow fell. While she waited, Eira paced, continuing to assess her options. She was in a small valley up on a ridge. Above and below her, the forest thickened. Given the altitude, she was either east or west of Solarin—closer to Oparium or Rivend. Eira was familiar with those two places...but she didn't recognize where she was now in the slightest.

After fifteen minutes, Eira made a second line, assessing its difference from the first. The shadow had moved in a clockwise direction and the two lines helped create her compass rose. At least...it should, according to the book on survival tactics Alyss had found in the Imperial Library.

Eira stared at the cart tracks. There was a notable pile of snow by a deeper rut—likely where the cart had come to a stop. This meant that the cart had entered from the east. So she surmised she was closer to Rivend and Solarin should be back...

"In that direction, right? What do you think?" Eira murmured to the howling wind. It pushed on her back, as if encouraging her to the west, south-west. "Yes, that way? Let's make sure."

Eira lifted her hands slowly, feeling her magic swell. She swept them across her body and her power surged. A tide of water was summoned from thin air at her command, freezing in place against the ridge rising at what she suspected was her south. Stairs formed in the ice and Eira made her way up.

As she walked, she twirled her hands around each other. Eira imagined herself as a Lightspinner, unraveling invisible strands of power that condensed in front of her feet as she rose higher and higher above the trees. At the top of her staircase to nowhere, Eira came to a stop, coating her feet in ice to her calves so she wouldn't fall.

Raising a hand to her brow, Eira squinted into the horizon. The snow and ice from the blizzard was blindingly reflective. But in the distance... *Was that smoke, or a cloud?* Smoke, it had to be.

Turning, Eira freed herself from the ice and raced down the stairs. Magic crackled around her, following her every step. Cold and quiet were welcome companions. The rustling of the trees were the only sounds she heard. Forests rarely had unintentional vessels to whisper at her.

Eira inhaled deeply. The air tasted like freedom. Her magic was alive here—*she* was alive here. She was untethered from the world. She was alone and the fact thrilled her rather than filled her with fear. This frozen landscape couldn't hurt her if it tried.

After about two hours of what was otherwise a pleasant hike, it did try.

The world had grown still, the air holding its breath. There was a low *whoosh* sound, like the earth itself let out a soft groan. It was followed by a rumble, almost like thunder on the horizon. But it was too early for the lightning storms that plagued the South in summer.

No...this was a different and terrible sound that Eira knew as well as the terror that followed it in her bones.

She spun, looking up at the ridges and mountaintops around her. A fraction of movement caught her eye. A sheet of snow was breaking off, sliding down the mountainside. An element of the trial or bad timing? Either way, she had to act *now*.

The snow and ice was already racing toward her, sweeping up the mountainside. There was no way she could confidently outrun it. She'd have to brace for it.

Eira planted both her feet, facing the impending avalanche. Holding her arms out wide, Eria spun her power around her. A cocoon of ice began wrapping in arcs supported by thick beams. She anchored it to the sturdiest trees nearby. If the avalanche was going to take her down, it'd have to take down three large pines with her.

The ice was a deep blue, the shade of the ancient glaciers and equally strong. It would hold because this survival technique was one of the first things her uncle had taught her and Marcus when he'd found out about their abilities.

Which was why Eira didn't miss the flash of magic up the mountain from her. Ice shot up like petals wrapping together into a bud with a point at its top. That was Marcus's framework. She knew for certain it was even if she couldn't get a good look before the rush of snow consumed the distant cocoon and her own ice closed around her.

Eira closed her eyes and took a deep breath. Either it was Marcus, and he'd be fine, or it was another candidate who didn't have the ability to defend themselves in time and Fritz or Grahm was protecting them at the last minute. She'd find out later. For now, she needed to keep her focus on herself.

The walls of her ice fortress were so thick that when the avalanche reached her it was little more than a dull thud. She could hear the groan of snow, ice, and debris rushing around her. But Eira remained safe and insulated, waiting until the sounds had vanished and the world was still.

She walked up a spiral stair of her making, leaving through a small skylight she opened in the top of her bunker. The mountainside was washed away with a slough of snow. Eira squinted up it, looking to where she'd seen the magic spark.

Whoever it was would be all right. She'd already run the calculations in her mind. There was only the illusion of danger in the trials…nothing real.

She needed to worry about herself and keep going.

Eira turned, starting in the direction of Solarin, her magic shoring up her footing. But her feet stopped, refusing to move another step. Her gaze swung back to that distant point—at least, where she thought she remembered seeing the magic.

"Come on," Eira murmured. She had to keep going. There were still eight Waterrunners in the competition and two were being cut. She had to be one of the first six to make it back.

Though…if she was the first or the sixth, it made no difference.

"Come on," she repeated, louder.

Still, there was no movement in the snow.

Worry got the better of her. Eira raced up the mountainside, the snow and frost meeting her feet to support her sprint. She was over a third of the way there when she saw a spark of magic erupt through the snow like a frozen volcano.

Eira pressed on anyway. She wouldn't leave until she made sure the other person was all right. Perhaps the avalanche wasn't part of the trial and was merely a freak accident. If that was the case, someone might have been actually hurt. The proctors hiding in the forest might not have eyes on her and whoever this person was.

She was over halfway when she saw someone, *finally*, emerge from the snow. Eira ran faster and forced her eyes to focus on the individual. She'd know that silhouette anywhere.

"Marcus, you ass!" Eira shouted, her voice echoing across the snow. He spun, dazed, before his eyes landed on her.

"Eira?" he called back. "Wait there." Marcus leapt in the air. When he landed, two strips of ice were underneath his feet, thin and strong; he skied down the mountainside to her. "What're you doing here? Did you get caught in it too?"

"Yes, farther down… I saw your magic but you took forever to surface. I was worried."

"I was pretty deep under. I tunneled slowly to make sure I didn't get buried the moment I opened the shell." His eyes scanned the track of the avalanche. "Do you think there was anyone else trapped in it?"

"Not that I saw." Eira followed his gaze. "But I can't be certain there wasn't someone farther down from where I was."

"I'm sure they're all right. After all, the illusion of danger, right?"

"Yeah...assuming this was part of the trial."

Marcus laughed. "I can imagine Uncle Fritz perched on a mountaintop delighting in messing with us all. I'm sure it's fine." He clasped a hand on her shoulder. "Now, we should go."

"We're supposed to do this alone. The point is to survive on our own," Eira said as he moved to set out once more.

"No one should have to survive alone. The first step to survival is trying to find someone to do it with. It's too unbearable otherwise."

"You explain that to them when they're trying to disqualify us," Eira murmured, the wound of Fritz's attempt still lingering.

"You were the one to help me first." His hand was heavy on her shoulder. "Why did you?"

"I was worried you were trapped under the snow."

"Not that... You helped Cullen find out about the second trial when I couldn't."

"You asked me to." Eira glanced away, knowing where this was going. She didn't expect to have this conversation here, *now*.

"You could've said no. I basically asked you to cheat."

"You didn't 'basically' ask me, you *did* ask me to cheat." Eira rolled her eyes and Marcus gave a sheepish grin. "Plus, I cheated on my own later."

"Yet you shared that advantage with me. Alyss I get you telling your insider information because she's your best friend *and* she can't take your spot as a final competitor. But I can. You want to win, don't you?"

"More than anything." Eira looked at him fiercely. "At first, I just wanted to show you that I could take care of myself. But then I...I wanted it for *me*. I wanted it because I thought I could win and deserved to. Then when I found out—when Mother and Father told me—well, you know...I think there may be a clue as to who my birth parents really are on Meru."

"And you want to know?" he asked.

"I think so." Eira shook her head. "It's all a bit confusing still. I don't know yet if I can live with not knowing... But even if I find I can, Meru calls to me in a way nothing else has before. I wanted to go before I found out all that and I still want to go now. I know that want is mine."

"If you want all that so badly, why help me?"

"Because, as far as I saw it, you have been my only competition from the beginning. You and I had to stay on a level field. Otherwise, I couldn't feel like I earned my spot. I wanted to beat you fairly."

He chuckled and pulled her close. Eira gave her brother a tight squeeze. "I don't deserve a sister like you."

"No, you don't," she teased.

He laughed softly, not releasing her. "I should tell you something. I should have told you a while ago but I didn't... because I'm not as strong as you, apparently."

"What is it?"

"Why I didn't graduate the Tower." He straightened and looked her in the eye. "It was because Fritz knew the tournament was coming. He wanted to keep me close, where he could train me and prepare me for it. He also thought I'd be a more compelling candidate if I were an apprentice still. So, yes, I was looking out for you, too. But it wasn't always about you, Eira."

Her smile was bitter. The confession gave new clarity to what she'd heard in the library months ago when he'd been speaking with Cullen.

"Thanks for telling me," Eira said softly. "I guess you were always the one destined to win this."

"We'll see. Destiny isn't written by mortal hands."

"Isn't that the truth?" Eira looked out over the snowy slopes and forests, back toward Solarin. "You know I'm still going to fight for it, right?"

"I'm counting on it."

"Good." She gave him a small smile.

"Then let's fight for it together; let's make sure it's you

and me at the very end." He patted her shoulder. "I've felt the same. You were my only competition from the start."

"Really?" The wind nearly washed out her word. He'd seen *her* as his *only* competition? That meant Marcus had seen her as his equal or better? Her perfect brother that she'd held on a high pedestal for years thinking she could never reach him...all along they'd been standing together.

"Yes, really." He nodded. "So, let's go back, you and I. We'll overcome this fourth trial and get to Solarin together. And then, we'll fight it out at the very end. Let the best Landan sibling win."

Eira beamed. "I wouldn't have it any other way."

THEY HADN'T BEEN skiing for a good month or two. Springtime brought the best snowfall to the mountains, but getting out to the slopes was tedious and the clinics had kept them busy this year. Eira hadn't realized how much she'd missed it until now.

Racing down the mountainside, swerving back and forth around each other, Eira couldn't stop smiling. The wind tangled in her hair like a lover, threatening to loose the ties on her braids and knot it hopelessly. Her traveling clothes—carefully chosen to be mobile for the trial—were plastered against her skin by snow and speed.

It felt as if she were speeding toward her destiny—racing to a land of infinite possibility that was now suddenly in reach. She traded grins with Marcus as she went on ahead. They'd stop soon. The tree line was looming. But for now, she'd go as fast as she could. She'd fly.

She crossed the first tree and twisted to the side, digging in with the sides of her ice skis and magic until she slowed to a stop. When Eira straightened, the ice was gone and Marcus came to a stop as well. They stared, breathless and grinning, before bursting out laughing.

"You've been sneaking out to the mountains without me."

"I have not!"

"You've never been that fast."

Eira shrugged, starting through the snow into the forest. "I've always been faster than you, though."

"But not *that* fast. What's your secret?" He approached wriggling his fingers.

"If you even try and tickle me I swear I will freeze you to your marrow." Eira shot him a glare. He roared with laughter.

"The last time I tickled you was before you were even a Tower apprentice."

"Let's keep it that way, shall we?" Eira regarded his hands warily before continuing to walk. "And the trick is to use your magic to smooth out the snow in front of you. Less resistance means you go faster."

"See, you are brilliant." Marcus swept a hand through his hair, shaking frost from it.

"I always knew it; you were the one who had to catch up." What she said was a lie. She hadn't always known it. Maybe part of her had. But the other part of her was so good at doubting herself that it had been able to speak the loudest words in her mind for years.

"I'm glad you knew—know it." Marcus slung his arm around her shoulders.

"Don't get sappy on me." She pushed him away. "And you're too heavy; I can't walk like that."

"Fine, fine."

They continued making conversation for the rest of the day as they trudged through the woods. Eventually, they came to a small game trail that Marcus swore he recognized from one of his maps as a hunter's thoroughfare from Solarin to Rivend. After only a brief discussion, Eira agreed to let him lead them, insisting it was a shortcut.

The sun was now hanging low in the western sky. So they knew for certain they were heading eastward. If Eira was right, they were headed to Solarin. If she'd been wrong about her initial placement then they'd end up in Oparium and the fact that his shortcut was wrong wouldn't matter anyway. They would've already lost the trial *and* she'd have to face their parents. Their navigation had better be right, because Eira wasn't prepared for either.

As the last dredges of sunlight were slipping away, Eira paused, knocking her knuckles against her tired thighs.

"Do you think we should make camp for the night?" she asked.

"You want to get back before everyone else, right?"

"Yes, but…would they have put us so far out if they hadn't intended for us to take shelter out here?" Eira looked over her shoulder at the molten sky. If they were going to set up camp, they needed to do it now, while they still had a decent amount of light.

"If they did, all the better. Groundbreakers will likely hunker against the cold. But Firebearers may continue. They can make light in the darkness and keep themselves warm with their flames."

"We're not competing against them though," she needlessly reminded him. Though her thoughts wandered to Alyss spending the night alone in the cold.

Only the illusion of danger, she reminded herself. Alyss may be frigid, but they were all being trailed by people, just out of sight. Weren't they? Even her and Marcus…unless they'd somehow given their trackers the slip when they'd moved quickly off the beaten path.

"The other Waterrunners will either settle for the night because they don't have light, or they'll continue on because they're impervious to the cold. Do you want to take the risk?"

Eira looked up to the sky. It was a full moon tonight. That would give more than enough light to see by. There were eight Waterrunners left. But two would be cut. That meant they couldn't risk coming in last. And nothing sounded more horrible than arriving in Solarin together and finding only one slot left.

"You're right, we should keep going," Eira decided.

"That was my thought," he said as they pressed ahead. "If I'm right about the cutoff we took, we should be well away from any of the other little tests they could throw our way. We should make it back to Solarin before dawn if we walk all night."

"If we walk all night," she repeated and added a groan at the end.

"You could always stop here."

"I'm not stopping here."

"Just saying." He shrugged with a grin.

"You and me, together at the end." Eira stared into the darkening forest ahead. Every tree looked like the last. She was grateful her brother had his bearings. "I should tell—warn—you...I know that the last trial is going to be a duel. We will have to actually fight each other."

"And that's different from when we were kids, how?"

She laughed at his deadpan tone. "We really did tear up Mom and Dad's kitchen that one time after my powers manifested."

"Absolutely destroyed it."

"You can't go easy on me, all right?" Eira glanced in his direction.

"Only if you swear to not go easy on me." He ruffled the hair on the top of her head. "I thought we established earlier—we want to earn our spot from the other." Eira nodded. "By the way, how did you get all this information, really?"

"I..." Eira bit her lip. "I sort of know someone who is helping organize the trials."

"Other than Uncle Fritz?"

"Higher up than him."

"Who?" Marcus whispered as though there was someone to overhear their suddenly scandalous discussion. "Was it someone you met at court with Cullen? He said you ran into Prince Romulin."

"Not the prince. It's Ambassador Ferro. I might have been meeting with him in secret."

"*What?*" There was a protective edge to Marcus's voice. But unlike in the past, it didn't make Eira immediately want to shout about how she could defend herself. This tone made her feel warm, safe. "What exactly have you been doing? Has he done anything inappropriate?"

"No! Of course not..." She filled him in just as she had Alyss. Marcus listened just as intently, but asked much fewer questions than Alyss had. Eira finished just before her last meeting with Ferro, keeping the kiss to herself.

"So, you like him, then?"

"Yes, I think I do," Eira said, softer than the pastel tones that were quickly being painted over by a starry brush in the sky above them.

"Do you love him?"

She thought about the question a moment, trying not to let her cold and defensive walls immediately shut her off from her feelings. Those walls, placed around her heart from having to survive Adam's cruelty and her subsequent life as the Tower outcast, had slowly come down over the last few weeks. They didn't seem like they needed to be as thick. The incident from three years ago no longer had a hold on her. Perhaps what Aunt Gwen had said was right.

Life went on. She could let the mistakes she made along the way, however grave, define her or teach her.

"I think I do," Eira admitted to both herself and her brother. "I know it may be silly, but—"

"It's not silly at all," he said softly, once more throwing an arm around her shoulders and pulling her in for a hug. "My sister, courting the elfin Ambassador to Meru. Well, I guess it's not *that* surprising."

"Stop." A scarlet blush burned her cheeks.

"There's nothing to be ashamed of." He chuckled. "Just promise me when you go off and move to Meru to be with your new elfin lover you'll come back and visit from time to time."

"I'm not moving to Meru." She tried to laugh off the wriggling, uncomfortable feeling the thought put in her stomach. Part of her was here, born and bred from the salt air of the sea in Oparium and the mountain frost of Solarin. The other part of her…was elsewhere in the vast unknown of the world beyond.

"We'll see about that."

Before Eira could object again, the forest opened up, surrounding a massive lake. The top of the lake was entirely frozen over, but thin at the center. Marcus approached and put his foot down on the edge of the ice. Magic pulsed out from him and Eira watched the ice thicken into an even consistency. When he lifted his foot, a blade of ice formed underneath it. He stepped out onto the lake, gliding over its surface on two frozen skates.

"Skiing and now ice skating?"

"I know, it's a crime we're having this much fun on a trial." He did a lazy loop. "Come on out."

Eira laughed with a shake of her head and stepped onto the ice as well. Making ice skates was one of the first things her brother had taught her to do. They'd sneaked out that night, too. It was the first winter after she'd manifested her magic in full and he couldn't wait to show her how to use it. He'd taken her to a nearby pond and they'd spun and spun on clumsily made blades until they were sick.

Now, they swerved around and around, making lazy progress forward. Eira tilted her head back and stared at the stars above her, swimming through the sky in her dizzy haze. The sky and all its vastness above her. Her brother's laughter filling her ears as he hooked his arm with hers. The smile they shared...were the last things she saw before the flash.

Light glowed underneath the surface of the lake. Bright and hot, there for only a moment. The darkness was twice as thick the second after it vanished.

Ice cracked underfoot, shattering with a violent explosion. Eira tumbled, her arm slipping from Marcus's, and they plunged into the inky depths beneath them.

Water rushed around her. Her waterlogged clothes tried to pull her down. Eira inhaled in shock and her magic activated from a base instinct to survive.

Water wouldn't hurt Waterrunners so long as they had magical strength.

A pocket of air surrounded her nose and mouth, the water pressing against it in a fight against her powers. Eira gasped and sputtered, getting her bearings underneath the water. Marcus was in a similar position, already kicking to the surface. She followed behind him.

Perhaps they weren't as far off track as they'd thought and this was a test. Or perhaps whoever had been trailing them decided that they had been having too easy of a time and saw an opportunity to make their lives more difficult—even the playing field. Either way, they would be up on the surface soon.

Or so she thought.

Light spun into existence, weaving from between the shadows. It snapped into place just under the surface of the water, stretching from bank to bank across the lake. Marcus slammed into the barrier first.

Eira didn't even try. She recognized this glyph. She'd seen it, night after night, on a much smaller scale.

Break my shield, Deneya had commanded.

Marcus summoned a spear of ice, slamming it as hard as he could into the barrier. The water slowed him down, but even if it hadn't, the result would've been the same. Eira watched as his spear shattered against the shield.

She felt removed from her body, detached from the creeping horror that was all sharp fangs and gnashing teeth making its way up her spine.

What kind of test was this? Eira's mind whirred around the question as she saw her brother pressing against, slamming into, and magically assaulting the shield that kept them underwater.

The shield couldn't be broken. Deneya had admitted as much. Why was it here?

She swam over to Marcus, grabbing his elbow before he could punch his bloody knuckles again into the shield.

Stop, she mouthed. It was impossible to communicate effectively underwater. They only had so much air in the small bubbles around their nose and mouth and he was using his up quickly with all the exertion. *Wait.*

Why? he worded back, looking frantically between her and the shield.

She brought her fists together and made a breaking motion in time with a shake of her head. *It can't be broken.* She hoped he understood.

His eyes continued darting between her and the shield. Marcus waited several seconds before trying to break it once more.

Stop! Eira tried to grab for him but he ignored her.

He was going to exhaust himself. This had to be a test of endurance. If his magic ran out, then the little bubble would collapse.

He'd drown.

Eira pressed her nose to the shield, seeing nothing of the dark world past the glowing, spinning lines. *Come on*, she thought. *This is enough; let us out.*

The reverberations of Marcus's attacks through the water were torture. Eira listened to their thrums as numbness set in on her, colder than the water around her, colder than the ice of the mountaintops. The shield wasn't going away.

Marcus's magic flickered as he tried to summon another club of ice. It melted away into the water. Eira saw the moment his power wavered and the bubble collapsed. It was back in a moment, him coughing and sputtering.

No, this is too far.

Eira turned to the shield, finally lodging her own magic against it. The moment she tried, she could feel how thin her power was already from trying to keep her alive. Fighting against the laws of nature took a toll on any sorcerer; there was only so long they could hold out. And even if her magic was strong enough, she'd run out of air in her tiny bubble, pass out, and then drown.

She began attacking with the same frenzy that Marcus had. She placed her hands against the shield, her own disk of ice forming beneath it, that Eira tried to push up against. It didn't budge.

She sent her magic to the other side of the shield, watching ice spike up on the lake top frantically. *Help*, she imagined the ice spelling. *Help!*

Marcus grabbed her shoulder with wide eyes. *Help.* His mouth made the word she'd just been thinking and Eira watched as the bubble collapsed.

Without thinking, Eira reached to her face, taking a part of her own bubble and attaching it back to his. She held it there with her own magic. Marcus coughed and sputtered, his eyes going hazy.

They had to get out, now. If they couldn't they were doomed.

Eira faced the shield and pressed her hands against it. She pushed her fingers so hard into it her nails splintered and bent back. Blood mixed with the dark waters. Eira visualized her magic stretching through the Lightspinning, weakening it, fracturing it.

Stop. Stop. Stop! she screamed mentally.

She imagined her icy tendrils extending all the way back to the person who made the shield. She'd kill them. She'd freeze them alive—Deneya, Ferro, someone else, she didn't care. She'd kill to save her brother if that's what it took—freeze over everything, close it all off.

Stop!

Her magic spiked and the world went dark. The bubble around her mouth collapsed and Eira inhaled a gulp of water. But the shield was gone.

She emerged on the surface gasping and coughing violently, shards of ice bobbing around her. Eira splashed. "Marcus?" she called weakly between coughing. Her throat burned. "Marcus!"

He hadn't come up.

Every bit of survival instinct rallied against her ducking her head under those dark waters once more and returning to where she had just been trapped. But Eira did so anyway. She summoned the last of her strength and brought ample air with her this time.

She swam down, into the inky depths, into the deep void of

the Father's realms themselves. She would leave this world if that's what it meant to bring him back. Marcus came into view, pale and ghostlike in the filtered moonlight.

Eira pulled him back to the surface. With her magic, she pushed them over toward the bank. The water deposited them onto the frozen ground with a disembodied hand that quickly collapsed back into the lake.

"M-Marcus?" Her teeth chattered. But not from the cold. Frost was already freezing her clothes to her skin, her hair to her neck, but that wasn't why she was shivering. "Marcus?"

Eira placed her hands on his chest and tried to feel the water in his lungs. Carefully, clumsily, she pulled forward. Like a horrible geyser it bubbled up from his throat.

"Breathe," she whispered. "Please breathe." She pushed on his chest as the sailors had taught them to do that day they were playing on the beach. But Eira knew her technique was wrong.

Maybe she could do something more if her uncle had taught her as much as he'd taught Marcus. Maybe if she had been stronger from the start. Maybe if she hadn't been in the trials at all, he would've stayed on the beaten path because he wouldn't have researched this alternative route.

"Come on, Marcus. It—it's just the illusion of danger. It's not real. This isn't real." Eira grabbed her brother's face with both hands. "Marcus, please," she whined. "*Please.*"

Letting out a cry, she went back to pushing on his chest. At first she was counting, but then her pushes lost all rhythm. They were hopeless and frantic.

"Don't do this. Marcus. You can't. You can't—" *Die.*

Eira tilted her head back and let out the most horrible sound she had ever heard. The stars shivered at her scream. The trees trembled.

And when she was done…

She let out another.

EIRA SCREAMED IN a long, fading wail until her ragged voice finally gave out. She would scream until there was no more sound left in her—until she was an empty cavern, hollow, void. *Numb*.

"Help!" she cried to the heavens. Her brother was gone. She knew that. And yet, she called anyway, "Someone, please, help! *Help!*"

She screamed on instinct…without considering that whoever may answer might be the person who had trapped them beneath the ice. That they might be someone Eira didn't want to draw any nearer.

"Help! He's—my brother—he is—" Her voice gave out.

Did this happen because we broke the rules? Eira wondered as she wept over her brother. *We were supposed to survive on our own…and we dared to survive together. We cheated on the second and fourth trials.*

And they were punished for it.

No.

The trials were hard…but they weren't supposed to be dangerous. She looked to her brother, gray in the last of the moonlight, and hiccupped a sob. No one was supposed to die. Least of all him.

It had to be a rogue elfin. Someone was out there who—

Her thoughts faltered.

There was a shadow moving between the trees that surrounded the lake. Eira peered through the darkness as she choked on ragged breaths. Ferro stepped into the pale moonlight.

"Thank the Mother," she breathed. "Fe—"

"Yargen," he snarled, continuing to approach.

"Wh—"

"The Goddess's name is Yargen, you heathen. *Mysst soto larrk.*" He held out a hand, his hateful words becoming a sword spun from light. "The people of Solaris are as annoying as weeds and as evil as the shade of the god they were born under. The one whom they have unleashed back into the world."

Eira open and shut her mouth several times, trying to make sense of his words. Her mind could only focus on one thing. "Please, Ferro, please, your Lightspinning. Help Marcus."

The snow crunched under Ferro's boots as he came to a stop before her. His violet eyes shone with malice. His hair was damp from snowfall and it clung to his head in clumps. He clutched his sword tightly.

The actions hardly registered to her. How could she reconcile the man who was standing before her now with the man who had spirited her away, who had kissed her, whom she had...she had loved.

"You should have died with him," he whispered, shattering the illusion of that man. "You should both be at the bottom of that lake."

"What're you talking about? Help my brother, please. I beg you. I'll do anything you want. Save him."

"Pathetic creature." Ferro leaned forward and grabbed her by the throat. Eira's hands closed around his wrist as she kicked her feet, struggling to find balance in the snow and mud as he hoisted her up. His hand was like steel. "You were useful when you had information I needed. But now you're nothing more than a loose end that knows far too much."

Ferro pulled back his sword, holding her out. Stars pricked at Eira's vision as she gasped for air. Darkness encroached all around her. He thrust forward.

Eira pressed her eyes closed, bracing herself. She'd be with Marcus again soon. It should have been her that died, not him. This was righting a wrong of fate.

But the sword sheered off her harmlessly. Her magic had

risen to protect her as a thick layer of ice over her skin. It had acted just as she'd read in the journals of that hidden room countless times over but could never consciously summon. Off balance, Ferro dropped the sword and his grip on her. Eira landed, rolling backward. Her side slammed into a rock by the lake bed. She gasped, wheezing. But the ice continued to protect her flesh. The covering stayed as she stood once more, staggering to her feet as Ferro approached.

"You...you made the shield on the lake," Eira whispered, trying to get her thoughts in order.

"You two were the last to die tonight and I got clumsy." He took a breath, opening his mouth once more. But Eira didn't give him a chance to say another word of power.

With a cry, she lunged forward. Ice flaked off of her. A weapon appeared in Eira's hand by instinct more than a conscious command. She thrust forward, ready to skewer him.

"*Mysst soto xieh!*" Ferro barely had time to react. Eira's trident shattered on his shield.

She spun in place, feeling the air around her condense. The moonlight shifted through her distortion. A copy of her—an illusion—jumped back as she spun around Ferro, invisible in the darkness.

"*Juth calt,*" he snarled, and Eira watched as her illusion was ripped to shreds.

She summoned a dagger to her palm and went to plunge it into his side. But Ferro was too fast and too well-trained. He dodged at the last second, her ice merely clipping his luxurious coat harmlessly.

"*Kot sorre.*" A glyph appeared between them. It charged into her, pushing Eira back. She tumbled through the snow, trying to fight against it. But the circle of light moved with the speed of a carriage pulled by a dozen invisible horses and she was just as helpless to fight it.

Her back cracked against a trunk as the glyph nearly doubled her around a tree. Eira let out a gasp of air and the remaining ice vanished from her skin. Everything in her body hurt. Everything was aflame with an agony she'd never known before.

The only thing that kept her moving was a drive deeply rooted in her—survival. She would do anything to survive. She would keep moving at all costs. She wasn't going to let him or anyone steal the breath from her lungs.

Especially not before she avenged her brother.

Eira groaned, plunging her fingers into the snow. She dug deeper than ever before for magic. Ice spiked upward, racing from her to Ferro.

"*Juth calt.*" He shattered her magic with two words, sending a spray of ice in all directions. "You can't beat me. You know that, right?" He laughed. "You're tougher than you look, I grant you. But I am the son of the Champion. I am destined for glory!"

Eira groaned, moving her hand through the snow, trying to leech its cold—its strength. But she was tired, so tired. There wasn't enough left in her to fight him. He was right. She didn't even know the first thing about combat.

Ferro came to a stop, looming over her. "Now, it's time for you to die."

Eira pressed her eyes closed. *Make it stop*, she begged her magic, the goddess, anyone. *This can't be it; I can't die here.*

"*Loft dorh*," he snarled.

Weight piled atop her, trying to hold her down.

No! The instinct to survive was back—even when her body broke, it persisted. Eira resisted against the invisible force. She pushed herself to her knees.

"*Loft dorh*," Ferro repeated with purpose. Eira saw the glyphs that hovered in his palms flickering, as if they were unstable, as if his own strength was fading. "How...how are you—"

She didn't give him a chance to finish. With her magic waning, Eira was left with no other choice. She punched him square across the jaw. Her knuckles split on his bone but she followed up her first punch with another. And then a third.

Ferro stumbled backwards, putting space between them. He wiped the back of his hand against his bloodied face. Eira knew she shouldn't ease up on her attacks but she was too weary to keep going. Every movement was leaden.

"*Maph*," he snarled. A glyph sparked like a tinderbox around his wrist. Barely there and fragile. Ferro looked at it in disgust and then back to her. He opened his mouth to speak but Eira wasn't going to give him the opportunity.

Running on the last of her power, she froze his mouth shut. He grunted and groaned in agony, raking his fingers down his face, his nails clipping on ice. But her magic didn't budge, and his lips could no longer move.

Lightspinning was powerful and incredible in its versatility. But it had one key weakness that Eira had just figured out—a sorcerer had to be able to say the words to summon the glyphs and use the magic.

Eira sank back, collapsing. She kept a firm hold on her magic. She'd die before she let him speak again.

Ferro charged forward, hands balled into fists.

With a look toward his feet, she rooted him to the ground. Ferro toppled forward, no longer able to move. Three points of magic—she had to sustain three points, his mouth and two feet.

As Ferro tugged against her holds, Eira stared at him listlessly. It was because of him her brother was dead. He had tried to kill them both.

Whatever remnants there had once been of her heart were now turning dark and cold. Part of her was dying alongside where her brother lay. Whatever goodness Eira had once possessed was leaving her.

Kill him, an ugly voice within her snarled. It grew louder by the minute. *Blood for blood.*

Eira stared at Ferro. He'd stopped struggling and now stared at her with an almost content gaze. He was going to wait her out. He knew how weak her magic was and the moment he was free, she wouldn't be able to put up a fight.

Her gaze drifted back to Marcus.

Pushing herself up for what felt like the final time, Eira made her way to her brother, ignoring Ferro. She knelt down, scooping him up—or trying to.

Marcus...the golden child. Marcus...the better one. Marcus...the true son of their parents.

His blood was on her hands as much as it was on Ferro's. She hadn't been fast enough. She'd told him to stop trying to break the shield. She'd gone out on the lake with him in the first place and skated in stupid circles when she should have insisted they keep pressing onward.

Her mind jumped from one dark thought to the next. Further and further down she spiraled until she was the one who had sunk into a dark abyss. But when Eira opened her eyes, she was the one still breathing.

Eira bowed her head and pressed it into the center of Marcus's chest. He was freezing over. The water had sapped the warmth from his body before they'd even come ashore.

"We promised... I promised you," she rasped. "We would go back together. Let's go, brother. One last time."

She didn't have much magic left and what she was about to do risked depleting the last of it. She was risking Ferro getting free to bring her brother back with her. But Eira couldn't have it any other way.

Eira lifted a hand and her brother rose off the ground, supported by a bed of snow and water. It gurgled and shifted around him. Marcus was carried on the tides of her magic as Eira began the long march back to Solarin.

Ferro sounded like he was laughing behind her. His throaty chortles and snorts echoed into the forest, chasing her with the promise that soon he would be as well. She ignored the noise and focused on her magic. One hand guided Marcus. The other was balled into a fist and held Ferro in place. She would keep that fist all the way back to Solarin. She would keep it until Ferro was captured by someone stronger than her.

It wasn't even an hour when Eira slipped the first time.

Marcus tumbled to the ground and she caught herself on a tree. Tears spilled down her face once more.

"I'm sorry." Eira hastily lifted her hand, bringing him upward on his bed of snow and water. "I never meant for any of this to happen."

Eira spoke as she walked. She told her brother of all the things that she should have said when he could hear her. She told him about her fears, about her wants, about her worries.

But her voice soon gave out. It was just as tired as she was.

So tired.

One step.

Then the next.

That was all she could think about. One step after another. A relentless march toward Solarin.

"I'll get you the Rites of Sunset," Eira vowed aloud as the sun rose. "I'll see your soul has a proper send-off to the realms beyond. I promise, Marcus." The tears were flowing again. "I couldn't save you, but I can do this."

Silence was her only reply.

One step.

Then the next.

The fingers of her left hand were sweating. They trembled with the strain of keeping a fist and a hold on her magic. Eira refused to release them. *She would die before she let that man free.* If she repeated that enough times, it would come true.

The trees blurred around her, eventually relenting to a road that appeared out of nowhere. Eira stumbled down the snowy bank. Tripping, and falling hard. The cobblestones bit into her. Red splattered gray and white.

Marcus tumbled next to her. Eira pressed herself upright, uttering a thousand apologies. Warm, wet tears thawed the chill on the cobblestones as they fell from her cheeks.

They were close.

Just a little more from her, from her magic. And then… She didn't know what then. She would sleep for a thousand years, maybe. She would sleep until the hurt stopped.

Keeping her left hand in a fist, Eira tried to stand. But her feet slipped on her own blood. She fell once more, clipping her chin. Her whole body was a mess of bruises and exhaustion. Eira lay on the road next to her brother. She stared at his lifeless face.

"I can't," she rasped. "I can't, Marcus. I can't do this alone. I can't make it back without you." He continued to lie there, lifeless. *"Please wake up."*

He didn't.

Eira lay back and stared at the trees above her. Every second was harder than the last to keep her hand in a fist. Her muscles had long since cramped and locked up.

Blinking slowly, she watched as dawn broke on a silent world. She imagined people waking and going about their business and she hated every last one of them for their ignorance to her suffering. She would freeze it all if she weren't so tired.

Every time her eyes closed was longer than the last. Yet Eira kept her hand locked. Maybe she was Adela's offspring after all. Maybe Ferro was right and she had elfin power. How else could she sustain for so long?

Eira hoped he was right. For the first time she hoped she was spawned from the cold and cruel pirate queen. That would make her life, and her blood, cursed. And she would inflict that curse on whatever existence Ferro had beyond her.

Just when Eira's eyes were closing for what felt like the final time, a rumbling echoed through the earth to her. It drew nearer and nearer until it could no longer be ignored. Eira twisted, barely able to lift her head.

In the distance was a rider, moving faster than the wind itself—as if the horse was flying more than galloping. Only one man could perform such a trick.

Eira opened her mouth, croaking, "Cullen." She swallowed thickly; it tasted of blood. "Cullen!"

TWENTY-FIVE

EIRA FELT AS though she was being lifted from the grave. Cullen's arms were sturdy as he hoisted her, supporting her on a bent knee, a hand cradling her head.

"Mother above, Eira, what—"

She knew by his expression what had halted him. His eyes had landed on Marcus, who was unnaturally still. Eira gripped Cullen's shirt with her free hand.

"Ferro, he…"

"Meru's ambassador?" Cullen shook his head, his eyes growing red with tears he was struggling to hold back. "What happened to you two?"

"Ferro attacked us."

Cullen stared in shock. Then, his face twisted with a rage Eira had never thought possible from him. It shattered all of her notions of the prim and proper man who was always in control. He looked as if he was about to level the forest with a twister.

"I know you won't believe me, but I swear—"

"I believe you." Cullen looked back to Marcus once more. His arms tightened slightly around her. "We need to get you back. You need medical attention."

"Yes, and I need your help to bring Marcus with me. I'm not strong enough to carry him and hold Ferro captive."

"*You* have Ferro captive?" Cullen let out a curse word that sounded impressed rather than angry.

"I think so." Eira lifted her fist. "I pinned him down and gagged him with ice. I can still feel my magic draining, so I think he's still in place…" Unless he had broken free and she was just sending magic to a patch of ice in the woods.

"You're incredible," he murmured.

Eira had waited years for someone like Cullen to say that to her. For someone in the Tower—other than Alyss—to see her as valuable. To see her magic as powerful as Eira had always known it was. And now that she had the praise and attention… She didn't care.

All that mattered right now was Marcus and bringing Ferro to justice. She didn't need Cullen's—or anyone else's—validation. She needed his help and strength.

"I have Ferro back by a lake, where he trapped us. I don't know how much longer I can last. I can feel him struggling against my tethers… I have to get back and then we can send the guard. That way they can apprehend him." If she could hold that long.

"Let him go; save your strength."

"*No*. He must be brought to justice. He killed Marcus!" She clutched Cullen with her free hand. Cullen staggered some, eyes darting to Marcus and back to her.

"I agree with you. I do. But we need to focus on getting you back. And we can't bring Ferro to justice alone."

"That's why I wanted to get the guard. My aunt—"

"Think of how this will look," Cullen said firmly. "You and I both know your history. If you return with a dead body and holding the *Ambassador to Meru* captive and demand he be apprehended, fingers will end up pointed at you."

"But I didn't—"

"I know how this works, Eira. Trust me, I know better than anyone. Let Ferro go. He'll be on the loose, yes, but then the guard can chase him down. We'll leave Marcus here—"

"You want to leave my brother here?" Eira nearly shrieked. She wrestled herself from Cullen's arms. He didn't force his hold on her and Eira tumbled to the ground. She shook her head, pushing against the icy cobblestones. She'd get her and Marcus back to Solarin herself, alone, if that's what it took.

"You have to listen to me, or you'll be a suspect in his death."

"I would've never hurt my brother." She hung her head. The incident from three years ago would haunt her forever. She could never escape its repercussions.

She'd killed someone. She was forever branded as a murderer.

"I know that, but he's not the only competitor who's died tonight!"

"What?" She brought her eyes back to Cullen's.

"That's why I came looking for you both... The proctors found the other Waterrunners dead. Traps had sprung early and wrong. The others...they had their throats slit."

Ferro had killed them. That's what he'd meant about having a long night and the "others." Eira's gut turned molten and she had to consciously pack her ice tightly around her mind to keep a cool head.

"All the more reason we must bring him to justice. We can't let him run free." Eira stood, swaying. "I'm going back to Solarin with Marcus, then I'll send the guard."

"If you do this—"

"I'm doing this."

"But—"

"This isn't a negotiation, Cullen!" Eira turned to face him. "I made a promise—the *last promise* I will ever make to my brother was that we would go back together. We would finish this trial together. I *don't care* what happens to me. I have let him down too many times in my life. I won't, I can't, let him down now. This is my last chance to do something for him. Don't take it from me!" Her voice was cracked and broken, shaking apart like the rest of her. But no tears fell. She'd cried out every drop of water within her. All that was left now was ice.

Cullen stared at her until he clearly could not bear to any longer. He looked away, back at his horse. Without a word, he strode over to the mount. Eira expected him to leave her. The Prince of the Tower couldn't be seen with a murderer, after all.

Plus, he had his secret to guard—whatever that was—and

he was right…they would suspect her. Even if she could prove her innocence, she would be under investigation. She knew how the events unfurled after something like this. She'd been here before. And the Waterrunners—her direct competitors—were the ones murdered. Eira's gut twisted. Ferro had left her for last because he knew, even if he didn't succeed, Solaris's justice would finish her off for him.

No, she wouldn't blame Cullen for leaving. It had been inevitable that he would. She was a risk to him and his family, a liability through association.

Except…he didn't leave.

Cullen led the horse back to her. "Get on."

"What?"

"You're dead on your feet, get on."

"But—"

"You need your strength to keep holding Ferro in place, don't you? Don't walk the rest of the way, ride. And before you ask, I'll carry Marcus."

"You don't have to do this," she whispered.

"I don't, and I likely shouldn't." Cullen frowned. "I'm risking a lot right now, more than you realize."

"Then why?"

"Because it's the right thing to do. Because Marcus was my friend and he would want me to look out for you and because I…*I* want to look out for you."

The last man that had "looked out for her" murdered her brother and tried to kill her. But Eira kept the thoughts to herself and gave a small nod. She needed Cullen's help right now. But she wouldn't be swept away by the kindness either. She would guard her heart from being vulnerable ever again.

Cullen helped her into the saddle and then faced Marcus. He stood in tense silence, head bowed, and Eira allowed him to have his moment. She had mourned through the entirety of the forest and would continue to mourn long after she'd returned to Solarin. When he was ready, he lifted his hands and Marcus's body hovered off the ground.

Together, they started their silent trek back to Solarin. The road they were on eventually dumped into the Great Imperial Way. From there, it wasn't far to the switchbacks that led up to the capital. The roads were empty at dawn, though in the distance, at the gates high above, she could see a group gathered on a platform that hadn't been there before.

As she approached the final switchback, she heard words from a distance. There was shouting. People began to move.

"I'm not going to be able to help you immediately," Cullen said softly as he came to a stop. Reverently, he set down Marcus's body.

"That's all right." Eira dismounted with his help. Her hand was still clutched tight, the muscles long since spasmed and locked into place. "I didn't expect you to help me this much. I can do the rest on my own."

"But you won't be alone, I promise."

Eira didn't have a chance to ask him to clarify. City guards rushed around them. Fritz and Gwen were close behind. Senators with their bright blue sashes lagged after the rest.

Fritz's hands closed around her shoulders and he shook her with unintentional aggression. Eira's head swung back and forth. Her muscles barely had enough strength to support her anymore.

"Eira. Eira! Thank the Mother you're alive." He yanked her close and then pushed her back. "What happened?" His eyes were soft with heartbreak as they turned to Marcus.

"I—"

"She must be arrested," a familiar voice spoke above her. Cullen's father, Yemir, had reached the circle of guards surrounding her. "Guards, arrest her!"

"No one move!" Gwen shouted, pushing past the guards. She was in her official plate armor, dressed to her neck in steel. "Senator Yemir, you are not the head of the city guard."

"And neither are you." Yemir didn't miss a beat. He made a show of looking Gwen up and down. "You're part of the *palace* guard. This is beyond your jurisdiction and falls under the purview of the senate."

"Please, let's let her explain," Fritz said firmly.

"She has murdered her fellow candidates. She has a track record of killing her peers. This is what we were trying to avoid by removing her from the Tower and bringing her to justice those years ago." Yemir spoke more to the handful of his fellow senators than to the guards, as if he was putting on a show for them.

"I didn't," Eira whispered, looking to Fritz rather than Yemir. "You know I wouldn't. I would *never* hurt Marcus; I'd never hurt anyone intentionally! We were attacked and I brought him back so he could have a Rite of Sunset. I didn't hurt him." Eira grabbed her uncle's elbow with her free hand.

"I know, I know," he tried to soothe. "But you must tell us what happened. Who attacked you?"

The senators had conferred in record time. "Solaris is under the rule of law. City guard, you will arrest this woman and take her into custody. There is too much suspicion surrounding her to allow her to go free."

"We were attacked," Eira insisted.

"A likely story," Yemir fired back. "We'll see if the evidence supports your claims."

"I didn't do anything!" Eira screamed at Yemir. Everything was playing out how Cullen had said. But it was somehow made worse by it being his father pointing the blame at her. Eira's breath was short. She was back in that senate hall, barely fifteen, awaiting trial, awaiting her fate.

"Then you have nothing to fear. Guards, apprehend her."

"No! I won't let you touch her!" Gwen pushed forward and brandished her sword.

"Auntie, don't." Eira was not about to see any more of her family suffer because of their proximity to her. "I'll go willingly."

Cullen finally spoke. "Take her to the depths of the palace."

"What?" Gwen's gaze was murderous. "You will not take her there. I have seen the cells and—"

"It's all right," Eira tried to soothe. *Enough people I love have suffered for me today,* she wanted to say. "Let me go." *I won't be a curse on your family any longer.*

"See?" Yemir preened. "My son speaks sense. Lock her away where the worst of Solaris goes. If she's speaking the truth, she'll maintain her story. If she's not…enough time there breaks the strongest of men."

Eira met Cullen's hazel eyes. They shone honey in the morning light, deceptively sweet. He'd said he'd help her, but the moment his father had shown up, he was throwing her into the dungeon. Cullen had to take his family's side. She knew it. Yet, somehow, it still managed to sting. How were there spots of her left to wound?

"We're going to help you," Gwen swore.

"We'll get to the truth of this." Fritz crossed to his younger sister, wrapping his arms around her to hold Gwen back as the guards closed in on Eira.

"Look after Marcus," Eira begged as cold, steel-coated hands wrapped around her wrists, wrenching them behind her. The shackles were heavy—a terribly familiar weight. More hands wrapped around her arms, carrying her more than pushing her in the direction of a palace entry. "Make sure Marcus gets a Rite of Sunset! No matter what, give him a proper send-off!"

The ground drifted beneath her as they manhandled her away. Was this how Marcus felt as she ferried him all the way back here? Helpless to do anything? The world drifting around him? Changing?

Her attention landed on him once more. Fritz and Gwen knelt at his side. No…he hadn't felt anything.

Because he was long gone.

"Goodbye, brother," she whispered.

The last thing Eira saw was Marcus's cold body, her aunt and uncle mourning over him. They would look after him. And she—

A sack was thrust over her head. A hand ripped the pin

from her breast. Eira was thrust onto a cart and another tarp thrown atop her. She gasped the stale smell, coughing up dust. They didn't want the masses to see a candidate dragged through town. This would all be hidden. They would try and blame her for the murders, but as long as Eira drew breath, she would not let that happen.

Because, no matter what they did to her, as long as she had strength in her marrow she kept her hand clenched into a fist. Ferro was still her captive. And maybe her last bargaining chip.

THE CELL SHE was thrown into was a cold, barren place. There was *nothing*. No bed, no chamber pot, no warmth, no light.

It suited her.

Eira leaned against the bars of the door. The footsteps of the soldiers had long faded into the dripping of some distant water. Someone had to be stationed somewhere to keep an eye on her. Iron bars, even strong ones, weren't effective at keeping sorcerers locked in. She wondered what sorcerer was given the order to kill her if she tried to escape. Who would be as eager to the task as Yemir had been at the idea of taking her captive for murders she didn't commit?

It didn't matter. She wasn't going to try to flee. Eira closed her eyes, finding it was hardly any different from having them open.

Darkness within, darkness around.

Time passed. The minutes slipped by, pouring into hours. Eira drowned in them just like she should have drowned in that cold abyss where Marcus had taken his last breath. Her numbed senses were beginning to sharpen. Thoughts of her brother returned in full, as though a dam had been broken.

Her eyes shot open.

"Hello?" she called timidly. "May I have some light?"

The darkness she'd once relished was suddenly oppressive. It closed in around her from every corner. Shadows lived in it, ready to make her weary mind into their shattered plaything.

Dark, just like the water of the lake they'd fallen into. Dark like the forests Ferro had emerged from, the forests she hoped her clenched fist still kept him captive in. Dark as the depths she'd pulled Marcus from too late.

Too late.

"Please?" she cried, louder. "May I have some light? *Please?*"

If anyone heard her, they didn't come. Eira curled into a ball, arms still bound behind her back. She'd begun using her other hand to hold her fingers and magic in place.

Pressing her face into her knees, Eira drew deep, shuddering breaths. Ferro was her prisoner. He was captured. He wouldn't harm her, and she could breathe. She wasn't underneath the water and ice anymore.

But Marcus was.

Oh, Marcus.

"Someone, please, light!" she begged with a sob.

Light suddenly appeared, brighter than she expected. Eira bounced away from it with a yelp, tumbling, scrambling backward uncomfortably. At least until she realized that the light didn't come from Lightspinning.

The empress stood, a lit torch hovering over her shoulder, magically supported by invisible currents of air around its base. Vhalla quickly unlocked the door and stepped inside.

"I'm so very sorry," the empress murmured. Eira panted softly, her nerves calming. Feelings returned, though still somewhat detached and surreal, as the empress of all of Solaris knelt behind her and unlocked her shackles. "I came as fast as I could. Can you stand?"

"Are you...are you a dream?" Maybe she had died with Marcus. Maybe this torture was the Father's realms beyond. Eira was being punished for her crimes—for the apprentice she'd killed and for the apprentices who had died because of the information she'd given to Ferro.

"No, I'm not," the empress said kindly. "I'm here to help. Now, are you able to stand?"

"I...I think so." Eira nodded.

"Good, let's go somewhere more comfortable. You've had a hard enough day as it is."

"But the senators—"

"The senate answers to the crown," Vhalla said sharply. Then her expression softened into something more pained, tortured even. "But we have to do a dance around the fact sometimes to keep the peace. Politics can be…complicated. I didn't understand it myself when I was in your shoes."

"In my shoes?" Eira asked as Vhalla helped her to her feet. Her legs wobbled, but somehow still supported her weight.

"Yes, a long time ago…" Vhalla's gaze swung around the cell. Her nose scrunched in disgust. "I'll tell you on the way. I have no interest in lingering here."

The empress left and the torch followed her. A very confused Eira hobbled behind, trying to keep up. It was that, or stay in the darkness of the cell forever.

The empress led her up a stair and down a hallway, where she returned the torch to a rung on the wall. She then lifted a tapestry to reveal a door that they passed through. Farther along, there were two more hidden passages, three more stairways, and several switchbacks, to the point that Eira was well and truly lost.

This all has to be a dream, her mind continued trying to insist.

No, dreams don't hurt this badly, her heart retorted.

Nightmares do, and you will never have a pleasant dream again.

Behind a locked door was one last hall that led to another locked door and, finally, into a lavish parlor. Vhalla closed the door—no, painting, it was a painting on this side—behind them and locked it once more. She said, "You'll be safe here."

"Where…" Eira was high up in the palace now, based on the view from the windows, in a room that dripped gold. Beyond that and all the finery, she didn't have a clue as to where she was.

"You're in the Imperial apartments. No one but my family, most trusted friends, and hand-picked guards are permitted here. You'll be safe." Vhalla crossed over to a low table between the sofas, where a pile of blankets was set out. "Come, sit by the fire and get warm."

"I'm not cold."

"No..." Vhalla paused, the blanket she'd been about to offer hanging limply over her arm. "I imagine you're not."

"I don't feel anything." Eira shook her head.

Vhalla slowly approached her, as if Eira were a wild animal. She waited a moment before draping the blanket over her shoulders. When she spoke, it was with a mother's voice rather than the Empress of Solaris'. "I know..."

Two words, in that tone, broke her once more.

"I-I don't feel anything!" Eira sobbed as the empress bundled her.

"I know," Vhalla echoed herself and then stepped forward and wrapped her arms over the blanket. Eira could hardly process the fact that the empress was holding her. But instinct had Eira burying her face into the woman's shoulder as she sobbed. The motherly position had her aching, longing for a love that Eira had needed desperately but her parents had left her wanting. "I know," Vhalla repeated over and over.

Something made Eira believe she really did know. There was a sorrowful need that bloomed from forgotten grief in the empress's voice. This was a woman who had been born into nothing and had risen up to power despite all odds to take on the Mad King. She had suffered greatly along the way, if the tales were to be believed. This incredible woman was holding Eira, of all people.

"I'm sorry," Vhalla whispered.

"I don't... *What do I do wrong?* Is it because of me? Because I cheated? Because I didn't drop out? Because I didn't listen to my family?" Eira hiccuped as the tears abated once more.

"Come and sit with me, for starters." Vhalla led her gently over to the sofas by the fire. Eira sat, at a loss for what else to do. Vhalla sat close, arm still around her shoulders. "I see so much of myself in you and my heart breaks for it."

"What?" Eira blinked.

"I was in that cell once. They don't talk about it much anymore… Does the Night of Fire and Wind mean anything to you?" Eira shook her head and Vhalla laughed softly. "I suppose I should be grateful it's long since fallen out of favor to speak of. That night is certainly not one I wish to be prominent in my legacy…if I get to choose what my legacy is at all." The empress shook her head and refocused herself. Vhalla pursed her lips in thought, her palm rubbing circles on Eira's back. "Listen to me, Eira. I was put on trial because there were twisted people in power and because there were forces at play greater than myself. I like to think my husband and I, for all our shortcomings and for all the good we could still yet do, are not twisted people in power. But there are powerful people maneuvering and you have ended up a piece on the board of their game."

"I didn't kill my brother." The words were accompanied by a violent shake of her head. "Or any of the other competitors."

"I know," Vhalla said quickly. "Cullen told me."

Eira stilled, her wide eyes unfocused. "What?"

"Cullen told me what you said when he found you."

"He…how?"

"First things first." Vhalla's hand fell on Eira's clenched fist. "Do you still have Ferro captive?"

"You know?" Eira whispered. Vhalla nodded. Eira looked to her hand. "I think I do. I still feel magic leaving me but… I'm so tired. I don't know if it's enough, he might be—"

"We'll find out soon. After you were taken, Cullen came to me and explained everything. He told me where he had encouraged them to lock you away." She chuckled softly. "I suppose being honest with him about that night in my past, long ago, and its aftermath resulted in something good. He knew where to put you where no one would look, where no one but guards of Imperial choosing could find you—where *I* could get to you."

"He…looked after me?" Eira slowly brought her eyes to the empress's.

"As best he knew how. Be gentle on him; there's more than you know riding on him as the first Windwalker after myself. He is not without darkness and struggle, either." She wore a sad smile and smoothed a hand over Eira's hair. The movement didn't even seem to register. Eira had only ever thought of the empress as a figurehead, her sovereign...never as a mother. The familial movements were making Eira's heart break further in a sort of beautiful torture. "He should be here soon. Along with the others."

"Others?"

At that moment the door to the parlor opened, revealing Fritz, Grahm, and Gwen.

"Vhal, you are truly the savior of Solaris." Fritz's voice broke with emotion as his gaze fell on Eira. "Thank you for getting her."

"Of course, Fritz." Vhalla stood to make room for Eira's family. Eira barely resisted asking the comforting woman to stay.

Gwen was the first to press her side against Eira's. Fritz and Grahm surrounded her next, completing a semicircle of protection. Eira dipped her head, trying to drown in the folds of the blanket still on her shoulders.

"I'm sorry," she murmured. Lingering underneath all the affection was how things had been left with her uncles and the revelations of her family. It all seemed so insignificant to her now, but would they feel the same?

"You have nothing to be sorry for. We'll get to the bottom of this," Gwen said with a squeeze. "And you're safe now. No more senators acting like they own all of Solarin."

Eira thought back to Yemir. What would he think once he found out Cullen had helped her? He'd been so eager to lock her away... Was he truly that committed to justice? Was it a score to settle from when she had "eluded justice" for the apprentice she'd killed as a girl? Or...was he afraid of her? Eira thought back to the day at court and his reaction to her power. She thought back to what Fritz had warned her of.

Her powers were dangerous, deadly, and the sort of magic men and women fighting to be at the top would want to possess or destroy.

"I should have listened." Eira met Fritz's sad eyes. "I shouldn't have entered the trials."

"Stop that; it's all right," he said softly, wrapping an arm around her shoulders. But nothing felt all right. In fact, everything felt very, very wrong. "We're thanking the Mother above you're safe."

Eira stared at the floor. It wasn't enough. *She* wasn't enough. Marcus should be here and not her.

They sat together for almost an hour, saying very little. Gwen made an attempt at conversation, but her voice kept cracking and eventually her words were swallowed up by the absence of Marcus. After that there were only a few words exchanged between them. What was there to say? Nothing was going to bring back Marcus, or fix the broken picture of their family. What was the point of speaking at all?

When the door opened again, every head turned except for Eira's. She was far too exhausted to even raise her eyes. Her magic was as brittle as her sanity felt.

Two familiar hands covered her trembling fist. Eira followed them up to a pair of sad, hazel eyes.

"You can let go," Cullen said softly. "We have him."

"Y OU CAPTURED HIM?" Eira repeated. "Ferro?"

"Yes. Deneya has him now. They're with the emperor and empress." Cullen's gaze shifted to her family as Eira's roved the room. She didn't remember Vhalla leaving. "The empress has instructed me to inform you all that she is working on sorting out Eira's situation. The plan is there will be an announcement to the city, after a brief period, of a mystery attacker. Eira's involvement will be cleared following an 'investigation' and the next random murderer taken into palace custody from the city will be convicted of the crimes."

"But…" Eira whispered. No one heard her, or no one listened. Eira continued to hold her hand in a fist; the truth hadn't sunk in yet.

"It should go without saying that you three should never mention to anyone beyond this room that Ferro was behind these heinous acts."

"Understood." Gwen dipped her chin, accustomed to royal orders being funneled through others.

"What will happen to him?" Grahm asked, clearly uncertain about being sworn to secrecy.

"That has yet to be decided. Given his position, and the upcoming Tournament of Five Kingdoms, this matter is being handled with the utmost discretion."

Discretion was far better than Ferro deserved.

"The Tournament is still going to happen?" Fritz stole the shock Eira was missing the energy to feel.

"It must. A landmark treaty between five nations cannot be stalled because of the actions of one clearly insane man."

"I'm not going to allow apprentices to be sent after this."

Fritz stood, sliding into the mantle of Minister of Sorcery. "We don't even know his motives. What if they were directed by the Queen of Meru herself?"

Cullen remained calm. "Those are all questions for you to take up with the empress."

"I will be certain to."

"In the meantime, Her Majesty asked me to send you back to the Tower," Cullen continued to Fritz. A young man, an apprentice of the Tower, was ordering around the Minister of Sorcery as though it were nothing. Even if he was just a vessel for the empress's wishes, Eira found herself envious of the skillful wielding of power. Though, she was more envious of his ability to remain composed. "There will be questions, understandably, following the deaths of candidates. You need to be there for the Tower to keep calm and try and quell any rumors."

"How many died?" Eira made herself heard this time. Though as soon as she asked the question, she regretted it.

"Seven." Cullen's expression was void of emotion. It wasn't that he was composed, Eira realized. He was functioning like she was—numb and detached. "All Waterrunners."

"And I'm the only one who survived," Eira breathed. No wonder Yemir was ready to pin her with the crimes and everyone was ready to believe him. All her conversations with Ferro from those long nights floated through her head. She'd told him so much about Waterrunners and their powers. She'd helped him every step of the way without realizing it.

She'd been the one to give him the information he needed about the terrain, about what Waterrunners could and couldn't do, about her own past. Numb shock finally eased her cramping fingers and her fist uncurled. She had no fight left in her. She'd been used and maneuvered.

"It's not your fault," Cullen said, soft and firm, while looking her right in the eye. "But...clearly...the fact that Waterrunners were targeted is going to work against you."

"Work against her?" Gwen glanced between them.

"They think I have a motive." Eira spelled it out for her aunt.

"You'd never kill anyone. I still can't believe people even suggest it," Gwen said with disgust.

She would never escape three years ago.

"I agree." Cullen's mouth pressed into a hard line. "But people will look for any reason to explain these horrific acts. In their grief, they won't care if the real killer is brought to justice or not, so long as they have someone to blame."

"I can't believe this is really happening." Gwen shook her head.

Cullen continued to wear his cold, unfeeling stare. "We're working with bad cards, Eira especially." Before anyone could say anything else, Cullen shifted his attention back to her family. "Fritz and Grahm, please return to the Tower. The empress said she would meet you there as soon as she's able to discuss things further. Gwen, the empress would like to ask you to keep the palace guard in order—help prevent rumors there as well and, most importantly, make sure that no one realizes Eira is missing from her cell. The imperial plan is to keep her comfortable here instead of in the depths."

"That I will gladly do." Gwen sighed, resigned, and gave Eira a kiss on the cheek before starting for the door.

"And what will I be doing?" Eira asked, dejected. Fritz and Grahm squeezed her tightly before leaving, a movement that hardly registered.

"You"—Cullen's hands rested on her shoulders as the door clicked shut—"are going to rest and recover your strength."

"I'm fine." Eira pulled away. Her magic snapped and her hand spasmed. Eira stared down at it. The muscles were so cramped and exhausted she could hardly move her fingers. "I don't have him captive anymore. Marcus is dead and I…I need to be doing *something.*"

"The best thing you can do is rest. You need to stay here in hiding and wait until your name is cleared. As far as the rest of the world is concerned, you're still in that cell and it'll spell trouble if the truth becomes known."

"But Marcus's Rite of Sunset, it'll be…"

"Tonight." He said the most horrible word she'd ever heard.

"I can go, right?" Eira stood and the world swayed treacherously. She went from hating Cullen and all his cold, calculating, trained pragmatism one moment, to needing him for it the next. He said nothing and Eira's good hand balled in his shirt over his chest. "Cullen, tell me, I can—"

"I don't know." His hands covered hers gently.

"He's my brother," she choked. "I have to be there for his send-off into the Father's realms." It was the last moment his mortal soul and hers would exist together on the same plane of existence until she met her final rest.

"I'll try. But you must understand, Eira, everyone is just trying to protect you."

"I must go!"

"Not at the expense of your safety." The kindness in his eyes was withering into frustration.

"Forget my safety!"

"Your safety is all that matters!" His hands lifted off hers and flew to her shoulders. Cullen gripped her tightly, shaking her. His eyes were wide with emotion. "Marcus is gone! Nothing you can risk now will bring him back."

"Don't you think I know that?" Her voice rose to meet his.

"Then stop trying to throw your life away!" Cullen was breathless, his soft panting washing over her wet cheeks. She was crying again. When did that happen? Eira didn't know. She felt like she would be a tangle of tears and hate for the rest of her days. His voice broke into something tender, heartbroken. "Eira, I…" His hand lifted off her shoulder. Before she even registered the movement it was on her cheek, his thumb stroking away her tears. A futile effort. "I mourn for him, too. But he would want you to stay safe. I'm trying to honor his memory by helping you."

She had been a burden to Marcus, and now that burden

had transferred to Cullen. Eira pressed her eyes closed. But her cheek, with no command from her, tipped slightly into his palm, seeking out whatever tenderness he could offer.

After only a second, Cullen pulled her close. One arm slipped around her shoulders, the other buried in her hair. She'd thought about his nails brushing lightly against her scalp again once in a while, but she hadn't imagined it'd be like this.

"Tell me you'll stay here and stay safe," he murmured. "I don't want to ever endure the sight of you in chains again."

"I will." She didn't have the first idea of how she would escape even if she wanted to.

"Good." Cullen slowly pulled away. "Try and get some sleep."

"I will," she repeated, sitting back on the sofa.

Cullen dutifully adjusted the pillows around her. When he was finished, she lay back and he draped the blanket over her. Eira studied every movement, looking for a hint of betrayal. She'd missed those clues with Ferro. She'd never miss them again.

"I'll see you when I can."

It sounded like a promise she hadn't asked for. Yet her treacherous heart was glad to hear it. She stamped out the emotion as quickly as it appeared.

"But it might not be for some time. I'm going to try and curb my father."

"He hates me, doesn't he?" She sought confirmation of her earlier theory.

Cullen hesitated, then nodded. "At first, he merely disliked that I was associating with you."

"Why?"

"Because he's been hounding me to begin courting for a politically beneficial marriage for years." Cullen gave her a weak smile. Eira swallowed thickly, ignoring whatever implication might be behind his words. She wasn't ready to face it. "But, then, when he saw your magic... Now he sees you as a threat to us."

Eira studied his face as Cullen lightly brushed his fingertips over her forehead. The movement was so tender, so gentle, it nearly ended her. *I'm not worthy*, she wanted to say, *Don't touch me; I'm death to everyone who dares draw near.*

"You know, I never wanted anything to do with you," Eira murmured.

"I never wanted anything to do with you, either," he whispered. "But here we are…and now I will fight for you." His knuckles stroked her cheek one last time and, without another word, Cullen left.

She didn't remember falling asleep, but she must've. The last time her eyes were open, it had been early dawn. Now, the room was cast in inky night.

A fire still crackled in the hearth and Eira's eyes, crusted with sleep, struggled to adjust to the light. Someone had been in to keep the fire burning. Cullen? The empress herself? Trusted staff? The thought of anyone sneaking in and out while she slept coated her in a nearly palpable feeling of discomfort. Eira tried to rub that thick, slimy sensation off her arms, but only succeeded in throwing off the blanket.

"Good, you're awake."

Someone sitting on the couch across from her did nothing to ease the uncomfortable sensations. Eira was upright in an instant, calming when the individual came into focus. Deneya stared at her, eyes bright, outlined in orange flame.

"What time is it?"

"An ungodly hour when most of the world is resting after a *very* long day," Deneya answered vaguely.

Eira settled back into her pillow, staring at the dancing shadows on the ceiling. She'd missed Marcus's Rite of Sunset. No one had even woken her so she could pray alone to the Mother and the Father for his safe passage. She wanted to weep for what she'd lost, but all the tears had vanished.

"Are you here to kill me?" Eira asked, finally. "Finish the job your master started?"

"Ferro was more mark than master." The words held an echo of offense. "I came to apologize." Eira looked to Deneya once more. "If I had done my job correctly, I would've known sooner. I could have prevented the misfortune that befell you."

"Is that true?"

"Yes. I was sent here to keep an eye on him. He was suspect back on Meru."

"Then I feel like I should hate you," Eira said softly. If Deneya was telling the truth, she could've put an end to all of Eira's suffering before it began.

"Go ahead." Deneya shrugged. "You wouldn't be the first, or last, person to hate me."

"It's too much effort to feel anything right now... Besides, it was just as much my fault as it was yours."

"Because of your meetings with him?"

"Yes. How did you find out about those?" Eira asked. Deneya hadn't known about the meetings mere days ago.

"I have my ways."

"It must have been Alyss." Eira had only told Alyss and Marcus. Ferro had burned the notes he'd used to summon her—fastidious in covering his tracks.

Deneya nodded, approval glimmering in her eyes. "She told Fritz, who told the empress, who told me. Now, I need to know what you discussed in those meetings."

"I already told you when I said it was all my fault. I told him about Waterrunner magic, about the Tower, about Solaris, about the forests and everything else he needed to—" Eira stopped herself with a hand over her mouth. She gasped, holding in her sobs. She would not cry again. She wouldn't allow Ferro to have power over her once more.

"I need every last detail," Deneya said once Eira composed herself. "There's more depth to this than you realize."

"Such as?"

"The less you know the better."

"My brother is dead, my peers are dead, I'm implicated in their murders and I nearly died. I think have a right to know." Eira straightened, sitting taller than she had before. She ached, but it was the deep pains of grief that had made their home in her chest. The pains of her body and magic were nothing in comparison.

Deneya assessed her for a long minute. Whatever measure she was performing, Eira met the mark. "We suspect Ferro might be part of an organization that seeks to sabotage the Treaty of Five Kingdoms. I suspect this attack is proof of that—as he was trying to capitalize on the seeds of suspicion Solaris already holds for Meru."

"That's why they're not bringing him to trial here," Eira realized. No matter what, Ferro had thought he would win. Either he would escape after murdering her and all the other Waterrunners—his disappearance would cast blame on him but he lived to fight another day—or he would be tried in Solaris and every citizen would see an elfin as a murderer, an enemy. He hadn't accounted for being captured, or the emperor and empress to stay one step ahead of him by not bringing him to trial.

"I will bring him back to Meru and bring him before the queen for a private verdict. I will see him brought to justice, I promise you this. But I want as much proof as I can find of what he was doing. Not just for his trial, but to find any conspirators he was working with."

"He's not acting alone—you said he's part of an organization."

"Just so." Deneya wore a grim expression.

"Who's at the top of the organization? Who would sabotage a treaty?"

"We have some suspects, but nothing concrete. I thought Adela could have been when I first suspected you might be an agent for her. Investigating you distracted me from Ferro... thus, anything you can tell me might help make up for lost time." Deneya leaned back on the sofa, resting her arm along the back. "We're unable to interrogate him. As you might suspect, he's gagged so he can't use Lightspinning. That means you're the best we have."

Eira stared out the dark windows for several minutes. She had been a suspect because of her perceived connection with Adela. Even after Deneya had said she'd written off Eira working for the pirate queen, the suspicions had no doubt remained. Their nights together were cast in a new light. That light also shone on Fritz's—and her family's—fears about the truth of her possible parentage ever coming out.

Her possible connection with Adela had contributed to Marcus's death. She was culpable in so many ways.

"I'll tell you everything I remember," Eira resolved and shifted to the edge of the sofa. As painful as every word was, she forced them out. She recalled every last interaction with such brutal precision that her heart stung and her hands trembled. She had replayed these meetings in her mind, time and again, but they were now smothered in the stink of betrayal. Whatever she had to endure now wouldn't be enough; it would never pay back all she had taken from the Charem family. "… and that's it," she finished.

Deneya sighed. Eira had been able to tell from her expression while she spoke that her information wasn't terribly helpful. "Thank you for telling me. I'll do what I can." Deneya stood.

"Wait." Eira stared into the fire, an idea suddenly illuminated. "I think I can help you further."

"Oh?"

"Take me to his room."

"What—*oh*." Deneya's eyes were alight with wicked amusement. A smile curled her lips. "You are a useful one, aren't you?"

"I will be whatever I have to be to avenge my brother," Eira swore.

Deneya didn't seem shocked or put off in the slightest. She no doubt heard the murderous tone in Eira's voice and remained unfazed. The woman wasn't made of ice, but shadow—equally as unfeeling as Eira strove to be.

"Very well," Deneya said, starting for the door. "Follow me."

D ENEYA HAD A frightening knowledge of the palace. She moved between the shadows, confident with every step. She knew just how to open secret doors with rust-covered hinges so they didn't squeal and alert everyone still slumbering. She knew the rounds of the guards and what passageways weren't lit by flame bulbs but with long, dark candles.

Eira did her best to keep up, but her feet were clumsy by comparison. More than once she tripped, falling hard to narrowly avoid taking down an expensive vase or suit of armor with her. The exits of the passages were awkward at best.

But Deneya didn't slow. Not once did she look back to make sure Eira was keeping up. Nor did she ever verbally instruct the next turn. It felt like its own trial to Eira. As if every step whispered, *Keep up. Prove to me that you can.*

They finally came to a stop outside an unfamiliar door.

"The study you mentioned, I believe it's right down the hall," Deneya whispered and pointed.

"I have no interest in going back there." The darkness thickened down the passage, obscuring her vision beyond shafts of moonlight with a sinister edge.

"I thought not." Deneya produced a key from her pocket, unlocked the door, and ushered them both inside.

Eira did a turn about the room. She wanted it to seem more nefarious. She wanted there to be maps and writings of Ferro's plot strewn about. She wanted to see daggers and implements of torture littered around stacks of dark literature.

But everything was so very…benign.

The dresser, bed, chair, and desk were all what she would expect of Solaris nobility—stately, gilded, crafted from cherry with an impeccable hand. The linens were freshly pressed and tucked around the bed. Ferro was fastidious with everything else; it only served he would be about his chambers, too. There was a quilt that was stitched with symbols resembling Lightspinning, a closed chest at the foot of the bed, and a locked lap desk set out on the dresser. They were the room's only personal touches.

"I already did a preliminary sweep, but he tidied up well." Deneya folded her arms and leaned against the door. "I didn't find anything suspicious. But perhaps you'll hear something my eyes missed."

Eira glanced over her shoulder and nodded. Taking a deep breath, she braced herself. No matter if she found something useful or not, she had no doubt she was about to hear Ferro's voice. She packed the ice around her heart and swore that she'd never let it feel again. She'd never let her heart dictate whom she trusted. From this moment on, it wasn't in control, it wouldn't guide her.

On her exhale, she imagined her magic filling the room. Tiny crystals of ice sparkled in the moonlight, each an anchor for her power. The room sparkled with her malice—a shining sea of hate—and Eira steeped every item with her magic.

She turned first to the bed, inviting it to speak with her.

Turn down… I can do it… Thank you kindly… Snippets of conversations drifted through her mind. Every one was a harmless discussion with what sounded like palace staff. She hadn't expected the bed to yield much and that was part of why she'd started there.

But even though the conversations didn't yield much, they still hurt to listen to. Ferro's voice was an arrow to her temples. It sparked searing pain that nearly made her ill. The warm sounds she'd heard in the study contrasted against the man charging for her in the night—the man who'd tried to kill her.

When she had her composure, she turned to the chest. It also had little information to give her and Eira pulled up the latch, opening it. The fact that Deneya had yet to move from the door or say anything to stop her was all the permission Eira needed to rummage through Ferro's effects.

A tunic was particularly chatty, the echo of some woman bidding him farewell during what Eira assumed was a going away party back on Meru. She listened for anything that could give her a clue, but there was nothing. The conversation danced around concrete topics. Every discussion he had seemed to be a carefully edited script.

Eira went to the lap writing desk last. She pulled it off the dresser and placed it on the bed. The tiny fractals of ice in the room moved around her as though they were drifting in invisible currents.

Lifting the top to reveal the main compartment, Eira found exactly what one would expect—three quills, two ink bottles, and a stack of blank parchment. Right when she was about to close it, the faintest whisper drifted toward her.

Yes, everything is going according to plan, Ferro said in hushed tones. There was a long pause, and then he continued. *No, they suspect nothing. Though Deneya might be a problem.* Another pause. *Yes, the Court of Shadows is no doubt onto us. But we will stay one step ahead. They are no longer in control of Risen.*

Eira touched the various objects in the writing desk. When her fingers met the middle of the three unassuming quills, Ferro's words were louder and clearer.

Once the treaty is dismantled, we can step into the void created by the ensuing chaos. The people will be starved for leadership they can trust. It will be your glorious return. Then, we will purge the heretics and any associations with them. We will—yes...yes, Father, I know.

A bitter laugh escaped her.

"What is it?" Deneya asked.

"Everything he said to me was a lie." Eira picked up the quill, twirling it in her fingers and, for the moment, silencing the words. "He said he was an orphan, like me."

"He was." Deneya shifted off the door. "At least... according to the best information I could find. What did you hear?"

"I'm not sure, but I believe this is one of your communication tokens." Eira held out the quill. "What is it? Narro hath?"

"Indeed." Deneya approached, the fragments of ice shifting around her. "Why do you believe this to be a token?"

"I've only read about them in books, but I hear a lot of conversation from this item—as if Ferro was speaking *to* it. But I can't hear any other voices. If it's a communication token someone else has, then it makes sense I'd only be hearing half of the conversation."

"Such an unassuming object." Deneya scowled, taking the quill from Eira and turning it over in her hands. "I would never suspect this thing to be a communication token. Usually, people keep their tokens on them. But perhaps he realized that would be too suspicious. Or if he was caught, we'd confiscate everything important-looking, and he assumed this would be discarded."

"Seems likely."

"What did you hear?" Deneya asked. Eira quickly recounted the brief conversation as she listened intently. "That's all?"

"For now, yes. I've only begun trying to actively use this power recently. Perhaps there are more layers I could peel back and get more snippets of conversation. But for now, that's all I've heard."

"*Heretics*," Deneya murmured, repeating Ferro's word with a deepening frown. She snapped out of her thoughts, looking to Eira. "Well, you have been useful. I'll take you back now before anyone finds you missing."

"Wait." Eira stopped Deneya before she could open the door. The magic of the room vanished as she released it. "I can be more useful if you let me. I'm the last Waterrunner; I'll be going to Meru."

Deneya played with the end of the quill in thought. "Do you know what you're asking?"

"I'm asking for the opportunity to avenge my brother." Eira leveled her eyes with the elfin's. "Whoever did this, I want to make them pay. I want to see Ferro brought to justice. Meru has called to me my whole life, perhaps for this purpose and perhaps for another." Had Ferro's claims about Adela and Eira's possible bloodline to the elfin been a lie as well? Eira no longer believed it at face value, certainly. But she knew one place that might have the truth—the Archives of Yargen. And if not there, the Court of Shadows.

"You still want to go to Meru, after what happened to you?" Deneya arched her eyebrows.

"Yes. And I want to help the Court of Shadows."

The elfin slowly stalked over to her, as much shadow as solid. A grin slipped onto her lips. "You still think I'm part of the Court of Shadows, do you?"

"I *know* you are," Eira said without hesitation. "And that makes you my best chance at revenge."

"If you come into my world…there's no going back."

"There's nothing keeping me here." She'd killed Marcus. Even if her family would forgive her for the actions she'd unknowingly taken that had led to his death, there was no way they would ever look past the fact that she couldn't save him when it had mattered most. Eira had taken her parents' son. How could she hope to ever look them in the eyes again without, at the very least, bringing to justice the man—and organization—responsible?

Deneya's eyes shone in the darkness. But whatever thoughts prompted the contemplative expression, she kept them from Eira. "Very well. Come to Meru and the Court of Shadows might just have a use for a woman of your talents."

She spent six days alone in the Imperial quarters. The same servant came in and out to attend to her needs—an elderly woman who was no doubt more loyal to Solaris than her own self interests. But the woman never made conversation. She never answered Eira's questions about the world beyond and what was happening. She muttered reassurances: "Trust the crown," she'd say, and then leave.

Eira's thoughts were dangerous companions to be left alone with. She went over the night with Deneya time and again to remind herself that it was real. But the more she dissected it and picked those hours apart, word by word, the more it all seemed like a dream. Something about late-night meetings with elfin was too unbelievable to be real. And, just like with Ferro, she had no token to substantiate her moonlit memories come dawn.

Deneya never returned, of course. One or two days, Eira stayed up way too late to see if she visited in the night to check in. But if Deneya did, she left no trace.

It was the lack of Fritz, or Grahm, or Gwen that really began to eat away at her. Surely, they were busy. Fritz was likely drowning in managing the crisis that followed apprentices dying. Grahm was helping him. And Gwen was overseeing the palace guard at the empress's order.

But...couldn't they stop in just for a little?

Her logical protests against the insecure portions of her mind grew weaker by the day. It was becoming all too easy to object to the notion that they'd ever loved her. They were so eager to cast her aside when she finally showed her true colors. This was their chance to finally be rid of her.

No! her heart would try and object. But Eira was done listening to her heart. She'd risked it with Adam, then with Ferro.

Never again.

On the morning of the seventh day, the same elderly servant appeared with a bundle of clothes and announced, "I'm going to take you back to the Tower now, dear."

Eira dressed and followed the woman out of the Imperial halls, secret passages once more—different ones from those Deneya took—until they got to a normal servant's thoroughfare.

"I know where I am." Eira adjusted the Tower robes on her

shoulders. The candidate pin was affixed to them once more. She had her freedom and her title as competitor—Yemir had lost. "I can go from here."

"I was told to take you to the entrance." She was insistent and Eira was too tired to object further. They came to a stop by an illusioned passage, the entrance shrouded with magic to look like the stone walls on either side of the tunnel. "There will be someone waiting for you on the other side."

"Thank you, for everything," Eira tried to say with sincerity, though it was so easy to resent the woman for withholding information at every turn.

"It's my duty to the crown." She bowed and left.

Eira slipped through the illusion into a dim passage. At the far end was a woman with thick braids cascading down her back. A woman Eira ran to.

"Eira!" Alyss planted her feet and stood firm as Eira crashed into her. Their arms wrapped around each other in crushing grips. "Thank the Mother you were finally cleared. I prayed every night. I heard they had you in a cell. How bad was it?"

Alyss had believed the lies spread by the emperor and empress: that Eira had been held as a suspect but declared innocent on investigation. She opened her mouth and shut it before she could tell Alyss everything. She might, eventually, but now wasn't the time.

"It was…very lonely." Eira continued to hold her friend, inhaling deeply the familiar and comforting scent of the lotions and perfumes Alyss used.

"I can imagine… Marcus, he… I went to the Rite of Sunset for him."

"You did?" Eira yanked herself away to meet Alyss's dark eyes.

"Yes. I would've regardless, but when I found out they weren't letting you attend, I had to go." Alyss smiled sadly. "I said a prayer on your behalf."

"Alyss, I do not deserve you." Eira pulled her friend close

once more.

"After all you've been through, you deserve someone far better." Alyss gave her a final squeeze but Eira was reluctant to let her go. "I saw your parents there."

"My parents?" News had certainly traveled quickly. "Did they…did you speak to them?" Eira asked awkwardly. Hope tightened her chest. Though she didn't know what she was hoping for.

"I didn't. It…didn't seem like the time." Alyss frowned.

"Right, of course," Eira mumbled. Fritz, Grahm, and Gwen had visited with her, briefly. Couldn't her parents have come? Had they wanted to?

Alyss took her hand. "We should go; your uncle is waiting."

Fritz was the last person Eira wanted to see, especially after the torment her mind had delighted in creating about her family for the past few days. But she knew she had no reason to object. So Eira followed Alyss dutifully back into the main spiral of the Tower.

Other apprentices stopped and stared as she passed. Eira heard whispers fluttering around her like small birds, ready to pick at her weary mind. They regarded her with skeptical glances and a few with outwardly hostile stares.

Cullen had been right. Everyone saw her as having a motive to get rid of her competition. Suddenly her known obsession with Meru was a liability. These people—her *peers*—thought she would kill them to get across the sea. They thought she would actually kill her brother for it.

Though, he wasn't her brother. Perhaps that rumor had finally leaked somewhere and begun to spread too. Maybe, to all of them, she looked like a raging, orphaned child, shunned and cast out, seeking to take vengeance on a family she'd never belonged to.

Eira kept her eyes forward and her mouth shut. She didn't trust what she might say if she opened it.

"I'll be reading in my room. So when you're done, if you want company, come and find me," Alyss said as they came to a stop in front of Fritz's door.

"Thank you," Eira said. What she really wanted to do was beg Alyss not to leave. "I'll see you soon."

"You better. I missed you." Alyss squeezed her hands and took a step away, waiting. Intentionally or not, her presence gave no room for Eira to run.

Ready or not, she had to face her uncle.

He was behind the desk, silently motioning to the seat in front of him. Eira shut the door and sat in her usual spot. The chair next to her—the one Marcus would fill—was painfully empty.

Eira broke the silence. "I've gathered I'm no longer a suspect?"

"In the eyes of the crown, and thus the senate? Yes. But there are many still skeptical of you." He sighed. "But, more importantly, how have you been?"

"Fine," she lied.

"I know that can't be true."

"You would've seen it if you came to visit me," Eira said casually. She'd practiced this conversation in her head.

"I had matters to attend to that I couldn't ignore—for your sake as well. None of us could risk coming to you and having it be discovered that you were no longer in that horrible cell."

"Thank you for your efforts on my behalf." Eira gripped the armrests of the chair lightly, bracing herself. "Did my parents make any efforts to come and see me?"

"I just said it wasn't possible." Fritz frowned and his eyes held a heavy sadness.

"Did they try and send a letter?" she asked. His silence told her the answer, but Eira pressed anyway. "Did they leave any message with you?"

"No."

One word, spoken so calmly, had never been so loud. Fritz said nothing else on the matter, but Eira didn't need him to. Her parents had written her off. And how could she blame them? After how she'd acted over the past few months, the revelation, Marcus's death?

Eira expected it to hurt more. But any chance of feeling pain had been drowned in the ocean of numbness that she was sinking deeper and deeper into by the day. They stared at each other for a long minute, neither saying anything.

"Is there anything else, Uncle?"

"Yes, I need to go over the next steps for you." His eyes dropped to the pin on her robes. "In light of the incidents, the fifth trial will not be happening. There aren't any Waterrunners left as candidates, save for you. However, one of your instructors has said he's willing to take your place."

"You…you're still expecting me to drop out?" Eira asked, incredulous. Her hand covered the pin, as if shielding it from his grasp.

"Eira…" He trailed off, staring at her. Was he somehow, honestly shocked she'd still want to go? Eira thought it'd be obvious. "Please, don't do this."

"I'm going," Eira said calmly, even though she wanted to scream at him for even thinking of asking this of her after all that happened.

"I know how you must feel. This has been hard for you— for all of us."

"You don't have the slightest idea of how I feel."

He ignored the remark. "Your family has had enough heartbreak. I can't sit here and send you off to Meru after… after Marcus's death. We love you and want you safe, here, with us."

"I must go." And Marcus's death was precisely the reason.

"This isn't the time to be selfish."

"I'm doing this to see that the men who killed my brother are brought to justice."

"Men?"

"Man," Eira corrected quickly. Fritz didn't know about the organization behind all of this. The fact filled Eira with a strange sense of power and duty. "I *have to* go."

"What do you honestly think you can do?" Her uncle

looked down on her, even still.

"Whatever I can."

"Your parents have lost one child. They need you. *I* need you. I'm sorry for the transgressions you feel I've committed against you. I'm not perfect, none of us are, but we're trying." The ghost of the surrogate father she'd once known him as passed over him. The sight of it nearly broke a part of her heart somehow still intact. But Eira banished it with a silent reminder of everything he'd done the past few months—every time he had held her back or stepped in her way. "Don't leave now, please."

Eira gripped the armrests of her chair tighter. But her magic stayed under her control. Not one speck of frost stuck to the velvet upholstery.

She had a million quips she wanted to say and a thousand objections. She'd had a lot of time to try and figure out what was best for her and her family. But the one thing she kept coming back to was that she couldn't face her parents. Not yet. Not with her brother's blood on her hands and his killer out there.

And especially not after they had abandoned her.

"I'm sorry, but I have to." Eira stood. "My mind is made up; I will go to Meru." *The Court of Shadows is waiting for me.*

TWENTY-NINE

IRA DIDN'T GO to instruction, workshops, or the clinic for the next three days. As long as the pin was on her breast, she was still a candidate and that meant she didn't have any obligations. It didn't matter that the fifth trial was canceled and she was the only Waterrunner left. She wasn't going to anything she didn't want to and no one dared to tell her otherwise.

She spent most of her time with Alyss in the back corner of the library. Alyss alternated between reading her romance novels or sculpting, oftentimes both. Eira always knew when Alyss was scared or nervous. She busied her hands and buried herself in other worlds and other people who existed neatly in a few hundred bound pages.

Eira retreated in a different way. She might have spent time reading before. But now, when she sat at the window seat of the library, she practiced listening. She stretched out her magic silently, invisibly, and targeted various objects around her.

Whispers heeded her command now. But Eira silently trained anyway. There would be a day Deneya would come— here in Solaris, on Meru, or wherever else destiny took Eira. The Court of Shadows seemed like something that didn't understand or respect borders. It was a living, breathing entity in Eira's mind, one from which she didn't want to escape. She wanted to be a part of it.

Whenever the court came to call on her, tonight, tomorrow, a year from now, she would be ready. She would help bring Ferro and anyone else who stood with him to justice.

She and Alyss were left mostly alone, the other apprentices in the Tower avoiding them in wide arcs. Rumors had continued to spread that Eira had somehow had a hand—despite what the Imperial investigation had turned up—in the deaths of her fellow competitors.

This cocoon of solitude made it all the more jarring when Cullen and Noelle approached them. Wordlessly, Cullen handed Alyss a letter and then gave one to Eira. He held out his hand, waiting, as she looked from the letter to the man she hadn't laid eyes on in a week.

A treacherous corner of her heart wanted to feel something toward him. She wanted to reach up and wrap her arms around his neck and clutch him to her. She wanted to mourn once more with him, held safely in the security he seemed to provide. She wanted him to brush her hair from her face and tell her everything would be all right.

But she couldn't. She wouldn't let herself.

"I know what this letter says. It's not a trap this time," he said softly, misreading her hesitation.

"I suppose it is like that night, isn't it?" Eira murmured. She reached out and took the letter from Cullen. The last letter she'd taken from him had been the night of Adam's cruelty and the start of a wedge between them. But Eira already expected the missive she held now was the beginning of them being bound together, like it or not.

Eira unfolded the parchment, recognizing her uncle's script.

"'Congratulations,'" she read, skimming the few lines of text he'd written.

"Doesn't seem like much of a congratulations after all that's happened, does it?" Alyss muttered, looking to Eira with somewhat haunted eyes. "The other Groundbreakers wouldn't back down. Since there wasn't a fifth trial, the minister and royals chose me based on my past scores."

"Welcome to the team," Noelle said, "fellow competitors."

Eira looked between the three people around her and then back to her letter. "I suppose we should start packing."

The next morning, Eira was up well before the sun. She moved through the silent halls of the Tower, ending up in the hidden room she'd spent so many hours in. Eira watched the dawn break through the small window and wondered how many times Adela had stood in the same spot she was now.

This room *had* been Adela's, Eira had long come to terms with. That meant the journals she had studied from could be the writings of her birth mother. Or, Eira was wrong, and her birth mother was lost to time. Nevertheless, Eira slowly collected those journals, stacking them in the bag she'd brought.

When she was finished, she spared a moment to bid the room farewell, leaving it behind for the next apprentice to uncover.

Eira left her bag in her room alongside one other and a large trunk. She then descended through the halls, down a secret passage, and was the first to arrive in a waiting room designated by a second letter that had arrived late last night.

Cullen was the second to arrive.

The moment he entered, his eyes met hers and he came to a halt. They spent a long minute staring at each other. A thick and heavy tension immediately occupied the space between them, much like it had the day before. Eira sincerely hoped this wasn't a new sensation that she'd feel every time she was around him.

"Are you ready?" he asked softly.

"I am." Eira looked to the window. Meeting his eyes now felt oddly vulnerable. "This wasn't how I wanted everything to happen. But I'm here now."

"Marcus would be proud of you."

Eira tensed at the mention of her brother's name. "Let's go and win, for him."

"We will," Cullen vowed.

Eira didn't clarify that she wasn't merely talking about

the tournament. There was another game at play. One she was willing to risk everything in.

"Eira." He whispered her name, close enough that it forced her to look away from the window and realize he was standing before her. "I know...you and I...we..."

"We what?" Eira looked up at him, guarding every tender edge of her still-bleeding heart.

"We had a rough start."

She snorted softly. "That's one way to phrase it."

He cracked a smile. "But I'm glad to be here with you now."

"You would've preferred Marcus."

"I would've preferred he be here to see you take this spot," Cullen said firmly. "I'm glad you're here...with me."

His hand rested lightly on hers. Eira stared at the unexpectedly tender touch. She followed it up his arm to his face. She didn't know what expression she was wearing, but whatever it was made Cullen pull away.

I can't, she wanted to say. *I can't risk giving you my heart. People die when I fall in love.*

"I think we'll make good teammates," Cullen said stiffly. It was his turn to ignore her and look out the window.

Despite her heart being walled in ice, it persisted to ache. She wanted touch. She wanted comfort. *His* comfort.

All things she couldn't let herself have. Cullen had his secrets. She had hers. And Eira couldn't risk bringing him into the world of shadows she was headed to.

The door opened again to reveal Alyss and Noelle. Alyss promptly crossed to Eira and Noelle hovered in the far corner of the room. Cullen went over to make small talk with her.

After about thirty minutes, Gwen arrived in her formal regalia. "Hello, competitors of Solaris," she said warmly. "Are you ready for your debut?"

They all nodded and followed behind her.

Gwen led them through quiet back passages, up to a hall that was familiar. The last time Eira had walked this path it was night, and she was chasing behind Ferro. She hoped the muzzle they had on the ambassador-turned-assassin was good and tight.

They came to a stop behind the large doors that opened to the Sunlit Stage. There were muffled cheers following unintelligible proclamations on the other side. All at once, the doors opened, and the four of them stepped into the sunlight.

Ferro and Deneya were expectedly absent. Eira had heard some excuse made about them having gone back early to Meru to help with further preparations. Eira had no doubt they would be traveling alongside them in secret. The emperor and empress stood on one side of the stage, Fritz on the other. Eira kept her eyes forward as she strode toward the stage's edge with her fellow competitors.

The four sorcerers lined up, sunlight glinting off their pins—the last four pins in all of Solaris. The pins that now marked them as competitors.

"Men and women of Solaris," the emperor boomed. "I present to you our competitors. The Windwalker, Lord Cullen Drowel—"

Cullen stepped forward at his name to thunderous applause.

"—the Firebearer, Noelle Gravson—"

Noelle took a wide step, flicked her hair, and raised both her hands in a wave.

"—the Groundbreaker, Alyss Ivree—"

Alyss braced herself before stepping forward. Eira could see her chest heaving with nerves but she managed to plaster on a bold smile. The effort was rewarded by more cheers.

"—and the Waterrunner, Eira Landan!"

At her name, the applause fizzled like an ember doused in water. Eira scanned the ramparts, watching the people as they clapped politely and uncertainly for her. They had no doubt been fed the same rumors of her killing for this spot. Even if her name was officially cleared, they were still skeptical of her involvement.

Eira forced a smile and a wave.

Let them think what they wanted, because by nightfall she would be in a carriage headed for Norin. Within two weeks she would board a ship of the Imperial Armada. Within the month, she would step foot on Meru. And within the year, Eira would bring Solaris victory, and her brother vengeance.

Eira's story continues in...

Learn more about A HUNT OF SHADOWS (A Trial of Sorcerers, #2) and grab your copy at:
https://elisekova.com/a-hunt-of-shadows/

Want to make sure you never miss a giveaway, cover reveal, or release day?

Sign up for Elise Kova's Mailing List:
http://elisekova.com/subscribe

You can get a FREE GIFT on sign up!

Want more from the world of Air Awakens while waiting for
A HUNT OF SHADOWS?

Read Vhalla's story in AIR AWAKENS. A library apprentice discovers she has a rare elemental magic and falls in love with a sorcerer prince.

Learn more:

https://elisekova.com/air-awakens-book-one/

How did the crown Princess Vi Solaris discover Meru, Lightspinning, and the elfin? Read her story of action, adventure, and love deeper than time itself in VORTEX VISIONS.

Learn more:

https://elisekova.com/vortex-visions-air-awakens-vortex-chronicles-1/

The Golden Guard is the most elite fighting force in all of Solaris. Learn about how they were formed in a series of three stand alone stories of action and deep friendship.

Learn more:

https://elisekova.com/the-crowns-dog-golden-guard-1/

About the Author

ELISE KOVA has always had a profound love of fantastical worlds. Somehow, she managed to focus on the real world long enough to graduate with a Master's in Business Administration before crawling back under her favorite writing blanket to conceptualize her next magic system. She currently lives in St. Petersburg, Florida, and when she is not writing can be found playing video games, watching anime, or talking with readers on social media.

She invites readers to get first looks, giveaways, and more by subscribing to her newsletter at:
http://elisekova.com/subscribe

Visit her on the web at:
http://elisekova.com/
https://twitter.com/EliseKova
https://www.facebook.com/AuthorEliseKova/
https://www.instagram.com/elise.kova/

See all of Elise's titles on her Amazon page:
http://author.to/EliseKova

MORE BOOKS BY ELISE...

THE
Air Awakens
SERIES

A young adult, high-fantasy filled with romance and elemental magic

A library apprentice, a sorcerer prince, and an unbreakable magic bond. . .

The Solaris Empire is one conquest away from uniting the continent, and the rare elemental magic sleeping in seventeen-year-old library apprentice Vhalla Yarl could shift the tides of war.

Vhalla has always been taught to fear the Tower of Sorcerers, a mysterious magic society, and has been happy in her quiet

world of books. But after she unknowingly saves the life of one of the most powerful sorcerers of them all—the Crown Prince Aldrik--she finds herself enticed into his world. Now she must decide her future: Embrace her sorcery and leave the life she's known, or eradicate her magic and remain as she's always been. And with powerful forces lurking in the shadows, Vhalla's indecision could cost her more than she ever imagined.

Learn more at:

http://elisekova.com/air-awakens-book-one/

ACKNOWLEDGEMENTS

My Tower Guard—this book is for all of you. You lift me up when I am down. You're there when I need feedback. Whenever I have a problem there is always someone among you who jumps up, ready to help. When I need something shared, you're there. Each and every one of you give so much to me, and it is my fervent hope that I can continue to give back to you with every book I write. Thank you for believing in not just the world of Air Awakens, but all of the worlds I write.

The Man—thank you for all you did to help bring this novel into the world. Every time you listened as I storyboarded ideas, every night you made dinner, or cleaned the house, or took care of "life" so I could focus on fictional worlds was essential in my making Eira's story a reality.

Mom—thanks for being one of my most excited ARC readers and biggest cheerleaders. I appreciate all you have done and continue to do for me. Oh, please give dad a hug for me, too.

Melissa Wright—without you I wouldn't have finished nearly as fast and the story wouldn't have been half as good. Thank you for your feedback and hilarious comments. I couldn't have hoped or wished for a better crit partner.

Danielle Jensen—I'm pretty sure I owe you a glass of wine. For what? *Shh*, I don't know. It's just an excuse to try and see you. Thanks for everything, friend.

Mary—my friend, thank you for consistently putting my body back together after I've destroyed it with bad posture and way more words than any person should write in a single day.

Lux Karpov-Kinrade—thank you for being the best sprint partner anyone could dream of. You're an incredible friend and author and I'm so excited to write more alongside you and all your projects. The turtles—you all are amazing and I love that I have truly found my community among you.

Michelle Madow—I love all our brainstorming sessions, happy hours, and hang outs. Thank you for being a part of my author journey.

Turtles—you all are incredible and I couldn't have dreamed of a better author community to count myself a part of.

Every Instagrammer, Facebook Expert, Twitter Guru, Blogger, and other influencer who helped spread the word about *A Trial of Sorcerers*—you are my heroes. I will never be able to thank you all individually as you deserve. But know I see you. Know I'm grateful for every one of you and, much like my Tower Guard, I hope that I can express that gratitude through the stories I bring into the world and the special exclusives that can come with them.

CPSIA information can be obtained
at www.ICGtesting.com
Printed in the USA
LVHW090052060321
679711LV00033BA/63/J